Josephine Moon was born and raised in Brisbane, and had a false start in environmental science before completing a Bachelor of Arts in communication and then a postgraduate degree in education. Twelve years and ten manuscripts later, her first novel, *The Tea Chest*, was picked up for publication and then shortlisted for an ABIA award. Her bestselling contemporary fiction is published internationally. Her books include *The Tea Chest*, *The Chocolate Promise*, *The Beekeeper's Secret*, *Three Gold Coins*, *The Gift of Life*, *The Cake Maker's Wish*, *The Jam Queens* and *The Wonderful Thing about Phoenix Rose*.

She now lives on acreage in the beautiful Noosa hinterland with her husband and son, and a tribe of animals that seems to increase in size each year. She wouldn't have it any other way.

The wonderful thing about Phoenix Rose

Josephine Moon

MICHAEL JOSEPH
an imprint of
PENGUIN BOOKS

MICHAEL JOSEPH

UK | USA | Canada | Ireland | Australia
India | New Zealand | South Africa | China

Michael Joseph is part of the Penguin Random House group of companies
whose addresses can be found at global.penguinrandomhouse.com

Penguin
Random House
Australia

First published by Michael Joseph in 2023

Cover design by Nikki Townsend Design © Penguin Random House Australia Pty Ltd
Cover photography by © Ulas and Merve/Stocksy (woman), Steicha/Shutterstock.com
(sunflower), Markovka/Shutterstock.com (pattern)
Author photograph by Anastasia Kariofyllidis
Typeset in 12/16.5 pt Minion Pro by Midland Typesetters, Australia

Printed and bound in Australia by Griffin Press, an accredited
ISO AS/NZS 14001 Environmental Management Systems printer

A catalogue record for this
book is available from the
National Library of Australia

ISBN 978 1 76104 620 9

penguin.com.au

We at Penguin Random House Australia acknowledge that Aboriginal and Torres Strait Islander
peoples are the Traditional Custodians and the first storytellers of the lands on which we live
and work. We honour Aboriginal and Torres Strait Islander peoples' continuous connection
to Country, waters, skies and communities. We celebrate Aboriginal and Torres Strait Islander
stories, traditions and living cultures; and we pay our respects to Elders past and present.

For Janelle, the best person to have by your side if you're going to chase horses down a main road in peak-hour traffic, or if you need a best friend

1

As she tugged the sleep mask from her eyes, Phoenix's first thought was that her sick leave had now officially expired. Over a decade of high-school teaching and a work ethic that propelled her to never let anyone down had resulted in a cumulated forty days' worth of leave. But now they were all gone. Pecking at her phone, she discovered the anticipated email notification. There she was, right on cue – Evelyn Godfrey, fearsome principal. Phoenix always fancied that Evelyn could have starred in the likes of a Roald Dahl children's book, with her piercing, interrogative eyes, unnerving ability to materialise from shadows, and a robust intolerance of any perceived weakness – from parents, students or teachers.

The principal had been 'pulled off the bench' at the beginning of the school year as an emergency (and entirely opposite) replacement for Levi Backhurst, a young and progressive-minded principal with a meteoric rise to the top, followed by a spectacular fall from grace over a buck's night incident involving underage strippers and a pocket full of pills. The media had cashed in on the clickbait for weeks and Evelyn had made it her personal mission to restore St Clementine's to a conservative, squeaky-clean, top-shelf girls' school of choice. And, as she repeatedly told staff and students alike, nothing would stand in her way.

Phoenix debated whether or not to open Evelyn's email now and get it over with, or put it off till later. She reached behind herself to click on the string of LED-light sunflowers adorning the crest of her bedhead, optimistic that their golden glow could shield her from the darkness she sensed was lurking in that message. If she didn't do it now, she would pace all day. Holding her breath, she tapped it open.

Phoenix

Your attendance is required for a discussion ASAP about your return to school. I'm sure you can appreciate how difficult it is to run a first-class institution when staffing is inconsistent and uncertain. Today? Monday at the latest. Email Linda to arrange a time.

Evelyn

'Coffee's on,' Zack called.

Phoenix heard him depress the toaster lever then pull out the frypan. Zack ate three fried eggs on toast washed down with two coffee chasers every morning, without fail.

'Coming,' she said, but didn't actually move, resisting the cold air of the early September morning in their unrenovated postwar rental house in Brisbane. It had fibro walls, bandy-legged stumps and a small chain-wire fenced yard with a rusting Hills Hoist at its centre. It also had numerous draughts. Her hands were frozen already, simply from holding her phone. She was also frozen on the inside, rendered immobile by Evelyn's summons.

Could she go into school today? She hadn't been back since *the incident* that had led to the forty days of sick leave. She knew that, schools being the festering gossip mills they were, all manner of shaming things would have been discussed in the corridors till they spilled over into the classrooms, texted between parents and sneered about by students. To stop herself from imagining all the terrible things that would have been said about her (nutjob, breakdown, weirdo), she navigated to Pinterest instead.

A soothing wash of yellow greeted her, calming her nerves. She pinned a magazine-worthy image of a glass filled with pale lemon curd mousse, a rich toffee-brown biscuit crust, tiny white flowers at the top. Her mouth watered at the sight of it. The photo now sat in her 'lemon board' collection, a visually balanced, inspiring layout of foods that made her feel, if not happy, at least hopeful.

Two months of intensive research since the day of her diagnosis – no, correction, her *identification* – with over a dozen books read, three online courses completed, and rabbit hole after rabbit hole of websites explored, meant she now had an entire catalogue of vocabulary to decipher her behaviour. Right now, this Pinterest organising activity was one she did when she was *dysregulated* and needed to *self-soothe*.

For a moment, her mind flicked back to a time when her mother's work as a festival coordinator had dried up and they'd temporarily stopped following the arts trails around the state. The two of them had stayed with Jac's sister, sleeping in the spare room of Jessie's ramshackle house, which was filled with dust, boxes of LP records and disused macramé plant hangers. While her mother drew the curtains against the daylight and tapped ash into an empty Coke can, Jessie and Phoenix lay on a blanket under the enormous lemon tree in the backyard and gazed up at the bounty of bright yellow fruit, pendulous and robust, like joyful party lanterns. It was the year Phoenix ate lemon butter and mayonnaise sandwiches for lunch every day. It was her year of calm. Jessie's two bedraggled orange chooks would sit on the blanket with them and snatch at Phoenix's fallen crumbs and Phoenix decided that no matter what she did with her life, no matter where she ended up, the only thing she wanted was a huge lemon tree, like Jessie's.

Until then, she had Pinterest.

'Coffee in bed this morning?' Zack arrived at her doorway, a steaming mug in one hand and a squishy stress ball in the other.

'Hey, you're looking rather fine,' she said, giving him a flirty smile and a suggestive raise of an eyebrow. For a moment, his frown smoothed and the corner of his mouth lifted, a gesture he reserved solely for her. He held her gaze for a second, fleetingly free of the stress he'd been carrying of late. But his worries were back a moment later.

'I've really got to go.'

He'd put concentrated effort into ironing his new shirt, and a new belt shone at his waist. His too-long trousers still bunched above his shoes, but that was just Zack. He was one part Phoenix's devoted partner, one part loyal employee and one part absent-minded professor. This new outfit was his attempt to lift his confidence in the face of upcoming staff changes at the centre. At the age of thirty-seven, he'd finally felt brave enough to put himself forwards for the senior radiographer position on offer, getting himself off the soon-to-end contract he was on and into a permanent role. He popped the coffee down on the table beside her.

'Oh, sorry. I got distracted.' She held out her hand and he took it, squeezing it tenderly.

'Stay there. The eggs can wait in the pan till you're ready.' He bent to kiss her, smelling of minty toothpaste. 'I've got to go.'

'You working late again?'

Zack flicked the stress ball from one hand to the other. 'Yep.'

'I'm old enough to remember when Thursday-night shopping was a thing. Now late-night X-rays are all the rage.'

'We never get through the lists each day as it is,' he said, matter-of-factly. The concept of overtime had never bothered him. His focus was one hundred per cent on his clients.

'You're a saint,' she said.

'I like to help people.' He ran his free hand over the top of his hair. He'd attempted to brush it down but the black springs resisted, popping straight back up again the moment his hand lifted.

'I know you do. Have a good day.' She let go of his hand, always warm compared to hers, which were always cold. It was one of the million things she loved about him, that he was invariably happy to have her climb into his bed and put her cold hands under his shirt to warm them up, or tuck her cold feet between his legs. The man was like a furnace, even in the middle of winter. She wished she wasn't so sensitive to light, sound and movement and could share a bed with him and actually sleep. She'd never be cold again, for one, but more than that she simply felt better with him beside her.

People keenly vocalised how weird they thought it was that she and Zack had separate bedrooms, but to the two of them it was a perfectly sensible accommodation. There wasn't a hallway long enough in the world to keep them apart if they wanted to be together. With the rest of her life imploding right now, at least her relationship was stronger than ever before. If only Zack's enormous love could be protection enough from Evelyn the Fearsome, she'd have nothing to worry about.

What was she going to say to the principal? If she disclosed her recent, surprising, late revelation of neurodivergence, she was bound to lose more credibility than she already had after *the incident*. Evelyn was the type of principal who rolled her eyes at maternity leave and was outright hostile about bereavement leave. She wasn't going to take this new information well, of that Phoenix was certain. The concept of accommodating differences was a complete waste of time in Evelyn's mind. *Shape up or ship out*, Phoenix had heard her mutter, more than once. Even if Phoenix felt able to advocate for her legal rights (which she didn't, right now), laws and the reality of workplace culture were two very different things.

Was she even ready to go back to school? No, she didn't feel ready. Would she ever feel ready again? She had no idea. She'd burnt out once; it was surely only a matter of time before it happened again. But was she ready to throw away a good career in which she'd invested everything she had? Absolutely not.

Taking a deep breath, she emailed Evelyn's assistant and told her she could meet with Evelyn on Monday. That bought her another few days to figure out what to say.

•

Downunder Auties

CarlaM78: Me, trying to change a ceiling light bulb in the wardrobe, variously ignore it and worry about it for a year, finally have a good day, locate a stepladder buried in hallway cupboard and pull it out. Wait another five days to remember to put the light bulb in my bag AND to stop at the hardware. They can't find the exact match but ASSURE me the new one will fit. Procrastinate for another 24 hours, then force myself to climb the ladder and of course IT DOES NOT FIT. Need to go to bed and numb myself with Netflix. Is this just me?

MagentaMel: Executive (dys)function is the pits. ☹

FidgetMan: I HATE changing light bulbs. I always think I'll electrocute myself or the glass will break in my hand.

VikingMan: I hear ya, Carla. I can run a successful courier company but it can take me two years to change a bulb. It's the little things.

MissWittyKitty: I have honestly never even thought about a light bulb! Mum and Dad must do it all. I better add that to my life skills list if I ever want to move out of home.

SnoopyDancer: Hey, has anyone heard from Olga lately?

Phoenix read through the comments, smiling. She had total empathy for the light bulb struggle. As well as having a memory bank that had gone on holiday to a warm tropical island without inviting her to come along, she'd also lost the ability to make dinner. The thinking about dinner was the first awful thing, followed by planning ingredients, buying ingredients and prepping vegetables, then the cooking, the not burning, and finally remembering to turn off the stove. She couldn't count the number of times either she or Zack had walked away with a stovetop still on. Truly, how was it that she could have a bachelor's degree, a postgraduate diploma *and* a master's and still not be able to make dinner? But this group helped. She wasn't alone.

She was about to respond when she re-read SnoopyDancer's comment.

Hey, has anyone heard from Olga lately?

Phoenix narrowed her eyes, thinking. Days blurred into each other in this weird in-between life she was living – not fired, but not working, on leave but with no clear return date, not sick, as such, except she couldn't think or function any more the way she used to. It was tricky to work out when she'd last connected with Olga.

SnoopyDancer, otherwise known as Therese, was a social worker in South Australia. It was consistent of her to notice Olga's absence from their usually active group. Phoenix scrolled

7

backwards through posts, looking for the last time Olga had contributed to their discussions, her worry increasing with the amount of time it was taking to locate her. But as she scrolled, a notification popped up from Olga herself and Phoenix hurried to read what her friend had to say.

She had posted a photo of her old black dog, greying at the muzzle, sleeping by the fireplace.

I have cancer, her message read. *Stage four. Please, could one of my friends here help me? I need to go to hospital on Monday to stay for a few days. I need help with my animals while I'm away and then, once I'm home again, to help me to find them good, new homes. I think I need you for a week? I hate to ask. I'm sorry. I've been unable to communicate. This is such a big shock. I've been paralysed with worry for my animals. But I have no one else and it's urgent. I don't care about me but my animals are my family. I worry for them. I wouldn't even be going to hospital except it will buy me some more time to sort out my affairs and make a will. You are my only friends. I need someone I can trust. Please let me know as soon as you can.*

Phoenix read through the sympathies from the others in the chat group as they emerged but didn't know what she could say that could possibly help Olga. Her friend didn't need sympathy, she needed action. Pushing her chair back across the linoleum floor, she got up and paced the house – down the hallway, past the bathroom with the cracked shower screen and the leaky taps the landlord kept promising to fix, past the loungeroom with the crocheted blankets and oil heaters and casement windows with arthritic hinges that would shudder open again once the weather warmed up – and back to the kitchen.

She couldn't go to Tasmania for a week, could she? Her mind was a mess and her body was in constant pain. The cold made her arthritis worse and Tasmania would be many times colder than here. She and Zack were each other's anchor points in the world but neither of them was a great communicator via phone. With her current struggles and Zack's promotion opportunity on the horizon, it wasn't a good time for them to be apart.

Then again, Zack was always the first person to put his hand up to help someone in need. Mud Army after the Brisbane floods? He was there, gloves on. Working extra shifts in the medical field during Covid? He was there. When his sister needed a new fence he was there the next day, tools in hand. When Phoenix's school needed volunteers to repair vandalised gardens, they made a date out of it, collecting fallen rosebuds and scattering the petals over their table for a candlelit dinner. She was sure he'd support her wish to help Olga.

Still, she was supposed to be recuperating. She'd never been a good traveller under the best of circumstances and this was a mission to help someone she'd never met in person. She'd be staying somewhere she had no control over, trying to rehome animals she knew nothing about. She was supposed to front up to the principal and assure her she was right to start work again at the beginning of fourth term, not drag herself on a stressful journey to help a stranger.

She stopped pacing. Olga *wasn't* a stranger; she was her friend. This online community of autists had saved her when she'd thought she was losing her mind. They'd taught her about herself as no one else had ever been able to do. They'd helped her piece together years of misdiagnoses and lack of support. They'd mirrored back to her a hundred inexplicable experiences they too had shared. She'd found her *neurokin*. When she was flailing with shock from a mature-aged autism diagnosis, this community had caught her and held her hand while she began to peel back the decades of masking and camouflaging she'd needed to get by in the world, and instead embrace her true self. She'd had Zack, sure, but he was only one autist, and a man, with a very different presentation and history. Where Zack had barely spoken till he was four, Phoenix's mother said the only time her daughter ever stopped talking was when she fell asleep, usually mid-sentence. This group had shown her the huge diversity within the autistic spectrum. They'd given her so much; it would be her honour to give something back.

She and Olga might not have met in person but that didn't discount the value or depth of the connection they'd made in daily conversations over the past two months. She knew more about Olga's childhood, fears, joys and daily struggles than she'd learnt about Anthea in the five years they'd been work buddies at school. She knew Olga must be terrified, alone, grieving for herself and her animals, and dreading the awful visit to hospital. She needed help from sympathetic friends who knew how to support her, who could help her make decisions, who understood she was non-speaking at times. She needed someone who respected her autonomy.

Phoenix needed to help. Setting up Olga's animals for the rest of their lives would allow her to end her life with as much peace as possible. It was important it was done right.

She stopped pacing and opened her laptop to check available flights, then texted Zack. His reply was swift.

You should go, as long as you feel up to it. X

Did she feel up to it? Honestly, no. But Olga needed help.

With trembling fingers, she emailed Evelyn's assistant and told her she couldn't make it into school in person on Monday but she could meet with Evelyn via Zoom, then she messaged Olga to tell her she'd be there on Sunday. She took a deep breath. A week away from home was a long time in Phoenix's life right now, but the challenges would be worth it to do this for Olga. Maybe it would even be good for Phoenix to get out of the house and feel useful and strong again instead of hiding away for fear of running into students or their parents at the supermarket or cinema. It might feel huge, but really it was simply an interstate flight and a week away at a friend's home.

How much could possibly go wrong?

2

Phoenix landed in Launceston on Sunday afternoon, finding the island state's weather bleak, cold, rainy and windy, which for Phoenix was the equivalent of the four horsemen of a mood apocalypse. She fought down nerves as she signed the paperwork for her rental car and tried to convince herself she was excited, not scared. Once settled inside, she kicked up the air conditioning to a toasty twenty-six degrees.

Olga had told Phoenix that her hometown of Wilmot sat roughly one hundred and thirty kilometres west of the airport. Twenty-five years ago, with a zoology degree under her arm, she had decided she needed to live like a hermit and thought moving to the bottom of the world would suit her perfectly well. As it was, Olga stopped in Tasmania, deciding that Wilmot, with fewer than three hundred people in it and bordered on two sides by rivers, was good enough, and bought herself the cheapest place on offer.

Phoenix's mood lifted as she motored through the small towns of Westbury, with its multitude of historic stone churches and

Georgian constructions, then Deloraine, set on the banks of the Meander River, and further on still through the farming town of Sheffield, with its colourful outdoor murals. Next thing, Wilmot greeted Phoenix with riot of zany homemade letterboxes – the town's claim to fame. Following the bright murals of Sheffield, these letterboxes lent her a sense of defiant, creative energy. For a moment, her doubts eased. She'd been right to come.

But then as she crossed the river and headed south towards Olga's home, the forest closed in. Trees climbed high into the sky, darkening the way forwards. The road turned to dirt, her mobile phone lost reception, and her hire car's wheels began to jolt painfully into ditches. Her surroundings felt gloomy and, frankly, like serial-killer territory, and she prayed the tiny rental would hold its own and not leave her stranded. Then the sat nav failed too. She grizzled at it, tapping uselessly at the screen.

She kept going, her teeth clenched, passing tree after tree after tree. She remembered Olga's street name, at least, and hoped there'd be a sign to point the way. A few minutes later, a hand-painted wooden sign announced she had reached the private lane of *Traveller's Rest*. There was, thankfully, just one dwelling at the end of the lane. It had to be Olga's place. She guided her wheels carefully over the potholed and water-damaged driveway, heading towards a glimpse of what looked to be a wooden cabin between the trees. At last she emerged into a clearing, the dirt driveway ending at what appeared to be two livable iron sheds covered in some sort of wooden veneer under an enormous, gnarled lemon tree, the last of the season's fruit low on its boughs and dripping to the ground.

'Hello, old friend.' She snapped a photo of the tree, moody in the late afternoon light.

Smoke puffed from a chimney in the first shed and even from inside her car she could hear Olga's dog barking furiously at the intruder. She took a deep breath and blew it out slowly, encouraging herself to get out of the car.

The dog's snarling continued, further escalating when she knocked on the red and gold Romani-inspired carved door. She expected Olga to be there, hushing the dog, but the animal kept up his tirade. She knocked again, worried now that she might have the day wrong, or even that Olga had collapsed from illness inside. She didn't know much about Olga's health in general but she guessed that late-stage cancer came with many complications.

'Olga?' she called. She itched to reach out and turn the metal knob of the door to check her friend was okay, but the dog's endless barking stayed her hand. She remembered the dog's name was Humphrey. She'd been expecting a big teddy-bear type, not this rather aggressive guard dog. 'Huuum-phrey,' she singsonged, cajoling him. A gunshot of a bark and a set of sharp white teeth shot up from below the window nearest the door. She jumped backwards, her hand to her galloping heart. Olga must be out. She would simply have to wait.

Phoenix backed away, instead heading towards the tree line by the road. There, she found a patch of semi-cleared land off to the right with strands of wire fencing, and followed the path. Reaching the metal gate, she spied the back end of a pony, a supremely hairy chestnut-brown Shetland by the looks of it. She smiled and called out to it in greeting, but it appeared not to hear her. She waved her arms back and forth instead and that got its attention. The pony's head rose from the grass, ears pricked in her direction, tufts sprouting from its mouth. Then it nickered to her and trotted to the gate, clearly hoping she had some sort of wonderful treat to offer.

'Sorry, lovely,' she said as it arrived at the gate – far friendlier than the dog, that was for certain. 'I didn't bring any food.' She offered her hand for the pony to sniff, and delighted in the feel of its soft lips and whiskers nuzzling her skin. 'Aren't you gorgeous?' she said, hanging over the gate now to rub its neck. The pony gave grunts of pleasure and leant into her.

'Itchy.'

Phoenix jumped at the unexpected noise and spun around to find Olga, she presumed, standing a few metres away. The woman's once-black hair was now heavily streaked with ribbons of white. Her shabby, overly long green coat hung baggy around her shoulders and Phoenix wondered if it had always been too large or if Olga had been shrinking.

'The colour of the eastern spinebill – *Acanthorhynchus tenuirostris*.' Olga squinted at Phoenix's head.

Startled by the observation, Phoenix touched her messily snagged hair. It was too orange to be brown but too brown to be orange, not enough highlight to be copper but too healthy to be dull. She'd often wondered what colour to name it. Now she knew – spinebill. She smiled. 'Hi. I'm Phoenix.'

Olga studied her a moment, swallowing a few times, her gaze meeting Phoenix's briefly before sliding away to rest on the pony, but didn't speak.

'Are you Olga?'

Olga nodded once and shoved her hands deeper into her pockets.

'Is this your pony?'

'Rita. Itchy and deaf.'

'She's a beauty.' Phoenix ran her hands through Rita's mane and the pony closed her eyes a moment. 'I used to beg my mum for a pony when I was young, but I was never allowed to have one.'

Olga turned and began to walk back to the house, so Phoenix followed her, nervousness leading her down a scramble of vocalised thoughts. 'Have you been out? I've been here a little while. I did come to the house first, not straight to the pony, I haven't

15

been wandering the property or anything, it's just that when I knocked Humphrey was doing a marvellous job at protecting the house and I was worried I was upsetting him too much, but then I didn't know if you were home and my phone has no reception so I couldn't message you so I thought, given how upset Humphrey was, that I should stay away from him and wait for you.' They were almost at the house now but Olga still hadn't spoken. Phoenix expected Humphrey to start barking again but he was silent. She fleetingly wondered if she'd given him a heart attack. That would be terrible luck to come here to help Olga find forever homes for her animals only to unwittingly kill one with her mere presence.

Olga opened the front door and entered without hesitation, while Phoenix froze to the spot, anticipating being leapt upon by the dog. But when he didn't appear, she peeked carefully inside and saw him shadowing Olga.

'Should I come inside?'

Olga turned, shrugged off her oversized coat and hung it on the hook, then beckoned her in. Phoenix wiped her shoes on the doormat then tentatively stepped inside, her eyes glued to the dog – but he was completely undisturbed by her entrance. His feathery tail waved slowly from side to side. Olga shuffled to a simple oiled wooden bench with a sink against the far wall, a half-open string of curtains beneath it to conceal plates and pots. A fridge gurgled in the corner. An open pantry exhibited canned and dry goods, as well as a bowl of bumpy lemons. From a shelf above the sink, she took down a pottery tea canister and began to make tea.

Phoenix hovered a moment, then eased into the single chair of the matching set of vintage brown and cream velour couches. Humphrey, satisfied he wasn't needed in the kitchen, climbed up gingerly onto the three-seater and flopped down with a satisfied groan. He was a border collie cross, by the looks of him, though totally black, other than his grey muzzle. He caught her looking at him and turned his head away in disgust. The old guy had personality, that was for sure.

She gazed around the space, taking in the concrete floor, covered almost entirely with overlapping mismatched rugs, and the pot-belly stove in the corner, currently blazing nicely and flanked by two tabby cats asleep in tight balls in baskets. Bookcases lined an entire wall, each shelf bowed under books stacked in no obvious order. A small wooden table was barely visible beneath towers of typed manuscripts, three-ring binders and a laptop perched precariously atop them all. A small staircase led to a loft above the kitchen. It was madcap and warm and she felt instantly at ease.

Olga placed a mug of white tea for her guest on top of a stack of *National Geographic* magazines so tall it served as a coffee table, then joined Humphrey on the big couch, a weathered hand with earth-stained fingers reaching out automatically to stroke his body. His tail thumped in return.

'Thank you,' Phoenix said, lifting her mug to her lips. It was another pottery creation. 'Did you make these?' she queried. 'And the tea canister and the other pottery pieces?'

Olga nodded. 'There's a wheel in the shed.' She tipped her head to the left, indicating the second shed Phoenix had seen upon arrival.

'They're wonderful.' Phoenix admired the tiny image of a ring-tail possum that had been carved into the belly of the mug. 'You're very clever.'

Olga jiggled the teabag in her cup, staring into the middle distance.

Phoenix opened her mouth to speak, then closed it again. She knew her own nerves were heightened by her day of travel and she knew Olga's preferred mode of communication was not the spoken word. How momentous to have intentionally lived as a hermit for twenty-five years and now being forced to open her home to someone she'd never met in person, someone who was there to help her finalise the care of her animals – her only true family. So Phoenix sat in silence, sipping her tea, and let the warmth of the fire and the deep calm and silence of their remote location settle into her bones and gently dissolve the stress of the day's travel.

She was almost to the bottom of her mug when Olga spoke.

'I'm sorry I didn't answer the door when you arrived.'

'It's okay,' Phoenix rushed to assure her, though she was quietly surprised that Olga had in fact been home when she'd knocked.

After another stretch of quiet, Olga continued. 'You here . . . makes it all real. This is the end.'

Phoenix bit her lip to ward off emotion.

Olga stared at Humphrey, her hand moving repetitively across his fur. 'How can I leave them?' she whispered.

Phoenix shook her head, lost for answers. 'I don't know,' she admitted.

Olga glanced at her, her own eyes bright with unshed tears.

'But I promise you this. I will not rest until I know all your animals are very safe and very loved, with homes for life that honour the great love you have for them. That is my promise to you, and my word is my bond.'

Olga smiled briefly and nodded. 'That's a good autistic trait to have.'

Phoenix smiled. 'Yeah. I like that one.'

Olga, apparently now energised, suddenly started. 'I should have asked you how you like your tea. That was rude of me.'

'It's fine, really. If someone's kind enough to make me a cup of tea, that makes me happy.'

'The cats will drink it if you leave it unattended,' she warned.

'Really?'

'Oh, yes. They shouldn't though. The caffeine's no good. But the pony loves coffee.'

'That's adorable.'

'I make her one every morning. She's quite grumpy without it. And the chickens love sunflower seeds.'

Phoenix cocked her head to the side. 'Chickens?' She didn't remember Olga saying anything about chickens.

'Four girls. Rarely lay.'

'Right, chickens.' Phoenix mentally adjusted the list of animals, wondering what else Olga might have stashed away. 'So, one pony, one dog, two cats and four chickens. Is that the lot?'

Olga pressed her lips together, murmuring, and Phoenix waited, wondering what she might reveal next. 'Well, there is Henry.'

'Henry?'

'But you probably won't want to, shouldn't really anyway . . . not legal.'

Legal?

Phoenix had a sinking suspicion she knew what Olga was talking about and her body stiffened.

'But after I'm gone . . .' Olga paused, playing with Humphrey's ears, making him grunt in pleasure. 'Someone will buy the place and probably knock everything down, build a big house, put in a pool, clear the land.'

'Olga, is Henry a python?'

She nodded. '*Morelia spilota.* A real beauty.'

Phoenix swallowed, unable to speak. Snakes filled her with utter horror. There was no way she could deal with one. She peered around the home, glancing upwards to the loft. 'And where exactly does Henry live?'

'In the shed,' Olga said. 'I'll have to get someone to come and catch him and relocate him,' she said sadly.

'Mm,' Phoenix said, as sympathetically as she could. Surprise chickens she could deal with. A snake, she could not. 'Just so I'm clear, is that *all* the animals you have?'

Olga gazed at the ceiling a moment, then nodded.

'Okay,' Phoenix said. 'We can do this. First thing tomorrow, we'll go through the local options and I can make some queries while you're in hospital. Then together we can make a start when you get back.'

Olga made them a simple meal of beans on toast for dinner. Phoenix had brought a loaf of gluten-free bread with her, always prepared. After that, Olga gave Phoenix the wi-fi password so Phoenix could message Zack to let him know she was okay, then handed over a set of clean sheets, plucked from a leather trunk on the ground floor. The aged, stale smell of them made Phoenix's eyes water, but she stuffed down her reaction.

Olga grimaced sharply.

'Are you okay?' Phoenix asked.

'Pain,' Olga gasped, closing her eyes and leaning against the wall for support. Her shoulders hunched high near her ears. 'My back.' She groaned, taking short, sharp inhalations. 'Sorry. I don't think I can make the bed for you.'

'It's no problem.' Phoenix put the sheets down on the steps leading to the loft. 'But what can I do for you? Do you have pain-killers or something?' Her eyes scanned the cluttered home for bottles or pill packets.

'No, it's fine.' Olga staggered back to the couch. Phoenix made her a cup of tea and found some paracetamol in her own bag, encouraging Olga to take those at the very least. By the time Olga had finished her tea, she said the pain had gone, lifted as swiftly as it had descended.

'That's good,' Phoenix said, relieved Olga would be heading to hospital the next day and able to get stronger pain relief. 'But I am not going to sleep in your bed. I will sleep on the couch. You must go and get some rest.'

But Olga would not be deterred. 'I won't be sleeping tonight. Far too many things to organise. I need to write you detailed notes on all the animals. Right now, I can barely think of anything past the hospital stay, but when I get back I'll be able to give all my focus to the rehoming. Still, I want to make a start on the notes for you, so you at least have something to go on while I'm in hospital.'

'But—'

'No arguments,' Olga said. 'My house, my rules.'

Despite endless attempts to get Olga to allow Phoenix to help her with the things she needed to do, to stay up with her through the night to keep her company, Olga rebuffed them all. Phoenix was left with no choice but to climb the stairs to the loft and make her bed. She was a terrible insomniac in any such unfamiliar space, not to mention the tangible sadness and tension of Olga's plight, so sleep was nowhere in sight, but at 5 am, Phoenix snapped to consciousness from the barest whisper of a doze to hear Olga crying.

She waited a few moments, her heart thumping hard, wondering if it was better to go to Olga and offer support or let her have this time alone to prepare for the coming onslaught of being in a bright, loud, odorous hospital. She pushed back the covers and rose, but paused when she heard the dog ease himself to his feet and whimper, his claws making soft scrapes across the old rug as he made his way to Olga. Phoenix crept to the loft's railing to peer over and watch as Humphrey climbed up carefully onto the couch and lay down with his person, his head in her lap, whimpering and licking her hands. Olga crumpled over him, her shoulders shaking as she poured her misery out to her best friend in the world. Her hands wove into his fur, holding onto him for what was left of her life. Phoenix watched them a while, her vision blurry with tears. She did not go down, certain that Olga wanted this special time alone with her beloved dog. She retreated to her bed, uneasy, for another couple of hours of restless drifts of slumber.

When she removed her eye mask and earplugs a short time later, the morning was grey, the room cold now that the fire had burnt itself out. The little house was silent. It made her happy to think of Olga at last finding some rest with Humphrey. It strengthened Phoenix's resolve. This was why she was there – to ensure Olga knew her loved ones would be cared for when she could no longer do it.

She threw her puffer jacket on over the soft pants and long-sleeved top she wore to bed, stuffed her feet into her ugg boots, and padded down the creaking wooden stairs as quietly as she could. She expected Humphrey to snap and snarl at her, but peeking across the room, she saw the dog was still snuggled up against Olga where she'd seen them earlier.

Phoenix hovered at the edge of the space and let her gaze rest on the sight of Olga and her dog, asleep. A relieved smile settled on Phoenix's lips, but a moment later, it vanished. A strangled noise barely escaped her constricting throat.

The pallor of her friend's face conveyed it clearly. Olga was dead.

3

Humphrey was still with Olga when the paramedics arrived.

'He won't leave her,' Phoenix said, her voice weak and wobbly through tears.

'That's okay, love,' the older paramedic said, smiling at her from behind his bushy grey beard. 'It's not uncommon.' He indicated for his younger partner, a nervous-looking woman with blue veins visible beneath her pale skin, to hold back a moment. Then he knelt down near the couch and offered the back of his hand to Humphrey to sniff. 'Hey, buddy. You're a great dog, aren't you? You're looking after your mum? Good boy. I'm here to help.'

Humphrey raised his head and considered the man, extended his nose and quivering nostrils to his flesh, then sighed and pulled away. Phoenix's eyes filled with tears. Gone was the fight she'd seen in Humphrey the day before.

'I'm just going to have a look at your mum,' the paramedic told Humphrey. Then, just as Phoenix had done, he laid his fingers against Olga's throat and her wrist, working gently to seek a pulse.

23

Rationally, Phoenix knew he wouldn't find one, yet her nerves drew taut, hoping. Olga had already been cool when Phoenix had touched her. The paramedic grunted, and continued with a variety of tests until he was satisfied. He straightened, patting Humphrey on the head, telling him again that he was a good boy.

Turning to face Phoenix, he flung his stethoscope over the back of his neck and took a breath before speaking to her calmly and clearly. 'You were right; she's definitely gone. She is dead.'

Phoenix nodded, biting her lip and blinking rapidly.

'We're going to call for a doctor now, who will come and issue a medical certificate of death, or decide if they think an autopsy is needed.'

'Autopsy?'

'It's always considered in these kinds of cases. But given what you told us about her advanced cancer and the pain in her back, I'd hazard a guess she either died from a heart attack or some other cancer-related complication. The doctor will be able to tell you more.' He nodded to his partner, who left the room, presumably to contact the doctor. Then he set about making Phoenix a cup of tea.

'Are you going to be okay here on your own, waiting for the doctor?'

'Oh . . .' She couldn't process his question. How long would she be there alone in this house with a deceased Olga? She imagined herself sitting there with her and Humphrey, alone, in the quiet.

'You could wait outside, if it's easier,' he said.

'I might do that,' she agreed, barely able to believe this was really happening.

By late morning, the ambulance officers had left, the doctor had left, and the funeral director had left with Olga's body. Phoenix had tended to the animals, trying unsuccessfully to get Humphrey to eat, then collapsed into the single armchair that faced the couch where Olga had died. Aside from trotting alongside the rattling procession of Olga's body out the door, Humphrey hadn't left the couch. He lay there now, not asleep, but not moving either, his eyes staring into nothing as grief overwhelmed him. When Phoenix finished another round of crying, she picked up her phone to contact Zack and discovered several displeased messages from both Linda and Evelyn about Phoenix's failure to turn up to their scheduled meeting.

'No, no, no,' she groaned, imagining a furious Evelyn pacing and muttering. She texted Zack and he called back the moment he could take a break.

'I'll come down on the next flight.' His keys jangled as if he was about to head out the door this instant.

'What about work?'

He paused and she knew he'd be pulling his watchband tight against his wrist as he struggled with this problem. 'They'll have to cope without me.'

'But the reason you're doing overtime is because you're already two radiographers down and it's still another month before the new one can start.'

'Yes, but that's work and this is *you*. I'd do anything for you.'

'I know.' If she hurt herself, if she got sick, if she was away from home, he was quick to panic. 'I love that you want to help me and honestly I do wish you were here right now. I could really use a hug.' She stopped as her voice began to crack.

'Then I'll do it.'

'Let's wait, okay.' Her head reeled, simply unable to keep up with everything that had happened. She pinched the bridge of her nose, seeking a focus point in the swirling thoughts. 'It will cost a lot to get you down here and it might even damage your chances for promotion. It's not a good time to leave them in the lurch.'

He grumped a few words of agreement under his breath.

'Give me till tomorrow to think. I can barely string sentences together at the moment.'

'When did you last eat?' he asked suddenly.

'The nice ambo made me some tea and toast.'

'When was that?'

'I'm not sure.' Time had warped with the panic and shock.

'You need to eat something to help your brain think straight again.'

She eyed the open pantry, wondering about the appropriateness of rummaging through Olga's fridge and cupboards, looking for food. It felt wrong. Was it stealing? A cold wave crashed over her. She was in a strange land . . . and she was alone. Suddenly, the thickness of the trees in the forest surrounding the house, the long dirt road with no mobile reception, the distance she was from Zack, and her isolation here in this moment, in a room still echoing with death, felt more than a little eerie. She flicked her gaze to Humphrey, flattened on the couch, not caring about his surroundings. She had no confidence he would rise to protect her the way he had Olga when Phoenix had arrived at the door. Zack was right; she needed to take care of herself. Olga wouldn't want her to be unsafe or unwell, because she needed Phoenix to be there for her animals. 'Okay, I will.' She ended the call, agreeing to talk with Zack again after she'd had time to process the shock of the day.

Clumsily, she made herself a cup of tea, extra milky and sweet. Resuming her place in the armchair, she rubbed her thumb over the possum on Olga's handmade mug, and held vigil over Humphrey. His breaths were shallow and Phoenix half expected him to simply give up. 'I'm sorry this has happened to you,' she said. To her surprise, he flicked up his dark eyes to meet hers and blinked. 'I promise you, I'm going to find you the best home.' At this, he moved his gaze away and stared into nothingness once more.

Heavy raindrops began to hit the iron roof and the pride she'd felt that morning at coming to Olga's rescue was extinguished. It was all too little, too late.

The larger of Olga's tabby cats jumped up unexpectedly into Phoenix's lap, nearly causing her to spill her tea.

'Ah, hi,' she said, placing her mug down and giving her attention to the cat. She checked the name tag. 'Audrey. You're the oldest cat, I think Olga said.' Audrey threw herself down in a half-roll in Phoenix's lap, a huge purr rumbling out of her throat, pushing her head into Phoenix's hand and drooling with pleasure. Phoenix returned the affection, already feeling better for having this warm, living being snuggled in her lap. She was less lonely. Less afraid. Calmer.

Again, she considered Humphrey, sad and alone. Who on earth would take this ageing, peculiar dog, one who could be a fierce beast one moment then slayed with depression and loss the next? Phoenix swept her gaze to the cat basket, where tiny Marilyn slumbered on her back, paws in the air. Then her ruminations turned to the outside animals – to the paddock and the dear deaf pony who loved coffee, and then to the motley crew of barely laying chickens. All of them aged. All of them vulnerable. All of them now orphaned. Then she thought about Olga and her promises to help her with her animals.

Doubts prickled up her legs.

What if she *couldn't* rehome them? Or what if she did rehome them but then the people wanted to hand them back? Or worse, what if they mistreated them or dumped them at a shelter? She already knew there was no way she would hand these animals to just anybody, and even then she felt that to truly honour her promises to Olga she would need to be an ongoing godmother figure who could watch over them from afar.

She let her gaze again rest on Humphrey's broken spirit and it took her all of three more seconds to make the only decision that felt right. *She* would take care of all of Olga's animals. She wouldn't waste Zack's time in getting him down here to help her try to rehome them. Instead, she would take every single one of them back to Brisbane with her – even the pony. 'I give you my word, Olga, and my word is my bond.'

Suddenly, she was bursting with ideas and action points. This was better, fuelled by urgency and planning rather than despair. She texted Zack, announcing she had a plan and that he should call her tonight so they could go through it. Then she jumped into her Downunder Auties group to let them know about Olga. It wasn't an easy message to write, and shock and sympathy flooded in from the group almost immediately. Their words threatened to undo Phoenix's composure so she switched out of there and got back to Evelyn and her assistant, apologising for the missed meeting, explaining about the sudden death of her friend, and asking to reschedule.

To keep moving, she turned to the notes Olga had written in haste the night before, her lists of animals and their quirks, their ages, medical conditions and feeding routines. Phoenix read through them, relieved Olga had managed to write them but dismayed that this was all she had to go on. Olga wasn't supposed to die so soon. She was supposed to be back here in a few days, her treatment giving her more time to make her plans. This was supposed to be the start of the preparations, not the end.

Still digesting this unexpected turn of events, Phoenix hit the web to research how it was even possible to get these animals home to Brisbane. Racehorses flew around the world but she was certain it wouldn't be in her budget to fly a pony. But complicating a road trip was the big old Bass Strait lying between Tasmania and the mainland before she even got to the thousands of kilometres after that.

Her research hit many dead ends and disturbing accounts of injuries, disappearances and deaths during animal transport. She pushed herself away from the table. As doubts began to gather, she returned to the Auties. What she needed now was the collective wisdom of the group.

PhoenixRising: Thank you all for your kind words and sympathy. It's been really difficult. But now I need our brains trust. I'm going to bring all of Olga's animals home with me from Tasmania to Brisbane. That's one old dog, two old cats, one old pony and four old chickens and I have no idea how to do it. I've looked at flights but I can't fly the pony. Also, I've looked at Olga's notes and the dog has a heart condition (I've found his meds) and extreme anxiety. That rules him out from flying.

I could pay for horse transport for the pony but I'd still have to drive anyway so I might as well take her with me. The only thing is that I don't have a vehicle big enough for the job and I've never even towed a garden trailer, let alone a horse float! I'm an anxious, stressed-out traveller and I really can't drive for more than a couple of hours at a time before fatiguing out. I want to be on the road by the weekend, which doesn't leave a lot of time to organise something like this, especially as I need both a vehicle and horse float. Zack offered to come down to help me but I don't want him risking his chance of promotion, so I'm going to have to handle it myself. All advice appreciated!

•

Zack called that night.

'Hello,' she said warmly, relieved to hear his voice after the silence of Olga's house.

'Are you okay?'

'I think so.'

'I still want to come down to be with you. I can get a flight first thing. What do you think?' he asked.

She cast her eye over Humphrey's deflated body, still on the couch, and took a deep breath. 'I was thinking about rehoming the animals and I did a lot of research and the reality is that rescues are overcrowded and old or sick animals rarely find their happi-ly-ever-afters. So, I feel the best thing to do, to truly honour my promise to Olga, is to keep them.' Zack was silent, absorbing her

29

words. She continued. 'Instead of you coming down, I think we all – me and the animals – need to come back to you.'

'But—' Here, Zack ran out of words.

'I know there're logistical challenges here. We are renting our house for one and currently have no animals on the lease, but we're buying a house soon and one dog and two cats in a home is not a lot.' Despite trying to convince herself about this, her voice lost its strength at the end – it was definitely a big jump for renters with no animals on their lease, especially in the current market. She opened her mouth to say more but decided to wait, giving Zack a chance to organise his thoughts.

'Didn't you say she had a pony?' he finally said.

'Ah, yes.'

'But we live in the suburbs.'

'True.'

'We don't have land.'

'Also true.'

'Then how can we keep a pony?'

'I'll find somewhere to keep her,' she said.

Zack fell silent once more.

'I know this is a lot to take in,' she said, bending down to rub little Marilyn's head as she smooched against Phoenix's leg. 'I think the best action we can take is to do the next right thing.'

'But what *is* that?' he asked, quite reasonably.

'I truly believe the right thing to do is to get these animals out of here and bring them home.'

'But I don't like dogs,' he said.

'Oh.' In all the stress of the day, she'd conveniently forgotten that. She glanced at Humphrey's lethargic, silent form on the couch. He may be placid now but she'd seen him at his boldest when they first met. If she had to sell the idea of a dog to Zack, she guessed someone small, meek and fluffy would be the way to go, not someone large, loud, unfriendly at best and aggressive at worst. 'Can we get them all home to Brisbane and work it out then? I really need to get out of here.' For a moment, she felt the walls closing in on her. Her skin flamed hot. She shut her eyes tightly and continued. 'The worst-case scenario will be that I have to rehome them once I get back, which is no worse than if I rehomed them here, but better in the sense that I might get home sooner, I can take my time finding them homes and I can be local to them so I can actively watch over them. I can still be connected.'

'That does make sense,' he said.

'The best-case scenario is that I bring them all home and it all works out beautifully. Maybe you and Humphrey will love each other and he'll be the first dog you connect with. If not,' she rushed to assure him, 'I'll find him a new home.'

'But that sounds like a lot of trauma for him.'

'It does,' she agreed. 'But honestly, if you could see him, you'd see that he is already broken. I don't think we can do much worse than what he's going through now, having watched Olga die.' She swiped at yet another tear rolling down her cheek.

'Okay,' Zack said, and inhaled deeply. 'Let's do it.'

'Really?'

'Sure. Two cats, a dog and a pony. How hard could it be?'

'Exactly,' she said, her spirits rising. Then, 'Oh, wait, there's *one* more thing.'

'Mm?'

'Did I mention the four chickens?'

4

There was a tiny second when Phoenix first woke where she'd forgotten what had happened. Then she was awake, remembering. She allowed herself a cry then abruptly pulled herself together. She needed to get out of there and back home and she was now responsible for one, two . . . *eight* animals, not including the snake, which she ruled out immediately. The python was a wild animal; he could take care of himself. She turned on her phone to find a message from Zack, checking on her, and she sent him a boatload of love back. She was suddenly full of regrets that she hadn't married him when she'd had the chance.

When Zack had first brought up marriage a few years earlier, she'd agreed straight away. But the moment she'd stepped towards a wedding dress shop, the sight of all the white dresses had paralysed her. She'd literally not been able to walk through the door. The whole idea of a wedding – of the organisation involved, of having everyone's eyes on her, imagining the tightness of one of those dresses, the fussy layers, scratchy synthetic materials, the absolute *whiteness* of it, the accessorising of shoes and underwear and clutches and make-up and hair – had completely undone her.

Through tears, she'd confessed that, while she wanted to be with him forever, she didn't want a wedding. Instead, they decided to buy a house together, a legal arrangement to signify their union as much as any marriage certificate could, and they'd been saving ever since. Right now, they were on track to go house hunting and buy something in time to move during the Christmas holidays.

But in the past two months, her whole idea of herself had been dismantled. Her idea of the rules of life had loosened its hold on her. While she was busy rebuilding her identity, it had been Zack she'd seen more clearly than ever before. He was her everything. She *did* want to marry him, though she still didn't know how to do it without the stress ruining it all. But he was her Southern Cross – the way home, every time.

She smiled at the wallpaper photo of the two of them on her phone, at his lopsided smile, the cowrie shell and leather wristband on his arm pulling her close, and the long dark lashes surrounding the deep pools of his eyes. Their cheeks were pressed together, eyes bright from a recent belly laugh.

She would propose to him as soon as she got home.

'Morning,' she called into the stillness of the cabin. Marilyn and Audrey raised their heads, meowed in return and hopped from their baskets. Marilyn trotted and talked as she made her way over. Audrey was slower, her bulk swaying slightly as she ambled, but no less chatty. Phoenix dropped two handfuls of biscuits onto the floor. She stroked them both as they ate, enjoying their low rumbling purrs, and they arched their backs up into her hands in appreciation.

With a heavy heart, she turned to the couch where Olga had been this time yesterday. Humphrey was there, completely still.

She held her breath, but a tense moment later, his ribs expanded. 'Oh, Humphrey, you're going to make me cry again.'

She made coffee, enough for the pony to share as well, then headed outside to feed the chickens and Rita, pausing to revel in the sight of the hairy Shetland snorting into her morning brew, covering her muzzle in it, licking her lips, her eyes glazing over with pleasure. Then back in the house, she settled into her favourite armchair and logged in to the Downunder Auties, crossing her fingers and toes for miraculous answers to all her tricky questions.

Jess (aka Reddotspartyfrocks), a drama teacher, had been away on a regional tour and was only now catching up on it all, from Olga's original plea for help to Phoenix's.

I can't think what I can possibly do but I want to help. At the very least, if you're coming past my place, I would love to come and see you.

The same went for Kitty (aka MissWittyKitty), who said she didn't even have a licence herself, relying on her parents to drive her around, so she didn't see how she could help either, but added that she would also love to see Phoenix if she was passing by.

It was a lovely sentiment, and something Phoenix would normally enjoy, but her mission was to get home as quickly as possible without detours or hiccups. She thanked them both and said she'd definitely keep it in mind, though couldn't imagine how it would be at all possible.

On the other hand, Shane (FidgetMan) had thoughts that left Phoenix feeling ill.

Look, I'm an accountant so this is how I think, and you probably don't want to hear it (most of my clients don't), but have you made a budget? I'm guessing not. You strike me as the idealistic dreamer type. I'm going to make a spreadsheet and get it to you ASAP.

The coffee in Phoenix's belly swirled uncomfortably. Shane was correct. She hadn't made a budget. Other than baulking at the cost of plane fares, she hadn't got much further in her financial research. She was good at saving money. She was also good at spending it. Her life's relationship with money generally swung from one to the other, rarely finding balance in the centre. Right now, she and Zack were in saving mode for the house. She well and truly had her head in the sand about the impact this trip might make on those plans.

Ignoring the discomfort the financial discussion elicited, she moved on to Carla's (CarlaM78) message.

Sounds to me like you need a travelling companion. We could check in our autie circles for someone. What do you think?

Phoenix was quick to give her enthusiastic agreement. A travelling companion would help ease the driving load considerably. Of course, she'd prefer to have Zack, but his promotion came first. And this had been her idea; she needed to sort it out.

Therese (aka SnoopyDancer) jumped in too.

It's your friendly neighbourhood social worker here ☺ I'll send you my phone number. Call or PM me anytime, okay? I live for these kinds of aspirational shenanigans.

It was welcome support after Shane's douse of cold water on her dreams. Feeling truly hopeful for the first time since Olga's death, she read the next message from Bruno (aka VikingMan).

Hey, I run a courier company. I have a fleet of vehicles on the road. I will see if I can sort out a van for you.

Phoenix could have jumped out of her skin with joy, but settled on jumping out of her seat with a whoop. This was really going to happen. So much was it going to happen, in fact, that by that very afternoon, Carla had lined up three interviews for Phoenix to do with prospective travelling companions.

•

There was something so calming about The Grind cafe in Wilmot, with sturdy red bricks on the outside and its almost-white greys, gentle muted blues and blond wooden tables on the inside, that Phoenix felt herself inhale deeply the moment she walked in the door. She'd returned to the world of the living. To her utter delight, a gluten-free baked lemon cheesecake sat in the glass cabinet and her mouth watered instantly. She wouldn't be leaving here today without trying that.

She'd arrived early so she could wolf down some freshly made food before her first interview with James F at 2 pm. She ordered a gluten-free turkey and cranberry sandwich with an extra strong flat white on almond. But as it turned out, she needn't have given herself indigestion in her efforts to finish it all before James F arrived because he was late. After forty-five minutes of writing to-do lists, Phoenix resigned herself to the fact he wasn't coming and messaged Carla to let her know, then ordered another coffee.

Constance W was also late, and Phoenix had nearly accepted the idea that no one would be coming to meet her today at all when a woman opened the front door, her blue hair and purple kaftan lighting up the entrance. There she paused, surveying the walls and the ceiling of the rectangular room, then carefully turned towards Phoenix.

'Hi,' Phoenix said, smiling. 'Are you Constance?'

Constance nodded.

'I'm Phoenix, it's lovely to meet you.' Phoenix held out her hand but Constance didn't respond and instead stared at the framed picture behind Phoenix's head, an indistinguishable murmur escaping her throat. Phoenix withdrew her hand. 'Would you like to sit down? You've come from Launceston, haven't you?'

'Forty-two Potters Road, eight kilometres out of town,' Constance said briskly, half sitting, then straightening, then trying again, this time succeeding. She turned her body to the left to gaze out the window.

'Right,' Phoenix said, not having a clue which part of Launceston that might be. 'Thank you so much for coming. Can I get you a drink or something to eat? Tea, coffee, cake?' She wouldn't mind a bit of that cheesecake about now.

Constance licked her lips several times before shaking her head.

'I'm so glad you're interested in making the trip. It's comforting to know I'll have a companion as it's quite a long journey – eight days by my current calculations. I think Carla said you have family in Brisbane, is that right?'

Constance crossed her arms to squeeze herself tightly. 'Of sorts.'

Phoenix waited for Constance to elaborate but when she didn't she prompted, 'Have you made long journeys before this? Would you say you're a "good" traveller?'

'Maybe. Not sure.'

'Do you like animals?' Phoenix attempted to get them onto common ground, assuming the animals would be a drawcard for the trip.

In answer to this, Constance covered her eyes. 'Can you stop looking at me?'

'Ah, sorry, I . . .' Phoenix began. She looked over Constance's shoulder to address the wall. 'I should have realised. It's my fault, I wasn't thinking.'

But now Constance was on her feet and striding from the cafe.

Phoenix sat frozen, her jaw unhinged until she felt the weight of the questioning eyes of the others in the cafe. She reached for the now empty coffee cup, turning it smoothly in its saucer, her face hot. She stayed there for several minutes, eyes downcast, disorientated and twice rejected. It was looking more and more like she'd have to make the long trek home by herself.

If ever there was a time for cheesecake, it was now. She ordered a piece and another strong coffee and returned to the table to find a message from Carla.

Constance has declined to take the road trip with you. She says she doesn't feel comfortable with you. Sorry ☹

Phoenix re-read the message. The refusal by a fellow autie hurt, her new identity still tender, her claiming of it still lacking in confidence. She'd been nervous to meet Constance, and sometimes when she was trying to make a good impression, her eye contact got stuck in one spot and she wrestled with how to move it on. In this case, she'd pushed away a fellow autie because of her inability to regulate. Phoenix had spent her life masking to pass as neurotypical. Eye contact was what the world demanded. It was a learned behaviour, one she'd thought she'd mastered. Had she become *too neurotypical*?

The sting of judgement brought to mind the sore point of Anthea's reaction to the news of Phoenix's identification. Phoenix's best workmate had had the final word in their conversation while weaving between peak-hour lanes on her way to school. *What rot. You don't look autistic at all.* Anthea's words, her instant, almost aggressive dismissal, still dogged her.

First Anthea – *you don't look autistic at all.* Now, Constance – uncomfortable with Phoenix's learned neurotypical behaviours. Would she spend her whole life being 'not autistic enough' to be autistic but not neurotypical enough to be considered 'normal'? She *was* different: that she'd always known. But maybe she was different enough for things to always be a struggle but not different enough to be actually accepted as 'different'?

The optimistic mood she'd started the day with plummeted and she felt dangerously close to tears, urgently close to getting up and leaving this cafe never to return, frighteningly close to calling Zack and asking him to come and get her. She couldn't do this alone and he was the only person who truly understood her.

She reached for the fork and carved off the tip of the piece of cheesecake, the sweet, creamy goodness filling her mouth and calming her, the way food had done when she was a teenager – the release of pressure and stress at the end of another day of simply surviving at school.

The base was soft and tasted of cinnamon. The lemon topping, tangy and bright. She reached for another fluffy forkful, inhaling wafts of vanilla. Another mouthful, and another, her brain registering the dopamine hit. She swilled the second coffee, then opened Pinterest, adding photos of lemon chicken soup and lemon garlic butter salmon. She'd managed to pull herself together into her 'teacher mode' by the time her third and final interviewee arrived

Lily Buchanon was a sight to behold. She was easily six feet tall and slender, not that long out of school at Phoenix's guess, with long, curly mermaid hair that was pinned above her ears and fell to her shoulderblades in a bushel of autumnal tones. Her clothes made Phoenix's mouth drop. 'You look incredible,' she said, managing to stop herself from asking if Lily had stepped off a film set. Her potential travelling companion wore a fitted dark velvet coat with brass buttons over a frilly white shirt, an elaborate gold and black belt above maroon riding pants, and tall brown boots. The young woman's arrival had engaged everyone's attention.

'I accept your compliment with pleasure,' Lily replied, in a rather good impression of a Jane Austen BBC series voice. She pulled out the chair opposite Phoenix, who was astounded to see how easily the young woman could move in her intricate outfit.

Phoenix couldn't imagine even being able to breathe in it. She tucked her own scuffed boots under the table, her attention to fashion being limited to what felt comfortable and warm.

'Thank you so much for coming,' Phoenix said, truly relieved. Lily exuded an air of grace that dared her to believe this meeting would go well. 'Can I get you a cup of tea?' She was about to suggest coffee but going with the Merrie Olde England theme decided tea was perhaps more suited.

'You may, thank you.'

'How do you take it?' Phoenix asked, trying not to copy the formal enunciation. The last thing she wanted was for Lily to think she was mocking her. She was anything but – she had a good ear for accents and affectations and often found herself unconsciously repeating them like a pesky parrot in the corner of the loungeroom.

'A slice of lemon would be delightful.'

Phoenix smiled. *Lemon for the win.* She ordered the tea and was thrilled when the owner brought out a fancy china teapot with two matching cups and saucers and small bowl of cut lemon. Having poured the tea, Phoenix proceeded. After Constance's startling exit, she wanted to make sure they began this conversation clearly. 'I'm thinking we should start at the beginning.'

'That is always a wise place to begin.'

'What has Carla told you about this trip?' Phoenix asked.

'The correspondence detailed a lengthy journey by road from Tasmania, heading north to Brisbane, accompanied by several animals – a dog, cats, chickens and a pony, I believe.'

'Yes, that's right,' Phoenix confirmed, much relieved.

'We shall need to travel by boat and vehicle across many counties until we reach our destination. Eight days is the allotted itinerary, is it not?'

'Exactly. Does that sound okay with you? Are you in a hurry to get to Brisbane? I very much hope we'll get there in eight days but in case we do run into trouble, will it cause you any distress if we need to extend by a couple of days?'

Lily delicately turned her cup on her saucer, considering. 'I should not think so.'

Phoenix smiled. 'Do you like animals? Do you have any of your own.'

'I have a considerable affection for bats,' Lily announced, her eyes widening with delight.

'Bats?'

'Incredible mammals and most regrettably under-esteemed.' She shook her head crossly. 'I have been championing their cause for many years now.'

'Ah, I see,' Phoenix said, smiling. Lily had leapt straight to her special interest, the thing that lit her up from within.

Lily continued. 'With regards to other animals, my mama and papa are landholders so I grew up understanding the ways of the land and its inhabitants. My childhood was filled with horses, poultry and stock of various kinds.'

'Oh, that's wonderful. I love horses but I don't know much about looking after them, so it will be a big relief for me to have someone knowledgeable along. And do you have a licence? Can you drive a car or pull a horse float?'

Lily smiled. 'I am accomplished at both of those things. There are many large vehicles on my family's estate.'

Phoenix couldn't believe her luck. 'This is wonderful. I know this is short notice but I'm hoping we can leave this weekend. I'm determined to have the vehicle and horse float sorted very soon and then we can set off to meet the ferry on Saturday. That was the first day I could get a berth. Does that work for you? Do you have a job or anything you need to get time off from?'

'I am not engaged in employment at this time, rather preferring independent means. I make a modest living as a seamstress and artist.'

That explained the clothes.

'I am available to depart on Saturday.'

At this, Phoenix exchanged mobile numbers with Lily – whose modern necessity was tucked away inside the billowing pockets of her riding pants – and said she would contact her as soon as possible for the trip north.

Lily hesitated. 'I am able to meet you sooner, if it is agreeable. I imagine there are numerous jobs to organise for this journey and many animals to care for.' She leant forwards eagerly in her seat. 'If it is not an inconvenience. But I am keen to get acquainted with our charges as soon as possible. I believe I could be of some service to you at this time.' She paused a moment, then added, 'Carla informed me of the passing of your friend. I am so very sorry for your loss.'

Phoenix swallowed. 'Thank you.' There was something urgent in the way Lily hoped to join her sooner rather than later, but she ignored it for the sake of gaining company. It lifted her spirits to think she might not be alone in that house in the forest for much longer. 'You know what? It would be a great help to have you on board as soon as you wish.'

'Wonderful,' Lily said, and gave a small but bright smile.

'Out of interest, who are you meeting in Brisbane?' Phoenix inquired. 'Carla said you had a friend to see, is that right?'

'An amour, in truth, and I cannot deny that intentions have been declared between us.' Lily's cheeks took on a rosy hue and she touched her hair a moment.

'Have you been separated from each other for long?'

Now Lily's cheeks flamed. 'Although we have exchanged extensive correspondence, we are yet to have the fortune of intimate introductions.'

'It must be exciting to finally meet, I guess.' Phoenix smiled in an attempt to make up for the lack of enthusiasm in her voice.

'Are you around the same age?' All sorts of worrying thoughts about scams and frauds raced through her mind.

'Her name is Bianca Mayberry and I won't deny she is my senior by some years. I am but twenty years, and just now coming out, while Bianca is not yet two score and one.'

'Ah.' The age gap, combined with the fact that their romance had been conducted entirely online, put Phoenix instantly on edge. She had many more questions for Lily but knew she should keep them to herself for now. There'd be plenty of time for them to talk in the car as they made their way to Brisbane.

5

The next morning, Lily texted announcing she would be at Olga's house by that afternoon. Taking encouragement from the forward momentum, Phoenix followed MagentaMel's advice and called the local vet to come and check all the animals. When Dr Gertie arrived – tall, mid-thirties, ponytail askew out the back of a white cap – Phoenix was instantly relieved. 'Thank you so much for coming,' she said, meeting the vet at her large and throaty truck.

'Absolutely,' Gertie said, pulling out a battered leather bag and slamming the truck's door shut. 'I'm so sorry to hear about Olga.'

'It was quite a shock.' Phoenix pulled her coat around herself against a sharp hand of icy wind that had slid down her collar.

'I can imagine.' Gertie followed Phoenix over to the pony's yard, her bag clinking with metal implements. 'Is it true you're planning to take all of Olga's animals back to Brisbane with you?'

Phoenix was rattled by the edge of doubt in the vet's tone. 'Yes.' She nodded, giving her an *I know it's crazy* shrug of the shoulders.

'Good for you,' Gertie said. 'More than a quarter of a million cats and dogs are euthanised each year in this country. Older animals barely stand a chance. The chickens don't stand any chance at all. And all but a slim minority of horses end up at the knackery,' she said grimly, nodding at Rita in the distance.

'Thank you,' Phoenix said, feeling the weight of the vet's words, appreciating the endorsement of her challenging plan. 'I thought it was best to have them checked before I go.' Their boots crunched on the path as they neared the paddock.

'It's a good idea,' Gertie agreed, her eyes locked on the pony meandering through the grass. 'There's not much in Rita's records but I did her annual dental about six months ago, so at least you won't have to worry about that till next year.' Gertie opened the gate; Rita spied them, lifted her head and gave a low nicker. 'Hey there, pretty girl,' Gertie said, then turned to Phoenix, gazing at her hands. 'Do you have a halter?'

'You mean, like a dog harness for walking? Or the thing with reins for riding?'

'You're not horsy, then?' Gertie said, smiling.

'No,' Phoenix admitted.

'Do you have animals of your own back home? Cats or dogs?'

Phoenix shook her head, feeling foolish.

Gertie nodded, patting Rita's back a moment while she thought. 'Okay, we'll take this from the top.' She pulled out her phone. 'Hey, it's me. I'm out at Olga Hoffman's place in Wilmot. I'm going to be here a while. You might need to call a few of today's clients and tell them I'll be running late.'

'I'm so sorry,' Phoenix said.

'Everything's going to be okay,' Gertie said, encouraging.

Over the next two hours, Gertie assessed each animal, prescribed treatments or medications and gave advice about feeding and travelling while Phoenix scribbled everything down.

Every animal received worming treatments, vaccinations and the paperwork required to board the ferry. Gertie warned Phoenix about Hendra virus (lethal to horses and humans alike), bumble-foot and lice in chickens, heartworm treatment for Humphrey, stress in cats leading to urinary cystitis or blockages, and flea and tick prevention. She advised against sedatives for travel on the ferry, especially for Humphrey, as the animals would be left unattended and no one would be there to help them if anything went wrong.

'However,' she said, standing at the couch, where Humphrey was still lying, largely lifeless, 'I would like to prescribe him an antidepressant. He's highly anxious and the tablets should help with that.' She wobbled her head from side to side. 'They may not quite kick in by the time you head to the ferry, unfortunately, as that will be a big stress for him. But hopefully somewhere on the road trip he'll bounce back.' She stroked his lacklustre fur. 'Poor fella.'

The cats, despite being old, were fighting fit and ready to go. 'They've both got tartar build-up so I recommend you book them in for teeth cleaning when you get to Brisbane.'

'Absolutely,' Phoenix said, her head swimming with the mounting medications, treatments and ongoing management . . . and the escalating bills. She kept scribbling on her to-do list, though at this point it was primarily a way to focus her mind against the rising panic.

She waved Gertie off then returned to the house on shaking legs, overwhelmed by all the details she needed to manage for her trip – and she hadn't even looked at Shane's spreadsheet yet. After pacing the room in circles for a while, she realised she was starkly hungry. She'd completely forgotten to eat breakfast and wasn't even sure she'd drunk any water all day. Without the school bell at regular intervals, or having Zack to remind her, she could simply forget to eat, drink or go to the toilet, missing her body's signals till her hands shook or she wanted to cry.

But despite the wall of canned goods on offer, she couldn't decide. Other than yesterday's trip to the cafe, she'd been subsisting largely on toast and baked beans, and what she really needed was fresh food and green vegetables. She found herself sliding to the floor, head in hands, willing herself to calm her breathing, to remember that she was okay, right here, right now.

Instead, the room spun and homesickness seared through her with hot desperation. How had everything fizzed so out of control so quickly? She pulled her knees to her chest, rocking herself.

You're okay, you're okay, you're okay.

But she didn't feel okay and couldn't imagine ever feeling okay again.

It was at this moment, her head down in her arms, that she heard scratching and rustling noises through the otherwise dead silence. She lifted her tear-stained face and saw Humphrey hauling himself stiffly from the couch. With four paws on the floor, he shook himself. At the sight of him testing his legs as though they were new, unfamiliar appendages, she felt her face abruptly transform into a smile.

'Oh, Humphrey, you brave boy. Well done, my love.'

She took a chair outside, carrying a plate of smoked mussels on toast (distasteful, but beggars couldn't be choosers). As though celebrating Phoenix's ability to feed herself, the clouds vanished and a rich blue sky stretched above. Humphrey trotted triumphantly around the property (a patrol replete with hind leg cocking, hole digging and sunlight appreciation) and Phoenix allowed herself twenty minutes to update her Pinterest board, adding Greek lemon potatoes, lemon and thyme creamy chicken, and lemon spaghetti. Mind calm once more, she reluctantly exited the perfectly styled and curated images and opened Shane's spreadsheet instead.

In answer to Shane's original question – had she actually tried to estimate how much a trip like this would cost? – the answer was a resounding no, the significance of which became clearer the more she worked through his colour-coded and annotated figures. The mode of transportation for both the humans and the animals was the biggest variable and the biggest challenge.

A motorhome would save accommodation fees, but adding a horse float wasn't necessarily even feasible given the towing capacity. If she thought she could send the pony on commercial transportation she could go for the motorhome but renting one that was big enough would be pricey. As well, the motorhome might be ruined by the animals and then she'd be up for costs there too. She may also need to return it to Tasmania.

Eliminating the motorhome left her with finding a more conventional vehicle with enough towing capacity to pull the occupied horse float. The downside of that, though, was that it would be squishy with so many animals on board, they would have to pay for accommodation along the way, and they would need to transport animal feed and supplies as well as luggage.

His calculations moved on to the various costs of accommodation, petrol, meals, animal feed, site fees, ferry fees, vehicle repairs, animal crates, the hire (or purchase) of a horse float, insurances, and temporary fencing for the animals for rest and exercise. The total figure at the bottom of the column resembled an amount Phoenix might expect to pay for an overseas jaunt.

Barely a moment had passed for her to process this when Gertie's list arrived, with due dates for ongoing treatments for the animals, a series of links on various animal ailments and the bill, an amount she could now plug in to Shane's spreadsheet, if only to make her feel like she was accomplishing something.

But before she could spiral too far into fretting, a perfectly timed message from Bruno arrived.

VikingMan: Hey Phoenix, I got ya a vehicle. Will do job. Well run in delivery van. 3m long x 2m high. Ya could sleep in it if ya had to. Plenty of room for the small animals. 2 tonne towing will be just enough for ya float and pony. Ya can pick it up this afternoon.

Whooping with joy to have this problem immediately sorted, Phoenix thanked Bruno then quickly texted Lily to arrange to meet at the airport this afternoon. That way, Phoenix could return her hire car and they could collect the van together at the same time.

So it was that a few hours later in the car park near the terminal, Bruno's driver handed over the keys and bade Phoenix farewell, leaving her to slowly circle the vehicle, a hand to her mouth while she simply tried to *absorb* the sight of it. To all intents and purposes, it was an ordinary rectangular delivery van, one of thousands like it on the road. Except *nothing* about this van was ordinary. This van was a spectacle.

A bustle of skirts caught Phoenix's attention. 'Lily! You look incredible.'

'Good afternoon, Phoenix. You are very kind.'

Phoenix stood rooted to the spot, keys in hand, taking in Lily's outfit today. A long, layered, khaki-coloured skirt swayed gently in the breeze. On the top, she wore a faux-leather underbust corset with shoulder straps over another frilly blouse, this one taupe. An aged gold locket graced her décolletage and her boots peeked out from beneath the length of skirt.

At the same time, Lily ran her eyes down Phoenix's body, likewise studying her companion's track pants and ugg boots.

'Are your parents here too?' Phoenix craned her neck, hoping to catch a glimpse.

49

'I took a cab,' Lily said, chin raised. Phoenix wondered if she was imagining it, but she felt certain she discerned a note of defiance in Lily's words. Did her parents not approve of this plan?

'Well,' Phoenix said, moving on, gesturing to the van. 'This is our home for the next little while.'

'It is commanding in its appearance,' Lily ventured, beginning to circle the van the same way Phoenix had, noting all the quirks.

The white Zebra Couriers van had been skilfully adorned with black zebra-style stripes. Long, curled, dark eyelashes waved gently in the breeze atop the headlights, as did the side mirrors' fluffy black ears. Phoenix followed Lily around the vehicle. When they reached the double doors at the back, Phoenix lifted the long zebra tail with a fluffy black tip, then let it drop, watching it sway jauntily back and forth.

After a long silence, Lily gave her appraisal, with great equanimity. 'It appears to be a fine carriage indeed.'

Phoenix rubbed her forehead, laughing. What on earth would the other drivers on the road think of them? 'Would you like to drive?' she asked, holding up the keys. 'It might be good to get used to it before picking up the horse float from the hire centre. It's a couple of suburbs away, but I chose one with a reciprocal depot in Brisbane, so at least we won't have to bring it back.'

'I should be delighted,' Lily said, then lifted her brown duffel bag, pillow and sleeping bag – even they somehow complemented her clothing choices – accepted the keys from Phoenix, yanked open the door with a metallic clunk, and tossed the bag over the back seat into the cavernous space behind. Lily was obviously not intimidated by the size of the beast she was about to command and, for the first time, Phoenix dared to believe that together they might actually pull off this crazy adventure after all.

6

Though Phoenix had tried her best to entice Lily to sleep at least on the couch near the fire, if not in the loft bed, Lily had insisted she would be fine in the van. Phoenix wasn't surprised to hear her travelling companion open the front door of the cabin not long after first light and begin making tea. She hurried downstairs to meet her, both to offer her assistance and also, she had to admit, because she was keen to see what sort of clothes Lily slept in.

She wasn't disappointed, taking in Lily's white cotton nightgown with lacy bell sleeves and a navy silk robe over the top. On her feet were the same brown boots as yesterday.

Phoenix was impressed with Lily's command of style. It made her reflect on a time in Year 8 when she'd turned up at school for a rare non-uniform day. She had put on what was comfortable – shorts and a T-shirt – but had quickly pivoted to great discomfort. Girls in overalls swirled through the quadrangle like colourful confetti. Overalls were it, and it seemed everyone had known it except her.

'Good morning.'

'Good morning to you,' Lily replied, nodding slightly, though not returning Phoenix's smile.

Phoenix wasn't sure if Lily was unhappy or if her outsides simply didn't match her insides. 'How did you sleep?'

'Rather well,' Lily said. 'When I was young, my family took my sister and me on outings to the woods to establish camp. I suppose it gave me a good grounding.'

'I'm glad,' Phoenix said with relief, both for Lily's sake and also her own. One insomniac on the road would be difficult enough, let alone two of them. She took the chance to find out more about her new friend. 'Are you close to your family?' This time, she didn't imagine Lily's reaction – her shoulders rose stiffly. 'My sister left home at sixteen and does not maintain contact. We quite genuinely do not know where she is. My mama and papa are rather strict. I believe that is what has kept Leonie at a distance.'

Not knowing how to continue from there, Phoenix pondered the pantry. 'I'm afraid there isn't much in the way of food. I'm sorry. I'm not very good at organising meals, not any more, anyway. I used to be but I seem to have lost it.'

'Have you deskilled?' Lily asked, gazing down at her. She really was very tall, especially in those boots. She was narrow and flat, with prominent fine collarbones – perfect for Victorian fashion. 'Have you endured burnout?' Lily's tawny-coloured eyes were piercing.

'Well, yes,' Phoenix said, instantly afraid Lily might feel tricked into coming on this journey with an only partly functional partner.

'I am sorry to hear it,' Lily said, with genuine warmth in her voice. She turned her gaze away. 'Rest and the passage of time really are the only remedies for it. You must be gentle with yourself.'

'Thank you,' Phoenix said.

'Now, let us share a pot of tea.'

•

The two days preceding their departure overflowed with jobs and tasks, animal care, planning and checklists. Phoenix was relieved to have Lily with her, both for the practical assistance but also the company. They worked well together, sharing high standards of excellence and a focus on details, enjoying minimal but purposeful conversation. They discovered they both loved reading, loved the feeling of disappearing into another world. Phoenix preferred fantasy stories, particularly reworkings of old-world mythologies, while Lily enjoyed Regency romance, all things Jane Austen, the Brontës, and Shakespeare too.

'I am enamoured with the very sound of the words,' Lily confessed while scrubbing the kitchen splashback. 'It is the very elocution of it all that captivates me and ignites my mind, the way the entire meaning of a sentence can change depending on which word or even syllable is promoted.'

Not only were they packing and sorting for their trip but they were cleaning and tidying Olga's place too. Food would have to be thrown away. Electricity turned off. The place locked up. With no will, no instructions and no known relatives as yet, the local police officer had instructed Phoenix to finish up as best she could before handing in the house keys at the station when they left town. At times it was desperately sad.

Phoenix found herself drawn to Olga's photographs, notebook sketches, observation journals and bound academic papers. She had left such a tremendous amount of knowledge behind. Phoenix marvelled at the many dissertations she'd written about the local fauna – everything from wombats and raptors down to the tiniest of bugs with Latin names Phoenix couldn't ever hope to pronounce. Decades of study, work and learning potentially set to be buried at the tip. Olga's life, the meaning of what she did, was here in every word. Phoenix wanted to protect it, to scoop it all up and take it with her, but knew she had no right to do so. Instead, she reached for her phone, found the contact details for the College of Sciences and Engineering at the University of Tasmania and emailed them with descriptions of what Olga had left behind, hoping that someone would be able to intervene in its preservation.

'What do you enjoy watching on television?' Lily asked, tossing spoiled food from the fridge into a garbage bag. The question was a welcome distraction.

'I don't watch a lot but I do love a good Aussie drama series. I also return again and again to *Buffy the Vampire Slayer*, or *Angel* or *Lucifer*, though both *Angel* and *Lucifer* are at times too gory. I can handle a bit of violence if it's fantasy, but real-world stuff freaks me out too much. I'm too sensitive.'

'I completely agree,' Lily said, pulling out a mop and bucket. 'I like to watch adaptations of books I know. They are predictable, for the most part, and therefore I am less likely to be traumatised, unless the director has taken wild liberties with the script.'

Phoenix packed Olga's papers into a box, patting the lid affectionately as she slid it snugly into place. 'Zack is a huge *Babylon 5* fan.'

Lily paused. 'I believe I have heard of it. Is it akin to *Star Trek*?'

Phoenix laughed out loud. 'Don't say that to Zack. He says, and I quote, "*Babylon 5* is far superior, far more nuanced, and its fans are way too good for *Star Trek*."'

•

Friday was both their last full day in Olga's house and the last day of the school term back in Brisbane. If this had been a normal day in Phoenix's life, she would be spending it collecting end-of-term history and English assignments from six classes, which she would need to take home in order to grade them over the next two weeks of school holidays. Even if she allocated herself a rate of ten minutes per assignment (which she never did, as she always wanted to give her best to each student's work), she would still have a minimum of twenty-four hours' worth of marking to do on her 'vacation'. She would also be expected at end-of-term drinks in the staffroom, where she'd be eyed suspiciously for refusing a beer or wine, and she'd have to make cheery small talk while every cell in her body was pleading to lie down in a dark, quiet room for the next three days.

In an environment like that, people noticed her awkwardness – the way she flinched at a sudden outburst of loud laughter from teachers on their third beers, or the way she struggled to keep up with and contribute meaningfully and promptly to conversations about families, diets and workloads. Last term Evelyn had raised her voice and demanded, 'Phoenix, what is all that hand-wringing about?' Chatter had ceased. All eyes had snapped to her. She'd quickly whisked her hands under the table, which was exactly where she'd wanted to go, too, just as she'd done as a kid when it was all too much.

No, she wasn't sorry to be missing that.

She was also not sorry to be missing out on planning and creating resources for Term 4 at the kitchen table, or worrying about the upcoming Year 11 camp (and having to patrol through the nights for students who were smoking, drinking, online bullying and sexting), an event that caused her so much anxiety beforehand and so much exhaustion afterwards it may as well have been a three-week commitment, not three days.

Finally, Phoenix received a reply from Linda, who said Evelyn would meet with Phoenix via Zoom on Monday at ten o'clock. Phoenix sent her acceptance and put her phone down. Marilyn jumped into her lap, the tiny cat nearly knocking Phoenix's mug from her hand. 'Careful,' she said, rubbing Marilyn's belly. 'We don't want to break your mum's beautiful mug.' She smiled at the ringtail possum Olga had carved into the pottery. 'She was very clever.' Marilyn purred in agreement. 'As for me, though, I have no idea what to do about school.'

It wasn't that she didn't appreciate the need for certainty for the school and for the students. She'd very much like it for herself too. Evelyn may want Phoenix to be *back to her old self*, but wasn't being her old self what had led to the incident in the first place? Knowing what she knew now, knowing why she'd burnt out – because her neurodivergent brain wasn't built for the environment she'd been forced into – meant she didn't yet know how to trust herself any more. She didn't want history to repeat itself.

She stopped patting Marilyn. The school couldn't fire her, could they? Were they able to terminate her while she had a medical certificate? She'd run out of paid leave, but surely there were laws against pushing her out straight away, weren't there? But then laws were only as effective as someone was willing, and financially able, to hold someone to them. Zack had experienced blatant racism at his previous job but without the financial and emotional reserves to fight it, it had simply been easier to leave. She'd seen Evelyn break down teachers before and knew the principal was capable of making Phoenix's life so miserable that it wouldn't be worth her staying, laws or no laws.

She didn't know who she was without that career and she didn't deserve to lose everything she'd worked for because she was different or because she had a disability – a notion she was still coming to terms with. She finished her tea, scooped Marilyn up into her arms and rose from the chair.

'Come on, Marilyn, we have a huge day ahead of us. We need to get you to your new home.'

While Lily was outside stocktaking animal feed, Phoenix took a moment to call Zack and update him on all the goings-on.

'How is the most fabulous man in the world today?' she said, smiling.

'Better now for hearing your voice.'

'How did you go with your application?' she asked.

'I got it in on time,' Zack confirmed, though he sounded unsure of himself.

'Congratulations. I know selection criteria take ages and are really tricky. I'm sorry I haven't been there to help you.'

'It was difficult,' he conceded and she knew that would be both because he had no idea how good he actually was and also because written communication had never been his strong suit.

'I can't wait to be home again,' she said, feeling small in the face of the thousands of kilometres keeping them apart. She'd been crazy not to marry him.

At the end of the call, she turned to the dog, who was lying in front of the potbelly stove. 'Hey, Humphrey.' He flicked an ear in her direction but otherwise ignored her. 'I'm going to propose to that man the second we get home.' Humphrey saw no reason to express any delight in this but she was nevertheless cheered that she could begin counting down the days till she was with Zack.

Back on her feet, she searched for animal transport cages. Not locating any in the house, she headed to the shed, the one Olga had said housed the pottery wheel, and the one where Henry the snake lived. Though deeply reluctant to step inside, she was also aware of the mounting costs of this trip and the need to save money – especially if she wasn't going back to work anytime soon. She could call for a snake catcher but she needed to cut costs wherever possible.

She scanned the grounds for Lily but couldn't locate her. With her heart thumping wildly from serpent phobia, she turned the cold knob of the shed door and shoved it open about a third. She craned her neck to peer inside. She noted a cacophony of items – the potter's wheel, cardboard and foam boxes, insect-collecting nets and jars, boots, a ladder and random rusty tools. Mouse and rat droppings speckled the floor.

She nudged open the door further still, her eyes scanning the tops of shelves and the towers of boxes, looking for a large python. Something was blocking the door's full opening, so she gave it a good thump with her shoulder. Immediately, a dark-grey diamond head rose into the air and moved towards her.

Phoenix yelped. She fled, promptly tripping and falling onto the rocks of the driveway. She propelled herself to her feet and ran, not stopping till she was back inside the house, slamming the door behind her. She stumbled, shaking and breathless, to the couch where Olga had died and fell onto it, gasping for air, feeling foolish for having such an extreme response.

Humphrey lifted his head from the floor to observe her, dropped open his mouth, letting his tongue fall out, panting gently, his eyebrows twitching. It was the most expression he'd offered her since losing Olga.

'Are you *laughing* at me?' she challenged him.

In reply, the dog's mouth wrinkled in the corners and he thumped his tail on the floor, just once, but enough to confirm her suspicions.

•

Departure day arrived and anxiety whooshed through Phoenix like a camp fire enraged by a gust of wind. As they liked to say on reality shows, they were getting to the pointy end of things. She still had no idea what to say to Evelyn on Monday, whether or not she was ready, or even wanted, to go back to work, and behind that worry was another festering shame. She'd planned to propose to Zack. What sort of proposal was she truly offering? She didn't want to be a burden to him and she definitely didn't want him to feel as though she wanted to marry him in order to secure her financial future.

Relieved to find her GP was working this Saturday morning, she booked a TeleHealth appointment to have a chat and, maybe, to get another sick leave certificate, just in case. But while she waited for her doctor to call, the dark thoughts loomed stronger still. She was engulfed by a swirl of hopelessness and uselessness and the lifelong despair of somehow being 'wrong'. How could she do *any* of this – teach, complete a road trip, marry Zack, look after all these animals, survive in a world that had broken her down not just this time but truthfully many times in her life?

She recalled the daily drives home from uni, hollowed out inside, the darkness in her mind and menacing hands grabbing at her ankles, yanking her down towards the abyss. Uni, where everyone played soccer or met at the bar for drinks or dated or had study groups or matching tattoos . . . and she had no one.

She ate alone in the cafe.

She sat alone in lecture theatres.

She writhed with the agony of forced group assignments.

She did want to connect. She wanted to be part of it all. But she never was. She was so *different*, always two steps, or twenty-two steps, behind the conversation. Always out of sync.

She'd made not a single new friend.

Each day driving home, she stopped at the boom gates at the train station near her house. Her rusted car's nose pointed downhill . . . and she would do the maths.

How fast did she need to go in order to smash through those red and white gates and into the oncoming train in order for it all to end?

Now, she jumped as her phone sprang to life in her hands.

'Phoenix, it's Dr Sara, how are you?'

'Not great,' she squeaked, then promptly burst into tears.

After the release of emotion Phoenix had felt while talking with her doctor, the ease with which she and Lily worked as a unified team strengthened her spirits. It was a little ironic that Phoenix had just been thinking about the difficulty of group work, yet she and Lily were a perfect match. Perhaps birds of a neurodivergent feather really did flock together. Like her and Zack.

Lily dropped the float door and practised loading Rita on and off, offering her patience, kind words and buckets of coffee as incentives and rewards whenever the Shetland baulked. Phoenix made her last trip into town for supplies, hauling into the van armfuls of temporary fencing and puppy pads to line crates to catch poo. Together they put the flat-packed cat crates together and checked off the long lists of animal food and equipment. They stacked hay bales, sleeping bags, their clothes and a broom to sweep out the float.

Lily, not intimidated by the snake in the least, braved the potter's shed to look for anything that might be of use on the road and returned with a large foam box, about the size of a hay bale, with a broken lid and *Camping* written on the side. 'I did not want to unpack it all, but it appears as if it may be of use.'

'Great find,' Phoenix said, rearranging crates to leave room for them to climb in and out of the back, as well as enough space to stretch out to sleep if necessary. She was so grateful for Bruno's van. It offered many more options than they would have had with a car.

In the final rundown to leaving time, they bathed Humphrey in the shower while he glared at them, before he succumbed to trembling so severe it made Phoenix's eyes well. She wanted to be bonding with him, not making him hate her. When it was done, she sat him by the fire and returned to sit with him from time to time while she and Lily took their own showers, then washed clothes and tossed them in the dryer for a head start on clean laundry. Before they left the house, Phoenix wiped down the kitchen bench for the last time and spied Olga's handmade mugs. She may not be entitled to anything in this house, but she wanted to save them; they were too special. She took two, one for herself and one for Lily, certain Olga would approve.

At last they were packing the animals into the van. First the cats, each in their own cage with soft baby blankets inside to keep them warm, then the chickens, all four in one large crate, an absorbent puppy training pad under their feet. The birds huddled together, eyes wide with shock. Phoenix pulled a handful of sunflower seeds from the container nearby and sprinkled them into the cage. 'Here you go. Olga told me you love these.' She shoved the rest of the seeds into her pocket, hoping the chickens' mood would lift soon.

Humphrey was the last one in, visibly displeased. He shook his head vigorously and scratched at his new purple collar and matching body harness. They had placed his foam mattress in the centre behind the front seats, where they could hook his harness to an anchor point. But he flatly refused to jump into the back of the van, forcing Phoenix and Lily to hoist him in.

Phoenix stroked his neck. 'I'm so sorry, Humphrey. You lost your person and now you're losing your home. You have a right to be sad for as long as you like.' She reached into a pack nearby and plucked out a soft pink teddy bear. She offered it to him but he turned his head the other way. 'That's okay. I'll leave it here for you.' She placed it down on the mattress and exited the van with a heavy heart, wondering if Humphrey would ever recover from this loss and disruption.

Lily returned from behind the float, frowning at her phone, then stabbing at it and pocketing it away.

'Is everything okay?' Phoenix asked, nodding to the phone.

'It is my mama,' Lily said, irritably, then changed the topic. 'All is well with the horse carriage,' she reported. 'Are we ready to depart?'

'Yes, I think so,' Phoenix said, closing the van's doors, trying not to cry at Humphrey's desolate eyes and body posture.

No one left behind.

As they pulled the van and float out of the driveway, Phoenix lit the strings of LED sunflowers she'd picked up in town – a comforting reminder of home – laying them like shawls behind their shoulders on the backs of the seats. She hung her head out of the window to watch Olga's little house and shed roll away out of view, swallowed by the thickening of trees. On cue, Humphrey let out a mournful whine and slumped to his bed. Phoenix retrieved the remaining sunflower seeds from her pocket and tossed them out the window, scattering them along the side of the dirt road, imagining them taking root and rising, their sunny faces bringing light and cheer in a salute to Olga's spirit.

They reached the dock at sunset. Creamy golden sand hugged the edge of the island, the jetty stretching out into the sea and their blue and white vessel looming large alongside it. Beyond that was nothing but the open water of Bass Strait. Long lines of cars, motorbikes, caravans and trailers waited their turn to approach the checkpoint.

'I can't imagine why they call that a ferry,' Phoenix said. 'Look at the size of it. It's a ship.'

'It is commanding,' Lily agreed.

'I feel very nervous,' Phoenix whispered.

'I do too.'

'We can do this,' Phoenix said, for her own benefit as much as Lily's.

'I quite agree,' Lily said, turning to her, her chin lifted. 'Shall we take our leave and strike out for the north?'

Phoenix swallowed. There was definitely no turning back now. 'Let's go.'

Lily rolled the van forwards to join the line.

7

The ferry entry was a maze of checkpoints down to and then across the water. At the quarantine scan, an official searched their car and float for fruits and vegetables, explosives and extra petrol. At one point, the chickens erupted into hysterical squawking and flapping and Humphrey growled so menacingly at the inspector that Phoenix had to remove the dog from the van. Cleared of contraband, they rattled up a steep ascent to meet the yawing black hole in the stern of the ship.

It was like being swallowed by a beast – one way in and no way back. Phoenix's anxiety peaked. For a moment, she forgot how to breathe.

She recalled her research – beloved animals lost at sea, dying in overhead baggage compartments of planes, frozen to death in cargo holds, suffocated in moving vans, fallen to their death from trucks. The images and headlines galloped unchecked through her mind.

What if she killed Olga's precious animals on the way to Brisbane?

They passed through the darkness and into a cavernous car park beyond, lit by fluorescent tubes and porthole windows.

'Are you all right?' Lily asked. She seemed calm, though Phoenix noted her knuckles were tight on the wheel.

'Not entirely,' Phoenix squeaked.

Lily inched the van and float forwards as Rita shuffled in the back, her movements tugging on the van. They heard a frightened neigh.

After a moment, Lily spoke. 'I cannot presume to know what your life has been like, but I have been told many times that I cannot do things, that I'm not capable.' She raised her chin. 'I used to believe them, Mama especially, but now I'm not so sure. I think we have far greater capacity than that with which we are credited.'

'Is this your first time away from home?'

'It is,' Lily said, a slight wobble in her chin, her gaze fixed straight ahead on the car in front of them. 'It has not been an easy escape.'

Phoenix pondered her choice of that last word. 'You are so brave,' she said. Then she snorted. 'And it makes me feel quite ridiculous.' Lily was not that much older than Phoenix's senior students. 'I should be the one encouraging you.'

'Would it help you if I was to sing?' Lily said.

'What?' The question was so unexpected that it immediately halted Phoenix's careering thoughts.

In response, Lily began to sing 'Somewhere Over the Rainbow'. Her voice was lovely but the song choice too melancholy.

'You have a wonderful voice,' Phoenix said. 'Do you perhaps have something more cheerful?'

'Oh.' Lily stopped and thought for a moment and Phoenix feared she'd squashed her new friend's enthusiasm, but then Lily broke into 'I Could Have Danced All Night' from *My Fair Lady*. It was perfect. Phoenix had recently taught *Pygmalion* to her

Year 8 English class and they'd watched the musical adaptation too. She joined in on the chorus and together they sang their way around the twists and turns of the deck, finally coming to a halt. The engine fell silent, as did their voices. Stacks of cold-looking metal cages lined a wall nearby, already half filled with pacing, barking, howling animals. The women climbed out of the van, moving towards them. A grey and white cat headbutted the door and yowled, sending ice water through Phoenix's veins.

'Do you think we should put both our cats together in the one cage or separate them?' she asked Lily.

'Are they firm friends?'

Phoenix lifted her hands. 'I've no idea. I don't know them well enough. From what I've seen they get along but that's in their own house. I don't know how they'd feel squashed on top of each other.'

While she pondered what to do, they busied themselves choosing cages, lining them with absorbent pads and blankets, knowing it would be a long time before the animals could properly toilet again. 'So undignified,' Phoenix muttered, unhappy at the idea of them being locked in with their own waste. Because of that, she decided to separate the cats to give them more space. She placed the four flustered chickens in one cage and worried for them due to the level of noise that ricocheted and echoed off the hard surfaces. Phoenix's sensitive hearing rang from the auditory assault.

'I'm so sorry,' she whispered to them, closing the door and sliding the bolt across. She grabbed a soft baby blanket and pegged it up over half of the cage door to give them some sense of nesting but still allow air flow from the draughty car park.

Then it was time for Humphrey. He staggered out of the van with wide, terrified eyes, panting so fast Phoenix wouldn't have been surprised if he'd keeled over right then. He tugged this way and that, looking for an exit, and Phoenix eyed the portholes warily. It took her and Lily together to manage him inelegantly into his ground-level cage. His protestations only encouraged the dogs around him into further high-pitched keening.

'Let us go,' Lily said, smoothing down her vest and billowing skirt. 'There is nothing more we can do here.'

Phoenix felt a great wrenching inside her. Every instinct told her she should not leave Humphrey there. But what could she do? He wasn't allowed off this deck. It was so much worse than she'd imagined – but Lily was right. They had to go. She double-checked that her identification tags were secured to each of her animals' cages and paused a moment, trying to find some calm amid the constant noise of engines, squeaking tyres, attendants' shouts and the mournful dogs.

Desperate now, she decided to pray, though to who exactly she wasn't sure. Was it St Francis of Assisi? She attempted some sort of communication but, feeling out of her depth, she decided to talk to Olga instead.

'Hey, Olga. If you're not busy, could you watch over these furry kids, please? I have to leave them and I'm not allowed back. It would make me feel better if you could lend us your, um, wings, or whatever you have now.' She paused, pressing her palm on each cage door as though leaving some sort of energetic shield there. 'Okay, I'll leave them in your hands.'

Lily turned to Phoenix. 'Would it be an imposition if I was to link my arm with yours in this moment?'

Phoenix blinked, then smiled. 'No! I love hugs. I'm a bit of an over-hugger, actually. I've definitely hugged people and then worried they weren't into it.' She wished very much that Zack was there right now. He was a great hugger.

Lily tilted her head, her eyes cast to the shiny floor at their feet. A little frown appeared between her perfectly thick brows. 'While I do not seek physical affection in that way myself, I would like to link my arm with yours to offer confidence and support in this most difficult moment.'

Phoenix grinned and cocked her elbow out like a little wing. 'And I would be so grateful to receive it.'

In a swift motion, Lily hooked her arm through Phoenix's, giving her a supportive nod. Phoenix couldn't have been more grateful. She may not be able do this on her own, but she didn't have to. She had this quirky, steady and capable woman by her side, Zack cheering her on from Brisbane, a team of helpful friends she had never met in person but who had dropped everything to help her pull this off, and Olga somewhere in the ether. She only had to do the next right thing – get to the mainland with everyone in one piece.

Upstairs, their cabin greeted them with neutral tones, two crisply made-up single beds with a small shelf between them, a rectangular porthole revealing the dark sky outside, and a small private ensuite. Having already eaten before boarding, and both rather exhausted from the day, they agreed to forgo anything further from the many decks of eateries. Neither was keen to join any onboard entertainment, and happily collapsed onto their beds, mobile phones in hand. Not long after, their vessel's giant motors started, the ship shuddered and they began to pull away from the dock.

'I hope we get calm waters,' Phoenix said, peering out the window. Thanks to a half-moon, they could see the inky water below, topped with shiny white reflections. 'I've read that this crossing can be super rough.'

Lily tore her eyes from her phone to gaze out the window, but didn't comment.

Phoenix collapsed back onto the bed, fatigue dragging at the backs of her eyes but her mind racing. She texted Zack a photo of the ship and let him know the ferry was leaving now, wishing him a good night and promising to speak to him in the morning. Then she turned what was left of her brain power to planning.

'I think we should aim for a limited amount of travel tomorrow,' Phoenix said. 'Who knows what sort of shape any of us will be in by morning, animals included?'

'I quite agree.'

'Looking at these maps, and considering horse-friendly accommodation, I think if we can get as far as Echuca that would be amazing. We'll have to get poor Rita out of that float as soon as we hit land and let her stretch her legs. Humphrey too. The cats will need some quiet space to toilet, the chickens to roam. Then if we head straight to Bendigo, we can rest there for a while and find food and supplies, then another couple of hours on to Echuca. That should give us some time before bed to allow everyone to settle for a good night's rest to recover. What do you think?'

'I think this is a most wise proposition,' Lily agreed, though her voice was flat. She laid her phone on the mattress beside her.

'Are you okay?' Phoenix asked.

'I am quite well, though I suppose I am a little heartsick. Bianca has not returned my texts today. I am not sure what has happened.'

'Do you normally chat each day?'

'Text message, yes. Or email. Or live chat.'

'Are you worried something has happened to her?'

'Perhaps. She may be working tonight, teaching a women's circle or the like.'

'What does she do?'

'Bianca is a *soulpreneur*.' Lily's face took on an aura of serenity, staring at the ceiling. 'She is the master of her own destiny.'

'That's interesting. Excuse my ignorance, but what does that mean, exactly?'

Lily gave Phoenix her direct attention. Her eye contact, which had been inconsistent, was suddenly fixed. 'Bianca follows her heart and builds soul-enriching businesses around her truest passions. She is a poet and writer.'

'Like Jane Austen,' Phoenix observed.

'Yes! Much like dear Jane, Bianca is ahead of her time. She has eschewed the outdated traditional publishing business and self-publishes her work to have total control. She lives on land in Samford. Do you know it?'

'I do. There are lots of horses there. I plan to find Rita somewhere to board out there when we get back.'

Lily nodded enthusiastically. 'Bianca nourishes the planet and grows organic food, offering free accommodation to those who also wish to nourish the planet.'

Phoenix chewed her lip, thinking. 'Do you mean WWOOFers?'

'I'm not sure what that is but she is the founding member of the community. Everyone is welcome there if they wish to live in harmony and work with the earth, the plants, the bees.'

'And you have farming skills,' Phoenix observed. She tried to keep the tone of judgement from her voice but may not have succeeded. Lily appeared not to have noticed though and was continuing to rave about Bianca's amazing children's guitar lessons and herbal products when the ferry gave an alarming lurch to one side, knocking the words from her mouth. Lily spun towards the edge of the bed but managed to stop herself from falling.

'Oh no,' Phoenix groaned, as the bed rose beneath her, carrying her up and up and then dropping her once more.

Lily scrambled for her phone as it slithered across the sheets. Her sleeve pulled back to reveal a small tattoo of a bat in flight. If Phoenix hadn't needed all her reserves to stay on top of the bed in that moment, she might have asked Lily about it. Instead, she groaned and braced one hand against the wall.

Throughout the night the rough and unforgiving seas continued. Waves rose eight, nine, eleven metres tall, crashing against their porthole. They held onto the sides of their beds and groaned and salivated as the snacks they'd eaten for dinner attempted a return. Lily was pale and sweaty, her knuckles white on the mattress. At one point, Phoenix managed to stagger towards the ensuite only to fall backwards onto Lily's bed as the ship pitched, falling onto Lily's ankle. Her companion cried out in pain.

'Sorry,' Phoenix gasped, struggling to get herself off Lily but taking two goes to do it. She just managed to make it to the basin in time to vomit. She slid down onto the toilet seat, pleading to the gods for medications, a miracle, even a quick death to end this torment. But none came, and so the minutes crawled by into one of the longest nights in Phoenix's memory.

By dawn, the sea had calmed. The morning sky bloomed pale, and Phoenix turned over carefully in her narrow bed to check on Lily. They stared at each other a moment, shell-shocked, sick and exhausted.

'Are we alive?' Lily croaked.

'I think so.' Phoenix checked her phone. 'If we're still running on time then we must be nearly there.'

Lily took a deep breath and let it out slowly, as one does when their stomach has liquified and is no longer to be trusted.

'Do you think you could keep down some food?' Phoenix asked. 'Some dry toast?'

Another deep breath and Lily nodded gently. 'Perhaps.'

'Let's do it.'

They supported each other through the hallway and into the elevator, the doors opening to the smell of fried bacon and brewing coffee. After toast and coffee and sunlight streaming through the windows off a now tempered ocean, they did feel improved, though still greenish around the gills.

Finally, the ferry docked and they were allowed to return to the animals' deck. The elevator descended. How on earth had their animals coped during that terrible night?

Stepping out into the echoing, squeaking, fluorescent-lit car park, they hurried along the path. Phoenix could see Humphrey in the distance, curled in a ball in the corner of his cage, unmoving. She increased her pace, Lily at her side. They passed the horse float first, Rita neighing at them the moment she spied them.

'Hello, Rita! We'll be back soon,' she promised, continuing to the cages.

Humphrey lifted his head on their approach and she sighed with relief. 'Humphrey! I'm so glad you're okay, you poor darling.' She put her hand to his cage door.

'The cats appear robust and well,' Lily reported.

'Excellent news,' Phoenix said, straightening. But then she went to the chickens' cage and lifted the blanket she'd half pegged there. Her heart plummeted. Her smile disappeared. Two chickens, one red and one black, lay motionless on the floor, their eyes closed. It was quite obvious that they were dead.

8

'So now I'm thinking, this is it,' she said, her voice high and strained, Rita grazing beside her, tugging at the lead rope as she picked at grass.

'What's *it*?' Zack asked.

'That this is going to be my whole trip – I go to bed and I get up and someone else has died,' she said, her voice catching at the end. A clutch of little girls hovered nearby, trying to catch her eye, clearly waiting for an invitation to come and pat the pony. The sand of Port Melbourne stretched silky smooth along the water's edge, a walking path and green space running parallel. Generally speaking, Phoenix never broke the rules, which was one reason teachers had loved her at school. But right now, while she was certain she wasn't supposed to unload her horse out of a manure-filled float and stroll Port Melbourne's promenade on a chilly spring Sunday morning, she didn't have a flying fig to give.

'Man, I hope not,' Zack said, setting the coffee grinder to work in the background.

'Zack!'

'What?'

'Do you really think that's what will happen – that I'm jinxed? Like I'm the grim reaper or something and I bring death everywhere I go?'

'Of course not,' he said. 'I legitimately hope this is the end of all the death and dying,' he finished, uncertainly.

'The bar is set low, hey? Just try not to kill anyone?'

'Fi, have you had breakfast?'

'Bit of toast.'

'Coffee? Water? Change of clothes?'

'Coffee yes, water no, still in the same clothes as last night. The bad weather got us before we had a chance to shower and we were both too shattered this morning to get it done.'

'People don't realise how many steps are involved in having a shower and how much energy it takes,' he said, a supportive smile in his voice.

Phoenix stopped walking and took a deep breath. 'I think I've got to go,' she said, eyeing the little girls. They had given up waiting for an invitation and were inching their way closer to Rita, whose chestnut coat was shining a deep treacle colour in the morning sun. Their hands were already outstretched.

'Call me anytime,' he said.

'Oh, before you go,' she said, while smiling at the girls and holding up an index finger to hold back their encroaching and vulnerable bare toes, 'do you have any idea how we can dispose of the bodies?'

In Bendigo, they stopped for food at the cute and stylish Percy and Percy cafe, a historic building with modern grey paint and smart white trimmings, a white picket gate and a white bicycle with a flower basket on the footpath outside. They chose seats under the bullnose verandah with Humphrey at their feet.

'Do you consider it best to continue straight to Echuca or should we invest time here and take the animals out for another constitutional?' Lily asked, sipping her green smoothie.

'Good question,' Phoenix said, scraping up the last of the feta and salad onto her fork. 'I'm sure poor Rita will be well over being locked in that float by now, but I wonder if it's better to keep going so they can all have a longer period of freedom before heading off again tomorrow.' She lifted her lemon and ginger tea to her lips.

'Quite so.' Lily nodded. 'And what about . . .' she leant forwards to whisper, 'the deceased?'

Neither of them fancied tossing them in the bin or cremating them, which left burial.

'We'll have to buy a shovel,' Phoenix said.

'That is a wise investment for all manner of occasions – burying chickens, shovelling waste, walloping night-time prowlers over the head.'

Phoenix laughed, then abruptly halted, not sure if Lily was serious about prowlers or not. She pushed her chair back from the table, bent down and patted Humphrey's head. 'Do you think you could dig us a hole, Humphrey? Huh? No? All right then. We'll buy a shovel.'

Somewhere on the road towards the northern Victorian border, they left the endless open fields and rumbled down an unpaved side road. Outside, the wind whistled, the long grass bending in response. Phoenix grabbed her black puffer jacket and the long-handled shovel from the van, as well as the plastic bag containing the two chooks that had lost their lives on the perilous seas. Lily joined her, stretching her arms high and then bending at the waist, stiff from driving.

They took turns digging, and, while Phoenix rested to catch her breath, she collected the other two chickens from the van to attend the ceremony and farewell their sisters.

'An avian funeral procession,' Lily observed, watching as they scratched at the grass and murmured with curiosity. Neither seemed compelled to wander too far, thankfully.

When the hole was deep enough, Phoenix removed the chickens from the bag and laid them in the grave. 'We didn't even know your names,' she said sadly.

'Rest in peace,' Lily said, then stooped and lifted a handful of earth, scattering it over their feathery bodies. Phoenix did the same and the other two chickens came and stood at the hole's edge, gazing down. Lily tossed earth into the grave and Phoenix dispersed more seeds for the chickens to enjoy. When Lily was done, they pressed the final seeds into the earth so they would one day grow and shine their yellow joy here in this spot.

After checking Rita into her overnight equestrian boarding paddock at Echuca, Lily decided to stay at their Airbnb house with the animals for some much-needed solitude and silence. Phoenix completely understood. In the short time since she'd learnt about her autism and how to manage her energy levels, she'd found there was nothing better to repair her fragmented mental state and drained energy than being alone in the quiet – preferably with sensory deprivation and smothered by two weighted blankets to calm her nervous system. Half an hour of that could revive her as much as a two-hour nap. But while she was also exhausted, her body was aching from the amount of sitting and she felt like taking a long, slow walk down near the river.

She was thrilled to find a paddle steamer anchored on the glistening Murray River, enormous gum trees lining the water's edge. It looked exactly like a scene from the miniseries *All The Rivers Run*.

The tune of 'I Could Have Danced All Night' was stuck in her head and for a moment she allowed herself to slip through a portal to the past. Pausing on the bank, she took in the two-storey wooden boat and the huge wheel in the centre of its belly. She could almost hear the soft scrape of shoes across boards and the live band as ladies and gentleman waltzed after dinner while the paddles slapped the water on their way between towns.

The ping of a text message jerked her back to the present time. It was from Anthea.

> I'm so sorry. I think I've done a
> bad thing.

Phoenix's heart skittered.

> What do you mean?

There was a long pause while Phoenix waited for Anthea's reply.

> You know how Friday was
> end-of-term drinks?

> Yeeeessss . . .?

> Well, I was a bit drunk, so
> I can't quite remember what
> I said, but the gist is that I told
> Evelyn about your diagnosis.
> Please, please don't be mad.

> What?! Why would you do
> that?

I overheard her complaining that you'd sent in another medical certificate but you still hadn't told her what was going on, so I thought that she needed to know. It's really hard for her to know what to do with staffing levels and she seemed really stressed. I was trying to help, honestly.

You're the one who told me NOT to tell her!!!

I know, but maybe it's a good thing? She had to know sometime.

No, she didn't. That is my personal information to share IF and when I am ready and not before. I can't believe you did that.

Phoenix slumped down on the riverbank, her legs not able to hold her up. She waited there, breathing hard, the edges of her vision turning dark, her whole body vibrating with anger and fear. Her very private information, something she was still trying to get her own head around, had been callously released into her professional arena.

She knew what the dominant autism stereotypes were – angry outbursts, monotonous voices, literal interpretations, no sense of humour, intellectual impairment, a cold heart, someone who couldn't manage life and needed to be taken care of. Television shows portrayed autists as young, skinny, white men who were usually savants or geniuses and the punchline of jokes. She never saw representations of autists as teachers, psychologists, childcare workers or nurses. The pervasive and false belief that autists were people with no empathy – as if they were psychopaths – still circulated the globe. Some autists might relate to the dominant profile but that didn't reflect what Phoenix was like. She was her own person, with her own gifts and challenges, not a collection of media bites.

Sure, she got angry sometimes and, yes, she could say things that might not come out the way they had sounded in her head, but that made her human, not autistic. She was also a caring, intellectually capable, successful teacher. She felt utterly exhausted at the idea that she'd have to explain herself to everyone every day for the rest of her life, and probably even then people would doubt her because once upon a time falsehoods had been let loose in the world and people repeated them without ever bothering to learn if they were true or not.

These thoughts tumbled through her mind while she waited to see what Anthea – the person she'd thought was her friend – had to say for herself.

But Anthea didn't respond.

Ghosted.

Phoenix thought about all the time they'd spent together, helping each other plan programs, bringing each other cake on their birthdays, commiserating over hot chocolate and cheesecake when impertinent parents harassed them via email and over wine when a student started bullying them. They were friends, weren't they? Or were they only friends because they were at school together, and now that Phoenix wasn't there, or maybe because she had been deemed deficient in some way, their friendship was dead?

She'd been cut loose and, in another timeslip, she'd been thrown right back to Year 10.

That was the year Phoenix had been growing quieter, tormented by ferocious pain in her back, an inflamed nerve that no one seemed to be able to fix, an inexplicable mystery. There was no definable reason for it to have started and no end of it in sight. Surgery was suggested but averted. Pain was everywhere.

Phoenix and Maryanne were paired up to work on a class project. Phoenix always had her head down, working, but Maryanne spent most of her time turned around in her seat, gossiping with the girls in the row behind. Phoenix said nothing, but stared at the questions on the page, focusing on those, blocking out the fact that Maryanne hated her so much she couldn't even talk to her about the work they were doing. Like a bolt of electricity, a stabbing pain hit deep through her thigh muscle. Phoenix jumped and sucked in air sharply through her teeth. Maryanne spun around, annoyed to have her conversation cut short.

'What's wrong?' she demanded.

Phoenix forced a smile, pretending she was okay, normal. 'Oh, nothing. You know how you just get weird stabbing pains in your body?'

Maryanne looked at her like she was crazy. 'Um, *no*.' She screwed up her face in disgust and turned away, hurling a final 'Weirdo' under her breath. That was when Phoenix realised for certain that she was not like other people. Her body was different. Her mind was different. She didn't care about boys and clothes and perfume, she didn't sleep through the night, she couldn't eat what other girls ate, she had pain other girls didn't, and sometimes she lost her words, sometimes publicly, like the awful time in Year 8 when she'd been chosen to read a paragraph of German at the whole-school assembly. Instead, she'd stood in front of hundreds of girls, eyes downcast, unable to look up, the microphone slick with sweat. Silent.

She could hear the words in her head; she knew every one off by heart. She'd practised them dozens of times till they were perfect. But she couldn't make the words move from her brain to her mouth. Laughter rippled through the audience. 'Do it!' a classmate ordered. 'Read it, go on!' Giggles erupted in the hall. More calls, demanding she speak. But the more they hurried Phoenix, the further the words retreated.

'Weirdo.'

When Phoenix returned to their Airbnb house for the night – a renovated wooden miner's cottage with an iron roof, a picket fence and a little metal gate surrounded by purple agapanthus – Lily had showered and changed. She was already in her flowing white nightdress and robe, even though it was not yet dark, and was taking photographs of the cats, who'd each found a spot to sleep on the leather lounge chairs. Lily straightened to greet Phoenix.

'These most wonderful felines have partaken of a hearty feast and tended to their ablutions, settling most proficiently into an untroubled respite.'

'That's really good news.' Phoenix looked around. 'Where are Humphrey and the chickens?'

'They are promenading in the rear garden.'

Together they walked through the hallway leading to the fenced backyard, a ramshackle affair of some grass, dirt patches and vestiges of vegetable gardens, where they found Humphrey lying flat out in the last of the afternoon sun and the chickens scratching enthusiastically at the old garden beds. The sight of them helped to ease Phoenix's racing heart and deeply depressed mood. It was lovely to see the black and red chickens getting on with life after the loss of their sisters.

Lily came to her side to show her some of the photos she'd been taking. 'Animal photography is one of my special interests,' she said, swiping through the photos.

'These are gorgeous,' Phoenix said. Somehow, Lily had managed to capture each animal's personality or particular emotion as well as their physical appearance. Humphrey stood gazing at the blue sky as though lost in philosophical thought. Marilyn was on her back, cute and playful, while Audrey stared intently into the camera like a queen. The chickens both had their heads cocked at exactly the same angle as they assessed a curio in the grass.

'Would it be acceptable to post these photos to my social media sites?'

'Absolutely. You really do have such an artistic flair. I wish I did. These will be a great memory for me when this trip is over. This is your trip as much as mine and I am more than happy to make you the official photographer.'

Lily shuffled from side to side a moment and then said, 'I must confess I have already posted some to my artist's profile, Austen Style. I apologise; I should have sought your permission first.'

'It's fine, really,' Phoenix assured her, immediately looking up Lily's profile. She found images of the animals but also of Lily's artwork and clothing designs. There were notebooks intricately adorned with lace and pressed flowers and snippets of Austen quotes, handmade vintage fabric tote bags, coasters, earrings and bookmarks, even metal jewellery. 'Lily, these are incredible. This is one of your special gifts, I suspect.'

Lily tipped her head to acknowledge the compliment.

'And this is how you support yourself? By selling these items?'

Lily frowned. 'I make a little money, certainly, but Mama enjoys reminding me that I do not have the means to support myself. She has always said that I will need to live with her for the rest of my life.'

'Well, I suppose working for yourself is always risky in terms of having a guaranteed income, but Lily, these items are incredible. You have a real gift, and you're a hard worker, and I wouldn't yet discount the idea that you could actually support yourself. You have many options.'

'Do you really believe so?'

Phoenix presented a wide smile. 'I really do.'

Lily considered this for a moment, then offered her thanks and began swiping and editing in earnest.

Phoenix spotted the antique-looking gold locket on the chain at Lily's neck. 'Is that one of your pieces too?'

Lily's hand fluttered to the piece, then clasped it tightly, her gaze sliding away to the floor. 'No. It was my grandmother's. She was very special to me.'

'What a lovely heirloom of hers to have so close to your heart.'

Lily nodded but said no more about it.

'I'll share the animal pictures with my Downunder Auties group,' Phoenix said, stepping back from Lily to give her space. 'They'll love them. I should update them anyway to let them know we made it across the Strait, albeit two animals down.' She was about to go, then remembered Lily's girlfriend's radio silence. 'Have you managed to get hold of Bianca?'

Lily continued scrolling through photos. 'I did. It was a silly misunderstanding. She had been giving moonlit permaculture instruction and lost her phone in a patch of kale. That was all.'

'That's good news,' Phoenix said, though her feeling didn't support it. She had no evidence to doubt the stranger's words but she absolutely didn't trust this Bianca person. If there was one thing she knew about herself it was that she could often see the truth of people earlier and more accurately than others did. And Bianca gave her a nasty feeling in the pit of her stomach.

9

Phoenix's plan was to continue along inland roads because it would allow them to find more equine agistment for Rita along the way and facilitate more affordable and, she hoped, more pet-friendly small-town Airbnb locations. To conserve energy, their idea was to drive no more than four or five hours a day, with an extended break for lunch in between. Today's itinerary included a stop in the tiny town of Jerilderie in New South Wales before heading on to Wagga Wagga. By the time they got to Orange on Tuesday, they would be at least halfway home.

As both Phoenix and Lily were early risers, they decided not to squander the opportunity to explore a little more of Echuca before they left. After tending to the animals, Phoenix put Humphrey in his purple harness and the three of them set off for the short walk into town. Along the way they passed houses with trailing vines of fragrant jasmine in bloom and lavender bushes bobbing gently in the breeze. Humphrey even appeared to be in reasonable spirits, stopping to sniff at many aromatic enticements on the way.

'I still haven't seen him smile properly though,' Phoenix said, as they waited for Humphrey to finish taking in a perfume-laden tree trunk. 'I've not seen him as happy as he was the day I met him. He adored Olga.'

'Such a violent sorrow as that shall not be relieved in haste.'

'True.' They began to walk again, rows of shops now visible nearby. 'Can I ask you a question?' Phoenix began, cautiously.

'You may.'

'When did you discover Jane Austen?'

Lily continued walking at a steady pace, her posture highly enviable, her eyes cast to the distance. 'It was in high school,' she began, carefully choosing her words. 'At the time, life was rather difficult.'

Phoenix took in a sharp breath in sympathy. 'I'm so sorry you went through that. The stats are awful for neurodivergent kids and bullying. Almost no one escapes it. For me, there was a year of it that left deep scars that still haunt me today. It was the same for Zack.'

Lily stooped to pick a handful of yellow dandelion heads, arranging them into a tiny bouquet in her hand, then continued. 'For me, it never really reached a natural conclusion. I exerted my efforts into appearing normal, into learning the language and form that I needed in order to assimilate, but it was all to no avail. The schoolyard's conventions were in endless flux and a constant mystery. The moment I learnt one rule, it changed. But then in Year 11, my theatre class put on an adaptation of *Pride and Prejudice* for the entire school. I was chosen to play Elizabeth Bennett.'

'The lead role. That must have been quite an honour.'

'Indeed. I fell in love with the language, with the rules of society that, while not balanced in a woman's favour, were entirely consistent. There was a proper way to act. Particular words to say.' Here, she almost smiled. 'In addition, the costumes were exquisite.

I excelled in the role, and for a short time I was held in a certain amount of esteem by my peers. When I spoke in "Austen-ese", my fellow students smiled, teachers smiled, parents smiled. They admired my exceptional work ethic and talent for memorising long prose so easily. Others in the play asked my opinion about the way to best deliver lines. They asked my advice on how to remember dialogue. They copied the way I held myself on stage.'

'You were admired and respected.'

'For many months,' she agreed. 'However, when all performances were finished, no one applauded me any more for my speech and manners. Where mere weeks before I had been a celebrated talent, now I was bothersome and repetitive. But I was entirely possessed by Miss Austen's words and characters. I could not release that world. The way I now spoke gave me form and structure. My Austen-inspired clothing and accessory designs allowed me something to focus on outside of school and, eventually, a small income began to trickle in, something of which I am certain Miss Austen would have approved, knowing that a single woman needs a means to survive.' Here she paused and shook her head. 'Now this is me. I do not have to wonder how best to choose words because the scripts are so firmly embedded in my mind. This *is* who I am.'

They walked on in silence for some time, coming to a stop at the entrance of the Echuca Chocolate Shop. 'How did your parents respond to your transformation?' Phoenix asked, admiring Lily's mahogany corduroy riding skirt, matching jacket and the cream lacy frills at her bust and cuffs. Lily ran her hands down her perfectly flat torso and Phoenix wondered what it would be like to move through the world without the sway of a substantial bust or a curved hip that constantly bumped into table corners and sometimes, embarrassingly, into other people.

'My style is more steampunk than they feel would reflect dear Jane herself but they appear to have come to a place of indifference about that particular aspect. The new aspect they embraced was my transformation into a body that is held together, now collected, and my obvious autistic expressions, such as flapping, now quietened. To this omission, they give their wholehearted approval.'

'But your flapping is part of you. It is essential to your self-regulation.'

Lily lifted her chin. 'That fact posed no barrier to their criticisms and physical restraint.'

'Physical restraint?'

'Mama would tie my hands together, trying to train me to grow out of it. Papa would force me to sit on them at the table or in the car, insisting I practise *being normal*.'

'But what is normal?' Phoenix fumed. 'Everyone is different or we'd all be cardboard cut-outs.' She wondered if Lily realised that her parents' behaviour was abusive.

'The opinion they possess is that there is a spectrum of normality, within which I do not abide.' Lily took Humphrey's lead, tying it carefully around the nearest post. Upon straightening, she smoothed her jacket once more. 'I have forced myself to accept that I must engage in more neurotypically acceptable forms of regulation in order to survive. Now, I smooth my attire, which appears to bother no one. I curl my toes tightly in my shoes, which no one can see. I clench my teeth. I arrange my hands together in my lap as Miss Austen may once have done and clasp my fingers until they are white. If necessary, I pinch the skin on my thumb.'

Phoenix didn't know what to say. Lily was describing masking and camouflaging, suppressing natural behaviours in order to be more acceptable. She now knew she'd been doing it too, more or less successfully, her whole life, until forcing herself to live the way the neurotypical world wanted her to live had broken her down. One thing she'd learnt was that an autist's stims became obvious when they were happy *and* when they were stressed. If Lily was suppressing them all the time, she was also denying her joy. Still, Phoenix was new at this; Lily was not. Though it was difficult to swallow her opinions, she decided to let it go.

'I'm so sorry your parents weren't supportive,' she said, controlling her own natural urge to reach out and embrace her new friend. 'But I'm glad you've found a version of yourself that makes you happy. I still have no idea who I am, really. Who am I beneath all this exterior cladding I've built up?'

'Life has now gifted you with the opportunity to find out.'

Phoenix let that thought hang in the cool morning air, simultaneously excited to get to know her true self, sad that she'd missed out on so much time already, and scared about where this was going. She nodded at the front door of the shop. 'Well, I don't know about you, but I could use some chocolate,' she said, bending to pat Humphrey's head.

'A fine plan of which I am most supportive.'

Inside the cream rendered building, the exquisite aroma of chocolate greeted them and they both sighed with pleasure. Tiered wooden trellis tables and shelves groaned beneath wrapped chocolate delights with colourful ribbons. They set to work, filling little white carry bags with enough chocolate to last the whole trip – *if* they could restrain themselves for that long. Continuing, they were lured into the Echuca Heritage Sweet Co shop with its high ceiling and wall-to-wall striped boiled sweets, tightly wrapped candies, ropes of licorice and shiny tins of caramels. They loaded up once more, Phoenix gathering everything in lemon she could find.

Back at the house, Phoenix was relieved she'd logged onto Zoom five minutes early because she arrived only a fraction before Evelyn did. The last thing she wanted was for the principal to add 'tardiness' to her list of gripes.

'Good morning, Evelyn,' Phoenix said, mentally putting on her mask and engaging her teacher voice so she would align more closely with how others expected her to be. Then again, any response from her now would have to be an improvement on the way she'd been when Evelyn last saw her.

It was a Thursday in July, fourth period.

'Miss Rose, are you okay?'

Phoenix blinked, landing back in her body with an ungainly thud. She'd been staring, her eyes fixed on nothing in particular, her mind somewhere else. Returning her attention to the room brought a rush of sound – girls talking and squealing, erupting into snickers and laughter. Serena Watson was brushing her hair, again. Jasmine Singh was drawing something up her arm with a purple marker. Phoenix opened her mouth to call out to her but in the split second of time that passed, the girl's name had disappeared. A barely audible *Jjj—* reached her lips before the word vaporised.

'Miss?' It was Lina, in the front the row where she always was, staring at Phoenix.

'Y-yes,' Phoenix squeaked, forcing out a smile, a smile she knew looked as awkward and insincere as it felt. 'Fine.'

Lina cast a glance sideways to Emma. Or was it Emily? Emmagen? Why couldn't she find the girl's name?

Phoenix tried to focus her eyes on the school laptop in front of her where the electronic class roll was still open. She scanned it for names. She had no memory of marking it off, yet a small tick appeared in every box even though the names looked as though they didn't belong there. Was that even the correct class list? She tried to swallow but couldn't get past the iron fist gripping her throat shut.

Water.

She needed water. Her mouth was stuck together. That was the problem. That must be why she couldn't speak. She reached across the desk towards her bottle but the light from the Power-Point bounced off the whiteboard searing her eyes and she yelped, covering her face with the heels of her hands. Fumbling, grasping, peeking through almost-closed eyelids to stop the blinding pain, she snatched up her water bottle and unscrewed the lid, bringing it towards her lips. But the shake in her hands made her drop it straight onto the open laptop, water gushing across the keys.

'Shit.'

The classroom of girls erupted into gasps, laughter, shrieks, whistles and slow, mocking claps. Inside her mind, she had words to say to them, to tell them to settle down, to ask someone to find some tissues or paper towels, to implore them to be kind in this moment, compassionate rather than cruel because she could tell she was a tiny puff of air away from collapse.

Was she having a stroke?

But no words came. Instead, the smell of perfume and deodorant and hair products swallowed her in an unexpected tsunami, knocking her sideways, forcing her to smother a retch.

She tipped the laptop upside down and water poured from beneath the keys. Her hands shook and she dropped it back to her desk before covering her eyes a moment, willing herself to find a place of calm.

One, two, three, breathe.

The school bell rang, long and ear-piercingly loud, and it was all she could do not to shove her hands over her ears to wait it out.

The girls packed up and left, throwing a few unhelpful remarks her way as they went, pulling their mobile phones from their pockets, not even trying to hide them, ready to tell everyone about their stupid, clumsy teacher.

Phoenix hauled herself to the staffroom, dropped her things on her desk, then locked herself in a toilet cubicle. She could not move. Not even when other teachers spoke to her through the door and asked her if she was okay, if she needed anything. Not even when the second break of the day ended and the quadrangle quietened and the other teachers left to go to class. Not even when Evelyn came in and told her that someone was covering her class and Phoenix needed to come out of there and talk to her and tell her what was wrong.

Not even then.

Now, Phoenix shuddered at the memories. Zack had been contacted and had to leave work. It had been he who helped her out of the cubicle and took her to the doctor and Phoenix hadn't spoken to Evelyn since.

With her superior's face glaring at her from her phone screen, she felt her confident teacher voice draining away. She struggled to maintain eye contact with Evelyn, wanting to hide under the coffee table in front of her.

'How are you, Phoenix?'

'Good,' Phoenix replied, an automatic response, like the one you give the person at the supermarket check-out whether you're doing well or have lost your job, your best friend and house all in one day. 'Good,' she repeated.

'Excellent. That's what I wanted to hear,' Evelyn said. 'I assume then you're planning to return to work on the first day of term.'

'Well, no, I'm not sure yet, but I have another certificate.' Phoenix struggled for words, feeling cornered.

'But you said you were good.' Evelyn narrowed her eyes.

'But that's just what you say, you know, whether it's true or not.'

'So you lied?'

'That's—' Phoenix took a deep breath, knowing her anxiety was scrambling her words. This particular line of interrogation irked her, and not only because Evelyn was playing games. She would love it if people actually *would* simply say what they meant. She'd replied 'good' because that was how the neurotypical game was played; it was a learned skill, like eye contact, or please and thank you, or that birthday presents should be wrapped neatly with a handwritten card attached. It was social lubricant, a way of greasing the cogs of communication. A sign that both people were playing the same game.

If Phoenix ever did reply with the truth – *not feeling so great, a bit tired, losing my mind right now,* or *my favourite TV show has ended and now I have no idea what to do with myself* – people looked at her oddly, or sometimes laughed. If she asked someone how they were, she genuinely wanted to know the answer. If the person told her the truth it would actually give her something to continue with. Instead, the ubiquitous 'good' was a door closing in the conversation. And yet the autistic person was the one supposedly lacking in social awareness. How completely backwards it all was.

She carefully put aside her desire to argue the point. 'Obviously, I'm doing my best to find a way forwards under the circumstances.'

'The circumstances of your autism diagnosis,' Evelyn said, with clear disdain.

Phoenix opened her mouth to respond that she preferred the term 'identity' over 'diagnosis' (she wasn't sick or dying; she hadn't caught a virus or been struck down with something incurable – she was literally exactly the same person she'd always been) but didn't know whether to confirm or deny anything at all. *She* hadn't revealed that information. For all Evelyn knew, Anthea might have been lying or mistaken in her intoxicated disclosure. Phoenix had no idea if the principal was even allowed to bring this up; nor did she know whether revealing her identity was likely to help her case or hinder it. For the moment, she decided to say nothing.

'I have concerns,' Evelyn went on, picking up a stack of A4-sized papers from her desk and tapping them officiously on her desk. 'Your sick leave has expired. You've sent in another leave certificate but you haven't filled out an application for unpaid discretionary leave.'

'I'm sorry about that. I've been dealing with a family emergency, of sorts, and—'

Evelyn cut her off. 'I have serious concerns for the ongoing reputation of this school.'

Phoenix gasped. Was Evelyn really trying to compare Phoenix's autism with the previous principal's strippers-and-ecstasy scandal?

'As you know, I was brought in to this school by the bishop himself, cherrypicked to rectify the abominable hit to traditional values from the unsettling direction in which Mr Backhurst was attempting to take this school in the name of social progress, not to mention his criminal acts—'

Phoenix could hold back no longer. 'Evelyn, excuse me, I am not a scandal! I am a senior teacher with over a decade of teaching excellence. That hasn't changed.'

'Oh, come now, of course it's changed. *Everything's* changed,' she said, in a low, fed-up tone. 'And I will not be letting this school sink any further.'

At the precise moment Phoenix opened her mouth to tell Evelyn she had to stop blaming her for things that had nothing to do with her, Marilyn jumped up into her lap and knocked the phone from her hand, sending it crashing first against the edge of table, before it launched into space and landed in the bowl of pet water nearby. When she fished it out, the screen was black.

10

The room exploded in a frenzy of activity: Phoenix swearing and ineffectually using her shirt to try to dry the phone; alarmed discussions about putting the phone in a bag of rice; Lily looking up the nearest convenience store to procure said rice; and a frantic search for some kind of pin that might be able to open the SIM card compartment to at least retrieve that. Cupboard doors and drawers flung open. Bags and wallets emptied. None revealed anything suitable until Lily remembered a silver bat brooch in her magical bag of steampunk attire and they managed to open the confounding device and extract the teeny tiny metallic card.

Phoenix collapsed back onto the couch, the SIM card pinched between her fingers, sickened by having cut Evelyn off mid discussion. Lily's cheeks were red with exertion and a noticeable tremor had appeared in her hands as she smoothed her long curls away from her face. The offending cat jumped into Phoenix's lap and rubbed her head under her chin. 'It's okay, Marilyn, I forgive you.' She stroked the length of Marilyn's body, the cat arching her back into Phoenix's hand and headbutting her affectionately.

'Have you noticed there's a theme running through Olga's animals' names?' Lily said, abruptly halting mid circuit around the room, her hands clasped neatly at her waist, Victorian-style.

'What do you mean?'

'Rita, Marilyn, Audrey, Humphrey.'

'Nope, I don't get it.'

'They're old Hollywood names.'

'Oh, yeah,' Phoenix said, scratching Marilyn under the chin.

It was lovely to think she could still learn more about Olga even after her passing. Phoenix could imagine her friend at home on her couch in front of the fire, her animals curled up next to her, watching old black-and-white movies together.

She and Lily fell into silence. The truth was that Phoenix craved silence. But unlike most other situations where Phoenix might feel the need to fill the space, to keep actively trying to engage someone, here with Lily silence was easy.

Some teachers spent their time on yard duty moving from one group of students to another, talking the whole time. But Phoenix only spoke if she needed to. Her job required her to speak thousands of words each day, to engage with hundreds of individuals from students to fellow teachers to the principal, to parents, to tech support, to bus drivers and tuckshop volunteers. Every one of those individuals was a communication puzzle to solve. Every one of them required something of her and she needed firm defences at all times, filtering everything she thought and said, conscious of the way she said it, the way she stood, how her face looked, and how her clothes sat.

She needed her lunchtimes to be silent but they never were. Staffrooms required interaction, and even if she wasn't interacting she was filtering – noise, words, conversations, gossip, loud debates about football games and politics, shrieking bells and metallic announcements, piped music on Fridays. She couldn't get a moment's rest and it drained her more than she'd ever realised. She'd learned to ignore and suppress her own needs – or so she'd thought – until they refused to be ignored any more. The truth was that she needed silence, and lots of it. While she sat appreciating the peace and quiet offered by Lily and the animals, she also felt a flaming fear. She would never find silence in a school setting. It was a miracle she'd lasted this long. But this was the world she lived in, one that didn't actively make accommodations for people like her. What were her choices, really? She could never fully escape into silence, so what choice did she have but to battle on?

At length, she took a deep breath, kissed little Marilyn on the top of her head and put her on the ground before addressing Lily. 'I suppose we should get going. We're almost an hour past our check-out time and I imagine cleaners will be here any moment. We'd better get these animals into the van and go. If I could please borrow your phone, I'll email Evelyn to apologise and text Zack to let him know my phone's out of action, then we need to pick up Rita and hit the road before we get too far behind schedule.'

'You can depend on me.'

Animals loaded once more, Lily took the wheel and they set off for the paddock while Phoenix used Lily's phone to email the principal, once again apologising, and promising to get in touch when she had replaced her phone. She also booked somewhere for them to stay in Wagga Wagga, as well as an overnight spot for Rita. At one point, the phone lit up in her hand and flashed the word *Mum*.

'Oh, your mum is calling,' she said, holding the phone towards Lily.

Lily kept her eyes on the road. 'Send it to voicemail, please.' Her tone was firm.

'Is everything okay with you and your mum?' Phoenix ventured.

'She is unable to let me go,' Lily said, her nostrils flaring. 'She believes I am incompetent and while she harbours such beliefs I feel we have nothing left to discuss.'

Phoenix murmured her understanding and tucked that line of conversation away to be explored in more depth later. Right now, she needed to sort out her phone. While many sites suggested a bag of rice was more myth than magic for drying devices, it was all Phoenix had available so they made a quick stop at a convenience store for a bag of shortgrain and Phoenix submerged her phone into it, hoping for the best.

When she found Rita in the corner of her dirt yard, she was snuggled up to a pony on the other side of the fence, a handsome fellow with a chestnut coat and flaxen mane and tail. Their noses were pressed nostril to nostril through the wooden rails and Rita was stomping one foot as though annoyed she couldn't climb over to be with him. In return, his soft grey lips mouthed at hers in kisses. 'I'm sorry, lovely girl. It can be hard to say goodbye.' She stroked Rita's neck under her mane and gently slipped on the halter.

'In Year 4, I made a friend,' she said, scratching Rita's shoulder. 'I could only ever make one good friend at a time and that year Heather was it – although I went to her house once and all she wanted to do was play Barbies, and I could never understand the Barbie thing.' She shrugged. 'Anyway, I still thought Heather and I were besties. When she left school a week early before Christmas holidays it felt like my world had ended. Nothing at school made sense any more.' She tugged on the lead rope and Rita began to follow. 'But at the start of Year 5, Heather had forgotten all about me.' The pony sighed. 'When we get settled back in Brisbane, maybe we can find you a pony friend, one you won't have to say goodbye to.'

With Rita back in the float, tugging at the new hay they'd bought in Bendigo, and Lily returned from her walk with Humphrey, they set out once more. The dirt road from the agistment lot was long and unkempt, bordered by trees and fields on both sides, with not a house in sight. Stones spat up off the road, tinging against the underside of the van. Phoenix had turned the sunflower lights on and settled down into her seat when they turned a corner and a black streak shot out across the road. Lily slammed on the brakes, the weight of the horse float tugging at the skidding van, causing it to rock and sway. Rita stumbled; Phoenix could hear her stomping and jolting, trying to regain her balance. Time slowed as Phoenix waited for either the van and float to buckle, for Rita to fall in the float, or the little black streak to crunch under the wheel.

Miraculously, none of those things happened and the van and float came to a sliding stop. Lily's hands flew to her stricken face. 'Did I hit it? Did I kill it?'

'I don't think so,' Phoenix said, already unbuckling her seatbelt. 'It was a cat, wasn't it? Or a kitten?'

Lily nodded, breathless. She moved the van to the side of the road in the shade and cut the engine before climbing out to help Phoenix search for the animal. All was silent, save for Rita's stomping. Dust clouds billowed out from the vehicle's underbelly.

Braced for the worst, Phoenix got down on the ground and peered beneath the van. She couldn't see any sign of a flattened cat, but did wonder if it could be up inside the engine somewhere. Straightening, wiping her hands down her hips, she circled the van and float, while Lily turned right to check the bush at the side of the road. Phoenix headed to the left, back the way they'd come. 'You had to be black, didn't you, little one?' she despaired out loud, failing to see how they could possibly find a black cat in this vegetation, especially if it was injured and unable to move, or vocalise.

But she couldn't leave an injured animal behind. Even if it wasn't injured, it was clearly not okay to be left out there in the middle of nowhere. 'Puss, puss, puss,' she called, her voice small and light, as inviting as she could make it given that she'd emerged from two tonnes of metal that had mowed down a defenceless kitten, or cat . . . or maybe a dog? No, she might have only seen it for a second but she was sure it was feline.

Carefully, she began to forge into the bushes, scratched by lantana, terrified of stepping on snakes, imagining ticks and other nasties jumping onto her and climbing under her clothes. 'Puss, puss, puss,' she called gently. 'Come on, baby, I'm here to help. Please let me help you?'

She stopped still. Was that a meow? She turned to see Lily was also waist-deep in the bushes, her pinstriped pants and her boots swallowed by green-brown tangles, with just her billowing white sleeves to show her location. When Lily looked up, Phoenix waved her over. 'I think I heard a meow,' she said softly when Lily reached her side. 'Oh! Your vest is ripped.'

'It is of no concern,' Lily said, wiping at the sweat beading under her eyes and momentarily lifting the weight of her hair from her neck to allow a breeze there. 'From where do you think the sound came?' she whispered.

Phoenix grimaced. 'I've no idea.' Together they waited, and waited, staying still and silent for so long Phoenix began to believe she'd imagined it. She was about to say she must have been wrong when she heard it again – a tiny, plaintive cry. 'Did you hear that?' she whispered.

Lily nodded, pointing. 'This way.'

Together they picked their way through horrible thorns and spikes and let out squeaks of fear when unseen creatures moved out from underfoot. It was midday and the sun beat down on their heads. 'Have we gone too far?' Phoenix said, coming to a standstill and swiping at an ant crawling on the back of her neck.

'I am not sure,' Lily said, sounding as desperate as Phoenix felt.

There it was again. A tiny mew. Closer now, within metres, surely. As one, they set off again. Two steps later, they saw them, curled against the base of a tree trunk. The little black fluffball who had darted in front of them and his or her friend, a smoky grey and white kitten.

Both Phoenix and Lily gasped at the same time. The grey and white kitten was injured, badly. It was filthy, blood having mixed with dirt and dried tarlike. How long had it been here? Its back leg was a mess. The skin was split apart, revealing glistening tendons and muscles also covered in dirt. It was clearly not far from death, by shock, or infection, or predation, whichever came first.

Lily stood frozen, her hands over her nose and mouth.

Phoenix could see the trembling in her friend's fingers. 'Okay . . . okay . . . okay,' she heard herself repeat. She stared at the mess of grey and white on the left and the terrified eyes of the black kitten on the right.

'Okay,' Phoenix said, once more, this time with a plan. 'We need to move very slowly. We can't lose them now.' Beside her, Lily nodded, wordlessly. 'I'm going to take off my shirt and wrap up the injured kitten. I'm pretty sure it's not going to be able to run away but you never know, I guess. Do you think you can get the black kitten?'

'I will try.'

Moving slowly, Phoenix removed her shirt, leaving herself in her bra, and knelt down, shuffling carefully and slowly towards the kitten. 'Hey, little one. I'm here to take care of you, okay? We're going to get you some help and then you'll feel lots better.' She spoke the words gently, ignoring the voice in the back of her head telling her that it was all too late for this animal. She refused to listen to it. *Thoughts are just thoughts and that doesn't make them real*, she instructed herself. 'I'm going to pick you up very gently.' She extended her arms, laying the shirt over the top of the kitten as carefully as she could. The kitten was breathing rapidly, distressed. It gave no resistance as Phoenix bundled it up, limp and light in her arms. There she stayed, hunched on the ground, perfectly still, while Lily made her move for the black kitten.

As Lily stepped towards it, the kitten opened its little mouth and hissed, flattening itself on the ground. Phoenix extended her own bundle of kitten towards to the black one, hoping to entice it to stay with its friend. Alas, as Lily reached for it, the black kitten launched off the ground, landing on the tree trunk and making haste vertically. As Phoenix's heart fell, Lily – nimble as a mother cat – pivoted, reached for the kitten and snared it, pinning it to the trunk until she could get a better grip. But the fierce little thing bit her hard on the hand and Lily shrieked. She let go and the kitten bounded higher still.

'No!' Phoenix cried.

But it was too late. The black kitten had scampered up the tree, well out of reach.

11

There was nothing else they could do but drive the ten kilometres back to Echuca to get the injured kitten to a vet. Lily drove while Phoenix cradled the broken wee bundle in her lap and phoned ahead to let them know they were coming. When they arrived, Lily pulled up at the front of a heritage house that had been converted into a surgery. She took the kitten gently from Phoenix and started for the building while Phoenix retrieved a new shirt from her suitcase. When she arrived inside, Lily was still holding the kitten while a vet, flanked by two nurses, shone a light into the its eyes and lifted its lips to check the colour of the gums.

'Right. We're going to need to get this one into surgery straight away,' the grey-haired vet said. She looked at Lily, as if suddenly taking in her appearance, then turned to Phoenix, who was still catching her breath. 'Are you together?' she asked.

'Yes,' Phoenix said. 'We just found him, or her. Their leg is split open,' she said, feeling her belly dip.

The vet turned to her team. 'Let's go.'

One of the nurses took the kitten from Lily's arms and hurried out the back. Then the vet turned to her clients still in the waiting room with their dogs and cats. 'This is an emergency. I'm sorry for the delay. Kelly at the front will take it from here.' Facing Phoenix and Lily the vet said, 'See Kelly. You'll need to fill out paperwork, including permission for anaesthetics, resuscitation, financials and DNR orders.' Then she swept from the room.

Lily's hand fluttered to her throat. Phoenix felt the tremble in her legs turn to a quake and made for a seat, Lily following. The bleached-blonde receptionist handed Phoenix a clipboard and pen, then began rescheduling the waiting clients' appointments. Phoenix filled in her own details, claiming ownership of the kitten. She turned to Lily. 'Is it okay for me to put my name down?'

'Yes, of course. I would keep it myself but I have now left home, and I am unsure of Bianca's openness to having a cat.' Phoenix might have imagined it, but it seemed as though Lily might have suddenly questioned exactly how well she knew Bianca.

Phoenix returned her focus to the paper, but her brain refused to work. She stared at the words, her pen poised, unable to answer any of these questions. Was the kitten a boy or a girl? How old was it? Where had it come from? Did it already belong to someone? What had happened to it? And what about the one they'd left behind? Maybe it was also injured but they'd missed it because this kitten was in such obvious danger.

'We need to go and find the other kitten,' Phoenix said, standing up.

'Agreed,' Lily said, also rising.

'What's happening?' the nurse asked, returning.

'There's another kitten,' Phoenix said. 'We tried to catch it but it escaped. It might be injured too. We need to go back and get it.'

Kelly nodded, eyeing Phoenix's empty form. 'Okay. Let's get the legal and financial parts of these forms done, and you can fill in the rest when you get back.'

With supreme effort, Phoenix ignored the suspicious look Kelly gave her – she would never abandon an animal or her responsibility towards it – and quickly filled in her debit card details, giving permission for anything and everything the grey and white kitten needed, then passed it to Lily to add her phone number. Phoenix handed the clipboard back to the receptionist. 'Our number's on the form,' she said. 'Call us if there's any news. We'll be back as soon as we can.'

Still hauling the horse float with Rita on board, Humphrey on his dog bed and the cats and chickens in their crates, they drove back and forth along the dirt road, trying to locate the tree the black kitten had ascended.

'We should have left something behind to show us where to stop,' Phoenix muttered, cursing herself for not thinking things through properly. It took longer than they would have liked to find it but, fortunately, their earlier trampling and bush-bashing had left a broken path and Lily cut the engine. They raced to the tree, tipping their heads back, shielding their eyes from bright spears of sunlight.

'There!' Lily pointed to a branch.

'Where?' Phoenix moved closer to Lily.

'Where the branch meets the tree, next to that hollow, to the right, behind that burst of foliage.'

'Oh, yes, I see it!' Phoenix's joy that they'd spotted the kitten was quickly dashed, however, as there was no way they could reach it. 'Puss, puss, puss,' she called, clicking her fingers and making kissing noises. 'Come on, little one, we need you to help us help you. We can't climb. We need you to come down.'

The kitten opened its mouth, revealing its pink tongue as it meowed in response. But it did not move. Phoenix waded out of the bush, flicked the zebra tail aside at the back of the van and flung open the doors. She pulled out a bag of cat food, dropped some into a bowl and returned to the tree. She rattled the biscuits, calling the kitten. With no luck, she left the bowl on the ground and she and Lily returned to the van to sit on the edge and wait. Half an hour later, the kitten had still made no move. Phoenix's eyes stung with despair. What were they going to do?

Humphrey whined, so she clipped on his lead and took him out for a toilet break, frustrated that the sight of him would likely frighten the kitten even more. She led him away from the tree, taking the time to breathe and settle her escalating emotions, but when she at last returned, thirsty but calmer, Lily shook her head, still gazing up into the tree.

They both jumped when the phone rang.

'You take it,' Lily said, handing it over.

'Hello, Phoenix speaking.'

'Phoenix, this is Estelle from the vet clinic. I've just come out of surgery with the kitten you brought in.'

'Okay.' Phoenix braced herself.

'Her injuries are consistent with a car accident. It's been a tremendous cleaning and stitching job and she has a drain in to help release any fluid that builds up. I honestly can't believe she hasn't got a broken leg but she does have a lot of soft tissue damage that will still require care and confinement for a few weeks at least.'

'Oh, the poor girl.'

'She's certainly not out of the woods yet. She is suffering from shock, which is a dangerous thing. I am going to keep her sedated for a while and on IV fluids and oxygen too. If she makes it through the shock, I believe her prospects are good, but the next couple of days are going to be important.'

'Okay,' Phoenix said, her mind reeling from the absolute scuttering of her road-trip plans. 'How long do you think she'll need to stay in hospital?'

'It's difficult to say for sure. There's a lot of trauma here. But if there are no further complications in the next two to three days, she should be okay to go home. That is, if you are intending to keep her?' Estelle added, as though suddenly remembering that Phoenix and the kitten had only met this morning. 'We did scan her for a microchip but she doesn't have one, nor a desexing tattoo, so she hasn't come from a shelter. I'd say she's likely only twelve weeks old and, given where you found her, I'm confident she's a stray or been dumped. She's yours now, if you want her.'

Phoenix almost laughed. It was absurd that it was only that morning that she and Lily had wandered at leisure through the streets of Echuca because they had plenty of time to get to Wagga Wagga by the afternoon. Now, she'd booked accommodation she couldn't use, booked agistment Rita wouldn't be able to use, lost her mobile phone, damaged her professional prospects with Evelyn further still, and hadn't eaten since the bag of chocolate. At this moment, she, Lily and her animals were homeless and hungry and the day was rushing to its end and they still had a lost, defenceless kitten up a tree they couldn't catch.

She knew many people, perhaps most people, would not have helped that grey and white kitten, except perhaps to knock her on the head, let alone hand over their bank details to pay for her care. She knew many people, perhaps most, would walk away from the kitten up the tree rather than ruin their road trip, leaving themselves in danger of having to sleep rough for the night. But there wasn't a cell in Phoenix's body that would even consider not helping. It was simply the right thing to do. For her, there was no option. She felt those kittens' pain and fear and longing to be loved and cared for – literally felt it in her body as physical sensations – exactly as she did with Olga's animals. She would never walk away from an animal in need if she was capable of helping. It was incomprehensible to her that anyone could possibly think differently.

But yes, please go ahead and tell me autistic people lack empathy.

'Yes,' she confirmed to the vet. 'She's mine.'

Phoenix and Lily snacked on more chocolate and lollies while they made new, complicated plans. Fortunately, the horse agistment centre was able to take Rita back and she even got to stay in the paddock next to her new best friend, calling out to him enthusiastically the second the float rolled onto the property. Phoenix paid out more cash, happy at least that the other pony looked thrilled to have Rita back, if their enthusiastic fence kissing was anything to go by. The agistment centre also allowed them to leave the horse float there on site, which meant they could then check themselves in to a two-bedroom cabin in a nearby caravan park. The sign by the road said that dogs were welcome. There was no mention of cats or chickens and Phoenix was not inclined to ask any specific questions.

They pulled up in front of the wooden cabin with its little verandah at the front and a young eucalyptus tree by the stairs. Phoenix waved at other park guests taking afternoon strolls with their dogs and enquired as to where they were headed, and every one of them stared at Lily.

'Are you working at a theme park?' one woman asked her.

Lily shook her head and turned away, then climbed into the depths of the van, shutting the doors behind her. The last thing they needed was for someone nosy to see the cages in the back.

'Fancy dress party,' Phoenix joked, and plastered on a fake smile till the woman moved on. Inside the van, they wrapped the cat and chicken cages in sleeping bags, pet bedding and coats and smuggled them into the cabin one by one.

'I feel awful,' Phoenix said, setting down the chicken cage in the bathroom. 'They've been trapped in there all day with not a blade of grass to peck at or room to stretch.' The wide-eyed, hesitant chickens stepped out carefully, made a dash across the two square metres of tiles, then came to an abrupt halt at the opposite wall. They hunched together, murmuring their displeasure, and pooed onto the puppy pads that had been laid out for that purpose.

'It is only temporary,' Lily said, checking the windows as though they were under siege and she was on the lookout for approaching enemies. Her tone carried an edge of *toughen up, princess*, which suddenly struck Phoenix as so amusing and out of character that it made her laugh.

'What is funny?' Lily asked, spinning around to search the room for the cause of such mirth.

Phoenix waved a hand. 'Nothing. Or maybe everything.'

In the loungeroom, they lowered blinds, set out litter trays and released the cats, who skittered about uneasily in their new environment, jumping onto the tabletop then over to the couch.

'Please, stay silent, all of you,' Phoenix implored, stroking both tabbies at once. They arched their backs up into her hands, though continued to take in their surroundings with big black eyes. 'Right.' She stood, taking in a deep breath, grabbed a glass and gulped down two full tumblers of water, only now realising how little she'd drunk today and that it was probably the cause of her headache. She filled another glass and handed it to Lily, who did the same.

'I better get back out there,' Phoenix said.

'I am coming with you,' Lily said. 'I know it is not the plan upon which we agreed but I cannot in good faith allow you to go out there alone.'

'But what about the animals?'

'They will be fine. We shall turn off the lights and no one will know they are here at all.'

'Unless they start yowling.'

'It is unlikely to cause any complications until tomorrow morning when the office is open once more.' Lily shrugged. 'Then they might ask us to leave but I estimate that we at least have this one night of grace. I do not want you out there unaccompanied.'

Phoenix had to admit she would rather not be out in the middle of the bush by herself. 'All right, then. Let's go.'

They had no plan other than to set up the van near the kitten's tree and leave food out, hoping to entice it down. Best-case scenario would see them back at their cabin in a couple of hours' time, with a new kitten in the mix. Worst case would see them sleeping in the back of the van, though Phoenix was sure little sleep would be had at all. They filled every bottle or container they could find with water, took warm clothes, and set off once more, taking Humphrey with them. If by chance he launched into nonstop barking while they were away it would most definitely attract unwanted and angry attention to the cabin. It was safer to have him with them if also a potential deterrent to the kitten.

They parked the van beside the dirt road and approached the tree just as the late afternoon light was seeping to red and flocks of birds were heading to roost. The kitten was still in its spot. 'Come on, beautiful,' Phoenix said. 'You don't want to spend the night up there,' she said, pushing away images of a hungry carpet python scaling the tree for a tasty snack. They rattled the biscuits and left a little trail from the base of the tree to the edge of the road, where they placed the bowl in a position easier for them to catch the kitten and where they could better observe it from the van. Then they climbed inside to watch and wait.

The last blush of sunset glowed on the horizon, then turned deep blue. The black silhouettes of bats streaked across sky, their noisy chatter filling the air.

'There must be roosts nearby,' Lily observed, smiling up at them. 'Did you know that if you examine the bone structure of bats' wings they look remarkably like X-rays of our own hands? They even have thumbs, like us.'

'I didn't know that.'

'They're mammals, but the only mammals that can fly. We have over ninety species of bat in Australia. A group of bats is called a cloud.' Lily's voice sang with the joy of sharing her special interest, making Phoenix smile. Neurotypical people might view this as info-dumping, but autistic people might understand it to be a sign of affection, the vulnerability of displaying one's most treasured thoughts and joy. 'There are the mega bats, which eat fruit and nectar, and the microbats, which eat insects. They are keystone pollinators of our forests, and without bats our forests would be in terrible danger.'

'That's awful.'

Here, Lily's forehead crumpled. 'And people are so awful to them. They shoot them. Poison them. Trap them in nets to die long, slow deaths. Demolish their homes.' Her voice trembled. 'But we need them!'

Phoenix nodded in agreement but could find no words of comfort. She too had always felt the pain of the world and had no idea how to handle its weight.

When the sky had turned black, she asked, 'Tell me about your bat tattoo.'

Lily laid her hand over the bat on the inside of her wrist. She didn't say anything for a long time and when her voice came it was quiet, but sure of itself. 'I think bats are like us – autists. They are shy, quiet, relegated to the shadowy spaces. They are intelligent and devoted to the ones they love yet they are misunderstood, terrorised, the subject of so much misinformation and subjected to mismanagement, yet they are essential for our planet. There is a small percentage of the population who love them and fight for them, but there are so many more who will never appreciate them, until they've been hunted to extinction, and then it will be too late.'

Phoenix struggled for something positive to say here, to refute Lily's bleak words, but after all the research she'd done, she had to admit things seemed bleak. The historical record documented cruel and deadly treatment of autistic people. They'd been sent to asylums. Confined in straitjackets behind locked doors. Refused education. Injected with poisons. Experimented on. Forced into cruel conversion therapies.

Killed.

To this day, in some countries, autistic people were 'treated' with electric shocks large enough to induce third-degree burns. Right now, there was a global scientific race to identify all the autistic genes, with one potential goal being to eliminate them.

Yet being here with Lily, though the truth was painful, it was lightened and eased. There was real joy to be found in the unique and immediate friendships autists might find in each other. Other than Zack, she couldn't think of anyone she'd rather be sitting with in a van on an empty road in the dark on a crazy mission to catch a kitten.

12

They'd finished all their snacks – chips, more chocolate, a bag of popcorn and a packet of trail mix – by nine o'clock. They'd taken Humphrey out for two walks. Each had done a bush wee. Twice, they'd jumped when they heard the cat biscuits rattling in the bowl, only to find a cheeky possum helping itself the first time and a passing fox at it the second. An owl had been hooting, slow and rhythmic, for over half an hour. The grass slithered and shifted in disturbing ways with unseen visitors, and sparkling bright stars now punctuated the velvet sky.

Phoenix used Lily's phone to text Zack and give him an update and he replied saying he was eating pizza and playing Scrabble online with a robot named King Pin. He wished her luck with catching the kitten. He was as worried about it as she was. She was about to hand the phone back to Lily when the screen lit up. 'It's your mum, again,' Phoenix said.

Lily's shoulders stiffened. She took the phone and sent the call to voicemail, then stared out into the dark, giving Phoenix the impression she wasn't open to any inquisition as to why, though given their conversation this morning about how Lily's parents had treated her, Phoenix wasn't entirely surprised.

It was cold now, Phoenix shivering almost constantly. Her nose ran, and she sniffed often. Her fingertips were numb. 'I think we should set up some bedding,' she said, and Lily quickly agreed. They unzipped their sleeping bags and laid them flat, two pillows next to each other with a quilt, smuggled from the cabin, on top. They lay side by side, teeth chattering, and Phoenix lifted her hand from behind her head to stroke Humphrey's fur. He had a full belly and she'd given him his medication, so he was content to snooze on his bed, which in all honesty was likely a lot more comfortable than what Phoenix and Lily had.

'Have you thought of a name for the grey and white kitten?' Lily asked.

'No. I'm not sure my brain has stopped careering around logistical challenges all day.' Phoenix's heart lurched at the mention of the injured kitten, willing her to survive. She turned to Lily. 'I'm so sorry. I just realised that in all the chaos today I haven't specifically asked if you are okay being delayed on your trip because of these kittens. If I've upset you, I'm really sorry. If you need to go, I totally understand.' She hoped she wouldn't, though, as she'd come to think of herself and Lily as an established duo, like Batman and Robin.

'No, not at all,' Lily said, shaking her head, a tendril of her mermaid curls tickling Phoenix's neck. 'I am completely committed to fulfilling this mission, whatever patience is required in order to help the kitten, or anyone else.'

'That's a relief, thank you.' Phoenix had no idea how she would be handling this moment on her own.

'I am truthfully in no hurry. Bianca has been occupied with work and I do not wish to get in the way. Perhaps this delay may be all for the best . . . for the moment, anyway.'

'Do you think . . .?' Phoenix paused, searching for the right words. 'I mean, what did Bianca tell you about coming to stay with her? Was it for a holiday? Are you staying at her place or are you supposed to look for something of your own while you two get acquainted, in person, I mean?' She grimaced. She didn't want Lily to think she was judging this relationship (though she clearly was). But she had a feeling in her belly, a feeling she rarely read wrong. Something was up in this relationship.

Lily stalled, as if searching for words, or trying to recall exactly what Bianca had said. 'She proposed that I should come so as to be with each other in person and I said that I would arrive as soon as possible.'

'So, not specifically to *stay* with her?'

'I believed she meant stay,' she said, but a small quiver ran through her words. 'I mean, I am travelling from three states away. What else might she expect me to do?'

Phoenix opened her mouth to say more but was interrupted by the far-off sound of an engine that was definitely coming closer. She sat upright, facing the open doors of the van. Lily did the same. Headlights from a distance, like searchlights, seeking. Fear zinged through Phoenix – two women in an open van, in the pitch dark, in the middle of nowhere, with who-knew-who coming towards them. Flashes of horror movies barrelled through her mind, setting her heart rate galloping. 'We should shut the doors.'

'Agreed,' Lily said, springing forwards on hands and pin-striped knees, crawling to the end of the van. The light from the truck – because it sounded like that now, throaty and diesel-ish – expanded through the trees and for a moment Phoenix saw the kitten's eyes reflected green in the tree. Still on her knees, Lily yanked at the door, but it stuck hard, the silly zebra tail giving a swish. She swore – very un-Austen like – and yanked again, while Phoenix scrambled forwards to take hold of the other door and pull it closed. Humphrey rose to his feet, growling. The truck's engine roared, inching closer. Any moment they would be in the headlights. Phoenix launched over to Lily's side, jumped out of the van, shoving the door hard from the outside then scooting around it to leap back inside, yanking it shut as the truck rounded the bend.

Humphrey emitted a volley of deafening barks and Lily clamped her hands over her ears. The oncoming truck's headlights seared in through the windows of the van's doors and both women ducked their heads. The vehicle rocked, whether from their own movement or Humphrey's fierce tirade Phoenix wasn't sure. The truck was nearly on them.

Tyres skidded, the truck having taken the corner too quickly, coming upon their van unexpectedly, and Phoenix wrapped her arms around her knees, squeezing her eyes shut. Stones sprayed across the van's side. The truck slid sideways, spinning in a circle, and Phoenix held her breath, braced for impact.

Instead, the truck came to a stop, music *doof-doof*ing. Phoenix's heart hammered. She turned to Lily, eyes wide with fear. Humphrey continued barking.

'Shh!' Phoenix urged, shuffling towards him. 'It's okay.'

What they needed now was for that driver to move on, not be wondering why there was a dog locked inside a zebra-striped darkened van, barking its head off. 'Humphrey, stop, it's okay. Please, stop.'

Humphrey settled for frustrated whining and grumping.

'Can you hear anything?' Phoenix whispered.

Lily shook her head.

Phoenix waited for the truck door to open. For a heavy foot to hit the ground. For purposeful footsteps to head their way. The truck's lights seared into the driver's-side window of the van. She watched for shadows, for movement. The *doof*ing continued, confusing her senses and thoughts. She was frozen.

114

Was the driver's-side door locked? She didn't think so. She had no memory of doing it when they'd arrived in the afternoon. Why would she? It was light. They were busy doing things. But now it was dark. Her pulse thundered in her ears. Humphrey was still struggling beneath her hands and she could feel the van rocking from his contortions. Would the driver be able to see the movement too?

Seconds ticked by, interminably slow.

A lifetime later, the truck's throaty rev began again and it rolled away at a more modest pace. Humphrey gave it a final *good riddance* bark then sat down, muttering with displeasure, the truck's red taillights reflected in his eyes. The women shuffled on their knees to peer through the windscreen, checking the truck really had gone, and let out groans of relief to see it vanishing into the distance.

They sat once more, flapping at their faces, rocking and babbling nonsensical exclamations for a few moments, part laughing, part crying, till they flopped down onto the sleeping bags, taking deep calming breaths.

When Phoenix had composed herself, she rose again, leaning forwards once more to peer between the seats to assure herself that all really was well. Humphrey, who had been doing the same thing, suddenly swivelled his head towards hers, managing to press his nose to her neck for a moment. He pulled back, shocked at his own action, and their eyes locked, as though they were in the middle of a rom com and had been furiously at odds with each other until this adrenaline-fueled moment had made them realise their mutual affection for the first time. Phoenix was about to melt into gooey gratitude for the breakthrough when Humphrey abruptly sneezed, turned his back on her and curled up on his bed, ruining her moment. Still, she smiled.

Despite the fright they'd endured, they stayed the night, though with more security measures in place, with both front doors locked, the key in the ignition, one back door of the van closed, the other at the ready to pull shut. Only one of them rested at a time. The warm glow of the two strings of sunflower lights offered comfort. Neither of them slept, not really, perhaps only drifting off in short snatches.

Dawn broke in a frenzy of bird calls. Sleepy foxes and possums retreated into undergrowth and tree hollows. Wallabies disappeared into the bush. And still the black kitten was in its tree, now sagging with fatigue.

'His back leg's shaking,' Phoenix said, groggily, pointing to the branch. He wasn't meowing any more either.

'The wretched little thing is stuck fast.' Lily's voice was croaky from lack of rest. 'He is weakened.'

'We need help. We need someone who can get up the tree and rescue him. It's too high for a ladder.'

They fed and walked Humphrey, then returned into town, stopping for a cooked breakfast at a cafe – the first proper meal they'd had in over a day – then drove to the vet surgery, which was already open. Kelly recognised them as soon as they came in, which was not that surprising since they were still in the same clothes as the day before and Lily was a pretty unforgettable sight.

'Have you come to see your new baby?' she asked, cheerily.

'We'd love to see her,' Phoenix said. 'But we also need some help or advice.' She explained about the kitten up the tree.

Kelly's face lit up. 'Say no more. I have the answer.'

'Really?' Phoenix's hopes lifted.

'You need Magician Ken.'

'What?' both she and Lily said at the same time.

'He's Echuca's famous magician – often performs on the paddleboats – and is also known as Cat Man Ken.' She whipped a business card from a holder on the desktop. 'He's the town's go-to for cats stuck under houses, in chimneys and up trees.' She thrust the card at Phoenix, delighted to have solved the problem.

Phoenix studied the card.

Magician, Cat Rescuer, Window Cleaner

'He also cleans windows?' Lily queried.

Kelly shrugged. 'It's a small town. It helps to be flexible. Besides, his ladders and harnesses act as both cat-rescue equipment and window-cleaning equipment.'

Phoenix was speechless. One coffee really hadn't been enough.

'Anyhow, would you like me to take you out back to see your baby?' Kelly asked.

They followed Kelly down a narrow hallway to a space that might once have been a loungeroom and was now filled with cages of cats and dogs, some attached to drips, some alert and anxious, waiting for surgery, one dog with half its body hair shaved off, revealing pink, spotted skin. In the furthest corner lay a tiny bundle of grey and white, runny eyes half closed with heavy sedation. A drip hung from the top of the cage door, the tube running into her front leg, bandaged tight. A bloody drain poked from her leg, through the bandaging, oozing. Phoenix knew that under that bandage, countless stitches held the skin together.

'Oh, you poor little girl,' Phoenix said.

Lily sniffed and wiped at her eye.

Kelly opened the cage door so they could reach in and stroke her head and shoulders. The kitten responded a little, moving her head towards them, attempting to open her heavy eyes.

'She looks terrible right now because she's sedated,' Kelly said. 'But when she comes off that she'll be able to open her eyes and respond to you. Have you thought of a name yet?'

Phoenix turned to Lily. 'What do you think? Should we give her an Austen name?'

'Oh, but she is your cat. You most rightly ought to do it.'

'Please. I couldn't be doing any of this without you. I trust you.'

Lily shuffled, then lifted her chin. 'All right then. How about Jane? I do not think we could do better than that for a strong woman – one who defied all odds.'

Phoenix nodded. 'Jane it is.'

At ten o'clock, the magician/cat man pulled up alongside their own vehicle in a purple and white Volkswagen Kombi van with several passengers inside. He climbed out, wearing a sequined purple jacket, a matching bow tie, bright white trousers and spiked boots. His assistants, all dressed in black, emerged carrying cameras and tripods and Lily quickly disappeared inside the zebra van, shutting the doors behind her.

'G'day, I'm Cat Man Ken!' he said, standing with legs apart and hands on hips like a superhero. 'Nice van,' he mused, flicking a long zebra eyelash on his way past the headlights.

'Hi,' Phoenix said, eyeing his gel-spiked hair and creepy pencil moustache. His crew of ninjas was swiftly setting up their equipment, popping open light reflectors and testing microphones, completely ignoring her.

'I must say,' Ken said with a flourish, 'I adore your name. *Phoeeeniiiixxxx*,' he purred. 'You'd make a wonderful magician's assistant.' He eyed her up and down but twitched his nose with obvious disappointment. She might have had the name but she clearly didn't have the flair for costuming. Lily might have, though she was hiding. 'Very magical of you,' he continued. 'Rising from the ashes and all that.' He snapped his fingers in the air with another stagey flourish that made Phoenix flinch. 'Instead of sawing you in half I could simply set you on fire and then bring you back to life.'

'Hm,' Phoenix murmured, uncertainly. 'So, what are we going to do about the kitten?' She pointed upwards. 'He looks exhausted. I'm worried he'll fall.'

Ken suddenly dropped his over-the-top performance and squinted upwards. 'Only a little guy. Been up there long?' He sounded more like an ocker Aussie now.

'About twenty-four hours.'

'Yes, yes, we need to get to him quickly,' he said, his words in a rush, and back to his flamboyant magician persona. He waved vaguely to the ninjas. 'My crew will capture everything. Everything has to be recorded these days. YouTube, TikTok, Instagram, all that. Video is it. It's the only way to get any attention. If you don't get it on film, it never happened.' He turned his back and headed to the van and the pile of ladders and ropes.

Phoenix was lost for words. He hadn't asked her if he could film and his tone left no invitation to discuss it. But she wasn't sure how to bring this up with him, given she had literally no other options for getting the kitten down. She needed this to be done quickly, for the kitten's sake and her own. The kitten might be needing attention, and she and Lily couldn't keep living out of the van on the side of the road.

The next thing she knew, Cat Man Ken was stepping into a harness, talking to the camera about the urgency of needing to get to the sick and injured kitten up the tree. It was a life and death situation, apparently. Time was critical! He hoped he could make it in time! Then he and his team fussed about with ladders and a harness. She missed how it happened but suddenly (magically?) ropes were looped over the branch on which the kitten was perched and a camera was shoved at her face.

'Tell us about how you found the kitten,' the ninja demanded. 'Tell us everything, every detail.'

'Well, we'—she cast a glance at the van where Lily was hiding— 'I mean, *I* was driving along and the kitten kind of streaked out across the road.' She touched her hair, which hadn't seen a brush in at least two days and was scraped back into a thoughtless bun. Did spinebill hair hide dirt and dandruff?

'I asked if you hit it?' the ninja demanded.

'What? No, but I was worried about it so I stopped.' She fumbled on, telling the story, editing Lily out of it, while also trying to watch what Ken was doing. He was smiling and laughing, pulling himself up inch by inch, hamming it up for the camera, straining and wiping sweat away one moment and playing *look, Mum, no hands* the next, spinning in circles and laughing.

Phoenix stopped talking, unable to take her eyes off him as he reached the bough. He must have said something funny because the sound recordist, who was listening to him through her earphones, chuckled and cast her eyes up to where he was hovering, horizontally, almost like he was levitating. Phoenix bet the video crew would somehow edit out his harness and ropes later on to really make it look like levitation. It would be impressive. Part magic show, part cat rescue. A crowd-pleaser for sure – if indeed he had much of an audience at all. She'd certainly never heard of him. Maybe he was just a big fish in Echuca's small pond.

He straightened himself, 'sitting' in his harness with great natural lighting on his face, waiting for the camera operator to zoom in. Once he had the signal, he performed many takes of talking to the kitten, smiling into the camera, even wiping at a non-existent tear. Finally, he pulled out a bag on a pole – like a snake catcher's bag – from where it had been stashed in his belt and made a great stagey show of getting it ready, of loosening his shoulders, of taking deep breaths, of opening and closing his fingers as though casting a spell. At one point, he put his fist in his mouth in pretend anguish, before suddenly grabbing the kitten by the scruff of the neck while it spat and hissed and dropping it into the bag before spinning it closed. Cat Man Ken turned to the camera and pumped his fist in the air, then laid his hand dramatically over his heart.

Despite the overwrought theatrics, Phoenix was ecstatic and cheered and clapped and even shed some tears of relief. The kitten was on its way down to her and back to Jane. Cat Man Ken handed the shaking, squawking kitten to her and she clutched it to her chest, kissing the little head.

'My gift to you!' Ken said loudly, arms outstretched, turning to smile into the camera.

'Thank you so much,' she said, her cheeks stretched wide, the kitten attempting to crawl up to her shoulder. She pulled him down gently, but with an unrelenting grip, and waved at Ken and his crew as they climbed back into the Kombi. She watched them reverse and drive away. When the crew was a little way up the road, Lily burst from the back of their van and rushed to Phoenix, a joyful smile transforming her face. She clasped her hands together, grinning, trotting up and down on the spot a moment before leaning down to kiss the kitten on the head. It clambered up towards Phoenix's shoulder and Lily had to step closer to continue plastering on enthusiastic kisses. The kitten was nearly around Phoenix's neck when Lily carefully unhooked its claws from her clothes, then tucked him into the crook of her arm.

'Let's get him back to the surgery,' Phoenix said. 'Jane is waiting.'

13

'I've done research and I've ordered a stack of stuff online,' Zack said. Phoenix could hear the pride in his voice and smiled as she raced to keep up with his chatter. 'Four cat bed baskets, two scratching posts, five cat litter trays, because apparently we need one for each cat and one extra, a recurring delivery of cat litter, flea and worming treatments, collars with bells – not that they'll be going outside, the research is clear on that, it's bad for the wildlife and bad for them too, with car accidents, dog attacks, cat fights and cruelty issues. Mind you, we can always get harnesses and leads and take them out for walks and I've even seen backpacks with portholes for them to look through. Oh, and I've got two brushes for their coats and dental chews for their teeth. *And* I've got a cat water fountain as well, which is supposed to encourage them to drink more because cats often don't drink enough. And I'm about to order some stuff to help them with fur balls. It must be such a pain to take care of all that fur every day.'

Phoenix laughed. 'It sounds like you've thought of everything. Also, I'd be lying if I said I wasn't imagining you in one of those calendars that show firemen stripped to the waist holding tiny kittens in their arms.'

'Now I know what to make you for Christmas,' he said.

'Only if I get to take the photos,' she said, giggling. She watched the chickens peck at seed on the floor of the cabin bathroom. The red one suddenly stretched tall, rapidly flapping her wings. They needed to get out of this tiny room and home to Brisbane where they could peck and roam.

'You know, I'm actually excited now, to have fur kids,' he said. 'I'm hopeful that Humphrey and I will get on.'

'Look at us – buying a house, raising fur kids, you getting a promotion.' She pushed away the thought of her own vulnerable career. 'I mean, I know the cost of this trip will set us back a bit.'

'It's only temporary. We'll catch up quickly.'

'I'll sort things out with Evelyn as soon as I can,' she promised. 'And you'll get the promotion; I'm sure of it. You've been there the longest. You work so hard. You're always praised for your perfect X-rays. You never compromise on quality. You're the first to offer to stay late. You even work with X-rays on your days off,' she said. Zack's collection of vintage X-rays was one of his special interests. He got them from eBay and from garage sales, sometimes from friends and family. Now that X-rays were digital, he valued them even more for the historical records they were and turned some of them into artworks. She loved the abdomen X-ray he'd worked on recently, adding colourful butterflies to symbolise 'butterflies in the belly' and the skull X-ray with all the bees to symbolise how his mind was busy as a bee.

'You're ready for this,' she assured him.

'Hm. We'll see,' he said, always the first to doubt himself.

The red chicken clucked and flapped, so Phoenix turned the phone to FaceTime so the chook could peer at her reflection on the screen and Zack could watch. His mood brightened immediately. She watched the worry line between his brows smooth and a smile light up his eyes as he chatted to the chicken. Then his hand flew to the top of his head, where he rubbed at his hair in circular motions. 'The chickens! I need to organise a coop.'

Before Phoenix could respond, a loud volley of barking erupted from Humphrey, followed by a knock on the cabin door, making her jump. 'I've got to go. Speak to you soon.'

She stepped outside the bathroom, shutting in the chickens. Lily, not long out of the shower herself, hair dripping down the back of her billowy white shirt, scooped up Audrey and closed her into her bedroom, then lunged for Marilyn, who was sitting on the kitchen bench next to a used cereal bowl, licking her lips. When she had also been safely shut in the bedroom, Phoenix cautiously opened the front door.

'Hi!' It was a woman, about Phoenix's age at a guess, with dark hair and glasses and a warm but no-nonsense vibe that instantly made Phoenix think she might be a teacher. 'I'm Claudette. I live over that way.' She waved vaguely over her shoulder. 'I founded and run the community newspaper here in Echuca and I heard about you. You're Phoenix, right?'

'That's me,' Phoenix said, forcing a smile while also trying not to open the door too widely.

'Great! Do you mind if I ask you some questions? Cat Man Ken is my brother so I heard all about your kitten rescue. I'd love to write a feature.'

'Ah, I see.' Phoenix wished very much now that she'd paid the cat man for his services, without which she felt unequivocally indebted. Claudette was hovering, peeking around Phoenix as though waiting for an invitation to come inside.

'Let's have a seat on the deck,' Phoenix said, squeezing out the door and heading to the little table and chairs. 'That way I can pat Humphrey at the same time.'

'This is your dog?'

'Y-yes,' she confirmed, momentarily forgetting that she was now a dog person, then again with conviction, 'Yes, he is.'

'What brings you to Echuca? How did you find the kittens? Where will you go from here?'

Phoenix smiled at Humphrey, who was glaring at Claudette. 'I've got this,' she said softly to him. He looked between her and Claudette, unconvinced at first, then sighed grumpily and lay down. Phoenix turned to face Claudette's eager face to find she'd placed her phone down with the voice memo recording.

'That's just so I don't have to scribble unintelligible notes I can't decipher later on,' she said, smiling broadly. It was her disarming tactic, Phoenix surmised. 'So, what brings you to Echuca?' she repeated.

'Well, it's a long story,' Phoenix said.

'Excellent. I love nothing more.'

Phoenix began her tale, more or less sharing the whole journey but editing out the parts about autism. After Anthea and Evelyn had reacted so aggressively to her identification, she was wary of uninvited and uneducated opinions.

'I love this story,' Claudette said encouragingly, taking additional handwritten notes as thoughts came to her. 'It's quite the pilgrimage, and such a wonderful thing to do for a friend in need. This story has loss, friendship, commitment, vulnerable animals, community. Wonderful stuff! I'm so happy Echuca is playing host to you. Tourism took a big hit during the pandemic and many businesses closed. We need some good news and human interest to lift our spirits and it's great to see travellers back on the road. I'd love to get some photos of the animals too.'

Phoenix hadn't factored in photos.

'And I'd love to meet Lily. Where is she?' She glanced towards the cabin.

'She's out for a walk,' Phoenix said, feeling the lie grate over her teeth. Lying of any kind sat badly with her and it was one of the things that made her instantly lose faith in someone. She definitely had the classic autistic trait of truthfulness and she expected it in return. In this case, though, she'd seen Lily hide from Cat Man Ken and their caravan park neighbours, so she was pretty sure she wouldn't want to be part of a photo now.

'Where are the cats, chickens and pony?' Claudette asked, glancing around.

'Boarding elsewhere,' Phoenix said, holding only the image of the pony in her mind and hoping very much Claudette wouldn't push for more.

'Out at the horse agistment place near the road where you found the kittens?' Claudette guessed, her knowledge of the town clearly thorough.

'Yes.'

'Great. I know Jillian and Mike.' Of course she did. 'I should be able to get photos with the animals there.'

Phoenix felt as if she was watching a car crash in motion. That lie was going to undo her. She was gathering the courage to confess the truth to Claudette and beg her not to disclose the fact that the cats and chickens were in fact mere metres away when a noise shot her through with fear.

Bok, bok, bok, bok, bekerk! Bok, bok, bok, bok, bekerk! Bekerk! Bekerk! Bekerk! Bok, bok, bok, bok . . .

On and on it went. The sound of a chicken announcing to the world that she'd just laid an egg. The first egg she'd laid in quite some time. An egg that was totally unexpected given her advanced age and something of which to be tremendously proud. Look what she had done! This was a day to rejoice.

Phoenix closed her eyes a moment, feeling her innards turn to stone. When she opened them, Claudette was staring at her, mouth ajar, but smiling. 'The chickens aren't at Jillian and Mike's place, are they?'

Fortunately, Claudette did see the humour in the situation and promised not to write anything that would give them away.

Still, having a chicken lay an egg and announce it to all and sundry clearly meant Phoenix and Lily had to leave. It would only be a matter of time before word spread or someone complained. They hastily packed up and scrubbed the bathroom free of chicken droppings, seeds, feathers and the chicken's precious egg, which she'd laid in a wet towel on the floor.

They couldn't leave town, though, because Jane was going to be in hospital for at least another couple of days. Upon the vet's suggestion, the black kitten, newly named Milo, was staying with his sister, free of charge, to offer emotional support. By all accounts, it was working, with the vet confidently taking Jane off sedation. After picking up another mobile phone in town – as the internet had predicted, the bag of rice had done nothing to save the wet one – they looked for food. To Lily's delight, they located a vegan cafe. The Sweet Meadow was decked out in natural wood, calming neutral tones, earthy handmade ceramics, wicker, natural fibres and pops of colour from dried wildflowers. They sat outside in the sun, Humphrey at their feet.

While Lily worked her way through a plate of gnocchi, she carried on a text message chat with Bianca. When Phoenix saw Lily's texting quickening and her shoulders inch towards her ears, she swallowed her mouthful of meadow-green breakfast and took her chance. 'How are things going with Bianca?'

Lily grunted, then put her phone down to address Phoenix. 'She says she has hung new curtains in my yurt.'

'Your yurt?'

'I was led to believe I would be in the same room as Bianca. That we would be as one. To the contrary, she has informed me she needs her private space and I will be required to reside outside, along with the others.'

Phoenix had mixed feelings about this revelation. On the one hand, she didn't trust Bianca at all and suspected she was stringing Lily along to use her as free expert labour on her organic farm. On the other hand, she respected the idea of Bianca needing her own room. After all, that was exactly the arrangement she had with Zack. But when she tried to explain that to Lily, Lily simply got up from her chair and wandered away to find a corner of the garden to herself.

It was near closing time for the cafe. Phoenix continued to eat, to ensure she had some brain power to solve their next logistical accommodation challenge. After the previous night's experience in the van, she would really like some solid walls to sleep within. She knew how lucky she was to have that option when many people did not.

She added homelessness to the long list of world problems she would like to solve one day.

Swallowing her last mouthful, she reached down and stroked Humphrey's soft ears, grateful to be changing *his* world for the better. Then again, that would only be true if he and Zack got along. She was suddenly speared with homesickness, for her home and bed, certainly, but more so for Zack. To feel his arms wrap around her, pulling her close. To breathe in his scent of shaving cream and aftershave. For the particular smile that was reserved for her alone. For the way he calmed in her presence only, the way he sank deeper into his bones, rather than tightening and hiding behind a mask.

They'd first connected online and agreed to meet at Lefkas Taverna in West End, for haloumi, souvlaki and lemon potatoes.

Zack was nearly an hour late getting out of work, though he'd been texting every twenty minutes with updates. He arrived covered in raindrops, a whirl of anxiety.

'I'm so sorry, I'm never late,' he said, though that assertion quickly proved inaccurate. Zack was late then and he'd been late every day since. He flung off his jacket and scraped a forearm across the wet hair on his forehead. Beneath his jacket was the *Babylon 5* tee she'd come to know soon enough.

She'd been irritated that she'd had to wait so long on her own, yet he gave her his undivided attention from the moment he arrived and they talked endlessly about, well, everything – education, politics, the environment, art, movies, travel. It was the easiest conversation she'd had for as long as she could remember. He was *different* and she loved that because she was different too, though she could never pinpoint in what way, exactly. They'd found each other in this big chaotic world, in a city of more than two million people, despite neither knowing exactly how alike they really were.

On the day he'd cautiously disclosed his autism identity to her a couple of weeks later, the news had been unexpected but also entirely okay. Although it wasn't a conscious recognition, it was as though his divergence gave her permission not to have to conform to others' exhausting expectations either. He was the first person who'd ever understood, and was completely unfazed by, the fact that she couldn't share a bed with him, just for a start. Their love had grown effortlessly.

She needed to go back to teaching. She owed it to him. He had been unwaveringly supportive of her while she had time off, and of any decision she'd needed to make about returning to school. He'd never once put pressure on her. She couldn't take that kind of trust and devotion for granted. She had to do her part, but she knew she couldn't quit and start relief teaching. There were too many variables to deal with: not knowing if she'd be called into work that day; navigating to unfamiliar suburbs and negotiating peak-hour traffic; not knowing any of the staff members' names; not knowing her way around the school; not knowing any of the students, or where to park, where the toilets were, how to work the photocopier or where 'Area 3' was in the school for yard duty; having to log in to unfamiliar computer systems each day and having to track down tech support when it inevitably didn't work; and on it went. It was all too much to deal with. For now, it was better the devil she knew.

Term 4 was only one term. Ten weeks. So what if the girls made snide remarks? So what if her colleagues looked at her differently, spoke to her differently, thought of her differently? Let the parents say what they liked. Let the P&C discuss her as an item on their agenda if they needed to. Would it hurt? Yes. Would it make each day a grind? Yes. But none of that mattered compared to being able to show Zack that she was there, in this equally as much as he was, grateful that he supported her to do whatever she needed to. It was just ten weeks. She had to do it.

With no pet-friendly accommodation to be found so late in the day and daylight running out, Phoenix and Lily decided to use their portable electric fencing kit, collect Rita from her agistment and find somewhere free to wait it out. Regrettably, it was back to the van for the night. They found a spot about half an hour out of town at a remote rest stop off the highway. Here, they manoeuvred the van and float behind the toilet block so they were partially hidden from the highway and set up the fence as a square yard for Rita that was roughly fifteen metres wide. Out on the grass, Lily set up the soft crate with its roof in place for the cats to hang out and catch the last rays of sunlight. While she monitored the chickens freeranging nearby, Phoenix sat herself at the wooden picnic table to connect with Evelyn via FaceTime.

'I hope you have good news for me, Phoenix.'

'I believe I do,' Phoenix said, smiling widely. 'I wanted to let you know that I will be returning to work at the start of semester.'

Evelyn shifted, leaning her weight back in her boardroom chair, interlacing her fingers under the bust of her lavender suit. 'Excuse me if I looked surprised, but this is a quick backflip on how you were feeling only yesterday morning.'

'That's true,' Phoenix said, her professional teacher voice determined to steer this in the direction she needed it to go. 'Upon reflection, I realised that fourth term is almost two weeks away. That should be more than adequate time for me to get my head back where it needs to be, focusing on what I'm good at, getting back to my students.'

'I see.'

'I have responsibilities in life, both to my own family and to the school. I will always be deeply grateful for the time I've had off so far to recover and now that I've done that I need to move forwards. Get back in the saddle,' she finished, with a rather too emphatic fist pump.

'I see,' Evelyn repeated. The principal stayed silent, her gaze boring into Phoenix's through the screen.

Phoenix adjusted her position on the backless bench seat, sitting up taller, then swatting at a mosquito that had come to feed on her calf.

'To be clear, then,' Evelyn began, leaning forwards and picking up a pen to take notes. 'You are telling me you are ready to resume a full-time workload, across six classes, resume communication with parents, attend break-time supervision duties, guide senior students to excel in their critical ATAR assessments, write programs for two subject areas for next year, audit assessments, attend the Year 11 camp and complete semester report cards.'

Phoenix swallowed then pulled her shoulders back. 'Absolutely.'

'You have no qualms about returning to the classroom to face students after your mortifying and abrupt exit? To face parental queries or the P&C as regards your fitness to offer the excellence in education that this school is famous for and sells to prospective parents?'

Phoenix felt a tremor run through her thigh. 'Naturally, I feel somewhat nervous about returning after such a dramatic event. Anyone would. But the point is that I'm ready and willing to earn back the trust my peers and students have in me. I thought you wanted me to say I was coming back,' she said, irritated now.

Evelyn raised one eyebrow, laid her pen down and picked up a stapled set of sheets, which she held in the air. 'I have consulted the board on how best to proceed with this situation. The circumstances of your diagnosis haven't changed, have they? You are still autistic, I presume?'

Phoenix waited an indignant beat, then nodded. What was the point of denying it now? Whether she confirmed it or not, Evelyn was going to treat her with suspicion and derision.

'After such a lengthy absence for something so serious as a breakdown during class time, I am required to provide you with a "return-to-work" plan. If I had it my way, things would be different. As it is, I need to work closely with you on this until I am satisfied you are an asset to this school and not a liability.'

'Thank you,' Phoenix said, tightly. Working closely with Evelyn was the last thing she wanted to do. And as for being a liability? She had to clamp down hard on the volcano of fury ready to explode. *It's just ten weeks*, she reminded herself. That was all. By next year, hopefully Evelyn would have been replaced with a new, permanent principal – one who valued people above shiny brochures. Until then, she had to stay focused and do this for Zack – to rebuild the house savings they were currently pouring into this journey and to support their new animal family, to have a well-paying, stable job to impress the banks with, and to prove to him she was working just as hard as he was for their future. He was chasing a promotion. The least she could do was fulfil her current role. He needed support and security as much as she did. They supported each other – that was what made a good relationship.

'I'll get something to you by the end of the week,' Evelyn said.

'Okay, thank you again.'

Suddenly, Evelyn's gaze snapped to the corner of the screen where a very tall, slender woman in a billowing white blouse and riding jodhpurs walked past wearing an asymmetric, broad-brimmed Edwardian hat that billowed with lace and flowers and two iridescent peacock feathers.

'Gracious, Phoenix, who is that? Where are you?' Evelyn's gaze flickered around the surroundings behind Phoenix, while Phoenix twisted in her seat to direct the phone away from where Lily strolled, walking the pony at her side.

'No one that I know,' she said, sounding unconvincing even to herself. 'I've been walking and just sat down on a park bench.' She waved her hand airily and chuckled uncomfortably.

Evelyn widened her eyes and shook her head as though she had simply no idea how it had come to be that she was the only sensible, level-headed person left on earth. 'I have to go now, Phoenix. I will do up this plan for you to sign off on and send it to your email.' Here, she held up her pointer finger and directed it at Phoenix's face. 'But whatever the plan says, whatever accommodations it may contain, know this – I will be watching you.'

14

'Have you seen this?' Lily asked, coming in the early morning light to sit at the picnic table where Phoenix was eating a breakfast of lemon candies. She sat heavily, still in her flowing white night-gown but wearing boots on account of the cold, damp grass.

Phoenix squinted at Lily's phone's screen, in desperate need of coffee, taking in the graphics. A new video had been posted to Magician Ken's page, entitled *Kitten Presumed Dead Until Magically Rescued*. 'Gosh, that's a bit of an exaggeration,' Phoenix said. Unthinking, she reached for her coffee but her hand met only empty air. Disappointed, she returned to the screen and pressed the play button.

'I cannot watch it again,' Lily said, handing over the phone before rising to pace circles as Phoenix watched the most spectacu-larly edited film sequence ever. There was Ken, close to tears in his piece to camera, saying he feared there was no hope for the poor bedraggled kitten. It was a dangerous ascent up an enormous gum tree (cue a shot from the camera placed on the ground, pointing straight up the trunk, making it look like an elder tree from the Amazon jungle). No one else would risk their lives for such a tiny lost soul, but he would. He would not give up.

Intercut with this were close-ups of Phoenix's face, staring up into the tree, looking distraught, when in reality she'd simply been in pain from squinting in to the sun. She'd sneezed at one point, covering her mouth to do so, but it had been edited to look as though she was going to be sick from worry. Music thrummed to indicate danger and rising heartbeats of anxiety. Phoenix rolled her eyes.

'At least you're not in it,' she muttered. 'I look like a fair princess waiting to be saved by the knight in shining armour, or purple cloak, in this case.'

'Keep watching,' Lily instructed, wringing her hands.

Phoenix watched on as instructed. Exactly as she'd predicted, the clever crew had removed Ken's harness, and a long slow-motion sequence of him levitating in space was given wonderful golden glitter effects. The video, only live since last night, had already been viewed thousands of times and garnered hundreds of comments. He had a supporter sign-up button as well. No wonder he could afford not to charge his rescue clients. He was effectively making commercial television.

Eventually, he rescued the cat and there were shots of Phoenix crying and laughing and hugging Ken, which made her cringe, except that her name wasn't on it so hopefully no one would notice the sleep-deprived dark circles under her eyes, her unbrushed hair, unsmoothed eyebrows and unwashed shirt. It would blow over fast enough. 'Nearly finished,' she called to Lily, who immediately rushed over.

Lily arrived in time for the final shot. 'There.' She pointed a trembling finger at the screen.

Phoenix inhaled sharply. While Ken's Kombi van had been driving away up the road, they'd kept a camera rolling out through the back window, zoomed in on Phoenix and the kitten . . . and Lily. There she was, jumping out of their zebra van, rushing to Phoenix and kissing the top of Milo's head as he scrambled up Phoenix's arm. But from that angle and at that distance it looked as though Lily was kissing Phoenix.

'Well, that was unexpected,' Phoenix remarked, rewinding the footage to watch it again. Yep, it definitely looked like they were kissing. 'Are you worried about Bianca seeing this and getting the wrong idea?'

Lily shook her head quickly.

Phoenix placed the phone down on the picnic table. 'Then what? I know we're not together and it looks like we're kissing but—'

'I have no concern for that matter,' Lily said, her face crumpling. Her bottom lip twitched. 'It's me,' she whispered, pointing at her chest.

Phoenix shook her head. 'I don't understand.' Lily turned in circles, muttering under her breath, still wringing her hands. Phoenix let her go on doing that for as long as she could stand it. 'Are you able to tell me what's going on?'

Lily stopped and covered both her eyes with her hands, taking several deep breaths. A kookaburra broke out into a long and bolshy explosion of laughter and they had to wait until it finished, flying off out of the nearby tree with a snap of its wings. Lily lowered her hands.

'There is a situation,' she began, staring at a spot above Phoenix's head.

Suddenly, they heard a rumble of tyres on bitumen. Lily looked towards the sound with huge ice-blue eyes, like a Disney princess, before bolting to the back of the toilet block to get to the van. Phoenix heard the van's doors slam shut.

She turned to watch the road and a police car came into view. She stiffened. In general, the police didn't appear in your immediate vicinity without there being trouble of some sort. A split second later, she got it. She *knew* what Lily was trying to tell her. She remembered Lily dashing into the van after they'd arrived at the camping ground and the dog walker came too close. Again, she'd dashed into the van when Cat Man Ken had arrived and stayed hidden until she'd thought he had gone. But then she'd been caught on camera. Now, the police were here and she'd vanished again.

Clearly, Lily was on the run.

The officers emerged from the car like dark birds emerging from a nest, their fluorescent bibs a warning. Phoenix plastered on a fake smile, as though they were nothing more than friends returning from a grocery shop. In return, they maintained neutral expressions and sauntered towards the picnic table, the radios on their chests crackling with life. Humphrey, currently tied to the towbar of the van on the other side of the toilet block, growled and barked furiously. 'Humphrey!' she called. 'Humphrey! It's okay. Shush now.' She needed him to stop barking, both to allay any suspicions the police might have that she was hiding something worth protecting by a guard dog and also because she couldn't think straight while his barks whizzed through the air like fireworks. She willed Lily to do something to intervene.

Both officers cast their gazes towards the noise. Half the horse float was easily visible. 'Humphrey!' she called again. 'I'm so sorry. He's very protective of me.'

The female officer studied Phoenix for a moment and Phoenix's insides turned liquid. 'It's a good thing to have a dog interested in protecting you,' she said mildly.

'He's definitely a comfort, usually,' she joked. Mercifully, he stopped barking. She imagined Lily had had to decide whether to stay hidden with an incensed dog drawing extra attention to her or risk sneaking out of the van to quieten him.

The officer continued. 'I'm Officer Lee and this is Officer Sharma,' she said. The other officer nodded at her.

'Hi.' Phoenix was still sitting and wondered if she should stand. She felt uneasy being this much lower than them. 'I'm Phoenix.'

Officer Sharma tilted his head. 'That's an interesting name.'

Phoenix shrugged. 'I have an interesting mother. Harry Potter hadn't even been published yet. She was before her time.' They both looked at her quizzically. 'Because the fifth book was *Harry Potter and the Order of the Phoenix*, which led to a spike in interest about phoenixes. I was born in 1987 and I was sixteen when that book came out. Lots of jokes about it – I'm sure you can imagine.'

She really should stop talking now. It was like they were waiting for her to say something to incriminate herself. Wait, *was* she a criminal if she was harbouring someone who was a criminal? But really, what could Lily have done?

'Phoenix,' Officer Lee began, 'we've stopped here now because we caught sight of your vehicle from the other side of the highway and thought we'd drop in to see if everything's okay.'

'Right, yes, all is well.'

'Did you spend the night here?'

Phoenix swallowed. She had no idea if it was better to confess to that or deny it. But as she was an incredibly bad liar, the truth came out. 'I did. I'm sorry. I know I'm not supposed to do that but I didn't have anywhere to go last night and it just kind of happened.'

Officer Lee nodded. 'Technically people in light vehicles can rest here for up to twenty-four consecutive hours but you have a horse and a horse float, which doesn't comply. Are you travelling with'—here she gazed around, taking in the pony behind the electric fence, the chickens currently drawing-and-quartering an unearthed bug between them, and the hidden dog behind the concrete block—'anyone else?'

Now her heart galloped. Tell the truth and possibly have Lily arrested – for who knew what? – or offer a bald-faced lie to officers of the law in order to save her, when that act of pardon might actually be protecting someone who'd done something really awful and who should in all good sense be handed over and in custody? Was Phoenix travelling with an armed robber? A fraudster? A murderer?

Her mouth was dry. Could she lie? All she knew was that her intuition about people was rarely wrong. She trusted Lily, with no evidence to suggest any reason why she should or shouldn't. In the short time they'd been together, Lily had carved a place in Phoenix's heart. She was her friend. And Phoenix was nothing if not a loyal friend.

She held Officer Lee's gaze. 'I'm on my way home to my partner in Brisbane. I have to go by road because my friend died and I told her I'd take care of her animals, hence the Noah's Ark of sorts.' She managed a wan smile before leaping into the most difficult part. 'And in answer to your question, no, there's no one else here.'

Officer Lee maintained eye contact for longer than was comfortable and Phoenix felt her chest rising and falling under the stress. Then the officer and her partner looked at each other a moment, silently communicating. Officer Sharma nodded and Officer Lee accepted his opinion. 'Okay, then, Phoenix,' she said. 'We'll be on our way.'

Phoenix bit her lip, now mute with terror. She had lied. Not only had she lied, she'd lied to *the police*.

'I hope you find somewhere suitable to stay tonight. If you need help, if you need a women's shelter, a good meal or legal advice, come see us at the station in Echuca and we'll connect you with the right people, okay?'

Phoenix nodded and accepted the business card Officer Lee handed her. 'Thank you,' she managed.

'You're welcome. Take care.'

Phoenix watched them go, dark birds flying away once more.

At The Sweet Meadow for breakfast again – Rita in the horse float, cats and chickens in their crates, Humphrey at their feet – Lily began to explain.

'I am deeply sorry for causing you such distress,' she said, having barely touched her scrambled tofu. 'But I am forever in your debt for leaving me out of their inquisition.'

'Why? What is going on? Why do you keep diving into the van when people come near us?'

Lily pursed her lips into a duck bill while she considered her words, staring up into a nearby tree. Her hand rose to her throat and clasped the golden locket. 'My mama has been calling, often. Pursuing me. She implores me to return home.'

Phoenix put her fork down, remembering the times she'd seen Lily's mother's name appear onscreen and Lily ignore her call, or the times she'd seen Lily stab at the screen in disgust before pocketing the phone. 'Why?'

'She maintains her opinion that I am unable to live on my own, away from the family estate, that I am too young and may never be old enough for independence. She is angry at me for leaving despite her explicit instructions that I should not.'

Phoenix shifted her gaze to where Lily's fingers were white around the locket. 'You *are* twenty, are you not?' she asked, momentarily adopting Lily's syntax. She really, really hoped Lily was not about to tell her that she was in fact underage and travelling in a van with a mature teacher whose job was on the line.

'That is correct. I will turn twenty-one next autumn; however, Mama still believes I am a child. She continues to threaten me, telling me she will lodge a missing person's report with the police.'

Phoenix frowned. 'But that would be fraudulent. You're an adult and you've been perfectly clear about your whereabouts, haven't you?'

'Indeed! She knows I am travelling to Queensland, though she does not know specifically where I am. I must confess I was nervous that she would follow me and cause an appalling scene in front of Bianca.' Her voice had risen to a pitch that was beginning to attract attention from other patrons.

'I can't imagine the police would take her very seriously,' Phoenix soothed. 'You're not a child.'

Lily closed her eyes, her lashes fluttering a moment as she thought. She inhaled deeply – two, three, four – repeating the motion three times. A calming technique. When she opened them, her voice was steady. 'She says she will report me as autistic, mentally ill, with high complex support needs. She says she will inform them that she and Papa have no idea where I am but they believe I have been taken by force. That would be the only possible reason for me not to come home, given my incapacity.'

Phoenix rolled her eyes, unable to stop the disgust from oozing out of her. 'For god's sake, you're autistic, yes, but you certainly don't have "high complex support needs".' She hesitated a moment, checking through the information she'd assimilated in the past couple of months. One of the reasons the linear scale of autism – from high functioning at one end to low functioning at the other – was dismissed by the autistic community was because any autistic person's needs could fluctuate throughout their life. Phoenix herself, on the day of *the incident*, in the weeks of recovery from burnout, had been far less capable of caring for herself than at other times in her life. Still, her gut feeling was that Lily was not as needy as her mother was trying to make out. 'And as for being mentally ill . . .' Again, she stopped. What did she really know about Lily's mental health?

'I am not mentally ill,' Lily snapped. 'I have anxiety and depression, certainly, as does half the neurotypical population!'

Phoenix nodded. That was true for her as well. More and more, Lily's mother was sounding quite unreasonable. Lily was still clutching the gold locket around her neck.

'What was your grandmother like?'

Lily directed her gaze to the tree, where golden morning sun danced in the red and green leaves and small sparrows flitted from branch to branch. 'For several years, when I was in primary school, Grandmother lived with us after the death of my grandfather. She was the safe place. The calm in the sea. The light in the dark. She sheltered me from the worst of my parents' displeasure. She was the safe place,' she repeated. 'When she died, it was like an eclipse, like the moon covered the sun and refused to move again.'

'She sounds like an amazing woman.'

Lily nodded. 'She was. I departed Tasmania to strike out on my own for the first time, leaving everything I knew behind me, for my one true love. I had to bring her with me,' she said, rubbing the locket.

Phoenix ignored the high likelihood that Bianca was not Lily's one true love – that she might in fact be a manipulator and a fraud. No one who thought they were in love wanted the veil to be lifted on their fantasy. Instead, she focused on more earthly matters. 'Do you think your mother will give up calling you?'

Lily shook her head. 'No. Once she gets an idea into her mind, it is very difficult to dissuade her. When the constables arrived today I was certain she had been true to her word and had sent them to take me away. I cannot return to that oppression.'

Phoenix let out a long sigh. 'No wonder you ran.' She handed a piece of toast to Humphrey, dangling it in front of his nose to wake him. His eyes flew open and he took the toast, crunching it up and licking his lips. 'And what do you think now?'

'I do not trust her – of that I am sure. She will want to hurt me, to exercise her power over me once more, even if it is for the very last time to show me that I will never be enough for her. That I am the great disappointment of her life.'

'More than your sister?' Phoenix wondered.

Lily frowned. 'I have not really considered that. Perhaps Leonie and I are equally disappointing to my parents. But Leonie was so capable. Mama would never have been able to hold her back, but with me she feels she has a chance.'

Phoenix let Lily's words sink in. If she was right – and Phoenix had no reason to doubt her – then she felt compelled to no other action than to support Lily's safe passage to an independent life. 'Okay,' she said, giving Lily an encouraging smile. 'We'll work it out, I promise.'

15

Phoenix held the phone up on FaceTime, the camera pointed at the kittens so Zack could see them. Little Jane was off the drip and the drain was due to come out later today. Jane was stumbling around the cage gingerly, and Milo shoulder-bumped her gently down to the bedding so he could groom the fur on her head. Jane closed her eyes in contentment as his little pink tongue ran over her steel-grey ears. Phoenix turned the phone back around so she could see Zack's face. He was on his lunch break in the staffroom, in the corner near the lone potted plant, the single piece of nature inside the sterile walls of the imaging centre. He had 'happy eyes' today.

'Is your good mood because of what's in your lunch box?' Phoenix asked, noticing it on the arm of the chair.

'Mum came for dinner last night.'

'Lucky you,' she said, with a pang of regret that she'd missed Elainah. The thought of Zack's mum, all beaming face, soft bosom and hugging arms, made her smile.

He tapped the blue box. 'This one's her baked fish, taro, sago and coconut cream.'

'Sorry I missed her.'

'She left more food than we could eat in a month,' he said, but he didn't sound unhappy about it.

Phoenix suddenly longed for a home-cooked meal, especially one prepared by Elainah. She could hear his mum's voice in her head. *Zamar! You've become too thin! Eat up!*

'We should get a bigger freezer,' she said.

'Definitely before the next mumu.'

Phoenix had been to two family mumus and had loved them both. It was a sensory wonderland to share food that had been prepared by many hands, that had been cooked in an earth oven dug with shovels while laughing over jokes, with a fire built by cousins, heat powered by clean rocks to slow-cook food to perfection, to be eaten from foil and banana leaves, all while uncles sang and aunts rocked babies. It was slow and it was calm and it was joyful. It was sensory healing, not harming.

She left Zack to eat quickly before his break ended, then stayed to stroke the kittens. 'We'll be on the road soon,' she said softly, while vet nurses cleaned cages or mopped floors, dogs whined and machines beeped. 'Then we'll take care of you for the rest of your life. You'll never have to spend another night in the bush again.'

After she'd said goodbye to the staff, her next priority was to find somewhere to stay. She wondered if they could risk returning to the rest stop. If they didn't get there till dark and left early in the morning, the chances of running into the police again were surely slim. The vet was hopeful Jane would be well enough to leave here tomorrow, as long as Phoenix could continue careful care while they travelled. They couldn't go back to the camping ground cabins. She could ask for Rita to stay at the agistment place again but she felt awkward and ridiculous given she'd already been there, left and returned. To turn up yet again would surely have the owners questioning her state of mind.

Lily drove on, wandering roads, while Phoenix searched online for alternatives, but as the afternoon stretched, they realised they needed to set up camp. The only spot they could find was back at the rest stop. There was no litter or fresh tyre tracks to suggest the space had been used by anyone else since they'd left. It really had been bad luck the police had found them last time. This time, though, Lily unhitched the horse float so they could park both it and the van side by side behind the toilet block, making themselves less obvious.

Phoenix took stock of herself. Look at her now – lying to the police, hiding vehicles, abetting Lily's run from her mother. 'What's next?' she muttered, popping Humphrey back into his harness and clipping him to the anchor point. She was too afraid to answer that question, but she didn't have to wait long for the answer.

In long shadows of late afternoon, while Phoenix coaxed the chickens back into their crate with sunflower seeds, Lily wandered over near the tree line to take a phone call from Bianca. The pony chewed rhythmically on hay and Phoenix used the hoof pick to clean out her hooves. Suddenly, Lily's pacing increased in tempo, her voice pitching high. Phoenix couldn't hear her words but her sharp and increasingly upset gestures were obvious. She straightened, her hand on the pony's shoulder. Lily shouted in a torrent of anger, then dropped the phone to the ground and kicked it hard, sending it flying across the grass. She wrapped her arms around herself and heaved. Spiralling to the ground in her full-length cream lace dress, she resembled a broken butterfly.

Phoenix carefully ducked under the electric tape of Rita's makeshift yard and slowly approached Lily's wailing, rocking body. She halted several metres away and crouched down at

Lily's level. She angled herself away to relieve Lily of the feeling of being watched.

'Hey, Lily.' Phoenix's voice was gentle. 'I'm just letting you know that I'm here. You're safe right now. I'm going to stay nearby until you feel better. Take your time.' She settled on the grass and gazed at the trees swaying in the wind. The earth's temperature was still comfortable beneath her but it would be cooling soon. Dampness was already in the air.

The first star made its appearance in the evening sky and Lily finally began to talk. She was curled in a ball on the ground, faced away from Phoenix, her arm supporting her head.

Phoenix turned to face her and shuffled crab-like across the ground to hear her properly.

'. . . said she wanted a heart-to-heart talk,' Lily was saying, sniffing loudly between words. It was all Phoenix could do to stop herself from reaching out and laying a hand on her friend's shoulder. But that was Phoenix's way of giving and receiving comfort, not Lily's. 'I thought she meant it would be a declaration of the depth of her affections for me, the strength of our love.' Lily cried. 'I was so stupid.'

Phoenix had to bite her bottom lip to stop herself from rushing to fill the silence to defend her friend. With supreme effort, she waited.

'She began to tell me that she had not been fair to me. I thought she was talking about the yurt, that she had realised her error and wanted me to be close to her inside the home. She said she wanted to make it right with me. She said she had to follow her truth, to follow her heart.' Lily sat up abruptly to face Phoenix and wiped her tear-stained face. Phoenix braced herself for impact. 'But what she really wanted to say was that . . . was that her heart, her truth, had led her to someone else. A man. There is no place for me in her life any more.'

'Oh, Lily. I'm so sorry.'

Lily ripped fingerfuls of grass from the ground and tore them into tiny shreds. 'She said that you cannot cage the truth. We must willingly go where spirit leads us.' She dropped her head back and let out an almighty roar, then hit her closed fists against her brow. 'Stupid, stupid, stupid.'

'Lily, please stop hitting yourself,' Phoenix pleaded, shuffling closer still. 'Please.'

With another roar, Lily did stop. She pulled her knees to her chest and squeezed tightly, rocking back and forth. 'You are absolutely not stupid,' Phoenix said, her voice low with contempt for Bianca. 'We have all been taken advantage of by someone.'

Lily gazed at her through liquid eyes, disbelieving. 'Even you?'

'Definitely me.'

Lily looked as though she was about to ask Phoenix about it, but dissolved into tears before she could. 'She said she loved me,' she hiccupped. 'But she lied. She *lied*.'

Phoenix felt the betrayal and loss in her own chest. 'That was a terrible thing to do to you. It was wrong.' She was about to say she was at least glad Lily had found out now, before she'd given Bianca a year of free labour and devotion, but caught herself in time. Lily didn't want to hear that now. In her pocket, her mobile phone vibrated. She quickly checked the screen. It was the school. She sent it to voicemail. Evelyn could wait. Lily was more important. 'I know everything feels awful right now but you will feel better again one day. This moment will change and you will go on. I promise.'

Lily struggled to her feet as fast as the tangled Victorian dress would allow. 'Love is not true at all. It is all a lie.'

Phoenix peeled herself off the ground, staggering as her knees pained. The cold had seeped into her joints. 'No, it's not. Zack and I share a wonderful love. Love can be enriching and supportive

148

and mutual. Just because things have worked out badly for you this time doesn't mean it will happen that way every time.' Her phone vibrated in her pocket once more. Again, she ignored it.

'Not for me,' Lily said, adamant. 'Your story is not my story and this was it. I left my whole life, my family, such as they were, the bed I had slept in my whole life. I left with barely any possessions, with only a promise of true love at the other end. Bianca was it for me. She was the first person who ever loved me for me. She was it, don't you see? I'm ruined now.'

Phoenix opened her mouth but words failed to come. She wasn't sure in what way Lily believed she was ruined but she could appreciate the black-and-white perspective. She'd given her whole heart away believing it would be held with care and it had been trampled. Lily had few life experiences to show her that people could actually treasure her for herself, and for the first time she'd thought she'd found it – acceptance, commitment, love.

'Had you . . . Did Bianca know that you're autistic?' Phoenix was angry. Had Bianca specifically targeted Lily? Had she deliberately manipulated her for fun? To play with her emotions? Had her intentions been impure and a last moment of guilt got to her and she cut Lily loose before she showed up?

Lily nodded and slapped a hand across her mouth in horror. 'I thought it was safe to disclose that,' she whimpered.

'Well, we don't know her very well, so we don't know what her true intentions were.'

'No! No one will ever love me!' Lily shouted. Then to Phoenix's horror, she turned and ran away from their camp site, towards the thick bushland.

'Stop!' Phoenix ran too, her phone vibrating still, but she couldn't keep up. Lily had the speed of a thoroughbred. Her long curls and lacy hem flew out wildly behind her. 'Lily!' she called, but it took too much breath to shout and so she ran, saving oxygen to make her legs pump up and down, up and down, across the wet grass. Still, she couldn't catch her. Lily melted into the black shadows of the bush.

Phoenix's foot hit an uneven patch of ground. Her ankle rolled and she fell, landing heavily on her right wrist, with an audible pop. Pain shot through her ankle, her wrist and her windpipe, raw now from dragging the cold evening air into her lungs.

She hunched on the ground, clutching her wrist to her chest, grimacing with pain, not having a clue what to do about finding Lily. She stayed there, coaxing her breathing back to a reasonable pace and her mind to slow down and think clearly. Lily would have to come back, wouldn't she? She didn't have her phone; Phoenix had seen her kick it across the grass. She wasn't sure if she had her wallet on her. They were kilometres from any form of shop or petrol station – which didn't mean she couldn't walk there, though Phoenix was fairly sure she wouldn't do that. She couldn't see her as the hitchhiking type, but then, she didn't really know what Lily was capable of at all. Still, the most likely explanation was that she simply needed time to self-regulate and find her balance and then she'd return.

Gingerly, Phoenix felt around her wrist. It didn't look visibly broken and she could move her fingers. In all likelihood, the popping sound had been a tendon or ligament. An icepack would be helpful right now, but she didn't have one, nor a freezer to keep it cold. She didn't even have a hot dinner to eat, only snacks. She was starting to feel like Scooby-Doo, constantly living between *snax*.

She was talking herself into getting up off the ground and testing her ankle when the phone began to vibrate yet again. 'What now?' she muttered, using her left hand to pull the phone from her pocket. It was the school, still. Her first instinct was to ignore it. She and Evelyn had only spoken yesterday. How urgent could anything be right now, after 6 pm? Maybe it was because she was all alone in the middle of nowhere, in the dark, and the phone offered some light, some kind of connection to the world, that she answered it.

'Phoenix, it's Evelyn. We need to talk.' The principal's words were clipped and loaded with foreboding.

'Okay?' Phoenix's heart had begun to pound once more.

'I've seen the vision.'

'What are you talking about?'

'Right now, you are in Echuca in Victoria. You are two states away when you are supposed to be on medical leave and you are galivanting around the countryside with your lover.'

'What are you talking about?' she repeated, utterly confused. Zack was in Brisbane and he wasn't her lover, he was her partner, and hopefully soon her husband. She said as much to Evelyn.

'May I remind you that you work at a private girls' school with Christian values and you signed paperwork to say you agree to uphold the values thereof by your word and deed and most importantly your demonstrated lifestyle.'

'And I do,' she said, though suddenly wondered about how much reach the school had in interfering with her living situation. Weren't there anti-discrimination laws now to prevent that sort of thing?

'Then explain to me, please, how it is that you ended up on the nightly news kissing a woman – a *young* woman—'

'Oh, no, wait—' Phoenix said, suddenly relieved, realising someone must have shared Magician Ken's footage with Evelyn.

But Evelyn wasn't waiting. '—all while hiding out in Victoria, when only yesterday you swore to me you were ready to return to school? I would expect that after such a lengthy delay in your return to a senior teaching position, you would be spending these last days devoted to nothing other than catching up on all you've missed and preparing for a flawless teaching term to prove to me, the P&C and the board that you were actually worth the wait.'

'Evelyn,' Phoenix interjected, sternly. Adrenaline fired. She couldn't flee – right now, she literally couldn't see two feet in front of herself – so she came out fighting. 'First things first, what I do with my private time is none of your business.'

'Oh, I beg to differ,' Evelyn all but hissed. 'As the principal of this school, everything you do is my business.'

Phoenix ignored that. 'I am down here because a friend of mine was dying of cancer and needed emergency assistance. I dropped everything to help her. And I promised her I would take care of her animals, which is what I am doing, honouring my word. I would argue that is precisely what someone with Christian values would do.' Her heart hammered. Her right hand, though throbbing with pain, clenched into a ball.

'Who. Is. The. Woman?'

'Lily is my travelling companion, someone to help me share the driving and manage all my deceased friend's animals on the long trip back to Brisbane. She is *not* my lover. And we were *not* kissing!' She almost added that it was none of Evelyn's damn business if they had been, but she managed to find some restraint in time to stop the words spewing from her mouth.

'The footage clearly suggests otherwise.'

'The operative word there is *suggests*. That was just a camera angle taken from a moving, distant van. Lily was actually kissing *the kitten*, who happened to be on my shoulder at the time.'

'I don't believe you,' Evelyn said, her voice now soft, almost a whisper, and more frightening than she'd been earlier.

After a beat, Phoenix replied. 'With all due respect, Evelyn, that's not my problem, it's yours.'

'Oh, it most certainly is your problem. I will not have more scandal and shame tarnish this school's good name. Not on my watch. The board has called an emergency meeting and I expect you'll be receiving your termination advice shortly.' Then she was gone, leaving Phoenix trembling with rage in the pitch darkness.

16

Rain fell, cold and sharp, each flurry a slap in the face. Phoenix scurried on her injured ankle, first to retrieve Lily's phone from the grass, then following the light from her own back to the van. She jerked the door shut behind her, forgetting she'd hurt her wrist and crying out. The pain inflamed rage that had filled her from the roots of her hair to her toenails. Her anger carved through her nerves and muscles till she was on fire.

She hunched on the floor in darkness, trembling till the wave calmed. Evelyn's words played over and over in her mind on a frustration loop she could no longer offer counterpoints to, though she argued them out loud, getting them right, even though it was too late. Eventually, her shaking eased and the energy coursing through her began to fall . . . and fall . . . and fall. Now there was nothing left but a throbbing wrist and her racing mind. She ached for Zack to wrap his arms around her, holding her tight, bringing her back into her body. She reached out a hand to stroke Humphrey but he didn't respond and his rejection made her cry.

Out of nowhere came the memories, unbidden, but always lurking just below the surface. This time it was Veronica's face, haunting her from as far back as Year 10.

Veronica was the cool one. Impossibly pretty, flawless skin, pursued by the boys from the partner school a few train stops away. She was turning fifteen and the most talked-about event was her upcoming slumber party. Phoenix and Veronica weren't directly friends but moved in loosely the same circles. One by one, Phoenix watched invitations handed to everyone who she thought was a friend – though evidence to the contrary was mounting, if her regular escape to the school library at lunchtime to hide between the books was anything to go by.

So when Veronica approached Phoenix in the classroom and said, 'You can come to my party on the weekend, if you want,' Phoenix jumped at the chance to be included. She didn't receive a paper invitation like the others had but this slight was balanced by the relief that she hadn't been left out after all. She'd been included! With a wash of relief, she felt hope that perhaps she wasn't the weird one after all.

On Saturday morning, Phoenix took and packed her pain medication, and her mum dropped her off at Veronica's house and drove away. Phoenix rang the doorbell, her heart thumping. She was late. Phoenix could hear the other girls laughing and chatting inside and her toes curled, knowing she was already behind and that every one of them would turn and stare at her when she entered and she wouldn't know where to look.

Veronica answered the door. 'Oh, you came.'

The words were a fist to the gut. Phoenix was utterly confused. Veronica had invited her. She'd said, 'You can come to my party.' Why wouldn't she have been expecting her? She trailed Veronica down the hallway and into the kitchen. The other girls were already there, plates of chips and lollies half demolished and plastic cups with each girl's name on them.

Veronica said, 'I didn't make you a cup,' but went to find a marker to put Phoenix's name on one, while her mum smiled at Phoenix kindly, *too* kindly. This was a smile Phoenix had come to know as one where adults felt sorry for her. Immediately, she realised the skin-peeling truth – she wasn't actually wanted there at all. She had only been invited because Veronica had thought she wouldn't show up, and probably only then because her mum knew Veronica's mum professionally.

Her words evaporated.

She'd sat silently at the table, not able to keep track of six people sharing the one conversation, not able to contribute about boys she didn't know. With every second, the mounting pressure to find some sort of words to speak, at precisely the right moment in the game of verbal ping-pong increased her distress. No matter how much she wanted to, she couldn't pull any words from anywhere inside herself. Time crawled by, second by second; she was mute. Panicky words flapped around inside her like trapped birds with no way to escape, beating themselves senseless against the glass window between her and the outside world.

In the afternoon, the group walked to the park and girls paired off and whispered. Phoenix's super-sensitive hearing meant she could hear every word. Bat ears, her mother called them. Maryanne scowled at her but Phoenix kept walking behind them all, pretending not to hear, because what else could she do? She was there but only as a ghost to drift by unseen, or a shadow to be stepped upon, dying inside. Either no one noticed, or no one cared. Pain struck through her leg and hip like electric shocks with every step. Stuck in this nightmare, she took herself mentally to her safe place – at home in her room, surrounded by her stuffed animal toys and books about horses and animals and fantasy worlds. She read the words of the stories to herself now, blocking out the reality around her.

Years later, she would realise she should have just called her mum to come and get her but there was no way her fifteen-year-old self could do that because she couldn't understand how girls could be that mean. *She* would never be mean like that. And she didn't understand why – why her? What was *wrong* with her? She would never be able to explain it to her mum and the utter shame of it, the pure unadulterated rejection of every fibre of her being, would never have allowed her to call for help.

Instead, she endured, sleepless on her air mattress in the loungeroom, her throat holding a lump so big and tight she thought she might need to cut it out in order to breathe again, surviving minute by minute as the fires of rejection ran through her and the whispers continued in the dark.

Now Evelyn was trying to freeze her out, just like so many others had in her lifetime, and she wanted this bloody dog to love her instead of turning his back on her. She wanted to go back in time to that day in the classroom when it had all unravelled. She wanted a do-over. Instead of pushing through, she would instead acknowledge the eczema around her hairline and take stock of how many painkillers it was taking to get through each teaching day. She would notice her racing heart, avoid the small talk in the staffroom and the ear-splitting school bell and simply take a sick day instead of forcing herself to go to work. If she'd only taken care of herself when she needed to instead of rigidly sticking to her sense of duty at the expense of her personal autonomy, if only she'd known who she was before it all went wrong, then maybe she wouldn't be sitting here now all alone, her reputation and career in tatters, one and a half thousand kilometres from Zack. She curled into a ball on the floor and allowed herself to drop into nothingness.

•

When her phone sprang to life, she fell on it. Zack, calling simply because he felt something was wrong. She'd never loved him so much. She explained about the video, about Lily and about Evelyn's determination to see what she wanted to see instead of listening to the truth. Zack was outraged on her behalf and Lily's. He suggested she turn on her LED lights and she instantly felt lifted just by being able to see the animals in the van. The light offered comfort against the relentless rain. She let the cats out of their crates and they wandered around, rubbing on her arms and legs. She talked and Zack listened. Audrey curled up in her lap, her purrs vibrating through Phoenix's body, calming her. She wondered how she'd ever lived without the warmth of a cat in her lap, a living weighted blanket. Two hours later, after Zack had apologised for yawning for the tenth time, she told him to go to bed, that she'd be fine.

But she wasn't fine. The silence rang in her ears. When the pony snorted unexpectedly loudly, it pierced Phoenix like a knife. She worried terribly about Lily. Every awful movie she'd ever seen where a woman was snatched, tortured and killed flashed through her mind in blockbuster detail. Having a long and superior memory for details was a double-edged sword. It was why she could now only ever read or watch anything she was certain wouldn't traumatise her.

Several of the Downunder Auties had confessed they liked kids' movies best for exactly that reason – though every one of them was still traumatised by the death of Bambi, and most by the death of Artax, the white horse from *The NeverEnding Story*. Phoenix herself had been locked in a house when she was nine years old with a bunch of teenagers, who proceeded to show her *Friday the 13th* parts one, two and three in a row, which had her vomiting that night and sleeping in her mother's bed for months afterwards. Her sensitive young mind had been forever branded with horrific images that still flew at her from nowhere at random times, filling her with terror and freezing her to the spot – as they did now. She was desperate to visit the toilet block but all she could see in her mind was the camera's point of view on a young woman's face as she rode in the front seat of a car and the voice of a teenage girl in the room that day saying, 'She's not going to make it, is she?' and Phoenix remembered thinking, *What is she talking about?* because she had no idea what was coming. And then everything happened. Everything Phoenix had no idea could happen or ever did happen. And six hours of it happening over and over had forever changed every cell in her body to be wired for danger.

She couldn't sleep now because she had to remain on guard, alert, and she couldn't get out of the van because Jason – the *Friday the 13th* murderer – could be waiting. And if he wasn't waiting for her, he could be waiting for Lily, out there in the forest while she stumbled around in the rain, just as he had for the young woman at the start of that first movie.

Her chest crushed in on itself. She needed to escape her body. It was so hot in here. So hot. She needed to crack open a window.

A chicken squawked in her sleep.

Phoenix yelped, her hands jammed to her ears.

Humphrey barked, the noise hitting her like hands grabbing her around the ribs.

Now her pants were wet with terror.

It was midnight when Phoenix remembered that Therese from the Downunder Auties had sent her phone number and told Phoenix to call any time. It was late but she was desperate and assumed that Therese would have her phone off if she was asleep, so she made the call.

'Hello?' There was music playing in the background.

Phoenix explained who she was and apologised for calling at this hour.

'Not at all! I'm doing my PhD so I'm always working late these days. You've given me a great excuse to stop for biscuits.' She laughed heartily. 'Don't worry, I'm hyperfocusing my autistic arse off and smashing through it – both the PhD and the packet of VoVos, or it might be my third packet for the week, or today – honestly I've totally lost track of time – and I've got energy to burn for days.' She cackled again. 'Where are you? How's the trip going? What's happening? Tell me everything.'

Phoenix felt better immediately, just for having a friendly voice on the end of the line. Her breathing deepened. She explained everything, which took a long time, finishing with the chicken scaring her so much that she wet herself.

'What a clusterfuck!' Therese snorted, and Phoenix even found herself reaching for, if not a smile, then less of a frown. 'There's nothing like peeing yourself to make you feel like utter shit, hey? You know, I have a young adult client who has to wear nappies and he writes a lot about how everyone is temporarily continent, which is so true, right? We come into the world incontinent and we go out the same way. It's only a matter of time.'

'I suppose we're all temporarily able-bodied too.'

'That's it exactly!' Therese enthused through a mouthful of biscuit. She swallowed noisily then gulped a few mouthfuls of drink. 'By the sounds of it, you had a meltdown.'

'I'm sure this never used to happen to me. I'm sure I never had a meltdown before that day at school, which I actually think was a shutdown. I'm still learning the differences between meltdowns, shutdowns and freezes. Why is this happening to me now?'

'For the same reason you shutdown at school – the amount of stress you're under exceeds the amount of resources and supports you have available to you. That's all. It's not your fault. It's not something you can control when it happens. It's all about maths, or *energy accounting*, in this case. What we need to do now is build up your supports. Have you ever written out your daily tasks and assigned them energy values?'

'I've never heard of that.'

'I can walk you through it. Do you have paper and pen in your bag?'

'Think so.' The back of the unbreakably binding contract for her new mobile phone would do.

'I'll teach you how it works so we can help find you some more energy so you've got a buffer against all the craziness going on.'

Phoenix looked doubtfully around the van. 'I can't see how that's possible given my current situation.'

'Actually,' Therese mumbled, through more biscuit munching, 'you're probably right, it won't work well while you're on the road, but knowing the basics is a good start and it doesn't sound like you'll be doing much sleeping tonight.'

'You're right about that. I'm worried about Lily out there alone and in the rain. She must be half frozen. But I don't want to take you away from your PhD. This can wait.'

'No way. This is what I do for a living. Let's go through energy accounting first and then we'll tackle each immediate problem you've got till we figure out a plan.'

'Okay,' Phoenix said, leaning down to Audrey to receive the cat's affectionate headbutt. 'Thank you.'

'Right, I just ran out of biscuits and I need to chew while I think. You get your pen and paper and I'll meet you back here in a tick.'

Phoenix's Problems and Action Plans
- *Lily is missing – action plan is dependent on whether or not Lily returns tonight or in morning. If she doesn't return, do we seek help from the police? Complicated by Lily's worry over the police. But what if Lily is hurt? Abducted? Fallen down a well??? Reconvene by 7 am.*

- *Phoenix can't drive the van and horse float – action plan is dependent on Lily (see above). Reconvene in morning.*
- *Phoenix's principal is actually a villain from a children's fairytale – action plan is to expect a formal notice from the school board, then, depending on the contents, delay, stall, threaten to sue, seek help from a union representative if necessary, perhaps turn up to school on the first day of class anyway. Resist, resist, resist.*
- *Food supplies are low – action plan depends on Lily's return.*
- *Phoenix misses Zack terribly – action plan to call, text, message, video chat as much as possible and hug the animals for tactile support.*

'Hang on a minute,' Therese interrupted. 'I'm looking up the Cat Man's footage online now. Nearly there . . . got it.'

Phoenix waited in anxious silence, hearing Magician Ken's voice in the background, the dramatic music, the sound of herself bursting into tears, and then the soppy music towards the end.

'Naw, he's such a cute kitten,' Therese said.

Phoenix smiled, imagining Milo now curled up alongside Jane in hospital.

'Hm,' Therese went on. 'It does look like you and Lily are kissing, though.'

'I know,' Phoenix sighed.

'So pathetic, honestly,' Therese muttered, tapping a pen on the desk repetitively while she thought, now apparently out of biscuits to crunch. Then she snapped her fingers. 'You need to make noise first, before the school has any time to even set up a case.'

Phoenix's reply stuck in her throat. She had no idea how to go about doing that and it went against the grain. She was the 'goody-goody'. She was the 'teacher's pet'. She followed the rules. She'd never even skipped school. She'd tried to, once, in her final year.

Another girl convinced her it would be better to skip maths and go to the nearby shops instead. Phoenix had tried – she hated maths and had all but given up on it anyway, prepared to fail in favour of topping her other subjects. Surely everyone should break the rules at least once before graduation, shouldn't they? So she'd set out, her heart pounding, but had only made it halfway down the school driveway before turning around.

Now, what – she was just going to become the loud, shouty, rebellious one? She had no idea how her flawless career had come to this moment. How had her life flipped upside down, leading to this conversation, which she was having at one-thirty in the morning, stuck in a van in the middle of nowhere, with a bunch of animals and her friend missing in the bush?

Soberly, she considered Evelyn's obvious resolve – her clearly stated intention – to remove Phoenix from her job, and the woman's long, distinguished, determined career, and knew she had no other choice but to rebel. With decisive penmanship, she updated her action plan.

Take the offensive.

17

Exhaustion had, eventually, claimed Phoenix. She drifted off around half-past four and woke not two hours later when Humphrey decided he needed a walk to relieve himself. Trying not to bear too much weight on her injured ankle, she shuffled the cats back into their crates to prevent them from dashing out the door, then painfully wrangled on Humphrey's harness with her injured wrist. As far as she could tell, Humphrey might tolerate her but he definitely didn't feel that he belonged to her. The last thing she needed was for him to take off into the bush after Lily's scent, or even simply because he was sick to death of this road trip.

For a microsecond after stumbling out of the van, she believed Lily would be sitting on the wooden picnic bench, but she wasn't. She thought of her, out there without her coat. At least it had stopped raining – though the subsequent chill in the air was the kind that sank deep into bones. She hoped Lily had found some-where safe and dry during the night.

She limped painfully after the dog. What she really needed were elasticised ankle and wrist braces, and icepacks. Hypermobile joints plus well-entrenched clumsiness meant she was generally carrying at least one injury at all times, not to mention the autoimmune arthritis she'd eventually been diagnosed with after its beginnings in high school. Back at home she had a whole cupboard dedicated to slings, bandages and braces of every kind, for every injury imaginable. This time, she'd simply have to ignore it.

She shuffled on, acknowledging the pale morning with a cordial nod – *here we are again* – grimly accounting that she'd left Tasmania five days ago but hadn't progressed further than the Victorian border. When she and Humphrey returned, she collapsed back onto the sleeping bag, her hip bones aching for lack of a mattress and the damp, dreary weather, and ignored the rumble of her belly. She was down to her last two protein bars and one litre of water. She couldn't drive off to find food and leave the horse float there, along with Rita behind her electric fence. She was stuck.

Right on seven, Therese called, got the update – Lily was still MIA – said she'd be back soon, and ended the call. Phoenix tottered about, busying herself with chores – feeding and watering the pony, setting the chickens up in their play pen with grain to peck and grass to scratch, rolling up the sleeping bag, and tying Humphrey to the horse float so she could let the cats out of their crates to wander the van and use the litter trays. She was just finishing her second-last protein bar when Therese called back.

'Okay, first thing's sorted,' she said, sounding like a drill sergeant. 'Bruno is on the road right now, on his way to meet you.'

'What?' Phoenix nearly choked on her mouthful.

'He's got delivery drivers everywhere and he was going to send one to you to teach you how to pull a float but when he heard you were in Echuca he said he was running a quick job out to Yass first thing this morning and it was only a six-hour drive to you from there.'

'*Only* six?' She could barely manage two hours of driving.

'It's what he does.' Therese dismissed Phoenix's shock. 'He said he was feeling up for an adventure. You just need to text him which rest stop you're at. I'll send you his number. I've got to get to work now but call me, text me, PM me or whatever. I've told the Downunder Auties what's going on and there are some lovely messages in the forum when you're ready to read them. We're all behind you!'

'You're amazing, Therese. Thank you so much.' She honestly didn't know what she'd have done last night without her on the end of the phone. Now, the thought of Bruno coming to help buoyed her spirits. It felt awkward, yes, as meeting anyone for the first time did, but the feeling of relief was greater.

'It's nothing. I'm happy to help. Oh, have you had any ideas about your principal?'

'Possibly, but I'll get back to you when I know more.'

Bruno texted to say he'd need a stop for lunch but his ETA was around 3 pm. She asked him if he could please bring her some food, anything gluten-free, and some water, to which he sent a thumbs-up emoji. She vowed that when this was all over, she would send him a lemon cake to say thank you, one of Nigella Lawson's, with the zest of a whole lemon and free-range eggs with bright yellow yolks. She would make it herself and pop it in the express post.

While she waited for Bruno, she took Rita for an amble outside her yard, heading towards the bushland that had swallowed Lily the night before. The pony stopped frequently, her head dropping like a stone the second she spied a particularly enticing tuft of green, and she lashed her tail often at annoying flies. Phoenix searched for clues, like a character in *Picnic at Hanging Rock*, her eyes peeled for fragments of lacy clothing caught on bushes or branches. But a bush tracker she was not and no clues revealed themselves, despite Rita flattening a path for them to walk. She called for Lily several times and even attempted a wonky *cooee* or two, but all she could hear was traffic in the distance and birds in the trees. She tugged on Rita's lead and limped her way back to camp. She swapped the chickens out of their crate and replaced them with Audrey and Marilyn, who lay down to groom their furry bellies in the weak sunlight.

To distract herself from fretting about Lily, Phoenix channelled her nervousness into action. It was time to *take the offensive*. She sat on the picnic bench and called Claudette from the community newspaper. After Phoenix gave a brief explanation of her situation, the journalist said she'd be right over and would bring extra-strong coffees with her. The moment she arrived, Phoenix fell on the coffee like a parched desert wanderer, while Claudette watched on, amused.

'And I thought *I* liked my coffee,' she teased.

'You've no idea how much I needed that.'

'Oh, here, this is for you.' Claudette pulled out a copy of her community newspaper, folded back to the article on Phoenix and the animals, with a heart-wrenching picture of little Jane sedated, with her drip in her arm, and one of Phoenix under a tree, the red chicken in one arm and Humphrey at her feet. 'It came out this morning.'

'Such a big article,' Phoenix said, taking in the three-quarter spread with local business ads below. She made sure she smiled to express her gratitude but did wish she'd maybe changed her shirt from the night before, washed her face and put on at least a sheen of tinted moisturiser. 'I'll have a good read later.'

Claudette paused a moment, taking in the pony, chickens and cats now basking in a sliver of sunbeam, and their surrounds. 'Is Lily here?'

'No,' Phoenix said, with a sigh.

Claudette met Phoenix's gaze evenly. 'Tell me how I can help you.' Her face had softened. That teacher-ish vibe Phoenix had picked up on the first time they'd met was back.

'Were you ever a teacher?'

Claudette blinked in surprise. 'Yes, I was. How did you know that?'

Phoenix shrugged. 'I don't know. I get vibes from people, I guess. Sometimes I just know things. Like once, I was having coffee with a friend and I suddenly knew she'd been a smoker, though we'd never discussed it. I asked her as much and she nearly fell off her chair because she hadn't smoked in almost thirty years. It freaked her out a bit.'

Claudette sipped her brew, considering Phoenix. 'Why do you think that happens?'

'I used to wonder if I had some sort of psychic power or something.' Phoenix pulled a face to let Claudette know she didn't take herself too seriously. 'But I could never conjure it on demand; it was always spontaneous. Recently, I've read things from other people like me, who expressed the same thing. They thought they were psychic until they learnt that what they really had was exceptional skill in decoding patterns. Not with computer numbers or dots or dashes – I've never been good at that – but subtle things in people, animals, weather, the environment. That made sense to me. I see things other people don't.' Feeling self-conscious now, she grimaced. 'But I miss blatantly obvious things, too.' She jiggled her knee like a piston.

Claudette waited, not rushing to fill the silence, which Phoenix appreciated. Then after a beat, she said, 'You mentioned something on the phone about your boss trying to push you out of your job.'

'That's right.'

'What do you do?'

'I'm a teacher.'

Claudette tilted her head to the side and laid her phone on the table. 'I'm listening.'

Bruno arrived in a van the same as the one he'd lent to Phoenix, though his was shinier, the tyres slick black with inches of tread. He stumped across the ground with a significant lurch, an affect that did not seem recent. His steel-grey hair was plaited down to his waist and he wore a yellow and green Brazil soccer T-shirt.

'Good day, good day, good day to you,' he said, dropping a bag full of food onto the picnic table. Humphrey, interestingly enough, didn't bark at him at all, but came to sniff his workboots and peer with interest at the bags of food.

'Good day to you,' he said, again, this time addressing the dog. To Phoenix's surprise, Humphrey offered a tiny wag of his tail in return.

'Thank you so much for coming,' she said, while Bruno's gaze roamed over the van, the pony, the chickens and trees. 'I honestly can't believe you drove six hours out of your way to come here.'

'Driving's what I do,' he said, smiling down at Humphrey. The dog smiled back. Phoenix felt thrilled to see Humphrey so relaxed but equally betrayed that he was bestowing this sudden burst of loyalty and affection on a complete stranger. 'I like the quiet. Lets me think. Ya should eat something,' he finished, abruptly.

On cue, Phoenix's stomach growled. 'I really should.' Inside the bags, she found a huge bowl of chicken and salad, several types of nut bars, a piece of orange and almond cake and two litres of water.

'It's all gluten-free,' Bruno said, taking a seat opposite her to better rub Humphrey's ears. 'My wife's coeliac too. Service stations don't stock much. I was lucky to get the salad.'

'You did amazingly well,' Phoenix mumbled, already tucking in to it. She'd never been so happy to devour lettuce.

'Eat up,' he instructed. 'Then we'll get ya on the road.'

She ate the whole salad and the slice of cake in record time, feeling the low-level shake that had set in to her hands dissipating with every mouthful. Then they began their lesson. Now the tremor in her hands was from nerves. Bruno's instructions on how to hitch the float to the van were enough to send her into panic. More than once, the discussion of handbrakes, jockey wheels, electrical cables and safety chains tempted her to flee into the bush after Lily. What if she forgot to slide the safety pin in, or if the electrics didn't connect properly, or the safety chain just *fell off* on the highway? What if she was driving and the entire horse float simply broke away because she hadn't put it together properly and poor Rita ended up in a rollover accident?

All this, and she hadn't even driven yet, let alone attempted reversing.

Suffice to say, try as she might, she couldn't reverse the van with enough efficiency to line up the tow bar and the hitch, not even using the van's reversing camera and not even when Bruno used her trusty broom to guide her, standing where she could see him in the camera. 'This is impossible!' she wailed. 'How is anyone supposed to line a big van up with something the size of a small apple?'

Bruno scratched at his cheek with the back of his fingernails. 'New plan. I'll hitch the float and leave it hitched till ya reach Brisbane.'

Phoenix thought she might cry but then snorted in defeat. She took a deep breath and blew it away. 'All right. Let's do that.' It wasn't a great plan but it was the best they could do under the circumstances. Besides, *surely* Lily would return any minute now.

They moved on to the actual towing. She sat in the driver's seat, Bruno beside her.

'Driving in a straight line is good, good, good,' he said. 'Keep doing that and ya'll be fine. No turns, no worries.'

Phoenix turned to him, her mouth ajar. 'You're not serious.'

He looked at her, a little askew, but grinned. 'Not *reeeaaaally.*'

'I'm doomed.'

'No, ya are not, not, not,' he said, and his shoulders shook with suppressed giggles as she slowly accelerated.

'Basic rules – start slow, stop slow and turn wide,' he instructed. They were now out in the open grass, heading towards the bush. 'Okay, stop here.'

Phoenix applied the brake, ignoring both the pain in her driving ankle and the weight of the float behind her, pushing into the van like a firm hand at her back. She had to hold her focus. Pain or no pain, she'd always had to keep going. This was no different.

'Now, to reverse in a straight line, ya watch the float in the mirrors. As soon as ya see the float more in one mirror, steer towards that and it'll straighten like magic.'

Though her late lunch now sat hard as rock in her belly, Phoenix did as she was told, commanding the wheel first right then left.

'Keep breathing, breathing, breathing,' Bruno said.

She breathed. To her delight, she did it. She fist-pumped the air, as if she'd just climbed a cliff with no safety harness and only her bare hands for tools.

'Now we try reverse turning,' Bruno instructed. 'Now, everything is opposite.'

Her short-lived pride in her accomplishment evaporated. 'What do you mean?'

'If the float needs to go left, ya steer right and vice versa, vice versa.' Bruno coached her every move and the van gently flowed its way backwards. But then he got out and asked her to reverse the float to line up with a particularly gnarled tree on the edge of the clearing. She backed up, turning the wheel the way she thought it should go but instead the float went the opposite way. Startled, she overcorrected, turning the other way. Bruno shouted and waved from his spot in the clearing. He moved behind her to wave her the way she should go, but she couldn't work out if he was indicating the way the wheel should go or the back of float should go. It was all so confusing. She spun the wheel and the end of the float shot straight towards Bruno, forcing him to leap to the side like a stunt man in a movie. Adrenaline shot through her. She overcorrected again and promptly jack-knifed the float so the van was stuck out at a ridiculous right angle to its appendage. She snapped off the engine, evacuating the cabin in panic.

She slumped to the grass a long way from the van and float, while Bruno hoisted himself into the driver's seat and patiently coaxed the whole thing back into a straight line. Humiliation ran hot through her blood. She couldn't drive the van and float, she just couldn't. Her brain didn't align with mechanical things. Almost daily she lost her temper at a computer or photocopier or even a kitchen drawer that got off its tracks. She reserved her choicest swear words for inanimate objects and she had zero confidence in her ability to tow this horse float, especially with a living animal on board and especially out there on her own.

A depression attack loomed – the deepest sense of uselessness imaginable, swallowing her whole, dragging her down, down, down. This was all so hopeless. She was probably going to lose her job, she was two states away from Zack, she'd lost Lily, and she couldn't get out of this rest spot where she was now illegally camping. She wasn't even able to go to the shop to buy food.

At last, Bruno had the van and float in a straight line once more. He climbed out and stumped his way over.

'Are ya ready to try again?'

'What?! No! I'm hopeless at this.'

Bruno studied her calmly for a moment, his deep brown eyes meeting hers for the first time. 'Ya're not hopeless. Ya're inexperienced in towing a float, that is all, that is all. Everyone struggles at first. It doesn't mean ya're a failure; it only means ya need more practice.'

It was a common autistic trait, she knew, to want to give up immediately rather than to risk failing. She gestured to the sky. 'But it's getting late and you have to go. What am I going to do, learn from YouTube?'

'I learnt how to make ravioli pasta on YouTube.'

Phoenix paused a moment, then laughed, teetering on the edge of crying.

Bruno waited, his hands behind his back, stretching. 'Take a break and then try again. I reckon we have a bit more time before the sun sets. If not, I'll bunk down in my van and we'll try again tomorrow, tomorrow.'

'Bruno! I have no idea how I can ever repay you for all this kindness.'

'Don't repay – pay it forwards,' he said, and beckoned her up off the ground. 'That way the world keeps turning.'

'All right.' She pushed herself up off the ground, brushing off grass and a couple of small ants that had decided to climb aboard. 'I will pay it forwards. And I'll give it one more go.'

She had to get this right; she needed to get out of there. She absolutely didn't want to go on without Lily (*no one left behind*) but at some point she knew she'd have to make that awful decision, or it would be made for her, likely by the police ordering her to move on. And when that happened, she would have lost her only means to reconnect with Lily.

Please, please come back.

18

Bruno did stay with her, their two zebra vans forming a mini herd. His presence at the site meant Phoenix could leave him with the animals while she drove into town to stock up on supplies and bring them both back dinner – ravioli, even gluten-free. She also picked up a camping mattress in an effort to improve her sleep. They retired to their respective vans not long after dark.

She awoke the next morning to Humphrey's ear-splitting alarm barks. Heart pounding, she climbed into the front seats in time to see a small truck spraying up stones as it whizzed out of the dirt parking area, black smoke pouring from the exhaust. Rita let out a chest-vibrating whinny, then another, and another. 'What the hell?' She stumbled out of the passenger-side door as Bruno exited his van and together they stared towards the picnic table.

Standing there, tied to the table by tattered rope, was a dishevelled grey alpaca (or maybe a llama?). He swayed from side to side, trying to escape the rope around his neck, which cut in tightly behind his jaw. 'What on earth . . .?' Phoenix couldn't finish the sentence. The animal's coat hung in nasty, matted dreadlocks that pulled tightly at his skin. He could barely see from beneath the ones that covered his eyes. His hooves were overgrown and curled and his spine was protruded. Diarrhoea matted his back legs.

'Did someone just dump an alpaca on me?' Phoenix muttered, slowly taking in the poor animal's condition.

'Looks like.'

'Why?' She was dumbfounded, then a moment later, she remembered the article in Claudette's newspaper. She sucked in a shocked breath. When she'd had time to read the story clearly, she remembered seeing the words *animal rescue* and *rescuer* and *no animal left behind*. 'This is because of the newspaper coverage,' she said. 'But how would anyone know where I'm staying?'

'Small towns,' Bruno said, as if that explained it.

Phoenix approached the animal slowly but hesitated when he flattened his ears back. She knew that was a warning sign in horses but she didn't know anything about alpacas or llamas.

A 'house' call from the now familiar vet confirmed that the animal was indeed an alpaca, not a llama, that he was actually white and simply looked grey from the filth, and was in need of treatment. Phoenix had already sent photos of him to Zack, who had raged about how dreadful the people were to neglect him so badly and told her they absolutely must help. She stood silently – still in shock at this latest development – and watched as the vet wormed and vaccinated the animal, then sedated him to trim back his long and dreadful toes. She gave him an antibiotic injection to treat any infectious cause of the diarrhoea and left Phoenix with some powder to mix into his feed. Fortunately, he could share Rita's chaff and pellets. The vet cut away the long dreadlocks from his eyes so he could see, and from around his bottom to remove the worst of the matted faeces, but advised that Phoenix would need to find a shearer to finish the job.

'He's thin, but once that diarrhoea clears up he'll start putting on weight again. Just needs food and lots of it,' the vet said.

After that, she delivered the recovering Jane and her brother Milo into the mix, giving Phoenix instructions for the ongoing care of Jane's healing leg.

'I really should swap my van for an ark,' Phoenix said, accepting the cage of kittens. 'Maybe then we could sail back to Brisbane.'

Grateful to have Bruno around for a little longer, she drove back into town to get yet more crates as well as some specific alpaca food. When she called Zack to ask him if he would like to name the alpaca, he answered at once.

'Linus,' he said, a smile in his voice. Linus – sensitive, anxious and deep thinking – was Zack's favourite *Peanuts* character, and the one most likely to be autistic.

Phoenix returned after a couple of hours, bringing back lunch for herself and Bruno, feeling more motivated than ever to learn once and for all how to tow the float now she had another passenger to go in it. But she couldn't hide her shock when she stepped out of the van to see Bruno at the bench seat holding a cardboard box that was almost big enough to obscure him from view. The box was moving. His brow furrowed as she approached.

'What's this?' she asked, almost not wanting to know.

'Ducks.'

'Ducks?' Her voice came out high-pitched, with a tinge of outrage. '*Ducks?*'

'A young couple pulled up and . . . and . . . they just handed them to me.' He looked bewildered, gazing out to the road as if expecting them to come back. 'Said they don't lay no more.'

'Don't lay?' Phoenix could feel her blood pressure rising. 'What is *wrong* with people?! Who cares if they don't lay? Why is everyone's worth attached to what they can *do*, rather than who they *are*?!' she shrieked. She kicked viciously at the ground, hurting her ankle and making herself cry out in pain, which only made her that much angrier.

'That's actually the ideology of capitalism,' Bruno said, looking confused by her anger.

She opened her mouth to argue her point – that life was valuable simply because it was life – but gave up and satisfied herself with stomping back and forth. 'So now I have ducks too. How many are there?'

'Dunno,' Bruno said. 'Haven't been game to pop the lid.'

Phoenix closed her eyes and sighed, gathering her wits. 'Let me swap the cats out of the outdoor crate with the ducks. Then we'll see what we've got.'

One, two, three, four, five ducks quacked and flapped their way onto the grass. They were heavy and sturdy-looking, with white bodies, yellow beaks and orange legs and feet. Beautiful brown flecks dappled feathers here and there, with patches of dark at their necks or wingtips.

'Know anything about ducks?' she asked Bruno, who was hopping from one foot to the other as he watched them dart about, testing the boundaries of their crate. He shook his head. Phoenix pulled out her phone to search for sites to identify the birds. 'The closest I can come up with is an Appleyard,' she said, showing Bruno the photos. He nodded in agreement. 'They really are beautiful,' she said, coming to terms with the fact that she was now the custodian of five Appleyards.

Back in the van, she checked on Jane and Milo while the senior cats flicked their tails with displeasure at the new feline intruders. She pushed her fingers through the wire door to rub them, wishing Jane's recovery was happening at home, with lounge chairs and heaters and fluffy rugs. 'One day soon, you'll get the royal treatment, I promise.'

Lily's phone tinged, interrupting her thoughts. Phoenix grabbed it, hoping it was a message from Lily, but the identification listed *Mum* as the sender, her text visible onscreen.

> Lily, I only want to make sure
> you're ok. Think how I feel. I've
> protected you your whole life.
> You still need me. You can't
> do this on your own.

Phoenix dropped the phone, feeling guilty to have seen the message but also torn. Lily was missing.

Should she contact Lily's mother? She had no other way to connect with Lily and she was frightened something bad had happened to her friend. But Lily had been adamant that her mother was not an ally. What did Phoenix really know of their relationship? Her teacher training would tell her to contact the family, but Lily wasn't her student, or a child. She was an adult. Though it wrenched physically in her gut, she forced herself to ignore the phone. One more day. She would wait one more day.

Instead of fretting, she tackled the job she most needed to do right now and that was to master towing that horse float. Well, if not master it, then at least fudge her way through it enough to give herself options. If nothing else, it seemed she needed to move on from this rest stop before any more animals were dropped in her lap. What would be next? A cow, a camel, an entire litter of piglets? She swayed at the very thought of it.

She got on with it, and it was late in the day when Bruno prepared to leave.

'Ya'll be right now,' he said, opening the door to his own van. 'Ya've got the basics.'

'I hope you're right,' Phoenix said. They had left the van and float parked strategically so all she had to do in the morning was simply pull out onto the road.

Bruno stretched the seatbelt across his body and clacked it into place. 'Remember, ya can ask for help, okay? There're always folk around willing to lend a hand. Try to park strategically in places where there are likely to be four-wheel-driving/bobcat/machinery types.'

'Got it. Caravan sites, camping grounds, boating ramps, produce stores, mechanics, showgrounds, landscaping places, that sort of thing.'

'Ya'll be fine, fine, fine. And I'm only a call away.'

Phoenix smiled at him. 'Thank you again, Bruno, a million times. I don't know what I'd have done without you.'

He looked straight ahead as he started the engine but gave her a two-fingered salute from his brow. 'Cheerio.' He thumped the horn with the heel of his hand.

The air bloomed with a jungle soundtrack of chattering, shrieking and braying.

Phoenix leapt back, startled.

'That's what zebras sound like,' he roared over the noise. His shoulders shook with mirth as he pulled out onto the road.

She was processing the shock of the unique horn when Claudette returned in her hatchback. She parked without fuss, which was to say without bothering to line up in a dedicated space, and hopped out, her eyes immediately on the alpaca grazing in the pony's yard. 'You weren't wrong!' she exclaimed. 'He's a mess.'

'Know any shearers?'

Claudette waved a hand. 'Plenty. You'll have no trouble getting one.'

'It's only that I really need to leave tomorrow morning. I'm pushing my luck staying here.' She knew it was true, but worry for Lily dogged her. Had Lily simply abandoned Phoenix or had something awful happened to her? She'd been gone two nights and it was late afternoon now and heading into the third. She didn't want to leave Lily – but it was looking more and more as though Lily had left *her*.

'Also, I'm risking becoming the dumping ground for more animals.'

Claudette pushed her glasses up the bridge of her nose and winced. 'Gosh, I'm so sorry about that. I didn't in a million years think my article would make that happen.'

Phoenix lifted her shoulders and let them fall. 'People are the strangest creatures.'

'That they are,' Claudette agreed. 'Now, I have a few more questions I want to ask you for the new article I'm writing.'

Phoenix put a hand to her belly, willing the butterflies to calm. Was she ready to see herself in print, to see her story reflected back to her, to see herself publicly outed as autistic, to fight for her job? No, but she imagined she never would be. Nearly forty-eight hours had passed since Evelyn's threat of an imminent termination. Honestly, Phoenix was surprised it was taking this long, though it probably meant they were ensuring they had every last duck in a row to make sure it was done properly the first time. Either way, whether she went back to school or she lost her job, she was in for a world of struggle, so she might as well follow the trail of discomfort that led to a job. She had her own bloody ducks to take care of. 'Let's do it.'

That evening, with an aching heart, she prepared to leave the site. In the light afforded by her sunflower LEDs, she packed and rearranged the van. With the addition of five sizeable ducks, she didn't have enough crates for all the cats to have their own. Fortunately, Jane and Milo were happy to snuggle, but Audrey and Marilyn were less so. They were friends, certainly, but they were also queens. Each wanted her own space. She would leave them to roam the van overnight but apologised that they would have to travel together by day.

She sorted which of her clothes needed washing and which were still acceptable to wear. She did a stocktake of food supplies – human and animal – noting she would have to travel with less hay as Linus would now occupy the second bay of the horse float. She threw out what rubbish she could, mostly a lot of soiled puppy pads that had been used by the chickens and now ducks.

Lily's phone lit up with another text message from her mother.

> I know you think we did badly
> by you. We wanted you to be
> accepted, to fit in. For that,
> you had to be normal. Is that
> so bad? Can you blame us for
> wanting that?

Normal.

It hadn't been Lily's job to change herself to fit in with the world, to lose herself, to squash her uniqueness.

Phoenix was still sick with worry for Lily, but after speaking to Therese they decided it would do Lily more harm if they got the police and her parents involved. Most likely, she was taking her time alone to sort out her feelings. Lily was raised on a farm. She had skills, probably enough to last a few days on her own.

Sitting down next to Humphrey at the back of the van, she exchanged some flirty texts with Zack that brought a smile to her lips and warmed her skin. After several pleasurable minutes of that, they changed tack and got down to the practicalities of their new, unfolding situation. He confirmed the new chook house had arrived for him to assemble this weekend and she sent him updated videos of the kittens and the ducks. A moment later, he called.

'What do the ducks need?'

'A paddling pool, apparently,' she said, searching the internet for advice.

'What about a house? Are there duck houses?'

'They are prey animals, like the chickens, so they do need protection from dogs and foxes and snakes,' she said, skimming an article on duck care.

'I'll do some research,' he said, and hung up. Sometime later, her text messages began filling with images of duck houses. Some had little ramps and railings, some had their own flowerboxes, some had attached runs, and some opened straight out onto the water. They were adorable. She looked around at the dog, the cats, the chickens and ducks, and thought of Rita and Linus only metres away. It was an amazing feeling to know she could bring so much joy to these animals for the rest of their lives. In this moment, she couldn't think of anything more important than doing that. She reached behind her to move a box of groceries and stumbled across the handmade pottery mugs. She touched the possum emblem on each. 'Thanks, Olga.'

Humphrey leapt to his feet, growling, splintering the quiet. His eyes were fixed somewhere beyond the back of the van's doors. A scatter of sharp barks followed. Phoenix strained her ears to hear whatever Humphrey could.

Not this again – not another night paralysed by fear.

Adrenaline roared through her. *No.* She was not going to be held captive in this van. Even if it was bloody Jason from *Friday the 13th* out there, she would take him down. With a firestorm of bravado, she grabbed the trusty broom, yanking it free of the van's clutter, rammed open the van doors and charged out into the night with a mighty roar, the broom head leading the way.

19

Phoenix shrieked a blood-curdling battle call, charging at the figure in the shadows. Time slowed, details shimmered. A flannelette shirt, black jeans and a baseball cap. She barrelled for him, feet pounding, no feeling in her ankle or wrist now. She was nothing but roaring blood. The stranger yelped in fright and crumpled to the ground as the broom arrowed towards his chest. He deflected it with a rising arm and cowered, arms over his head. Phoenix hauled the broom high, preparing to smash it down. Attack or be attacked.

'It's me, it's me!' the figure pleaded.

'Who? Who?' Phoenix shouted, barely able to stop herself from completing the assault. She danced on the spot with muzzled energy.

'Lily!'

Phoenix jolted backwards, staggering over her own feet. The broom fell to the ground. 'What?' It wasn't a man at all. It was Lily. Wait, what? Her voice was different. Then again, Phoenix had been threatening her with a weapon.

'It's me, Lily,' she repeated, peeking from under the arm still shielding her face. 'It's me,' she panted, now sounding close to tears.

'You scared me half to death!' Phoenix threw the broom to the side and hopped up and down, her rational brain racing to keep up with the fight-or-flight hormones flooding her system. Her legs rattled and she dropped to the muddy ground to contain herself. 'I thought I was going to have to kill you. I thought I was about to die.' Her hand clutched at her chest, checking to make sure she was, in fact, still alive.

'I'm sorry,' Lily said, exposing her face now that the threat of a beating had subsided.

'Where the hell have you been?' Phoenix demanded.

'Out bush.' Lily threw her hand to the side to indicate the direction.

'And why are you dressed like that?'

Lily's eyes reflected the starlight above. 'I needed to escape myself.'

'I've been so worried about you,' Phoenix squeaked.

'I'm sorry.'

They sat in silence for a few moments, each getting her bearings after such a startling reunion. Phoenix was suddenly aware of the crickets singing in the long grasses and the whooping night birds in the bushland beyond. She shivered.

'Let's get inside.'

'Okay.'

Phoenix clambered to her feet and held out her hand to help Lily, then picked up the broom.

'Were you really going to hit me with that?' Lily asked.

Phoenix stared at the wooden handle clenched in her fist. 'I think so.'

'You were terrifying.'

'Thanks,' she said, and snorted with amusement. *Take that, Jason.* 'What made you come back? And *are* you back, for good?'

'Yes.'

'What about your plans with Bianca? What will you do now?'

Lily shrugged. 'I have no idea. But I can't go home to my parents. I can't go backwards, not after coming this far.'

Phoenix nodded. She got that. She stopped and turned to Lily. 'You're brave. I don't think you know how much.'

'Thank you.'

'You can stay with us when we get back, till you get on your feet.'

'Oh, no, I couldn't impose.'

'You absolutely can,' Phoenix said, smiling encouragingly. 'We have a spare room we can clear out. Zack works over fifty hours a week and I'll be working crazy hours too in that final term of school. We'll hardly ever be at the house. It will give you time to work out a plan. Besides, Humphrey will the need the company. I'll probably have to hire a dog walker otherwise to come and care for him during the day. You can think about it, but the offer is there.'

'Thank you. That is very generous.'

They were about to climb into the van when Lily stopped, staring in the direction of Rita's yard. 'Is that an alpaca?'

'It is.'

Quacking emanated from inside the van. Lily turned to Phoenix. 'Do we have ducks now?'

'Long story,' Phoenix said. 'I'm glad you're back.'

Lily smiled. 'Me too.'

•

Saturday morning burst into the campground with a perfectly blue sky and a huge ball of sun that warmed the earth so quickly

186

Phoenix could see steam rising from the ground. It also brought with it several new surprises, the first being that Lily knew how to shear.

'We had sheep on the farm. Shearin's no worries,' she said. That was the other surprise – Lily had shed her Austen-ese and with every passing hour sounded more and more like a character from *Crocodile Dundee*. She was still wearing the black jeans and flannelette shirt.

'Where did you get those clothes?'

'Took 'em off a line.'

'Right.' Phoenix was taken aback by this.

'Livin' off the land, ya know.' She lifted a shoulder and let it drop. 'She'll be right.'

They departed their makeshift camp site as soon as they could. Phoenix was determined not to let Bruno's tutelage go to waste and took her place behind the wheel. After taking several deep breaths and reminding herself of the tips he had given her, she pressed the accelerator and they rumbled and clanked their way out of the rest stop. Finally, she was on the move again and heading home to Zack.

'First stop is a petrol station for a newspaper so I can read Claudette's article,' Phoenix said, accelerating more now they were on a clear run of road.

'Can ya check it online?'

'No, terrible paper. I don't subscribe.'

'Have ya heard anything from yer principal?'

'Not yet. I suppose she's either not read it, or she's spitting fire that she didn't get to me first, or she's rewording her letter of dismissal.'

They filled up at the first petrol station they came to and picked up the newspaper Claudette had sold the story to, then got straight back on the road.

'Want me to read it to ya?' Lily asked.

'I don't think so, not yet. Let's get to the Gumtree person's house to pick up the shears you found, then we can swap driving, if that's okay.'

'No worries.' Lily snapped on gum in a way that made Phoenix's skin crawl.

Why had Lily turned into this? She said she'd 'slept rough' for her time away, finding corrugated iron animal shelters to hide in, pulling water from stock water troughs, and 'borrowing' fruit and vegetables from farms as she needed (as well as the new clothes). She said she needed time on her own to decompress and process what had happened with Bianca. Phoenix believed all of it, though it worried her that Lily had abandoned her previous style and way of speaking. Lily was 'loose' now, her body no longer straight and tall, her limbs no longer contained. Now her leg was pulled up under her, her elbows jutted, a foot constantly jiggled, her fingers knotted and unknotted, her jaw worked overtime on the gum. Phoenix was sure that some of that loosening had to be a good thing, letting herself go, perhaps rediscovering herself, unmasking from all the constructs she'd built over the years. But she suspected there was more to it. Lily hadn't thrown away her whole duffel bag, which was full of her steampunk and Victorian pieces, so maybe that version of her was still here too.

They picked up the shears, swapped places behind the wheel, and Phoenix opened the newspaper with a deep breath. A few pages in, she found herself, standing with the skinny, matted alpaca, but not smiling. She looked directly into the lens, her mouth serious, her shoulders set.

More Woes for Disgraced Girls' School

Phoenix winced at the title. The shouty headline's description of St Clementine's Girls' School as 'disgraced' would set Evelyn on fire. Her sense of control over her situation vanished. But then, had she ever had any control? Evelyn had made it blindingly clear she would get Phoenix out of the school one way or another. Wasn't that the point of her asking Claudette for help? She read on.

A prestigious Brisbane girls' school has set itself up for an unlawful dismissal case after it threatened to sack an autistic senior teacher.

At this point, Phoenix had to close the paper for a moment while she stared at the scenery racing by outside. With one sentence, she'd been taken out of the autism closet and there was no going back. She reminded herself why she'd done it – because there was nothing wrong with being autistic, because young autists needed to be able to see grown-up autistic people living and working in the world, because her being autistic didn't mean she was an unfit teacher, because the public narrative around autism was outdated and needed to change, and because she was sick of living a lie, of pretending she was one thing when she was actually something else. All of the camouflaging and masking had been slowly but thoroughly strangling her like a patient python intent on squeezing the life out of its prey. These were all good reasons, but it was still terrifying.

'Ya right?' Lily asked, casting a sideways glance.

Phoenix felt outside of her body, a flapping fish ripped from its world and thrown to the sand, unable to breathe.

She continued to read.

Senior teacher Phoenix Rose has worked at St Clementine's for twelve years, regularly receiving promotions and excellent peer reviews. Mid-year, Ms Rose took medically supported extended sick leave. But when it ran out, she broached the subject of an extension with the acting principal, Evelyn Godfrey, who did not support the continuation of unpaid leave.

'She made it clear she wasn't happy about me taking more leave and she made it perfectly clear she considered my recent autism diagnosis a scandal.'

Ms Godfrey was parachuted into the school as acting principal earlier this year when the then principal, Mr Levi Backhurst, was caught on film in a nightclub with underage strippers and ecstasy in his possession. Mr Backhurst has been on 'gardening leave' ever since, awaiting court proceedings.

Ms Rose claims Ms Godfrey said she had 'serious concerns for the ongoing reputation of the school'. However, after Ms Rose informed the acting principal that she'd decided to return to teaching in Term 4, Ms Godfrey seemed displeased. The principal informed Ms Rose that she would have to create a return-to-work plan for her and threatened that she'd 'be watching'. But instead of providing the return-to-work plan, Ms Godfrey phoned Ms Rose a day later claiming that she had breached the terms of her Christian 'lifestyle' contract and she would be receiving a letter of termination.

'For one, what she claimed wasn't even true,' Ms Rose says. 'There is footage of me and my travelling companion online. It looks as though we are kissing, but it's just the angle of the camera. My companion was kissing the rescued kitten I was holding. It was a silly misunderstanding, but I think Evelyn's using it as a way to get rid of me rather than saying she wants me gone because she sees my autism as a "scandal". I think she believes she has firmer grounds for a lifestyle dismissal than one based on disability.'

Phoenix skimmed the rest of the article, which gave the story of why Phoenix and 'her travelling companion' were on the road with the animals in the first place. She had to admit Claudette had done a good job. Phoenix came across as a sympathetic character, the animals gave it all a feel-good tone, and there were some great quotes from disability organisations about her right to employ-ment and accommodations in the workplace.

It was difficult to see herself so exposed but at the same time she felt a tiny pinprick of pride that she could stand up for not only herself but other autists too. That feeling was quickly dashed, though, by the storm of fury and fight she knew would be coming from Evelyn.

A short drive away from their scheduled pit stop in the tiny historic town of Jerilderie, Zack called.

'I'm sorry for taking so long to get back to you,' he said. 'I worked late last night and slept in this morning. But I got the paper and read the article and I think it's good. You did well.'

'All I can think is how angry Evelyn will be and what sort of lies she'll spread about me now.'

'Maybe. We'll have to wait and see. Hey, how's Linus?'

'He's eating well and his diarrhoea looked better this morning. The medicine seems to be helping. Now that Lily's back, she can shear him, so that will help him feel a lot better.'

'Send me photos when you can.'

'I will.'

A second after she put her phone down, it buzzed. Phoenix picked it up to find a text message from Anthea.

Are you crazy? What were you thinking, talking to the papers???

Paper, singular.

You know what I mean. I can't believe you. We've all suffered

enough after Principal Pants
Man, don't you think? At
least Evelyn is putting the
school first.

If she was truly putting the
school first, she'd be leading
the way in embracing the kind
of diversity that strengthens
the world and gives hope and
support to the autistic girls
already in our school, and
prospective enrolments too.

Phoenix tossed the phone facedown. She didn't want to see anything more from Anthea. If she'd had any hopes that there might still be a shred of their friendship left, those delusions were dispelled for good.

They arrived in Jerilderie eager for food. An online list of places to eat included four petrol stations, a closed hotel, a sports club and a bakery, none of which looked promising for vegan and gluten-free options. They decided to head to the two-storey Royal Mail Hotel, with its golden rendered walls, oversized windows, wide arches at the entrance and Ned Kelly iconography. The bushranger featured frequently in the town, they quickly realised. As Lily searched for a decent parking spot for their van and float, Phoenix read out bits off the internet about Ned Kelly's connection to the town.

'This is where he wrote something called the Jerilderie Letter, which is apparently the only piece of writing directly from him, all about his innocence and the plight of the poor Irish settlers. However, he did capture and lock up the town's police officers, stole their uniforms and impersonated them, robbed the local bank and broke into the telegraph office, which kind of undermines his arguments of innocence. Oh, and the Royal Mail Hotel has the original safe that Ned Kelly broke into.'

'This'll do,' Lily said, checking her side mirror once more before unclicking her seatbelt. 'I'm starving.'

'Me too.'

Lily stayed with the animals while Phoenix went inside to Kelly's Bistro and ordered them what takeaway she could from a menu that was heavily gluten and meat inspired. The woman at the counter was friendly, though, and did her best to work around what they had, offering Phoenix grilled fish and Lily a sizeable salad.

But when Phoenix returned outside, she found Lily pressed with her back against the side of the van and her shoulders hunched, Humphrey growling from inside the vehicle. A broad tower of a man hovered over Lily, blocking her escape.

Phoenix rushed over. 'I've got the food,' she called, her eyes darting between them. The slab of a man turned his head towards the sound of Phoenix approaching, but didn't move away.

'Is everything okay?' Phoenix asked, forcing herself to smile because people responded better to smiles than to accusations. 'Are you lost?' she asked the man, as though trying to be helpful. This was what women had to do – soften, soften, soften, not say what they really wanted to say, avoid the conflict if possible, defuse the situation. Get away with their lives.

He flicked his brooding gaze to hers. 'Are *you*?' he growled, through jumbled teeth.

'What? No, not at all. We're just passing through.' She forced another smile though her heart was beating so hard he must surely have been able to see her ribs jumping.

He worked his jaw as if trying to dislodge something from between those teeth, and looked at each of their faces, the corner of a lip snarled. 'Your kind's not welcome here.' A fat and grimy finger thrust out and poked Lily hard in the chest. She flinched, her face still turned away. Disassociating. Frozen. Phoenix knew that feeling well. Animals did it too when they were cornered with no escape – when they thought they were about to die.

'Hey!' Phoenix snapped, adrenaline kicking in, barely able to stop herself from slapping at the man's arm. She wished she had that broom in her hand now. 'Stop that.' They were the only words she could pull from a racing mind.

At the sound of her voice, Humphrey snarled, unnerving the man. He eased back a little, then hoicked up a ball of something disgusting and spat at Lily's feet.

'Don't let the door hit you on the way out,' he ordered, then looked Lily up and down in a way that might as well have been a physical assault. He turned to go. But as he did, he suddenly jumped towards Phoenix, shouting 'Boo!' into her face, his hands raised, and she yelped, dropping the lunch and covering her head with her hands.

A woman walking past the hotel called out. 'Hey!'

'Ah, shut up, bitch,' he retorted, then moved on.

Phoenix watched him go, mouthed a *thank you* to the woman, then turned to Lily. She had slid to the ground, her knees pulled up to her chest, rocking.

'It's okay,' Phoenix said, though she felt far from okay herself. 'He's gone.' She glanced up the street. He was still in view and she would like to get out of there as soon as possible. 'Do you think you can get into the van? I can drive. We need to get out of here.'

But Lily was frozen, shaking, her eyes staring at nothing on the footpath, making a groaning sound. Phoenix didn't want to touch her, lest she make things worse. The woman who'd tried to help came over and got down to Lily's level. 'We should call the police,' she said. 'Him poking you like that was an assault.'

Lily shook her head.

'He can't just come up to people and harass them and assault them,' the woman said. 'Who knows what else he's been up to or who else he's hurting? I've got a pretty good description of him.' She turned to Phoenix, trying to get her to see straight. 'If she won't do it, we can do it anyway.'

Phoenix struggled for words. She knew the woman was right but she also knew Lily was scared of the police and would never agree to report this. If Phoenix made a report without her, it could cause Lily to run away again and this time she might not come back.

20

Jerilderie's Luke Park was green, leafy and had a lake to sit by. Phoenix parked the van and float in a shady spot and began to organise the animals. She took Humphrey out first, then handed his lead to Lily, who stood with crossed arms and her eyes downcast. She hadn't said anything yet. She'd stopped shaking, though Phoenix thought that might mean the shock had simply sunk deeper into her bones.

'Why don't you head over to the water?' Phoenix suggested. Lily did and moments later a dozen domestic ducks glided across the lake towards her, hoping for food. Their happy quacks and flaps were soothing.

The woman outside the hotel had organised new food to replace the meals Phoenix had dropped in fright and Phoenix took them over to the bench seat, handing Lily her salad and a fork. Lily whispered a thanks and accepted it but made no effort to open it.

'It would help if you had something to eat,' Phoenix said, gently. 'Low blood sugar isn't a good combination with shock.' She opened the container for Lily. 'Here, I brought you some water too.' She cracked the top of the bottle. Lily took a small sip.

Phoenix ate her meal in silence, watching the ducks squabble and dive and appear again, miraculously dry. They cruised along the glassy water; it appeared effortless. That was what autistic masking was like – appearing totally fine on the surface but paddling like crazy beneath it just to stay afloat. Phoenix couldn't shake off the bad stuff as easily as the ducks shook off water droplets, though.

'You know, what that man did to you isn't your fault,' she said, putting her fork down. 'You didn't do anything wrong.'

After a moment, Lily said, 'He asked me if he could bum a cigarette off a mate. I told him I didn't smoke. He stared at me really hard and said something about me not being a bloke at all. That was when he forced me back against the van.' She no longer spoke like someone from an iconic movie, but neither did she sound like Jane Austen. Her voice was flat, empty.

Phoenix shook her head in disgust, wondering what exactly that man had considered to be the problem. Was it that he felt tricked and therefore stupid? Or was he outright homophobic? Or was he a random thug? 'That's awful. I'm so sorry that happened to you. He sounds quite—'

What? Unreasonable, stuck in the Dark Ages, brainwashed, insecure?

'—scary,' she finished. 'Scary and prone to violence and probably a repeat offender. That wasn't an acceptable response, no matter who he thought you were. It was callous and ignorant and threatening.'

'All my life, I have been wrong. I have been called stupid, embarrassing, weird, gay, lazy, lezzo, crazy, a moron, ugly, useless, a burden, retarded, broken. Never good enough. *Wrong.* Always wrong. And I tried so hard,' she said, her voice hitching, 'to be whatever they wanted me to be. For a time, I thought I had found it.'

'In Jane Austen.'

'But then there was Bianca.' Lily's voice broke over the word. 'I still was not good enough. Despite giving up everything, risking everything, I still wasn't enough.'

'Oh, Lily.' Phoenix felt her own eyes well up now too. 'I wish you could believe me when I say that you *are* enough. You are perfect just as you are. You feel terrible right now but I promise you things will change. These feelings will change. Nothing stays the same, not even our thoughts. You've had a terrible shock. You are bound to feel really low right now. Your parents took away your authentic self, the kids at school took away your sense of safety and belonging and esteem, Bianca took away your beautiful open-hearted trust and joy in finding a connection with someone, and that man took away your right to feel safe in your own body. That's a lot for anyone to deal with.'

Lily moved some leafy greens around in her container. 'I suppose it is.'

'That man and his issues – whatever they were – it was just bad luck. You're not a magnet for bad people.' Even as she said the words, though, she knew the stats for abuse and assault of women were unacceptably high. Women were abused, simply because they were women, and those stats were even higher for autistic women, LGBTQIA+ women and women of colour. In many ways, they *were* magnets. Instead of being celebrated for their unique ways of being, they were hunted.

Growing up, Phoenix too had been the recipient of much unwanted and frightening attention. With her mother working in festivals around the state, Phoenix found herself in all sorts of temporary housing situations, some couch surfing and long periods in caravans. When she was thirteen, a man her mother was seeing took it upon himself to frequently tell Phoenix that she was a really attractive young woman, his gaze roaming unchecked over her body, and Phoenix would lose her words. She didn't have the wisdom or education to know it was a warning sign, nor the voice she needed to express her discomfort.

Before she was even ten, her mother's then boyfriend often stayed in their caravan while her mother worked, and he would ask Phoenix to sit on the floor and use her feet and legs to push against his hands and thighs. 'You've got really strong legs,' he encouraged. Had he been using the moment to peek up her shorts? Had he been getting off on this technically non-sexual but ultimately inappropriate touching?

One day while crossing an oval on her walk home from school, singing a jingle that was stuck in her head, she encountered a man on a tractor. She moved out of his way. He followed her. Her voice fell silent. She ran. He chased her to the end of the oval, over the gutter, onto the road and up the hill. She was a fast runner but was no match for a tractor. Nearing the top of the hill, she dived into the driveway of the nearest house and ducked behind the fence. He rumbled past, laughing, enjoying his frightening game.

Why had that happened? He'd chased her and scared her, simply for fun. Maybe his initial plans had been darker still. But why? Was it because she was a little girl . . . or was it something else?

Then there she was as an adult, a student teacher on duty inside a gymnasium that heaved with sweaty teenage bodies pushed up against each other in the dark. Impossibly loud music blared and strobe lighting splintered her vision. Everything was discombobulating. She could barely walk in a straight line. She felt fractured into pieces, nauseated, her senses overloaded, making the world spin.

From nowhere, a tall boy moved towards her in the black-white-black-white strobe-fragmented world. Her eyes were averted from the pain of the lights. She stepped aside to get out of his way. Instead, he stepped into her, expertly and with absolutely no mistake cupping her breast with his hand, a thumb roaming over her nipple, before zigzagging away, disappearing into the dark. She stumbled, shocked and disoriented, every cell screaming at her to flee.

Bursting outside into the cold winter air, she made her way to a group of her supervising teachers. They were complaining about the dance, at having to be there on a Saturday night.

'Yeah, well, I just got felt up by a Year 12 boy,' Phoenix blurted, her brain still not comprehending that this was an assault. She was shocked – frozen. Her body knew she'd been attacked but her mind hadn't caught up.

Some of the teachers raised eyebrows, surprised but not motivated enough to help. Then another teacher, drinking rum, going through a divorce, said, 'You see! That's men for you.' Another sip of rum and that was that. No one did a thing to help her.

Later still, there was the radiographer who'd told her not to bother putting on the usual paper gown but to take off her bra and leave her shirt on for an X-ray. And though it made her feel weird, she did it anyway, because what could she say? Words were not her friends in these moments. It was only when she was standing in front of the plate, the lights beaming on her chest, that she knew he could see her nipples, erect in the cold air conditioning, and that was why he'd told her not to change. Clearly, he'd done it before.

On and on these traumas went, adding up and adding up. No wonder women suffered from so much anxiety – they were constantly being shown they weren't safe in the world. For autistic women, born with brains wired to look for danger at every turn, yet perhaps out of tune with the danger signals themselves, often having a brain that shut down the words they needed to say or scream, there was no recovery from these events. Just endlessly compounding anxiety.

But if she had *known* she was autistic, if someone had taught her how to be safer in a neurotypical world, some of it might have been averted.

When Lily finally began to eat, her spirits buoyed somewhat by a snow-white duck that had waddled onto the shore and sat at her feet, much to Humphrey's tail-wagging amusement, Phoenix excused herself to make a phone call. All her musings about childhood events had made her think about her mother, and she'd realised with a start that being in the newspaper meant there was a good chance her mum would stumble across the article, or have someone else mention it to her. She really should tell her first. She wandered over to the metal windmill sculpture in the park and stood at its feet to make the call.

Jac answered on the sixth ring.

'Yes, who is it?' That was the way she answered the phone, even though Phoenix's number would have been clearly displayed.

'It's me, Mum.'

'Oh, darling,' she crooned, sympathetic, 'have you and Zack broken up?'

'No. Why would you say that?'

Her mother sniffed. 'You sound a bit off, that's all.'

Phoenix had to hand it to her mother, who was many things – scatterbrained and inattentive for a start – but also uncannily intuitive when her focus was right. She felt her eyes well, longing for some maternal comfort.

She paused, swallowing hard over the emotion that had suddenly risen. Where could she even begin? 'I have news.'

'Hm?'

'A couple of months ago . . .' Phoenix did a quick calculation in her head. Yes, it really had been at least that long since she and Jac had last spoken. Her mother was an unsentimental type and was always 'extremely busy'. In general, Jac considered phone calls a waste of time, something that took her away from her work. An occasional perfunctory text was considered enough communication from her only child. Phoenix took a deep breath and continued. 'I had a bit of a collapse at school.'

'What sort of collapse?' her mother asked, with a note of trepidation that suggested there were a variety of collapses to be had but only some of them were acceptable. 'Oh no. You're pregnant.'

'What? No.' Phoenix's sentimental emotions evaporated with her instant irritation.

'Then what?' her mother prompted.

Phoenix inhaled and let it out heavily. 'I couldn't cope any more, I guess, and I couldn't stop crying.'

'Oh, Phoenix,' her mother said, as if her daughter had come home with an impromptu tongue piercing.

'The short of it is that I've been formally, officially identified as autistic.' Phoenix's heart tap-danced in her chest. She really had no idea how her mother would respond to this. She had read many accounts of people's parents and family members reacting badly to the news. She had a few key dot points stored in her mind, ready to offer as insight. She was prepared for anger, denial, shock and dismissiveness.

'Oh, this again,' her mother said, sighing.

Okay, she hadn't been prepared for *that*. 'Wait, what do you mean *again*?' She heard the paper tip of a cigarette crinkle as it ignited, the pause, then the heavy exhalation of her mother's first soothing drag.

'They were on about it when you were three.'

'Three! Who?'

'The doctor, and some other guy he sent me to see. They were awful, in my opinion. So you liked to twirl. So what? Twirling is fun! Twirling is self-expression. Twirling is dancing. Twirling is feeling the symphony of the earth's soul in your body—'

'Yeah, okay, I get it. I twirled. *A lot.*'

'Sweetheart, you sound angry,' her mother observed, genuinely perplexed by her daughter's outraged tone.

Phoenix rubbed at her forehead. 'I don't even know where to start with this. You had this information from the beginning and you never told me.'

'But what difference would it have made? Why would I want you to stop twirling? It made you so happy.' She chuckled at the memory. 'You especially liked to twirl with the neighbour's gosling in your arms. The dear thing seemed to love it too and would honk and flap its little wings when it saw you coming. You two made quite the dancing pair.'

'Goose twirling,' Phoenix muttered, trying to conjure a memory to match this testimony.

'Yes! It was who you were, as a person. Do you know how rare it is for someone to know themselves so clearly at such a young age? I wasn't going to saddle you with a label for the rest of your life.'

A label. Phoenix thought of all the labels Lily had been given in her life – stupid, retarded, weird, embarrassing, *wrong*. Phoenix had been called most of those things herself at one time or another. They'd both been saddled with labels anyway, whether they'd wanted them or not, and they'd all been incorrect, painful and unnecessary. There was only one word Phoenix had needed in her life, one word that could have opened the door to a rich culture, to history, language, identity, belonging and most importantly, to healing.

Autistic. It wasn't a dirty word.

Jac continued. 'If left alone, a child will show you their innate knowing of who they are. I wasn't going to put you in therapy to stop you twirling. What nonsense! You already knew exactly who you were.'

Phoenix's mouth was open and she made herself close it, inhaling a steadying breath. A lifetime of feeling like an alien who had landed on the wrong planet tumbled through her mind. A lifetime of always being two steps behind. A lifetime of not knowing why friendships ended. A lifetime of wondering why she was so sensitive to everything – clothes, foods, sounds, light, smells, shopping centres, parties, noise of every kind. A lifetime of wondering why everything seemed so difficult all the time. A lifetime of being exhausted and not able to keep up with everyone else. A lifetime of being even more vulnerable than most women already were. 'But I didn't, Mum. I didn't know myself at all.'

21

Linus the alpaca was relieved to be out of the float. He wandered through his overnight agistment paddock with his nose to the ground, sniffing and snorting, wagging his little tail. Then he buckled, forelegs to the ground, and rolled and rolled and rolled. His awful shaggy coat was near black now. Rita took the hint and did the same and when they both finally got back to their feet and shook all over with satisfied grunts, they had matching hairdos festooned with straw.

'Is it just me, or does Linus look as though he's put on weight in the past two days?'

'To be certain, I do not feel qualified to offer an opinion as we have only recently become acquainted,' Lily said. Phoenix was relieved to hear her voice returning to her chosen identity, the one that empowered her. 'I will unburden him of that dreadful coat tomorrow morning. His eyes are bright and he looks strong. I would suggest he is only young.'

Phoenix hadn't thought about the lifetime they would share, hadn't thought about it much for any of the animals. 'How long do they live for?'

Lily murmured and narrowed her eyes, thinking. 'I presume it is into the high teens. Fifteen to twenty years, perhaps.'

'So about as long as my own child would live with me, if I had one.'

Lily giggled, unexpectedly. 'Exactly.'

Phoenix let this sink in. Where would she be in fifteen years' time? She'd be *fifty*, for one. Would she still be teaching? Or was all this the beginning of a whole new way of life?

Their Airbnb house was on the northern side of the Murrumbidgee River in Wagga Wagga. It was a low-set rendered brick abode with three bedrooms and a garden, and dogs were allowed to stay too, though Phoenix hadn't confessed to the rest of the animals she had with her. The house turned out to be quite close to the neighbours, which unnerved her. She'd been hoping to let the chickens and ducks have free range in the garden. Still, there'd been no sign of the neighbours yet and this entire trip had been about taking risks, so she took the chance and released the flock to forage. Humphrey stretched out in a long spot of afternoon light to snooze in peace now that the van was no longer rumbling beneath him.

Both Phoenix and Lily were desperate for long showers, hair washes, teeth cleaning that didn't involve relying on bottled water, and fresh clothes. While Lily was in the bathroom, Phoenix let out the mature cats to have the run of the main areas. Milo could then have a bedroom to himself, with Jane staying in her crate nearby.

The injured kitten meowed plaintively, not understanding why she was still locked up, and Phoenix sat with her, rubbing her chin and singing to her. At last, Jane settled and began to purr.

206

Phoenix strode into the living room as Lily emerged from the shower. The sight of her made Phoenix smile. Lily was wearing an outfit Phoenix hadn't seen before, a new steampunk ensemble with an increased level of sass. On her top half she wore a high-necked, short-sleeved, black tunic shirt, with an oval of white at her chest and the black silhouette of a woman's head, the kind seen on antique cameo brooches. A brown belt wrapped around her underbust corset. On her legs, she wore what looked to be black faux leather riding breeches, with her usual brown boots below. On her head, she wore a black square hat with driving goggles snug around its girth.

'You look amazing,' Phoenix said.

Lily's cheeks coloured. 'I needed to rid my person of those clothes I so wrongly pilfered while I was away in the bush,' she said. 'They are not my style.'

Phoenix quite agreed.

'They were once my fashion, when I laboured on the estate with my parents. But after I saw my papa chop the head off my most beloved duck, I never wished to be witness or accomplice to such brutality again.'

'Well, I am in awe of your style. You've got such flair, such vision, a touch of brilliance I could only dream of,' she said, gesturing to her own jeans and filthy shirt.

'I could assist you, if you would like,' Lily said, her eyes alight. 'I love reimagining things. But, of course, there is not anything incorrect or unsatisfactory with you or how you dress now!'

Phoenix laughed, knowing full well that she could use some help. She had a standard work wardrobe – natural fibres preferably, nothing scratchy, nothing tight, nothing short-sleeved, nothing firm around her waist, tinted moisturiser and eyebrow pencil only. A simple tie in her hair, worn up in a bun, always, because having hair around her face bothered her, but she also didn't enjoy short hair. No bangles or bracelets that made noises on the desk. Natural deodorant. No perfumes or hairspray. Nothing fussy. No dresses – nothing she couldn't trip over in without flashing her students (because she tripped over a lot). But other than her small wardrobe of school clothes on high rotation (at least these days minimalism was in), she put little thought into her clothes other than that they were comfortable.

'It's okay,' she assured Lily. 'I know my style is basically "no style". I find it tricky with all my sensory issues to find something that's not distracting me every minute of the day.'

'I can be of help, truly,' Lily said, gazing up and down Phoenix's body with an artist's eye.

'Okay, one day, after we're off the road, let's do it.'

'Really?' Lily beamed, truly beamed, for the first time since they'd met.

'Absolutely.'

Lily put her washing on and Phoenix showered and changed clothes, pulling her wet hair up in a bun. They headed outside to check on the poultry, and by good fortune they unearthed a blue clam-shaped wading pool.

They released the ducks into the pool in a delightful cacophony of quacking and flapping wings that beat powerfully at the air.

'Can they fly away?' Phoenix was suddenly worried. She had visions of chasing them down off rooftops and washing lines.

'No. They have been bred to be too heavy to fly far off the ground,' Lily said.

Humphrey trotted over and began to circle them, nosing at their wagging tails. 'Do you think he wants to eat them?' Phoenix asked.

'I am inclined to believe he favours to round them up,' Lily said. 'He is a border collie. It is his birthright.'

They spent several pleasant minutes discussing the amazing way certain breeds of dog just seemed to *know* what centuries of selected breeding had prepared them to do. Border collies rounded up sheep; retrievers retrieved, well, almost anything; Alsatians guarded people; Maremmas guarded flocks of chickens and rookeries of endangered penguins; and bloodhounds tracked and sniffed. They were beginning to wonder what poodles were supposed to do when they were startled by a voice.

'Hey there!'

A young woman about Lily's age, Phoenix guessed, had come to the gate carrying a shopping bag. She grinned at them and waved with her free hand. Carefree as she pleased, she opened the gate with a metallic click and Humphrey stopped fussing with the ducks, raised his hackles, and growled.

'Oh, hey theeeere,' the woman crooned to him, not perturbed in the slightest by his bravado as she crossed the grass towards them. She smiled at the chickens and her eyes opened wide with delight at the ducks. She wore pale tattered jeans with iron-on patches of suns and rainbows and kittens. Her short, wild curls shone bright red in the sun, and freckles blanketed her cheeks and nose. Her shirt was a shiny, glittery red.

Phoenix rose to her feet, Lily a second behind her. 'Hi,' Phoenix said, her mind racing to work out who this could be.

'Hi, I'm Talia.' She waved and a leather bracelet with a silver dolphin jangled as she did so. 'My parents own this place,' she explained.

'Oh.' Phoenix immediately began to panic. What must this girl be thinking about their ducks and chickens?

'I love your ducks,' Talia squealed, and bounced up and down. 'I've always wanted some but the 'rents would never let me 'cause of the poo. They're big pooers. Make lots of mess. We have a pool. Mum swears they'd end up in the pool somehow and it would be ruined forever. She's probably right.' Talia cackled with laughter. 'It would probably be me that put them there.' She laughed again and slapped her thigh.

Beside Phoenix, Lily was still and silent, and wide-eyed at this vibrant visitor. But if she wasn't mistaken, Lily also seemed rather awestruck.

'But how could you not?!' Talia went on. 'Look at them! They're adorable. Look at their eyes, their wobbly backsides, how much they're loving this water! Why wouldn't you let them enjoy a pool party? Honestly, who would eat these gorgeous creatures?' she said.

'Not me,' Lily said, her enthusiasm to connect with this stranger taking Phoenix by surprise.

Talia's eyes sparkled as she gazed up from where she was crouched beside the pool, splashing the nearest duck with water. 'Are you vegan?'

'Yes.'

'Me too!' she enthused and stood up.

'I wouldn't eat duck either,' Phoenix said.

'Are *you* vegan?' Talia turned to Phoenix.

Phoenix thought the girl might actually jump into her arms if she said she was. 'Ah, no – I don't eat much meat but I would never eat duck.' Her words trailed off. Talia had grown bored already and turned her attention back to Lily as she quizzed her about her favourite plant proteins and so on.

'Um, sorry to interrupt,' Phoenix said, chewing her lip with anxiety. 'I'm wondering if the bag is for us?'

'Oh, yeah,' Talia said, thrusting the bag at Phoenix. 'Mum asked me to drop it over. She forgot to leave you dishwashing detergent and extra loo rolls.' She rolled her eyes.

'Okay, thanks.' Phoenix took the bag.

Talia was standing quite close to Lily now, close enough that Phoenix felt the need to step back to give them space.

'I love this outfit,' Talia said, giving fairy claps and enthusiastic bounces.

'You should know that I am an autist,' Lily blurted, suddenly, lifting her chin – she'd patently had an absolute gutful of being judged and abused for one day and was challenging Talia to accept her exactly as she was before she invested any more time into this conversation. Phoenix applauded internally.

'Oh, what kind?' Talia asked, curious.

'What?' Lily and Phoenix said at the same time.

Talia ignored Phoenix, directing her gaze and words at Lily. 'Painter, potter . . . oooh, street art?' She gestured to Lily's clothes.

Lily shook her head. 'No, not an artist, an *autist*.'

'Ohhhh!' Talia slapped her head, then frowned. 'Is that in Texas?'

'I do not understand.' Lily looked irritated, yet Phoenix could see a trembling smile tugging at the corners of her lips.

'Or one of those Midwest states?'

Lily laughed, a proper laugh that came from inside her chest, a laugh that gathered energy, a tonic for the trauma of earlier in the day. But a second later, she covered her mouth in horror, then held out her hands, appeasing. 'I must apologise. Please, accept my remorse. I did not mean to laugh. I was not laughing *at* you. It is most upsetting to be laughed at, I should certainly know, it was only—'

Talia screeched with laughter and slapped Lily lightly on the arm. 'Stop it! You're adorable!'

'Excuse me, I might go and . . .' Phoenix indicated over her shoulder to the house, but neither Talia nor Lily acknowledged her departure. Phoenix knew where she wasn't wanted, and in this case, the knowledge made her smile.

Two hours later, after Talia and Lily had been talking and playing with the animals, and Phoenix had been planning out the rest of their journey home, they ordered gluten-free vegan pizzas to be delivered for dinner. They flipped open the cardboard boxes at the dining table, while Marilyn and Audrey headbutted their legs. Their raucous purring left no doubt as to what they wanted.

'If we can do a slightly longer trip tomorrow,' Phoenix said, tossing a pizza crust to Humphrey, who caught it midair with a crocodile snap, 'then we should be able to make it to Brisbane in four days.' That would leave Phoenix less time than she'd like to settle and recover before starting school again, but it was the best she could do. 'We're heading a little further inland than is ideal but I'm limited by the horse agistment on offer along the way.'

'Which towns are in your itinerary?' Talia asked, taking a fourth slice.

'Tomorrow, we head to Young, which should take a couple of hours, break there, then on to Dubbo, which is over three hours, unfortunately. It will be our biggest leg yet, other than the ferry crossing.' She and Lily both shuddered at the memory of that awful night.

'Dubbo, hey,' Talia said, licking several fingers, one at a time, much the way the cats washed each toe.

'After that, we'll head to Tamworth, then Tenterfield and finally land in Samford on Wednesday, where I've found a paddock for Rita and Linus.'

Lily was quiet, though Phoenix thought she had probably used up a lot of words in the hours chatting with Talia, who could talk for all of them at once.

'Hold on,' Talia said, pulling her phone from her pocket. Her fingers moved rapidly over the screen, while Phoenix began to clear plates and pizza boxes. For many long minutes, Talia frowned, tsked, smiled, nodded, shook her head and finally fist-pumped the air. 'Yes,' she hissed. She looked up, a huge smile on her flushed face.

'I'm coming with you,' she announced.

22

They sheared Linus early in the morning, Lily working method-
ically and expertly. Even though he was sensitive over his bony
areas, he remained stoic, flinching and side-eyeing Lily, but
holding his ground. She praised him and guided him through
the long process. It was tough going and she had to stop often to
allow Phoenix to cut through the worst of tangles and matting that
were pulling painfully at the alpaca's coat. After they'd found their
groove, Lily cleared her throat, and spoke.

'I have been meaning to ask you about something,' she said, her
eyes on the clippers and wool.

'Sure thing.'

'That night when Bianca broke off our attachment and I was
quite wretched, you said even you had been taken advantage of,
and I am curious to know what you meant by that.'

Phoenix reached out and rubbed Rita behind her ear, making
her lean into her hand and grunt with pleasure. 'My first serious
relationship wasn't good,' she said, dragging up old memories.

'We both worked in the same department store. I would come home after a shift and he'd be waiting for me on the verandah. Mum was away a lot but kept paying the rent so I could go to uni and she had a home base to come back to between gigs.

'He totally love-bombed me. He kept telling me I was exactly what he needed, that I was so different from anyone he'd ever met before. He'd recently broken up with someone and said he shouldn't be jumping into something so soon, but he simply couldn't stay away because I was so special. He brought me gifts, flowers. He wanted to be with me all the time. He got what he wanted, but the moment I was truly invested in us, he stopped answering my calls.

'I heard he'd taken up with another girl from our store and a day later at a work gathering he was there with her, entwined on the couch in front of everyone. I fell mute, watching from the shadows. I was heartbroken. When I confronted him, he told me I had it all wrong, that we were never really going out in the first place.'

'A disgraceful gaslighter,' Lily muttered.

'He made me feel like I was crazy, that I'd imagined it all – but *he* had driven all of it.' Even now, the memory burned. 'So, yeah,' she smiled, weakly, 'you're not the only one.'

Lily nodded. 'Thank you for sharing your story. I am sorry he was so cruel.' They continued shearing in silence, each with her own thoughts, till Linus was finally free of the enormous weight he'd been carrying around, a weight that had been left on him entirely by someone else. Phoenix breathed deeply at the sight of the last blobs of wool hitting the ground.

'There you go, Linus. I promise you, you're going to be okay.'

Lily drove the zebra van to Young, Talia following them in her small Honda hatchback, the colour of which nearly matched Humphrey's dark coat completely. Although Phoenix had been uncomfortable with Talia following them for 'something to do' on her holidays from uni, and although it seemed odd and convenient that Talia had 'always wanted to head to Brisbane', she couldn't really come up with any good reason why she should protest. Talia was making the journey under her own steam. She was young, hadn't had her licence long, and it was surely safer for her to follow in convoy than attempt that long drive alone. Yet Phoenix's instincts prickled.

When Talia arrived as planned to join their journey, she wasn't alone at all, confirming Phoenix's instinct that something was up. She had brought her friend, Jordan, along. Where Talia's attire screamed 'cute kittens and fairy floss', Jordan wore black jeans and a black shirt with red, bloodlike writing that splashed *Anarchy*. Apparently, Jordan was also looking for something to do on the holidays and had, amazingly, always wanted to visit Brisbane.

Phoenix was about to voice her concerns to Lily when her phone pinged with a message from Zack. Her delight was short-lived, however, when she saw the contents of his message. It was a photo of an article in today's newspaper, this one presenting the 'other side of the story', featuring Evelyn Godfrey. The headline alone made her want to vomit.

Principal Keeps Watch Over Autistic Teacher

Veteran principal Evelyn Godfrey has defended her actions to supervise an autistic teacher if she returns to her role at St Clementine's Girls School. 'My job is to ensure that this school and every teacher in it is offering the highest level of education to our students at all times.'

The teacher in question, Phoenix Rose, has complained that Ms Godfrey undermined the success of her return with a comprehensive return-to-work plan and threatened Ms Rose by saying she would 'be watching her'.

'Naturally I would be watching her closely,' Ms Godfrey says. 'Any teacher who has had a mental health event while on duty would be closely supervised upon their return. I make no apologies for running my school in a hands-on way. We expect excellence from our students and we expect it from our teachers too. Ms Rose has a condition that may affect her work. What else am I supposed to do? Our students deserve better.'

Chair of St Clementine's P&C, Mr Robert Kendall, said he gave his full support to Ms Godfrey in her role of acting principal. 'The reality is that students in a mainstream school deserve better than mentally impaired teachers. Maybe a teacher like that has a role in a special school but in my opinion a school like ours deserves the best of the best.'

Phoenix's hands trembled so much she had to shove them into her armpits and wrap herself tightly. There was a high-pitched ringing in her ears. She closed her eyes against the landscape whizzing past the windows of the van, forcing herself to take in slow breaths.

She had been labelled mentally impaired in a major newspaper, and thanks to the internet, news was no longer something that was here one day and gone the next. That incorrect statement would live on in cyberspace forever. The moment a student or parent searched her name, there it would be. The implication was that she lacked capability to do her job, and such a falsehood could impact her professional life forever.

In and of itself, autism was not a mental illness; it was a neurological difference. It was about the way her entire body processed information. Some autistic people also had intellectual impairments, but she did not. But she doubted Evelyn or Mr P&C could care less about that difference. They'd made up their minds about her without even knowing the facts, never once having asked her

216

what she needed from them to continue her career. She wasn't too proud to admit that she needed support for some things in her life, but her teaching ability was not one of them. It never had been.

She was weary to the bone.

They arrived in the cherry capital of Australia in time for lunch at S&AJ cafe. Distressed wooden floor boards, black light fittings and green plants greeted them. Its vegan options were the drawcard for them, but it was the incredible coffee art that arrived on Phoenix's much-needed flat white that helped lift her spirits. The barista had created an intricate artwork of a cherry tree, dark trunk and bright pink flowers growing out of toffee-coloured earth. She decided immediately to order a second to see what else she might get, cheered by the joyful creativity. For a fleeting moment she considered quitting her job immediately and becoming a barista, simply to make such amazing images. The reality was, though, that the ear-splitting banging, grinding and milk frothing would break her on her first day. Shame.

Talia and Jordan talked nonstop about a movie they'd watched and how it had changed their world and would eventually change everyone's mind about eating animals. Phoenix tried her best to tune them out, not because she was unsympathetic or even necessarily in disagreement, but because she had no emotional reserves left to process the images their descriptions created in her mind. She excused herself to head outside and check on the animals, collecting Humphrey to stretch his legs.

They wandered slowly along the wide streets of Young, past old brick buildings and the blue clock tower of the town hall. An expansive sky stretched above. She allowed Humphrey to take his time to sniff the posts as much as he sniffed the air. He often looked up at her as if checking she was still there, assuring himself he was doing okay. She felt that maybe they were approaching, if not friendship, then a mutual understanding. Her heart lifted. He needed her and, right now, after reading that newspaper article, she needed his reassuring presence too.

Back at the cafe, Humphrey still at her side, she found Lily, Talia and Jordan gathered on the footpath, waiting for her, and to her surprise they had been joined by two others. The young woman wore flannel, had spiky green hair and an eyebrow ring, while the young man wore a faded blue tee and ripped jeans.

'Sup?' he greeted her with a tilt of his head. The young woman beside him said nothing.

'Hi,' Phoenix said, uncertainly, looking from one to the other, waiting for some sort of explanation.

'Great, you're here,' Talia said, with the air of one who had taken charge of the itinerary. 'Just in time.'

Phoenix was about to ask her what she was just in time for, given that this was, by all accounts, her road trip, but Talia clapped her hands and announced to everyone that it was 'time to get moving'.

Phoenix clamped her jaw shut, clenching her teeth till they hurt.

'Who are those people?' she hissed at Lily as her companion climbed into the passenger seat of the van and Phoenix checked her mirrors and mentally gave herself a pep talk about her towing capabilities.

Lily shrugged. 'I swear I do not know. We were finishing our most wonderful meal when Talia received correspondence on her phone and the very next thing we were gathering our belongings and meeting Sale and Morgan at the front of the establishment.' Lily sounded confused and possibly a little hurt.

'Sale? What sort of name is that?' Phoenix muttered, pulling the van and float out slowly into the street. 'And is that the boy or the girl?'

'The young man, I believe. Morgan is the young lady.'

Phoenix drove on in silence for some time, waiting for her choppy feelings to settle. Why were they being followed by four people? Because that was what it felt like – not like they'd made friends with fellow travellers on the road, but like they were being used, somehow. She decided to voice her concerns to Lily, as carefully as she could.

'I need to say that I'm feeling uneasy with this group of people following us,' she said, and left it at that.

After several long moments of silence, in which Phoenix had decided Lily must surely be offended and was not going to respond to her, Lily said, 'I think I feel the same.'

Phoenix let out a sigh of relief. 'It's like their energy is off, somehow.'

'I quite agree and I feel most befuddled, because Talia appeared to genuinely favour me and we got along really well. She claims she has a cousin in Brisbane and I have no reason to disbelieve that, but I feel as though she was one sort of person when she was having dinner with us but now, I do not know. She is different.'

'I think it's good to trust your instincts,' Phoenix said, carefully. 'Obviously I don't know anything about them so I can't say for sure what is wrong, if indeed anything is wrong, but I do know we need to listen to our inner voices.'

Lily wiped a knuckle under her eye and nodded and Phoenix felt deep regret for her. It could be so very difficult for auties to make friends. So many times, Phoenix had thought she'd made a connection with someone – a teacher at school, a fellow participant at a weekly yoga class, even one of Zack's cousins – but then they'd made it to the part when they 'caught up for coffee' and they met up, drank the coffee, they talked easily and Phoenix thought it had gone well, and hope rose like a helium balloon racing for the clouds. She was sure she'd made a friend.

And then, nothing. It went nowhere and a familiar creeping shame seeped along her veins. She'd misread the situation, or got it all wrong, or she'd somehow scared the new friend away. Perhaps she'd shared too much, gone too deep too fast, because going deep was the only way she knew how to be authentic. Surface-skimming small talk was tedious and difficult but authentic thoughts and feelings were meaningful.

Poor Lily had been dumped unceremoniously by Bianca and days later she'd been showered with affection and praise by a vivacious young woman who'd enjoyed her company so much she'd packed up to follow her, only to pivot to other friends and bring them into a circle they'd never been invited into. Lily hadn't been enough for Talia. It was a sick, cold feeling, and Phoenix knew it well.

'If you would like me to,' Phoenix began, 'when we get to Dubbo, I can tell them we need to continue alone.'

'What possible reason could you offer them that will not cause offence?' Lily asked.

'I have no idea. But you are my friend and a much higher priority to me than whether I upset them. This is what friends do – we help each other.'

Lily smiled. 'Thank you. I am honoured to be your friend.'

It took over three hours to get to Dubbo, with Phoenix and Lily swapping driving halfway. The cats hadn't stopped vocalising their displeasure nearly the entire time and the van felt stuffy and smelt of duck poo. So it was with much relief that they arrived at their accommodation at half-past five to find a converted iron shed with no neighbours in sight. It was deeply quiet. This place wasn't the loveliest option Phoenix could have chosen but it had the added benefit of being on acreage with a small but securely fenced paddock.

Before they'd even finished unloading the animals, Talia's car pulled in to the driveway. Phoenix gave Lily a reassuring smile and commanded her brain to think of something both tactful and effective to say to Talia that would have her stop following them. Instead, though, Talia hopped out of the car from the passenger side, closed it firmly and waved goodbye. Phoenix watched in shock as the dark car motored away, leaving Talia standing in the driveway, stretching her arms and legs.

Leaving Phoenix no time to reconfigure her plan to break up with Talia and her friends, the young woman approached them confidently, beaming a smile.

'Hey, Lils,' she said, ignoring Phoenix. 'I asked the guys to drop me here while they head into town for supplies. I was feeling really bad that we hadn't had any time to hang together today, what with all the driving and all the sudden enthusiasm from everyone to come on a road trip.' She tinkled laughter. 'That all got out of hand really quickly, didn't it?'

'It was a surprise,' Lily admitted, her arms tight across her navy corset. She scuffed at the ground with her boot.

'I've been low-key stressed all day about not being able to hang,' she said, arching her back now to stretch some more. 'Man, long drives are tough! My neck's like a corkscrew.'

Phoenix put a cat cage on the ground. Jane and Milo stuck their paws through the bars and meowed. 'Where are you all staying the night?' she asked, nervous the answer was going to involve this place.

'Don't worry, we're not crashing on you. We're saving money and taking turns sleeping in the car,' Talia said, making Phoenix feel both relieved and guilty that her reluctance to welcome them with open arms was so obvious. Talia moved towards the van. 'Here, let me help you unload all your fur babies.' With that, she jumped into the back of the van.

Phoenix's gaze met Lily's. Lily shrugged, helplessly. Phoenix felt defeated by the fact that Talia was there and she couldn't send her away because her car was not. She was too exhausted to speak any more, so she continued to unload and settle the animals while Lily made conversation with Talia. She led Rita and Linus into the paddock, deposited cats in bedrooms, poultry in the bathroom and Humphrey in the lounge, fed and medicated them all, addressed the need for fresh cat litter and puppy pads, issued clean water and checked Jane's bandage. Her limbs were weighted with wet sand. She was teary, again, devastated by the morning's newspaper article, utterly drained by the endless decision-making this trip was forcing her to do, and physically burning with the pain of sleep deprivation, bad beds, drinking water that smelt and tasted different in every place they stopped, unreliable and not always nourishing food, endless driving and hauling around animal cages. She honestly couldn't take one more step. What she needed was half an hour of sensory deprivation to try to reset her mind and body and refresh herself, before even trying to think about food and dealing with Talia and her friends, let alone that newspaper article.

As Talia and Lily made cups of tea, Phoenix wrapped on her eye mask, inserted her earplugs, and burrowed under as many coverlets and quilts as she could to at least try to recreate her much-missed weighted blanket from home. Slowly, her jangling nerves and pounding heart began to calm.

Almost three hours later she awoke to a dark house. Lily was gone.

23

Phoenix felt as though she spent twenty per cent of her life looking for lost things – her keys, her wallet, her shoes, the last place she put down her coffee mug, the nail scissors, and of course her mobile phone, which seemed to very much live up to its adjective. It was this wandering phone that she was hunting for now, in between working out which switches in the unfamiliar house turned on which lights, repeatedly bumping her knees and kicking her toes into corners as she fumbled for them.

'Think, Phoenix,' she commanded herself.

Marilyn approached and slinked her way around her legs, purring hopefully. Phoenix picked her up to cuddle, rubbing her cheek across Marilyn's soft head while she tried to retrace her steps. Maybe she'd left it in the van? She kissed Marilyn and put her gently back on the ground then headed out the front door. She rummaged through the front cabin by the van's weak interior light, shoving her hand down backs of seats and into all manner of nooks and crannies and was finally rewarded when her fingers snagged the device where it was jammed hard and deep between the driver's seat and the console. As she'd hoped, there was a message from Lily.

> I have accepted an invitation
> to dine with Talia and the
> others. I ventured to invite
> you too but you were deeply
> asleep and I could not wake
> you. Talia will return me later. L

Okay, great. I'm up now. Have fun.

She headed back to the house. Maybe she'd been too quick to judge Talia. She truly did seem to like Lily. Maybe Talia hadn't yet worked out that her companions may not be true friends.

Relieved to have found her phone and to know where Lily was (sort of, if 'out' was any kind of clue in a strange town), she committed herself to finding something halfway decent to eat for dinner. A Thai stir fry delivered to her door wasn't quite what she was looking for – it was a bit greasy – but at least it had vegetables. She and Zack ate together via FaceTime on their phones and her mood continued to improve, having him nearby.

'We could sue that guy for defamation for saying you're intellectually impaired,' Zack growled after swallowing a mouthful of his mum's boiled chicken and cabbage in spiced coconut cream.

'Probably,' Phoenix said, noncommittal. It would take a lot of money to sue the P&C president, money they needed to buy a house, rather than being tied up for years in a lengthy and possibly unsuccessful legal battle. And then there was the stress of it all. She didn't have the bandwidth to get past getting home to Zack and going back to school. Whatever way the next few days played out, she was determined not to lose her job. That was her baseline. Anything else was a bonus.

'Can we Netflix something together?' she suggested as Audrey leapt into her lap and thrust her nose into her empty bowl to lick the sauce. Phoenix lifted her out of the bowl and carried it to the sink while Zack listed off a few possibilities. 'Something happy,' she called from the kitchen sink.

'Movie or episodes?'

'Let's go with episodes.'

After a lengthy discussion of what to watch, they decided on *Frasier*. Phoenix settled herself on the couch, the cats both jumping up to lie with her, Audrey settling her weight in her lap, forcing Marilyn to curl at Phoenix's feet.

Frasier was the perfect antidote to a difficult week and an upsetting day. She and Zack laughed, properly laughed, over and over again.

'I love that they're psychiatrists and yet they're so messed up,' Phoenix chuckled, her skin singing with happy chemicals from so much giggling.

'Niles is my favourite,' Zack said, as he always did. 'But they're all brilliant. Even the dog.'

They watched four episodes together until Zack's yawns started to run together and Phoenix told him he really should get to bed, as he had to be up for work tomorrow. 'Any news on when you find out about your job application?' she asked.

'Possibly tomorrow,' he said, yawning again.

'That's exciting.'

'Maybe.'

'I believe in you,' she said, her longing to be back by his side suddenly billowing out like a bedsheet on the washing line, caught in the breeze. 'I wish I could give you a big hug.'

He smiled sleepily at her, his hair even more voluminous from

where he'd been rubbing at it while relaxing and watching *Frasier.*
'Me too. Not long now, though.'

Audrey took the moment to headbutt the phone screen. 'Audrey
wishes you good luck too,' Phoenix said.

'Appreciated, Auds.'

After a lengthy collection of soppy goodbyes between them all,
Zack ended the call. Phoenix sat for a moment, stroking Audrey
under the chin while she purred and drooled happily. It was nearly
midnight. She hadn't realised it was so late. Her long afternoon
sleep had given her a boost of energy and altered her sense of time.

Where was Lily? Surely she should have been back by now.

> Hey, just checking you're
> okay? Do you know when
> you'll be back?

Phoenix stayed where she was, the phone in her hand, hoping
for an immediate reply. She couldn't imagine Lily was much of
a nightclubbing person and she certainly couldn't imagine much
of anything would be open in Dubbo at this time on a Sunday
night. Her flickers of anxiety began to gather strength. She pushed
Audrey gently off her and carefully pulled her feet out from under
Marilyn, rising from the couch in order to pace. Lily was twenty. It
wasn't unusual for a twenty-year-old to be out late with friends. But
Lily wasn't usual, and only today she'd confessed to feeling uneasy
with the others. Maybe they'd decided to get some beers and head
out to drink somewhere? But then who was driving? Maybe they'd
designated Lily as the driver and she was stuck, waiting for them.
Then why hadn't she answered her phone?

For a moment, anxiety flared. This was an all-too-familiar
feeling. Lily had left Phoenix once before, gone for two whole
nights and days with no word and no messages of reassurance

she was coming back at all. If she'd decided to disappear again, where did that leave Phoenix? She simply could not lose any more time on this trip. She *had* to get home. Her career depended on it.

Then her phone lit up.

> I need help. Can you come?
> Explain later. I will drop a pin
> so you can find me. Leave
> the float behind. The road is
> rough.

Heart thumping, Phoenix pulled on her shoes, grabbed her backpack, got the house keys and headed to the door. Her hurrying around had alerted Humphrey, who was sitting up on his bed, watching her. She was about to leave, then paused. Should she take him? She had no idea what she was walking into and the dog had proved he could deter people when he wanted, like the guy outside the pub in Jerilderie. At the same time, his barking could be problematic, like the night she and Lily had been in the van and that truck had skidded to a stop next to them. They'd wanted him to be quiet in that moment. Should she take him?

She groaned in frustration. 'Sorry, boy. I think you should stay here.' She closed the door behind her, locking it, hoping she'd made the right choice.

She unhitched the float, working through the photos she'd taken during Bruno's lessons. It was difficult in the dark, but she got it done. Climbing into the driver's seat, she turned the key in the ignition. The van clicked, clicked, clicked. 'Come on, van, don't let me down now.' She turned the key again and it shuddered to life. 'Good van!'

She skidded out of the drive, checked herself, took a breath, and continued. The sat nav directed her towards and through bushland, but as it was midnight and dark out, there was very little to see. The headlights offered a short tunnel of illumination but they could only reach so far as the van gobbled up bitumen below. She worried a kangaroo might bounce out of the bush at any moment or a tawny frogmouth might swoop into her windscreen. A tyre could blow, leaving her stranded and alone as well as Lily, with no way for them to reach each other.

The absolute pitch darkness could swallow her whole, not a trace left behind. If she did make it to Lily, there was trouble that needed to be sorted, whatever it was. Phoenix's highly visual, overly active mind came up with dozens of potential scenarios, each one worse than the last.

'Breathe, Phoenix,' she instructed herself. 'Just breathe.'

Closer to her destination, she saw lights in the distance. There was so much light, in fact, that it looked like a small city was awake in the middle of the dark bush, casting a solid haze across the horizon. The navigation commanded her to drive past it, and she saw that it was a factory of some sort, set a long way back from the road. Floodlights, like she imagined would shine on a prison yard during a breakout, illuminated huge, white, windowless buildings squatting on the ground, a few storeys high at least. Its brightness made the adjacent darkness seem that much darker. She couldn't pick out any details. Couldn't see any signs.

Monstrous towers belched acrid, putrid smoke, which seeped into the van despite Phoenix having the 'recirculating' option chosen on the dashboard. It was utterly vile and overwhelmed her. She held her breath till she was woozy then gulped small mouthfuls of air only when desperate.

Finally, she could turn off down another road, leaving the awful factory behind. Two police cars whizzed by, their lights flashing, and the sight of them further heightened her nerves. Something bad was in the air and it wasn't just that hideous smoke. She locked the doors. The van's wheels rumbled and crunched over the unsealed road, surrounded by forest. No streetlights. No houses.

'Lily, what are you doing out here?' she muttered. Was she being held against her will somewhere? She had given her an address at a corner of two roads and Phoenix couldn't possibly fathom why. Was she there alone, standing out in the open, waiting for Phoenix to get her? Had the others dumped her there as a practical joke, or something more sinister?

She arrived at the pin's location, a T-junction, and slowed to a stop. Her headlights speared through the darkness into a paddock full of grass as tall as herself, bordered by barbed wire. She waited, wondering if she should proceed and look for Lily, or if she should cut the engine and simply wait. But the idea of turning off the engine, especially after its reluctance to start, was unappealing. She couldn't turn her lights off, either. Those lights, her locked doors and the phone at the ready were the only things keeping her together right now.

A minute went by. Maybe two. She wished she had Humphrey now. She was about to turn down the new road, to inch along it slowly, looking for clues, but paused. Headlights had appeared, coming closer. She waited, counting, for no other reason than it gave her mind something to do. She used to count things all the time when she was younger. Right now, she counted heartbeats.

The car came to a stop on a grassy verge and extinguished its lights. It was a small dark car – Talia's. The van's headlights illuminated Lily in the driver's seat, alone. She got out and rushed towards the van, clutching something to her chest. There was blood on her arm.

24

Lily leapt into the car, the bundle still pressed to her chest.

'What is—'

'Drive!' Lily ordered.

A thousand questions ran through Phoenix's mind but she clamped them down. They had to get out of here.

'We must locate a veterinarian, with great haste.' Lily unveiled a bleeding animal in her arms and fished in her pocket for her phone.

'A pig?!'

'A mere infant,' Lily muttered.

'What's happened? Where are the others?'

But Lily was calling for a vet and didn't reply. Phoenix turned back down the road she'd arrived by. They'd have to return to how they'd ended up in this situation later.

Having located a vet, Lily entered the address into her phone and the GPS directed them to head back past that awful factory. Phoenix turned off the unsealed road. 'You should know there's some sort of hideous factory coming up,' she said, wanting to give Lily warning. 'The smell is unbelievable.'

'It is the abattoir.'

'Ugh. That explains the smell.' Phoenix's stomach turned in anticipation of having to endure it again. Then, a thought. 'Is this piglet something to do with the abattoir?'

'Yes.'

'Lily! What's happened?' Her companion gazed in shock at the animal in her arms. He was very still and quiet, and Phoenix feared he had already died. Lily didn't respond for several moments while she stroked the piglet's ear with the tip of her finger. Finally, she spoke.

'She kissed me.' There was a lot in those three words – disbelief, awe, confusion.

Talia. Phoenix's hands tightened on the wheel.

'You were asleep.'

Phoenix felt a stab of guilt. If she hadn't fallen asleep, then whatever was going on now might not be happening at all.

'Talia proposed that we allow you your respite and instead travel into town for supper. Alas, the group's plans changed almost immediately. Sale suggested some *recon*. This confounded me. At length, we ended up here. I swear I had not a clue of their sensibilities.'

They had reached the outer limit of the enormous abattoir and the smell invaded the van once more. 'I was nauseated and dis-orientated by the putrid odour and was hiding my face in my hands. Jordan was upset with me and informed the others that I would be *useless*. Somehow, despite the fact that it was only intended to be "recon", the situation changed again. Jordan noted an opportunity to breach the perimeter. The plan was brought forwards.'

They were passing the meatworks now and, to Lily and Phoenix's horror, police cars sat inside the high fences topped with barbed wire. 'They've been caught,' Phoenix said, her eyes watering from the stench. 'I passed the police on my way to you. They must have been heading here.'

Lily continued. 'They insisted I must be their getaway driver, as it was clearly *all I was good for*,' she said bitterly. 'I did not want to do that. I did not want to be anywhere near this awful place. Talia was excited, grinning, energy emanating from her like green electricity. She told me I was the key to their success. Then she *kissed* me, hard, and vanished.'

Phoenix took a careful breath to test the air and, finding it was safe to breathe freely, wound down the windows to freshen the van's interior. The tyres hummed in the quiet night.

'Was that your first kiss?' she asked, softly, glancing towards the passenger seat.

Lily nodded. Then after a moment, she spoke again, her tone wretched. 'She kissed me . . . and then she *left* me.'

Phoenix had many choice words to say about that but settled instead on focusing on practicalities. 'How did you end up with this pig?'

'While I was trapped there, awaiting Talia's return, two trucks arrived. The abattoir continues its industry around the clock. Animals keep pouring in. I could see the pigs through the bars of the truck, their large floppy ears. In horror, I watched as the trucks slowed near the entrance. As the second vehicle turned, this piglet slipped through the bars, tumbling headfirst to the road. I rushed to him, fearing he was dead. But when I touched him, he grunted, so I hastened with him to the car. Sirens and shouting followed, and I fled to safety.'

Phoenix parked the van outside the vet clinic, which was already lit up. 'Okay,' she said, sounding much calmer than she felt. She was worried. The others would certainly mention Lily to the police. At the very least, Talia would be wondering where her car had gone. She didn't know whether Lily's actions had been criminal in any way, but she wasn't about to voice her concerns, conscious of Lily's fear of the police. She unclipped her seatbelt. 'Let's get this little one seen to, then we'll sort out the rest, okay?'

Lily nodded, her eyes bright with unshed tears. 'Do you think the piglet will survive?'

Phoenix considered the unmoving creature in Lily's arms. 'I hope so.'

Inside the surgery, they were met by a blinking, bleary-eyed young vet, who took the piglet from Lily and placed it on the examination bench. He asked few questions and Lily answered only what she had to.

'He's alive,' he said, bluntly. 'He's got a concussion. These will heal,' he said, studying the piglet's legs. 'I'll give him some injections to help with the wounds. He can stay here overnight or you can take him home now but, to be frank, he's either going to make it or not.'

'Right,' Phoenix said, then she turned to Lily. 'Shall we take him home?'

'I suppose so,' Lily said, her brow furrowed. 'I am, however, concerned about other complications,' she whispered. 'I am in possession of Talia's keys.'

'I'll get those injections,' the vet said, excusing himself.

It was almost two in the morning and Phoenix was struggling to make decisions. She reached out to stroke the piglet's nose, thinking. 'Well, we don't know what's going on with Talia—'

Lily's phone sprang to life and her eyes grew wide. 'It is a local number,' she said. 'What should I do?'

In every cell of her body, Phoenix knew it was the police. Talia likely had handed over Lily's number as soon as she was questioned. 'I think you have to answer it,' Phoenix advised.

Lily nodded, reluctant, but accepted the call. The police asked her to come to the station right away, so they arranged to leave the piglet in the vet's care till morning.

The station was also brightly lit. Phoenix tensed, assaulted by the unforgiving fluorescent glow, voices that ping-ponged off hard surfaces, and a powerful smell of bleach. Beside her, Lily trembled and wrung her hands, her eyes downcast.

Phoenix had read enough to know that an autistic person was in danger in this type of situation simply because their stress responses – avoiding eye contact, avoiding touch or restraint, or sensory overwhelm – could make them appear suspicious, unco-operative or dangerous to neurotypical people. She thought of a young man in the US who went for a walk and never came home because he looked 'odd' and had been waving his hands while walking – and because he was Black – so he was deemed suspi-cious. Officers and paramedics were charged with his death but it would never bring him home.

Though rumbling with nerves herself, the first thing she did when presenting with Lily to the front desk was to explain. 'I am here as Lily's support person.'

The weary officer looked between the two of them, clocked Lily's unusual Victorian attire, and turned back to Phoenix. 'Why does Lily need a support person?' she asked, curious.

'Lily is autistic. Do you have specialised training in autism or have someone on staff who has?'

The officer focused her attention now, less sleepy and more engaged. 'No, I don't, and I don't think anyone here right now does either. But I'm open to you explaining to me what you need.'

'Thank you,' Phoenix said, so relieved she felt tears rush to her eyes and blinked them quickly away. 'Do you have a quiet room, somewhere with low lighting? Autistic people can become very overwhelmed with noise, lights, smells and touch and it makes communication difficult.'

The officer closed the folder in front of her. 'Yeah, I think we can do that. One of our officers has recently returned to work after having a baby so we have a breastfeeding space set up for her for when her hubby brings the bub in to visit.'

Phoenix and Lily followed the officer down an echoing hall and into a room that was part filing cabinets and part comfy lounge chair and cushions. A lamp in the corner offered soft lighting.

'You can take the lounge, Lily,' the officer said kindly. 'I'll get us another couple of chairs.'

'Are you feeling okay?' Phoenix asked as Lily perched on the edge of the chair, taking in her surroundings.

'I am not completely well of spirit but I am still here,' she said. 'Where do you think Talia is? And the others?'

Phoenix shook her head. 'I don't know.'

When the officer returned, she had a clipboard tucked under her arm and carried a tray of three glasses of water, which she arranged on the coffee table. 'My name is Officer Wentworth, but you can call me Kamille.'

Lily nodded in reply. 'Where is Talia?'

'Is that one of the activists at the abattoir?'

'Yes. She deserted me, requiring me to stay in her vehicle when the party stormed the barricades.'

Kamille smothered a small smile at Lily's choice of words.

'I swear I had no knowledge of their plans. One moment we were venturing out to secure provisions for dinner and the next there was spray paint and sizeable, menacing tools. They deserted me, allowing me no clue of their true intentions.' She looked away here, the pain of the group's exclusion clear on her face, perhaps thoughts of Talia's kiss silencing her words.

After a moment, Kamille spoke again. 'Talia will still be at the abattoir. She and her friends managed to chain themselves to equipment. They're being cut out now.'

'Oh, wow,' Phoenix said. While she did not agree with their actions, she was impressed by the speed and efficiency with which they'd pulled their stunt together.

Kamille took a deep breath. 'Before we get further into your story, let's start with some details, Lily. Can you give me your full name?' Kamille clicked her pen above her clipboard. Lily shut her mouth and chewed her lip. 'Lily? Is there a problem?'

'My name is Lily Buchanon.'

'And where do you live? Do you have a driver's licence on you?'

Lily turned to Phoenix with wide eyes.

'It's okay,' Phoenix said, smiling at her.

Lily did not speak but retrieved her licence from the pocket of her maroon riding pants and handed it over.

'Thanks,' Kamille said. 'I'll be back in a moment.' The door closed quietly behind her, and Phoenix and Lily waited in silence. When Kamille returned, she resumed her seat and handed back Lily's licence. 'Lily, are you aware that your mother has reported you as missing?'

25

The piglet came home in yet another animal crate the next morning. He was awake, though quiet and shell shocked, and likely sore with all those red raw wounds. Humphrey immediately came to snuffle him through the bars. The piglet gazed at the black shaggy face and made small squeaky noises, which sent Humphrey's tail into a gentle wave. The big cats circled warily, backs arched, tails fluffed in alarm at the pink intruder.

'What are you going to name him?' Lily asked, startling Phoenix with her presence. It was the first time she'd been out of her room since they'd got back from the station in the early hours.

Phoenix smiled at her, happy to have her company. 'In the absence of anything halfway sensible or creative coming from my mushy brain today, I might just go with "Lucky".'

Lily nodded, fetched a glass of water, and glided back to her room in silence, shutting the door behind her.

Phoenix sighed, disappointed. She wasn't entirely sure of all that Kamille and Lily had discussed last night, as she'd had to leave the room to find a toilet and jump online to secure the rental for another night, given the officer had asked them to stay in town today while they worked through statements from the others. But she had heard Kamille say that since Lily was an adult, they couldn't make her return to her family. Nevertheless, the officer did encourage it.

'Sometimes we find ourselves out of our depth,' Kamille had counselled. 'Sometimes, home is a good place to be while we find our feet.'

Obviously, Lily's mother had done a good job of sounding like a supportive, loving parent, and not one who had tied her child's hands together to force her to stop showing her autism.

Phoenix set about making Lucky a bottle of formula and then knocked on Lily's door. 'I'm going to give Lucky his first feed. Would you like to help?' She very much hoped Lily would be drawn out by the idea of seeing the animal she'd saved from death now guzzling milk, but Lily simply said, 'No.' Phoenix wasn't sure if she should push it, arguing that surely Lily would be better at this, given she'd hand-raised many young farm animals while Phoenix had not, but Lily was in a dark and silent mood, so she left her alone to recover from her ordeal.

'Okay, Lucky, it's just you and me,' she said, placing the piglet on a towel on her lap and offering him the bottle. He took no notice of it, instead taking in the strange sights of furniture, appliances, cats and a human, blinking his pale lashes. 'I think you'll feel better if you get some food in your belly.' She rubbed the teat near his mouth and tiny droplets fell to his lips. He sneezed in surprise. 'Come on, Lucky, you can do it.' Humphrey nosed at the piglet's belly, then licked his ear. 'See, even Humphrey thinks you should eat.'

Lucky tested the teat, pushing his snout at it in what Phoenix assumed was a motion to let the milk down from his mother. That's where he should be, she thought – with his mother, out in a field, drinking milk till he fell asleep with an enormous fat belly, sleeping in the sunshine. Phoenix's anxiety fizzed. Somehow, the success of this feeding attempt had become superstitiously intertwined with her own positive outcomes. If Lucky drank, if he lived, she'd be able to save her job. If he didn't, she would lose it.

She squeezed the teat to let out a spray of milk onto his nose and lips. He grunted, wobbled, turned away and then, with a whoosh of determination, grabbed hold of the teat and yanked on it, milk dribbling down his chin. Phoenix smiled and Humphrey wagged his tail. 'We did it,' she said. 'Well done us.'

In the early afternoon, as Phoenix was feeding Linus and Rita, a near-black hatchback pulled in to the driveway. She set the pellets down outside the paddock and marched to meet Talia.

'What do you want?' Phoenix would never usually forgo the standard niceties but right now she had no spoons left to give, and the last thing Lily needed was to be messed around.

Talia was pale, her eyes red-rimmed. She took a step backwards as Phoenix approached. 'I-I came to apologise to Lily,' she stammered.

'For which part, exactly? For pretending you liked her and cared about her? Or for trapping her in your stupid, dangerous and illegal scheme?'

'I did like her! I still do!' Talia said, her jaw muscles flicking. 'I thought we had things in common, both being vegan and all.'

'Loving animals, being vegan, and breaking the law are not all related activities. You could have been badly hurt last night and so could Lily. She had no idea what she was getting into. You didn't even give her the chance to consent to that or not. The only thing you did right was not to drag her into the abattoir with you, and even that is a slim margin of care.'

'I know,' she said, defensive now. 'I'm not an idiot.'

Phoenix scoffed loudly. 'You need to leave.'

'No, wait.'

Phoenix spun around to see Lily.

'I'll hear what she has to say.'

Phoenix reluctantly turned to leave, but Lily held up her hand.

'You can stay,' Lily said to Phoenix. 'This will only take a moment.'

'Thank you for seeing me,' Talia said, her hands twisting as she spoke. 'I'm sorry everything got out of hand last night. I never intended to drag you into that. We were only supposed to go and look around, get some intel, but then Jordan—'

'You retrieved your car, did you?' Lily interrupted.

'What? Oh, yeah. Thanks for leaving the keys with the police.'

Lily nodded, her lips pursed. Phoenix was pleased to see her shoulders straighten, her chin lift. 'The constables required me to stay here today while they concluded their interviews with you all.'

'They're done now,' Talia said, quietly. 'We've been charged. Between the four of us, there's quite a few charges, actually.' She chuckled, but it was empty and betrayed her fear. 'We have to front up to court this week. A trial date will probably be set after that.' Her eyes brightened. 'I really don't know how it all happened.'

A long stretch of silence passed between them, broken only by a round of excited quacking from the ducks splashing in the small dam in the corner of the horse paddock.

'You kissed me,' Lily said, her voice stern. Phoenix was startled by the edge to her words.

Talia swallowed. 'I like you.'

'You kissed me, without my permission, in a rough and thoughtless manner. My first kiss was outside *an abattoir*.'

Talia bit her lip, her cheeks colouring with shame.

'These,' Lily began, briefly pressing two fingers to her mouth, 'are lips that should have burned with passion but instead were left coated with the vile stench of death.'

'I didn't mean—'

'How dare you?' Lily murmured. 'You thrust some sort of declaration of love onto me then ran away, leaving me to fend for myself in the middle of the night. Our time together is over,' she said.

Talia's freckles were distinct against her pallor.

'If the constables have no further requirements of me, I will be moving on,' Lily said. 'I wish you well.' With that, she nodded curtly, turned on her boot heel and headed back to the house, her long-line wool cardigan flapping behind her in the breeze.

'Drive carefully,' Phoenix said, nodding to Talia's car.

Talia hopped in without another word and drove away.

When Phoenix returned to the house, Lily had tucked herself away inside her bedroom once more. She was desperate to talk to her, to find out what she was thinking, to tell her how proud she was that she had stood up for herself just now. She wanted to share the next piglet feeding with her, which would, she was certain, cheer Lily up. No one could possibly resist the charms of Lucky's happy little grunts, milk chin and wagging curly tail.

Instead, she went about her afternoon without Lily, collecting the Appleyards from the dam – not an easy task, as the ducks were most reluctant to return after such freedom. The chickens had also spent the day out and had to be brought inside. She sent videos and photos to Zack, who loved them all. He still hadn't heard anything about his job application, though, which was stressing him out, and she tried to ignore her rising sense of doom that he wasn't going to get the promotion after all. If that was the case, she knew he would be devastated and she wouldn't be there to support him.

The Downunder Auties also loved the new photos she sent them, especially the ones of little Lucky asleep in his crate or covered in milk. Somehow in the last feeding he'd managed to get it up his forehead and behind his ears. They were shocked about the abattoir incident and the danger it had put Lily in. And they had many gratifyingly angry things to say about the second newspaper article and the incorrect labelling of her as intellectually impaired.

By five o'clock, Lily hadn't reappeared from her room and Phoenix breathed a sigh of relief. The police must not have needed to call her back after all. That should mean they were free to set off again first thing in the morning. They'd lost another day, but she could still get back to Brisbane by Thursday. She also hadn't heard anything from the school yet, but couldn't decide if that was encouraging or a loud warning sign of worse to come.

She was getting out a loaf of bread to make vegan cheese and tomato toasties for their dinner when another car pulled in to the driveway. 'What now?' she grumbled, anticipating Talia's return, this time with a huge bunch of flowers and a melodramatic plea for Lily's forgiveness. But it wasn't Talia's car. It was a silver sedan. Phoenix frowned, wondering who it might be. The owner of the house? She swept her gaze over the assortment of feathered, furred and curly-tailed creatures, wondering if she could magically sweep them all into a cupboard before the driver got to the door.

Peering through the window, Phoenix saw a woman step stiffly out of the car. She was older than Phoenix. Late forties, maybe? She adjusted the bun of dark curls on her head and shook out her denim-clad legs. She stretched, her hands behind her back, then pulled out a wool coat, shrugging into it before closing the car door. With an accelerating heartbeat, Phoenix watched her stride towards the house with purpose. The woman's jaw and lips were set, her face lined with determination. When Phoenix registered her height and straight posture, it all clicked. This was unmistakably Lily's mother.

No sooner had she made the realisation than Lily was at her side, opening the door.

'Mama.'

'Lily,' her mother said, stopping in her tracks a few feet from the open door. She let out a heavy breath, not one of relief, but of frustrated exhaustion. 'Are you ready to go?'

'Go? What?' Phoenix instinctively reached out to place her hand on Lily's arm. Lily looked down at it, as though deciding whether or not to pull away. 'What are you doing?'

'She's coming home with me,' the mother said, highly irritated. 'Who are *you*?'

'Mama, this is Phoenix.'

Phoenix released her hand from Lily's arm and turned to the woman in front of her. 'It's nice to meet you . . .?' That wasn't true, technically, but Phoenix needed to know her name. She let the question hang in the air, but the woman didn't fill her in.

'This is Marcelle,' Lily said. Then, with a small voice and eyes that could not meet Phoenix's, she added, 'I asked her to come.'

Phoenix knew she failed to hide her shock from Marcelle, who now stared smugly back at Phoenix. This was why Lily had been avoiding her all day. She didn't want her to know. 'How did you get here?' she asked Marcelle.

'I flew,' she said, as though Phoenix was an idiot. Then she turned to Lily. 'I've been up since 2 am, when the police called me. Do you have any idea what that was like? I thought you were dead! I caught the first flight I could get to Sydney and then hired a car to get here.'

'I apologise,' Lily said, her shoulders slumping. She stared at the ground, her hands clasped in front of her, her knuckles white with the force she applied to herself.

'I should think so,' Marcelle said. 'So selfish.' She shook her head in disgust. 'Get your things.'

Lily turned.

'Wait!' Phoenix said. 'Let's just slow this down. Lily, why do you think you need to leave?'

'I—'

'She wants to come home. It's none of your business. This is a family matter.'

Phoenix gritted her teeth. 'With all due respect, Lily is an adult and is entitled to make up her own mind.'

'Lily is autistic and doesn't know what's best for her,' Marcelle snarled. 'Get your things, Lily, I'm exhausted. Let's go.'

'No,' Phoenix said, throwing out an arm to halt Lily. Then she closed the door in Marcelle's face and locked it.

'Hey!' the woman yelled, banging on the door. Humphrey immediately launched at it with a ferocious roar, causing Marcelle to emit a round of unpleasant and aggressive expletives, but also to stop banging.

'Lily,' Phoenix said, trying her best to calm herself and speak soothingly. 'You don't have to go with her if you don't want to. Do you know that?'

'But Officer Wentworth was correct. I lost my way. As soon as I left home, I lost my way. My plans to start a life with Bianca were ruined. A man assaulted me in the street. Then I met Talia and I thought I had made a friend – a friend who kissed me and threw me away. Not only did she discard me, it landed me with the constables. I nearly ended up in a position that could have had me jailed.'

'What happened with Talia was not your fault. Everything you're describing is painful, but it's part of growing up. Not everyone is like Bianca and Talia. You told me that you can't go backwards now. You tried running away after Bianca broke up with you but you decided to come back, because you *knew* you had to keep moving forwards. This is no different. You still have a place with me and Zack in Brisbane. We can help you work through this.'

Marcelle banged on the door again. Humphrey snarled in reply.

'It is too late,' Lily said. She looked as though her spirit had truly broken. 'It is not safe for me out here, on my own. I cannot trust people. They persist in hurting me and betraying me.'

'You're not on your own. You have me. You can trust *me*!' Phoenix's vision blurred with tears. 'You do know your own mind. You are smart and resilient and caring and a great friend. You are an artist with incredible talent and a potential career. Your whole life is in front of you. Please don't go now. Don't give up when you've only just begun.'

Three more thumps on the door. 'Lily!' Marcelle shouted.

Lily jumped. 'I have got to go,' she said, hurrying to her bedroom, returning with her bag. She halted in front of Phoenix and put her free arm around her, pulling her close. 'Thank you for being the best friend I have ever had.'

And then she plucked open the wooden door.

'Lily, *please*,' Phoenix begged. 'Please don't go back to her. She'll only hurt you more.'

Marcelle started to protest at that slur, but Humphrey jumped up on the screen, showing his pearly whites, and she stepped back instead.

Lily hesitated, then took a shuddering inhalation. She nudged Humphrey out the way. Phoenix grabbed him by the collar to ensure he didn't launch himself at Marcelle and Lily slipped out the screen door, marching towards the rental car without looking back. Marcelle gave Phoenix one self-satisfied snarl of her own, then got into the car and drove away, running over the edge of the flower bed and flattening a row of happy gerberas on her way.

Phoenix managed to get herself to the couch before her knees gave way.

26

Phoenix sat perfectly still, staring into space, her eyes open but unseeing. What the hell had just happened? Humphrey stayed at the door, his nose pressed to the wood, whining gently. It was the sight of him sitting there, having lost another person in his life, that made her bottom lip begin to tremble.

She was alone.

Lily was gone. Her *friend* was gone.

She was alone, hundreds of kilometres from home, with fifteen animals to care for and get safely back to Brisbane.

Her phone tinged. An email.

To: Phoenix Rose

Your presence is requested at a Special Board Meeting at 9.30 am on Wednesday at school. More than twenty families have called for the special meeting, fulfilling the requirements to do so. You will be issued with an Official Improvement Plan and you will be required to argue your case for your continuation at this school.

The trigger for this meeting was your decision to speak to the media as an employee of this school without first going through formal channels for permission to do so. This is a serious breach of your contract and is grounds for dismissal. The online discourse that has followed the media article has brought our school under tremendous scrutiny at a time when we should be rebuilding our reputation, not defending it from more attacks. To say we are disappointed is an understatement; however, we have agreed to consider the Official Improvement Plan at this time to show our good faith in resolving this matter in a timely and mutually beneficial way. Consequently, part of that improvement plan is that you state your case at the Special Board Meeting.

Your failure to attend this meeting will be seen as confirming your inability to fulfil your duties in the eyes of the parents, the board and the wider school community. I advise you to think very carefully about your personal level of commitment to this school.

Evelyn Godfrey
Principal, St Clementine's Girls' School

Phoenix read and re-read the email, her stunned brain taking several attempts to pull apart the many alarming points within.

Evelyn had signed off the email as 'Principal' not 'Acting Principal'. She must have been officially appointed as the head of the school. There was no longer any chance for Phoenix to 'just get through' the last term and hope to start afresh next year with a new principal. Evelyn was there to stay.

From what she'd seen in the past, Official Improvement Plans were only given out to teachers as a formality. What it really meant was that the school would push her out. There was no genuine way to get through a plan like that, not if the school didn't want her to. They could create endless obstructive scenarios to break her down. They could force her to teach Japanese or PE. They could take her off her current classes and give her the notoriously difficult Year 6s in Term 4, when they were at their most volatile, or load her classes with all the behaviourally challenging students they could find. They could give her every extra class cover and every extra bus duty and yard duty they could find. They could put her under supervision while she taught, undermining her power with the students, interrupting her flow simply to 'make a suggestion' and criticising each lesson, rightly or wrongly, till they broke her down again. Evelyn herself could sit in on every class, or turn up unannounced whenever she wanted, or only come to view the most difficult classes. They could remind her of 'the incident' every day to drive her mad. There were a million ways to break a teacher down.

As for her supposed transgression in speaking to the media, that was a move of self-defence. Now that she'd outed her autism, it made it much more difficult for them to terminate her. It would look bad and they knew it. She hadn't said a single thing that wasn't true. As for her not asking for permission to speak, well, that idea was utterly repugnant. She would not be silenced by people who were more interested in polishing their superficial reputations than in making real, meaningful change in the world.

But the biggest, most awful part of that email was the deadline. There was no way she could make it to Brisbane in time to front up to a board meeting at 9.30 am on Wednesday with her body and mind primed to fight for her job. Her original plan was to get home by Wednesday before dark, and that was with two drivers. Now she'd lost a whole day out of that plan as well as her co-driver. Some people in the world could drive twelve hours in a day but Phoenix was not one of them. And she knew any attempt to explain her situation would only make her sound more unreliable and flaky, as though she was prioritising animals over people.

She was doomed. She felt the blood draining slowly through her body. Her feet tingled. Her chest tightened.

Think, Phoenix, think.

She couldn't fly back and leave all these animals behind, even if it was possible to get a flight, which didn't seem likely from a rural airport. She checked the time. Could she drive through the night? No, she'd never risk it. She was a nervous night driver at the best of times, let alone towing a float with a pony and an alpaca on board. And . . . Oh god, the float! She'd disconnected it last night when she went to get Lily. Now she'd have to work out how to put it all together again.

She curled up on the couch, heavy with the loss of her friend, her career and her identity. She'd been cast adrift.

She was still balled up on the couch when the sun had set, the house now in darkness, the cats meowing at her and climbing over her, demanding dinner, when Zack called. With a jolt to her heart, she answered.

'Hi! Did you get the job?' Hope spiked.

'No,' he said, flatly. 'Michael Smith got it.'

'What? No! He's only been there a few months, hasn't he?'

'Yep,' Zack said, clearly pissed off. 'And he's five years less experienced than me. But hey, why would you want to promote someone named Zamar Kerowa when you can have bog-standard Michael Smith.'

Phoenix was about to reassure him that wasn't true, that the colour of his skin surely hadn't played a part, but then wasn't that worse? If it hadn't, then it must have been for some other reason.

'Actually, the real reason they gave me was, obviously, not because of my island hair,' he said, bitter, 'but because while I clearly had the most accurate techniques and great commitment to client care and service, the team leader position required someone who had "stronger demonstrated abilities to build, maintain and strengthen intrateam relationships".'

Phoenix stumbled in the dark to find the lamp switch, blinking as the light filled the room. 'What does that mean?'

'It means that in my selection criteria, I didn't have a lot to say other than valuing clear, direct and honest communication, whereas Michael Smith could demonstrate that he'd started an employee ten-pin bowling night and timetabled social drinks down at the pub.'

Phoenix groaned. 'I thought the key position description was in mentoring and coaching junior radiographers in skilled techniques and quality control, and you are a master of both.'

'Yep,' he said, his anger dissipating, his voice quietening.

'So basically they've promoted the popular guy over the more qualified science nerd.'

'Yep.'

'They're valuing the ability to play the social game of the neurotypicals rather than your ability to elevate the clinic's quality of work.'

'Yep.'

'Oh, babe.' Her heart broke for him. 'You so deserved that role.'

'Thanks,' he said, quietly.

'I wish I was there for you right now,' she said. She'd once read that if you played a single note on a piano over and over, in a room full of pianos, that all the other pianos in the room began to play the same note. She and Zack were like that. Sometimes that wasn't always great, as they were so sensitive to each other's moods that they could pull each other down, but it could also work the other way. When one of them was down, they could co-regulate with the other to find their way back to peace again. They could play the same note together, lifting each other.

She couldn't tell him about Evelyn's email now. He was already struggling too much.

'It gets worse,' he said.

'Surely not.'

'Lindy, the woman whose role I've been filling on contract . . .'

'Yes?'

'She's decided to come back in November. There's no place for me there after that.'

Phoenix sucked in a long, slow breath. Words failed her.

'I'm so sorry.' She jiggled herself, determination rising. 'This is not your fault. This is just such bad luck.' She heard him take in a shaky breath, but he didn't respond. 'We're going to be okay,' she said. 'You'll find another job. You will. We'll be okay.' She hoped she sounded convincing because she truly didn't feel it.

Two weeks earlier she'd left Brisbane thinking she had a job to come back to when she was ready and that Zack had a job and that they were going to buy a house and that she would ask him to marry her. And now? Olga was dead. Lily was gone. The school wanted her out. Zack was losing his job. They'd spent a ton of money on this trip and now had fifteen animals. They would likely have to find another rental in order to keep all the animals with them, but the real estate climate was the toughest it had ever been.

Zack said he needed to go and zone out for a while gaming and Phoenix reluctantly said goodbye, but she texted his mum and sister, asking them to check on him.

She hovered on the couch, numb with shock and disappointment and rage. It was completely unfair that Zack's superpowers – his ability to hyperfocus on his work, his perfectionism and his exceptional attention to detail – the very things that made him a brilliant radiographer, would also be the things that stopped him from progressing in his career. He would rather work late and hone his craft again and again than goof off in a brightly lit, noisy,

251

smelly bowling alley or down beers and talk rubbish with the guys (because they were almost all guys where he worked), yet his dedication to his craft would never be as valuable as being popular. It was completely unfair that her superpowers – her high sensitivity to other people's emotions and characters and to her environment, her ability to rapidly acquire knowledge and package it in a way that made sense to others, and her dedication to creating comprehensive and engaging lesson plans – were the very things that made her a great teacher and also kept her mind working on the job around the clock and burnt her out.

For her and Zack, autism was a disability not because of autism itself but because the world and people around them constantly disabled them. They led a life of constant rejection and correction, which meant they forever doubted themselves and were always healing from trauma. They were the ones deemed *wrong* and having to change – the way they spoke or sat or moved or used eye contact or enjoyed interests or wanted to be touched – rather than it being an effort on the part of both parties to understand each other. They were never going to win. It was a losing battle and Phoenix and Zack would always be the losers: of time, energy, friends, relationships, jobs, self-esteem and health.

At that moment, Humphrey got up from where he'd been lying in despair at the front door and trotted to his bed, where he found the pink teddy bear Phoenix had bought him before they left Wilmot. She'd never seen him give it any sort of attention before now, but he placed his jaws around it, lifting it as a mother might her pup, and carried it to Phoenix. He stopped at her knees and awkwardly placed it in her lap, nudging it towards her with the tip of his nose.

'Is this for me?' she said, accepting the teddy. Humphrey stared into her eyes and wagged his tail slowly. Phoenix held it to her chest, tears brimming. 'Thank you.' At that, Humphrey hopped up on the couch, lay down and rested his head in her lap. She placed a hand on him. His companionship calmed her, and she remembered why she was here.

The piglet awoke with a start and immediately squealed for food. Humphrey cast his gaze at Lucky, then back up to Phoenix with the eye roll of a teenager who was sick of having to look out for his younger brother. Phoenix barked out a short laugh. 'We better feed him before he sends us all deaf,' she said. Humphrey sighed and slid off the couch, stretching in a downward dog pose.

Phoenix gazed around at her menagerie, the sleeping ducks and chickens in their crates, the hungry, yowling cats, the squealing piglet shoving at the cage door, and Humphrey, her new mate, and realised she was abundant in friends. They were different from what society told her they should be. Her friends were feathered, furred and hooved; they were online; and her best friend of all was Zack, her partner. The typical world might not understand her but her A-typical world did, and it gave her strength she'd never even known she had.

Determination arrived in a rush. She might not win this fight. She might not win the next one either. But maybe she was at a moment in history that was simply not ready to let her win . . . yet. Maybe right now all she could do was show up, for herself, for Zack and all the other autists who were to come, the ones who never even had the chance to fight and the ones who were too tired to fight any more.

Like Lily.

She had no idea how she would do it, but she was going to make it to school by nine o'clock Wednesday morning. If she could do nothing else, she could do that. She could show up and be counted.

That was *if* she could get the bloody horse float reattached to the van.

27

Sweat beaded Phoenix's brow. This was her fifth attempt to line up the ball of the tow bar with the coupling. She'd missed it by mere millimetres the time before. It wasn't made any easier by the fact that when they'd first parked the van and float in this driveway they'd been on a bend, so she couldn't go straight back. She gave herself a talking to, closed her eyes and took deep breaths. Then her phone rang.

'How's my favourite adventurer?' Therese's voice was loud and cheery. 'Thought you'd be up at the crack of dawn. No rest for nomads, especially when you've got a zoo onboard.'

Phoenix welcomed the chance to break from wrangling both her brain and the steering wheel, put the van in park and sat back.

'How the bloody hell are you?' Therese said.

'I'm not sure where to start.' The smile in Phoenix's voice belied her frazzled state.

'Start anywhere. Linear conversations bore me.' Therese chomped into something crunchy. Corn chips, perhaps.

Phoenix filled her in on Talia and her friends, the abattoir, the piglet, the police, Lily's departure, Zack's loss of his promotion and his job, and the school's demand that she be at school in a little over twenty-four hours' time.

'Holy crapballs!' Therese uttered, her loud chewing having been halted by disbelief. 'And you're in Dubbo now?'

'Yep.'

'But you're going to drive all the way to Brisbane today, which is'—she tapped away on her phone—'ten hours' drive on a perfect run, without stops, without being slowed down by a van pulling a horse float. Didn't you say you're only able to drive for two hours at a time before losing concentration?'

Phoenix felt sick. 'I don't see what other choice I have.'

Therese was silent a moment, though by the sound of it she was clicking a pen rapidly. 'Send me your planned stops, okay?'

'Why?'

'I'm working from home today. I'm going to be your desk jockey.'

'My what?'

'I'm going to manage you and your trip from here. No arguments. You need support and I can help. You're so close to the finish line. You're not going to fall on my watch.'

'I don't know what to say.' Phoenix felt intensely guilty at the idea of Therese spending her day at home working to help her but, at the same time, she knew she was totally out of her depth. She would feel better knowing there was someone who knew where she was at any given time in case the enormousness of the country somehow managed to devour her whole. It boosted her confidence to know Therese would be on the end of the phone if she needed her. 'Thank you,' she said. 'That would help a lot. I'll text you my plan now.'

'One more thing before I go,' Therese said. 'Is there anything that would make your trip more bearable?'

Phoenix considered this. Other than having Lily back or Zack by her side, there was really only one thing that came to mind. 'Cake,' she said. 'I think I'm going to need a lot of cake.'

Therese laughed. 'You're singing my song. I give you permission to eat cake at every single opportunity.'

Following their chat, Phoenix rallied her focus and determination and on her seventh attempt she lined up the tow ball and float coupling perfectly. She didn't quite believe it till she wound down the jockey and it connected with a satisfying thump. She shouted with joy, hooked her thumbs into her belt loops and kicked her legs out to the side in an impromptu line-dancing jig. Humphrey barked at her from inside the house where he'd been watching.

'I did it!' she called to him, and he danced a little circle behind the screen door.

Before she let herself get too carried away, she FaceTimed Bruno and had him check it all again.

'Ya did it, did it,' he confirmed, sounding proud as punch. 'Ya're on your way home.'

Phoenix drove with Milo and Jane in their crate on the front seat so they could watch the scenery passing by. Jane was getting stronger each day, though she still wasn't allowed to gallop around. Phoenix would be able to get the stitches out in a couple of days' time in Brisbane, but right now the cat was clearly frustrated and bored, yowling and headbutting the confines of her crate. Having them in the front seat would be enrichment for them and company for her.

Since discussing the float's safety chain with Bruno, she'd had Tina Arena's 'Chains' stuck on repeat in her head, and she sang it loudly to the kittens while she wound down the windows. Phoenix's hair was quickly windswept and wild. It was probably because she was on a high after her not insubstantial win with the horse float, but she wasn't complaining. At this moment, she felt she could take on the world.

True to her word, Therese was on the job and had organised Mel (aka Magenta Mel) from the Downunder Auties to connect with Phoenix in Coonabarabran. They met in a small park, where Mel's two home-schooled kids were climbing the brightly coloured play equipment.

'I can't believe you're here,' Phoenix said, happily accepting Mel's warm hug, her friend's tight curls tickling her nose. 'Do you live here in town?'

'No, we're an hour and a half away in Coonamble,' she said, passing a sandwich to the youngest child, six or so at Phoenix's best guess, who'd come over to poke around in Mel's backpack for food. His sister, slightly older, fair-headed like her mother and wearing a floral fleecy top, smiled shyly at Phoenix from behind Mel. Phoenix smiled back and waved to her and she grinned before running off to climb the monkey bars.

'Oh, Mel, that's such a long drive for you to come and see me!' Phoenix said.

'I wouldn't miss it,' she said, her rosy cheeks, blue eyes and forest-green attire making her look like a Celtic nature spirit. 'It's so good to meet you in person.'

'Gosh, you too.'

While Phoenix walked Humphrey and introduced the kids to all the animals in the van, which quickly loosened their tongues and got them chatting excitedly, Mel went to a nearby cafe and brought back a piece of quiche, coffee and a gluten-free lemon cake with strawberry buttercream.

'How did you know I love lemon?'

'Lucky guess.'

'And lemon and strawberry is the most perfect combination.' She was truly touched and pulled out her phone to take a photo of the cupcake with its silver foil paper and pink icing, flecked with whipped strawberry pieces. 'I'm going to put this on my Pinterest board as my top favourite yet.'

While Phoenix ate and drank, she asked Therese about her kids. 'They're both autistic and ADHD. Neither of them fit in at school and they were miserable there. They're much happier with home learning.'

'That's a huge undertaking,' Phoenix said, admiringly.

'I made the choice to radically accept them and their need for something different. People value different ways of thinking when you're an adult. I don't understand why we try to knock it out of them when they're young. Mainstream schools are built for the majority, not people like us.'

'I totally agree.' Phoenix licked the last of the strawberry butter-cream from her fork. 'That was *sooo* good. I feel well caffeinated and sugared.'

'Although I'd love to keep chatting with you, Therese has instructed me that you're on a wickedly tight time frame and I need to feed you and send you on your way,' Mel said, collecting food scraps from the kids before they rushed off to the swings.

Phoenix groaned. 'I so wish I could stay longer and talk more.'

'You definitely don't have time,' Mel said, widening her eyes. 'Long way home yet.'

'So true,' Phoenix said, the reality that she'd only begun this marathon trek now sinking in. 'It means the world that you came to see me.'

Back on the road, she had Humphrey up front this time, buckled in with his safety harness. He sat up straight for the first hour towards Tamworth, barking excitedly at trucks that passed by, especially if they had horses or cattle onboard, but then when he clearly needed to lie down, she pulled over to the side and swapped him with the piglet, who was due for another feed. Lucky grunted and shoved at the bottle, nearly knocking it out of Phoenix's hand, then spun around in excited circles before finally collapsing and sleeping again.

Two hours out of Tamworth, she'd grown weary of the trip. The caffeine and sugar high had waned and she found herself yawning. She wound down the window to blast her face with incoming air, a long road of nothingness through cleared grazing land ahead of her. She pulled over to turn on her strings of LED-lit sunflowers and play some music, deciding on Bon Jovi for some energy. The lyrics were apt – for her, it *was* now or never.

Finally, she rolled into Tamworth midafternoon. A text from Therese instructed her to head to the dog park, where she would meet Kitty (aka MissWittyKitty) and her parents, Mahalina and Ramil. The park was busier than Phoenix expected but she wagered the dog owners were probably the kinds of people who might not mind if she was to unload her horse and alpaca here to stretch their legs. She certainly needed to move. She was stiff from driving and struggling with an awful afternoon slump in energy. She needed to feel sunlight on her skin. She was, and always had been, a solar-powered person. A dull and overcast day could wrap itself around her, draining her life force like a Harry Potter Dementor.

She unloaded Rita first, coaxing her down the ramp slowly on unsteady legs, well and truly sick of all this travel. When all four hooves were safely on the ground, Phoenix rubbed her neck and shoulder. 'Well done, Rita. I promise you, this will be over by tomorrow afternoon.' Rita snorted, her eyes wide and head high, taking in the sight of dogs zipping after balls in the enclosed dog area and the high-pitched yaps of excitement. Inside the float, Linus kicked his long, thin legs and pulled on the rope attached to his yellow halter. 'I'll get to you soon,' she soothed.

She led Rita away from the dog enclosure, the pony's muzzle to the ground, sniffing and snorting. Unexpectedly, she folded her front legs under herself and dropped to the ground.

'No, no, no,' Phoenix protested. She tugged at the lead. But it was no use; she had nowhere near the strength of a stout and muscly pony. Rita hit the earth with a thud. She stretched out on one side of her body, rubbing her face and neck on the grass, then flicked her legs up into the air to roll to the other side.

Phoenix struggled to keep the lead rope out of the flailing legs as the pony continued to throw herself from side to side.

Next thing, the heavy metal gate of the dog yard banged shut.

'Boomer, no!' a man shouted.

Phoenix looked up. An enormous shaggy grey dog bounded across the grass, its long legs covering the distance between them as fast as a gazelle. Rita leapt to her feet, tossed her head, yanking the rope clear of Phoenix's hand, and took off.

Phoenix watched in slow-motion horror as the dog made ground on Rita, whose nose was in the air, her tail streaming behind her.

On instinct, Phoenix gave chase.

Humphrey barked from within the van. She was torn between not abandoning the animals and keeping sight of Rita. Dog walkers and cyclists stopped and stared at the streak of chestnut flying across the open expanse of green, the shaggy dog in focused pursuit. The dog neared Rita's back legs. The pony lowered her head, spinning to change direction. And bolted.

Phoenix staggered to a stop, hands on hips. There was no way she could get anywhere near the pony, now in a flat gallop. The dog gave up too, tongue lolling, sides heaving.

Her head and tail high, Rita's hooves drummed thunder over the ground as she weaved between trees. She'd nearly run out of parkland, heading straight for the road.

Phoenix yelled, 'Stop!' But it made no difference.

Rita careered onto the road and into traffic.

28

The screech of braking tyres filled the air. Phoenix froze, watching in horror as the pony clattered across bitumen between two cars coming from different directions. How she avoided being crushed was inconceivable and yet there she was, wheeling to the right and cantering down the road. Phoenix ran. Others joined in. Two boys abandoned their soccer ball and joined the chase, as did a wiry man on a racing bicycle who wheeled around, rose to his feet and peddled like an Olympic velodrome sprinter. A tradie in denim and boots left his car and gave a few good metres before a hacking smoker's cough brought him to his senses. There they were, the cyclist in the lead, followed by the soccer boys, and Phoenix over-taking the tradie, racing through the streets after Rita like some sort of topsy-turvy running of the bulls.

Phoenix ran with the futile hope that Rita would see sense and come back to her. At the same time, she was aware she'd abandoned her van, float, animals and all her possessions back at the dog park. Still she ran around corners, dodged prams and narrowly avoided potholes. She ran until she could run no more.

Gasping for breath she doubled over, dragging in oxygen despite the painful stitch in her side. The two cars that had narrowly avoided a head-on collision had righted themselves and slowly moved on, one of the drivers throwing some random abuse Phoenix's way as he did so. She was trying to work out what to do, how to get Rita back, when a shiny gold Mercedes Benz pulled up alongside her.

'Phoenix?' the driver said as her window slid down smoothly and silently. The man beside her in the front grinned at her. Phoenix stared at them, still oxygen-starved, confused. 'It's us,' the woman said. 'This is Kitty.' She pointed over her shoulder to the backseat where a teenage girl was waving two hands furiously at her. 'Hop in!'

'Oh my god, thank you,' Phoenix managed to grunt, staggering on jelly legs to the back door. Kitty slid over and popped the door for her before rustling back to her side in a shimmering, multilayer blue skirt. Quiet, calming classical music floated easily through the surround speakers. The vehicle smelt clean but not invasively so. Just . . . clean.

'We'll help you find the pony,' Ramil said, encouraging Mahalina to continue driving, pointing at side streets Rita might have taken.

'Thank you,' Phoenix managed again, deeply grateful while simultaneously horrified that she was covered in dog and horse hair, dirt, piglet milk formula and spilt coffee, and had who-knew-what on the soles of her boots while she was sitting in a pristine car with pure white lambswool seat covers.

Kitty clapped her hands with joy, grinning at Phoenix.

'I love the purple,' Phoenix said to her, between steadying breaths. She gazed at the incredible shade of violet drenching the lower half of Kitty's black hair.

'I love colour,' Kitty said. Given Kitty's green pumps, red-and-white striped tights, blue skirt, yellow shirt and purple hair, she'd nailed the brief. She beamed like the rainbow she was.

'Turn left,' Ramil instructed, and when Mahalina did so, Phoenix nearly burst into tears. There was the pony, standing on the footpath with two police officers at her side. She was simultaneously delirious with relief that Rita had been caught and embarrassed by the number of times she had met up with the police on this road trip so far. She couldn't remember speaking to an officer once in her life before arriving in Tasmania, not even for a speeding ticket.

'Here you go,' Mahalina said, gliding to a smooth stop.

'Thank you.' Phoenix couldn't say it enough. She hopped out and headed straight to Rita. 'Is she okay?' she asked, placing her hand on Rita's hot and sweaty shoulder and running her eyes down her legs, looking for cuts or gashes.

'She seems okay,' the first officer said. 'She was very lucky. The streets can get a bit busy around here this time of day.' He didn't seem angry but he certainly wasn't shrugging it off. The second officer, with a Wyatt Earp moustache that moved like a living thing, asked her if she had any ID on her.

'I left everything when she bolted,' she explained. 'It's back in the van at the dog park.'

Mahalina, Ramil and Kitty had all joined them and Mahalina at once said, 'We'll go back there now and watch everything for you.'

Ramil asked Kitty something in Filipino and Kitty said, 'No, I want to walk with the pony.'

'Okay. We'll meet you both back there,' Mahalina said, and she and Ramil nodded at the officers and turned to go.

'You won't miss it,' Phoenix said, trying to lighten the mood. 'It's the van and float with all the animals in it.'

'You know you're not supposed to have horses in that park,' the moustache said. 'A bolting horse could have caused serious injury to people and property.'

'I'm sorry.' Phoenix's face flamed hot. 'I'm on a long road trip and I think Rita here has some energy to burn.' She tried to smile but wasn't sure she'd done so effectively.

The moustached officer asked her some more questions and tapped details into his mobile phone. 'We need to note the incident down,' he said, flat-toned. His colleague was smiling, rubbing Rita around her ears, amused when she snorted on him.

Finally, they let her go and she and Kitty began walking Rita back to the van, slowly. Both Rita and Phoenix were knackered from the chase.

Kitty skipped and clapped alongside them, a radiant beam lighting her up. 'That man's moustache was like a ferret on his face,' she said, cheerily. It made Phoenix snort, then laugh, then laugh some more till she was on a rolling wave of belly laughs that made her halt because she couldn't laugh that hard and walk at the same time. She pulled Rita up near a tree and leant against the trunk, giving in to the convulsions till tears ran down her face, laughing away all the stress and fear while Kitty twirled, her shimmering blue skirt held wide.

For a moment, Phoenix believed everything would be all right.

Before she left Tamworth, she texted Lily to check in and see if she was okay back at home with her parents.

Call or text me anytime, okay. Miss you x

Then she called Zack to see how his day was going. He was driving home, he said, and his voice was distant through the hands-free speaker.

'How was work?' she asked, picking up the cake Kitty and her parents had brought for her. This one was a triple-layered lemon velvet, with bright yellow lemon curd between soft layers of cake and lemon ganache on the top and sides. Obviously, knowledge of her love of lemon had spread through the Downunder group. She'd taken a photo of it, too. It felt good to collect images of food that she didn't only aspire to enjoy, but which had come to her through the thoughtfulness of friends – friends who'd turned up exactly when she needed them most.

'Pretty humiliating, really,' he said. 'All that extra work I did, all for nothing.'

'I wish I could hug you,' she said.

'I need you to,' he confessed, and his voice was so sad it made her want to cry.

'I'm leaving Tamworth now,' she said. 'I'm trying to get home as fast as I can.' She didn't mention that she was attempting to break all records possible to make it to school by 9 am tomorrow. It was after five now, Rita's escapades having added a delay she couldn't afford. On the upside, the fright and intense exertion had infused her with renewed energy at a time of day when she normally felt like a zombie.

'You can only do what you can do,' he said. 'Your safety is the highest priority. Nothing else is worth it. We think our jobs mean something, that our employers care about us, but it's all a lie,' he said, bitterly.

That was possibly true, but still, she was determined to try. 'I love you.'

'You too,' he said, and his voice felt like home. She needed to get back there, right now. Disconnecting the call, she finished off the last of the cake, sent a thank you text to Kitty and family, updated Therese on her whereabouts, made a bottle for the squealing pig and fed him on her lap, fed and medicated the other animals, apologised to them for the tedious confinement, gently shushed the quacking ducks, then buckled herself in and set off for Armidale. The van was starting to stink, the cats, ducks, chickens and piglet having been confined for more than twelve hours. But there was nothing she could do other than wind down the window and keep driving.

She had at least eight hours to go but likely more with the float slowing her down. And it was a mere fifteen hours before she had to be at school. With any luck, she'd be in Armidale by 8 pm. She updated Therese of her plan, assuring her she would eat and caffeinate some more once she got there, before pushing on to Tenterfield. There, she could sleep for a few hours (or at the very least, rest), then drive through the night to get home in time to shower and change clothes before the real fight began.

At the back of her mind, her inner voice whispered.

It's impossible.

'I'm not listening,' she replied, and pulled the van out onto the road.

29

The petrol light came on an hour away from Tamworth. Phoenix pulled in to the next fluorescent-lit service station, her glowing sunflower lights casting beams onto the windscreen and windows. The squealing piglet in the front seat attracted raised eyebrows from the dusty, weathered man at the bowser next to hers. For his timely entertainment, the chickens awoke under the bright lights and emitted scattergun-like clucking, then Rita let out a float-shaking whinny, stomping on the floor and rattling the whole shebang.

She ignored the man's stares, already irritated by the necessary but time-consuming interruption of having to stop. Inside the shop, she took a can of Coke from the fridge, more water and a likely toxic so-called energy drink, then collected chocolate and emptied a checkout display of its highly perfumed lavender sachets, hoping they'd mask some of the less pleasant aromas in the van.

The man was still openly staring at her as she returned to the bowser. She climbed in, started the engine and pushed hard on the horn. The man startled, ducking his head as the air filled with the jungle cries of chattering, braying and barking. She grinned and headed for the exit.

Back on the road, she set her music to play Neil Diamond's 'Sweet Caroline' and sang along at the top of her voice to give herself a lift, steadfastly ignoring the tug of fatigue at her eyeballs. The road to Armidale felt three times longer than it actually was but she arrived as predicted at 8 pm, greeted by Jess (aka Reddots-partyfrocks), who was waiting for her in a red-and-white polka dot dress with matching red shoes and hair band.

'I dressed like my online name so you'd know who I was,' she said, excitedly, bouncing up and down on her red pumps and grinning with red lips. 'It's so good to see you! Can I hug you?'

'Yes, please,' Phoenix said, walking stiffly towards her, as though she'd been riding a wild donkey for the past twelve hours, not sitting in a car. Jess's arms wrapped her in a strong hug and Phoenix took a deep breath, coaxing the iron hold of her anxiety to relax a fraction. She stepped back. 'I must look a terrible fright,' she said. She sniffed her hands. 'And even though I swear I've washed my hands I can still smell the piglet formula.'

Jess waved a hand. 'Plenty of farmers around here wouldn't blink an eye. Come on, I've got a table waiting.'

They sat at a round wooden table for two in the Luniva Momo Nepalese-Himalayan cafe and ate samay baji, a plate with rice, barbecued vegetables, boiled egg and legumes. Jess was great company, happy to talk about her life in the local theatres and on the road and the new position she'd started, tutoring at the university, as well as her ginger cat called the Doctor, after the central character in *Doctor Who*, and her love of baking and sewing.

'I think you'd get on well with Lily,' Phoenix said, missing her company. She wondered what Lily was doing now, if she was okay, if she'd collapsed in on herself and locked herself in a dark room, or if she was simply getting on with life. 'She's a bit younger than you but she loves Jane Austen and had the lead in her school play, and she can make her own clothes too.' She resisted the urge to check her phone to see if Lily had returned her text. 'She's wonderful.'

'I would love to meet her. She's the one who's been travelling with you, right? Therese told me a little bit about her. I'm sorry to hear she left you.'

Phoenix felt the need to defend Lily. 'I think she got scared.' She shrugged. 'She lost confidence in herself. She didn't believe she could keep going.'

'Maybe she just wasn't ready.'

'Maybe.'

They finished their dinner and Phoenix used the facilities while she could before apologising that she had to keep moving on.

'Of course you do! It's quite exciting, this last bit.' Jess fairy-clapped her hands. 'Like the end of a movie when the heroine is rushing to the airport to stop her love from getting on the plane.'

'Something like that,' Phoenix said, and laughed. She couldn't imagine herself as the heroine. 'Thank you so much for coming to meet me. It's been great to have your company to keep me from losing my mind with nothing but me, the road and a long night ahead.'

'Before you go, Therese said I should bring you sustenance, so I whipped this up for you this afternoon!' Jess handed over a cake box inside a shopping bag. 'Sorry I didn't have a fancier carry case for it.'

'Are you kidding? You made me a cake?' Phoenix carefully extracted the box and opened the lid to find half a cake inside.

'It's only half because it has cream cheese frosting, therefore really should be in the fridge. I know you can't eat a whole cake on your own overnight – or maybe you could, I don't know, no judge-ment here – but I thought if I give you half you'll be able to enjoy a few pieces without then having to toss the last of it.'

'It's unbelievable,' Phoenix said. The cake was the most adorable triple-layered lemon and blueberry creation she'd ever seen. 'It looks like a professional made it!' Purple juice seeped from around the edges of the fat blueberries that sat between each layer of light cake, and the cream cheese frosting boasted dainty curls of candied lemon peel. The aroma alone was heavenly and infinitely more appealing than the inside of the van right now, though the lavender sachets were valiantly battling the rising tide.

'Oh, and here, I brought you some wooden spoons, forks and paper napkins too,' she said, pulling them out of her handbag.

Phoenix pulled her new friend into another hug. 'Thank you. You're an absolute star.'

She left Armidale at half-past nine after taking Humphrey for a walk so she could get oxygen to her brain. But still the drive was difficult. She'd been on the road for the better part of the entire day and now evening too. Her body was screaming at her to lie down and rest. Her mind was starting to imagine things leaping out at her from the shadows at the side of the road or ruminating on the idea that she would break down in the middle of nowhere and be killed by a lone madman or disappear without a trace, her life told in photos and newspaper clippings on some crime investigation show.

She kept telling herself she was simply tired, that none of those things were true. Yet she *was* in the middle of nowhere. Kilometre after kilometre passed with nothing but blackness on all sides. The headlights that loomed up behind her didn't offer the comfort of not being alone but instead were portents of threats she hadn't yet begun to imagine. Australia was utterly enormous, a fact that became starkly real when one tried to actually cross it by vehicle. Though she absolutely did not want to stop before reaching Tenterfield, her eyelids were dropping involuntarily and she felt dozy, as though starved of oxygen, and no amount of air coming in through the windows helped. She simply had to stop and rest before she killed herself – or someone else on the road – and every one of these animals in her care.

She pulled in to a rest stop much like the one she and Lily had parked at in Echuca, careful to ensure she could turn the horse float around to drive out again, then cut the engine. The dramatic silence engulfed her, ringing in her ears. The animals were, for once, quiet. No scratching or shuffling from the birds. No meowing from the cats. No snoring from Humphrey. Even the piglet was fast asleep. In the weak moonlight, Lucky's chest rose and fell rapidly as he dreamt of greener fields. Silence boomed. She cracked open her window, night sounds drifting in.

A car on a lonely road far, far away in the distance.

The ticking down of the hot and bothered van as the engine cooled.

The wind in the treetops.

Humphrey, breathing behind her seat.

The beating of bats' wings.

Her heart squeezed, thinking of Lily and her deep love for bats. She wished she were here too. Blinking away tears, she popped open the driver's door to step outside. She needed to jump up and down on the spot and swing her arms back and forth. She needed to lunge and stretch and shake and spin. She needed coffee but in its absence settled for cracking open the energy drink to wash down several large mouthfuls of Jess's incredible cake, feeling the sugar hit her bloodstream in time with the caffeine. She had to keep going. Failure was not an option.

She pulled out her phone to update Therese on her location and dropped a pin. At least now if she disappeared, the nightly news would rejoice in having 'the last pin' on Phoenix's location to share with the country. After that, she logged in to the Downunder Auties to thank everyone who'd come out to greet her today on the journey. A mosquito bit her on the back of the neck and she slapped at it, annoyed.

That was when she noticed a Facebook message from Anthea – still an online friend though clearly not an IRL one any more. It was a video. With a fist clamped at her throat, she clicked on the play button.

Like being stuck in a bad dream, she watched herself at school on that last day. Video Phoenix looked dazed, confused, staring into space. The girl who had made the recording could be heard giggling while she filmed with her phone. Phoenix watched herself searching for water, the PowerPoint light on the white-board blinding her. Her painful yelp and recoil, hands to eyes. Then shaking hands bringing the bottle to her mouth before she dropped it and water gushed over the laptop. Here, the videographer had helpfully added a little GIF of two beer glasses, full of amber liquid with frothing heads. A ripple of laughter in the room. Her audible swearing. *Shit.* Her attempts to shake off the water to a chorus of whistles, laughter and slow clapping. The screeching bell. Her hands covering her ears in pain. The scrape of chairs as girls got up to leave, pulling out their phones as they went.

She pressed replay, barely able to breathe, barely able to believe it was real, and yet it most definitely was. This footage of her, at her most vulnerable, being mocked by students, was online, right now. It had been shared hundreds of times. The name of the person who posted it was not familiar – fake, no doubt. People had added in links to the newspaper articles about her and the school's response. Now this video was out there, public, for anyone in the world to see. Students. Parents. Friends. The entire school board. The P&C. Her mother. Zack's whole family. Evelyn Godfrey.

Phoenix watched the footage again, trembling. Who had done this? How was it allowed? Weren't there moderators that should take care of this? All schools had a way of having these things taken off social media platforms. St Clementine's had a documented process to remove things swiftly. They'd certainly been efficient in cleaning up online posts about Levi Backhurst. Why hadn't they done the same for her?

Oh. But *of course* the school hadn't contacted the service provider. It served the school's agenda to have Phoenix humiliated in this manner. This was their *proof* that she was not fit to teach. It didn't matter if that was true or not; it was all about perception. That and making sure they broke her down enough that she'd resign and go quietly.

She was still six driving hours away from Brisbane. So close, yet so far. She was exhausted, beaten. The surge of adrenaline that had flooded her body only moments ago had gone. She was defeated. She'd given this trip everything she could but she couldn't do it any more. She'd tried her best but her best simply wasn't enough.

They'd won.

She roared into the night, her screams silencing the chatter of bats and the scuttle of possums. She stamped her feet on the dirt, narrowly managing to stop herself punching the van. She was furious with Evelyn for being such a hard-arse, with Anthea for betraying her and then sticking the boot in with this video, with the students for being so unforgiving and uncompassionate and for making the bloody video in the first place, with her mother for not letting Phoenix understand who she truly was till it was too late and she was losing her career, with Lily for abandoning her when she needed her most, with Zack's awful workplace, where drinks and mateship were valued over real skill and dedication, with the ferry ride across the Bass Strait for killing Olga's chickens, with the people who dumped Linus and the ducks on her, with Bianca and Talia and her cronies for making Lily feel like she couldn't trust anyone, and with this bloody world for believing that entire populations could be ignored and shunned instead of welcomed and included.

Tears came, and she leant her forehead on the side of the van while she let out all the anger and resentment and fear and humiliation and loss. If she'd had a bottle of vodka she'd have used it to numb herself into nothingness. Instead, she crawled back into the van, locked the doors, rolled out the sleeping bag and laid her aching body down. Humphrey nuzzled her hair, then sighed heavily, dropping his head next to hers. She reached up and stroked his soft ears, feeling the last of her fight draining away. She closed her eyes, begging sleep to claim her, welcoming the darkness, the reprieve, not caring when she next woke.

30

Phoenix had been drifting somewhere out in space, but now a small part of her brain was telling her she was being slowly towed back to the confines of the van. She resisted the pull, vaguely aware that Humphrey's nose was snuffling at her hair. She didn't want full consciousness. Not yet. That way led to pain. But Humphrey was insistent, making small vocalisations, as though apologising for dragging her back to reality.

She lifted heavy eyes. 'What's wrong?' She patted his shoulder. He *wuffed* at her softly and nudged something hard towards her hand. She opened her eyes and squinted at the lit screen of her phone, on silent, but the bright light announcing a caller. It was Zack. She levered herself up onto one elbow, her spine protesting with sharp stabs. Wincing, she tapped the green button.

'Hey, why are you up so late?' she croaked. It was after midnight. She'd had less than an hour of catnapping and her insides swayed as if she were seasick.

'I'm glad you answered,' he said, relief in his voice. 'I'm outside.'

'What do you mean?' She couldn't imagine what he was doing out in the yard at midnight.

'I'm here, outside your van.'

She snapped upright. 'What? What do you mean?' She scrambled to her hands and knees.

'I didn't want to knock on the window and scare you and make you think I was Jason in a hockey mask.'

Confused, she managed to pull herself to the front of the van. Sure enough, she could see Zack's white sedan parked a few metres away. There he was, leaning against it. He was in shadow, but she'd know the outline of his body anywhere – the way he always leant against something with the sneaker of one leg crossed over the other ankle, the slope of his shoulders in his favourite *Babylon 5* tee, the length of his waist. His right hand pressed the phone to his ear while the other waved at her.

'What are you doing here?' she asked, trying to pull her foot out from where it was tangled in the sleeping bag. Beside her, Humphrey sat at attention, watching Zack through the window, but not barking. Why wasn't he barking? The dog always barked. Instead, he had his ears pricked, his head tilted to the side. Then his feathery tail began to beat gently against her side.

She tossed her phone into the console and opened the driver's door, nearly falling out in her effort to get to Zack. He rushed towards her to help and the feel of his strong hands on her arms, steadying her, flooded her with liquid warmth. He was here. He was really here, in the middle of nowhere. He helped her straighten and she fell into his embrace, holding him tightly and barraging him with questions – how, where, when, why?

'Therese called me straight after she'd spoken to you, when you told her about the deadline to meet the school board by the morning and your crazy plan to drive nearly nonstop to Brisbane on your own. She was worried about you.'

Phoenix stepped back a little so she could see his face. He was smiling down at her and ran his knuckles down the side of her cheek and neck, sending tingles down her spine. 'I knew you'd need help to get home, so I took the day off work.'

'But you never take a day off work.'

'But I'd do anything for you.' He shrugged. 'Besides, what does it matter now? I'm leaving anyway, so I rested at home and had a midday sleep then started to drive. My plan was to surprise you in Tenterfield. I was even going to be on time for a change,' he said, grinning. 'Luckily you dropped that pin to Therese to let her know where you were or I would have been waiting in Tenterfield a long time.'

'I can't believe you're here.' She ran her hands over his shoulders and down his arms, his chest and back to be sure he was real, relishing the feel of him. 'I've missed you so much.'

'Me too.'

He pressed his lips to hers. She was home. The rest of her world could go to hell – and right now, it seemed it pretty much already had – but if she had Zack by her side, she would always be home.

'I love you so much,' she whispered in between kisses, running her hands through his curls.

'I love you too.' He straightened, taking a deep breath of relief to be back with her, their bodies still pressed together. After a moment, he stepped back, surveying the van and float. The animals were unusually quiet. 'So, should we get going?' he asked. 'I can drive first and you can rest. Then if I get tired we can swap. We'll do it together.' Even in the darkness she could see the determination in his eyes and the way he held his jaw.

'But what will you do with your car?'

'I already sorted it with someone on AirTasker who'll bring it to Brisbane in a couple of days' time. You've got nothing to worry about.'

Phoenix covered her face for a moment with her hands, the reality of her situation hitting her all over again. 'I'm not going,' she admitted, quietly, her face hot with her failure. 'I mean, obviously we need to get home, but I'm not going to the board meeting.'

Zack frowned. 'What do you mean?'

Phoenix groaned. 'A lot happened today. I'm sorry you've wasted all this time and effort to make this huge romantic gesture by coming to be my knight in shining armour when there's no need. It's too late,' she finished, bitterness giving her words a hard edge.

'It's never too late,' he said, lifting his chin. 'Okay, to be totally specific, sometimes it *is* too late, like when the plane has left, or you missed the start of the hundred-metre final at the Olympics. But not in this case. We can still make it back in time. I know it's a tight time frame and it's not ideal to drive through the night and turn up to a board meeting with next to no sleep, not only on this night but for the past two weeks, and you've had no time to prepare'—he glanced at his Apple watch, tightening and loosening the strap while he calculated driving hours in his head—'and you might not have time for a shower.'

She cocked her head to the side and raised her eyebrows in amusement. He got the point. It was an ambitious plan, to say the least.

'All right, in fairness, it is an uphill battle. But we can do this, together. That's why I'm here, right now, ready to go,' he said, determination filling his voice and posture.

In response to his argument, she pulled up the school video online and showed it to him. He watched, his nostrils flaring and his jaw muscles flexing. When it ended, he swore and paced in circles between his car and her van, muttering and gesticulating while he thought through arguments and tactics. He watched it again, still pacing. At last he slowed and returned to her side. He drew in a long, slow breath and let it out heavily.

'Look, I want more than anything to tell you that you need to go to that meeting, to turn up and argue your case and fight for your right to work and have your accommodations met in the workplace without anyone seeing it as "special" or "extra" or considering you to be a burden. Everyone gets what everyone needs in order to thrive – that's the way it should be.' He paused and his shoulders eased away from his ears. 'But I'd be a hypocrite in saying that. I left a job because it was more stressful to deal with the racism head-on than to find another position. I am losing a job now because of ableism, and racism *again*, and I know it really is too big for me to fight. I wouldn't survive the battle.' He gazed down at the ground, perhaps disappointed with himself. 'I can't ask you do to what I can't. If you want to walk away now, I completely support you.'

Phoenix wiped at the blurriness in her eyes with the back of her hand. 'I appreciate that. I know right now that I'm dragging us down.'

'What? That's not true.'

'We're supposed to be buying a house and now I'm about to lose my job and I've brought all of this'—she flung her hand out towards the van and float—'into our life and I promised Olga I would support them, and then more animals arrived, and you've been so amazing at agreeing to keep them all while I have no real idea whether I'd actually even be able to do my job again, if I manage not to lose it.' Tears fell freely now. 'I don't trust myself any more.' All the emotion of the past couple of months and especially the past couple of weeks rose in her chest, threatening to spill over, but she managed to go on. 'And I wanted to ask you to marry me but how can I when I have nothing to offer you?' she confessed, sniffing loudly and wiping her nose on her shirtsleeve. (It wasn't like she could mess up her shirt any more than it already had been.)

'Wait,' he said, emphatic, stepping towards her to put his hands on her shoulders. 'Go back a step. It's not *amazing* that I'm taking on these animals. It's completely normal. This is what normal people do. They support each other, without strings. Olga needed help. These animals needed help. It shouldn't be seen as *amazing* to step up and help. It's normal baseline human behaviour. Or at least I think it should be.'

He lifted her chin a fraction. 'And as for the latter'—one corner of his lips twitched into the beginning of smile—'your value as a person isn't determined by what you can do; it's determined by who you are.'

She blinked away tears. 'Like the ducks.'

He shook his head slowly. 'You lost me.'

'Never mind.' She couldn't waste time on ducks because Zack looked like he was about to talk about her kind-of-proposal. 'Go on,' she urged, needing to hear whatever he had to say, good or bad.

'Did you really want to propose?' Starlight twinkled in his eyes as he watched her.

'Yes,' she squeaked. She gathered the last of her bravery together. 'I knew I wanted to propose early on in this trip but then I got caught in Echuca and everything started to spiral out of control, and I started to feel like it was a terrible time to ask you because everything was going wrong and I was spending our house deposit money and I want to be an equal partner in this relationship, someone who brings *something* to the table.'

He snorted gently at that. 'You do realise this is not a dowry situation, right?'

'Yeah, I know,' she said, a little irritated that he wasn't taking her concerns seriously.

'Listen. I hear what you're saying and I think I understand how you feel. I'm not saying I agree with it, only that I understand it.'

'Thank you.'

'The good news is that now I'm unemployed too,' he said, holding his arms wide, his face splitting into a grin.

'That's true.'

'And call me crazy if you like, but I think committing to each other when we're at our lowest is pretty romantic. I mean, it's easy if everything is going great, right? But if you ask me to marry you right now, while our life feels like it is somewhat imploding, and our finances are going backwards, and our careers are taking twists we didn't see coming, and we're standing in the middle of nowhere, in the dark, and you smell like . . .' He leant forwards and sniffed her. 'What is that, exactly?'

'Piglet formula,' she confessed.

'Fetching,' he teased.

'It's better than duck poo.'

Zack continued. 'As I was saying, if you ask me to marry you right now . . .'

'I want to marry you, Zack. Not in a big white dress because that makes me feel like running in the other direction, and maybe not with lots of people watching because that makes me feel like passing out, and I know you have a big extended family and that's tricky, but I *do* want to marry you, somehow, in our own autistic way. You're my one. My forever person, the one who understands me more than anyone else, the one who lights up my world, the one I want to grow old with. Somehow in all the craziness we found each other, and I don't ever want to be without you again. So, yeah, will you marry me?'

He paused a moment, then grinned, looked up to the sky a moment, then back at her. 'Yes, I will marry you, a hundred times over, in this life and the next.'

Phoenix melted into his body and breathed deeply while his arms held her tight. She wasn't even sure her feet were still touching the ground.

31

Despite Zack's long-held belief that he didn't like dogs and despite Humphrey's firm view that his life wasn't worth living without Olga, the man and his dog hit it off immediately. Zack's face lit up in response to Humphrey, who, despite everything he'd been through, and his reluctant acceptance of Phoenix and this ridiculous road trip, greeted Zack by rolling over to reveal his belly. His little paws hung in the air and his feather tail brushed patterns into the dirt, his liquid eyes focused on Zack's.

'I think he likes you,' Phoenix said, hardly believing what she was seeing. How did Humphrey possibly know that Zack was a good guy when he pulled up in his car at the rest stop? How did the dog know to wake Phoenix to take Zack's call? Why did he not bark like he had every other time a stranger arrived? But then, Zack was a gentle soul, a loving, generous, kind man. Why wouldn't Humphrey be able to see that straight away? She had.

Although usually nervous with dogs, Zack lowered to his haunches to rub Humphrey's chest. 'He's so soft,' he murmured, and Phoenix could hear the surprise in his voice. 'Albeit a little stinky.'

Phoenix laughed. 'Trust me, we're all at least a little bit stinky.' She sniffed her shirt, wrinkling her nose. 'Speaking of which, that piglet will be awake again soon and needing another bottle. I better introduce you to everyone before he squeals the place down.'

Zack crawled his way through the back of the van, meeting animals, while Phoenix called out their names and stories from the front seat and scooped formula into a bottle. It was her last clean one, she realised. They'd have to find somewhere with hot water before they got back to Brisbane. Right on cue, Lucky began to screech. Zack covered his ears till the teat was in the piglet's mouth and his eyes were rolling back in his head with joy, his delightful slurping now filling the space.

Zack ran his fingertip down Lucky's spine, making the piglet wiggle his curly tail. After a moment, he checked his watch, clucked his tongue and said, 'I hate to interrupt this sweet moment but if we're going to get you to that board meeting, we really need to make a move.'

A tight fist squeezed at Phoenix's heart.

'What do you think?' Zack prompted. 'Do you want to try? Or do you want to let it all go? It's totally up to you. I support whatever you decide, a hundred per cent.'

Phoenix closed her eyes, adjusting the piglet in her lap, his hard pointy trotters digging into her thigh through her jeans. She tried to look inside herself, to sift through the tangled wool of feelings.

She thought back to what had made her want to be a teacher in the first place. It seemed so long ago now. The decision had been influenced by her own time at school, certainly. She remembered as Year 12 drew to a close the intense sadness and fear, the desire not to leave. She remembered saying as much to one of her favourite teachers and him saying, 'You can't stay here forever,' and maybe that was part of it. She *could* stay there, if she was a teacher. She knew the system, she knew how it worked – the routine, the predictability of it all, the rules, the timetable, the yearly pattern. It all made sense.

But it had been more than that. She loved learning. She loved facts and information. Accruing knowledge brought her great joy and power. She was skilled at absorbing information and structuring it in a way that made sense to others. She wanted to share that love with students, ignite minds, inspire lives.

Outside of the awful year of bullying, school had, mostly, been a safe space for her. The kindly librarian who'd protected her in lunch hours, who'd welcomed her to retreat into the bookstacks without even needing an explanation as to why, had been the light in her darkest days. She wanted to be that light for other students too. At a deep level, she wanted to make the world a better place and the most obvious way to do that was through teaching.

She'd worked hard. Damn hard. She was a good teacher. And knowing what she knew about herself now only made her more valuable in a school, not less. The bullies might have beaten her in Year 10 but that was then. This was now. Like it or not, life had called her to this moment. It was her time to lead.

'Okay,' she said, wishing her voice was stronger but allowing it to be true, even if it was small. 'I want to try.'

'Yes,' Zack hissed, and fist-pumped the air. 'Step aside, Miss Rose. I'm taking the wheel.'

'I have to do one last thing before we go,' she said, closing the piglet's crate door. She pulled a handful of sunflower seeds from her jacket pocket and threw them out the window into the rest stop, seeding another little piece of Olga to light the way for future travellers. 'Okay, let's do it.'

Zack drove and Phoenix reclined, allowing her nerves to disentangle themselves, like long jellyfish tentacles slowly floating away with the current.

They stopped in Tenterfield to offer Rita and Linus fresh hay, give them the water bucket, apologise for the endless incarceration, and sweep the manure from the floor. They found a service station with hot water, and while Phoenix gave herself a hasty little bird bath and washed out Lucky's formula bottles, Zack took Humphrey for a wee walk and even managed to change the liners of the duck crates (without losing a single duck), mercifully improving the air quality. Now, the upliftingly scented lavender sachets could do their job unencumbered. He talked to the ducks and chickens about the new wooden houses he'd built and painted – yellow and white, because yellow was Phoenix's favourite colour. 'And we'll be able to add these sunflower light strings to the front of their houses too,' he said, indicating the nearest glowing flower.

'I think you're loving this quite a lot,' Phoenix ribbed.

'Maybe I am. Maybe I'll be a man of the land now.' Zack put the van into drive and they set off again. Phoenix knew she couldn't sleep but she sat a pillow up against the window, put in her earplugs, pulled down her eye mask and let herself drift. She felt her nervous system calm immediately, both from the sensory deprivation and also knowing Zack was there, that she wasn't alone any more. It was such a deep relief that she might have dozed a little, images flashing through her mind – a farmhouse on open green land, she and Zack surrounded by their menagerie, a sunflower field in the distance, a huge lemon tree bursting with bright yellow fruit against dark green leaves. The tyres thrummed ever onwards, minute by minute narrowing the distance and the time between them and the board meeting.

They followed the New England Highway. Stanthorpe, then Warwick. It was now 4.30 am. A stretch break for them both and Phoenix took the wheel, this time heading up the Cunningham Highway to Ipswich, arriving at 6 am. Out of the car for a rather unsatisfying breakfast of hash browns from a food chain and thick black coffee, nasty and bitter, then back on the road, Zack at the wheel once again. This was it, the last stretch. In theory, they should make it back to Chermside by 7.30, leaving enough time for Phoenix to have a quick shower at home before presenting herself to the board.

Her belly flipped like the pancakes she wished she'd been able to eat. Surely they'd make it. Surely nothing could go wrong now.

32

Nothing extraordinary happened on the road to Brisbane. There were no multiple vehicle accidents to block the roads for hours. There were no natural disasters like floods or fires to cut access. There were no wild horses or endangered koala parades. Not a single unusual thing to stop their progress and prevent Phoenix getting to school on time for that board meeting. Not one.

Instead, there was just the absolutely bloody ordinary. Traffic. Kilometre after kilometre of snarling snail-paced peak-hour traffic, all the way from Ipswich to Chermside, on four-lane freeways and tunnel bypasses, and roadworks that narrowed multiple lanes to one. Bumper to bumper. Red light to red light. The clock ticked on.

Seven o'clock. Phoenix had to pull Lucky from his cage, make a bottle and feed him in her lap.

Eight o'clock. Phoenix's insides were hard as rock with fear and her knee jigged up and down. The happy conversation between her and Zack all but disappeared as each withdrew inside themselves in their own patchwork of anxiety, frustration and sinking spirits.

Eight-thirty. Humphrey sighed and whined repeatedly, his tolerance for this shit show exhausted.

Nine. A chicken laid an egg and nearly burst Phoenix's eardrums with her raucous announcement, and at least two cats began yowling and butting their heads against their wire doors, desperate to be done with this.

She knew exactly how they felt.

Zack broke the silence between them. 'I don't think you're going to have time to duck home for a shower.'

'I know.'

'Do you have any clean clothes within easy reach?' he asked.

'Nothing that smells like fresh washing, no, but probably something better than this.' She gestured to the pizza-topping-style combination of assorted stains and aromas on her shirt. She twisted in her seat but, try as she might, she couldn't reach her bag. There was no way they could pull over and waste the precious minutes it would take to extract the bag and lose their place in the creep of cars.

It was hot, too, a burst of spring heat pushing the temperature towards 30 degrees today, and the burn of the sun was already piercing through the windshield and bouncing off the hard surfaces of the vehicles around them. Phoenix turned up the air conditioning to help cool the animals in the back.

Nine-fifteen. Rita let out several long, float-shaking neighs. People in the cars around them stared at the float. Phoenix agonised that Rita and Linus had been stuck in there for so long. Straight after this meeting, despite how desperately she wanted to go home and fall into bed, they would take them to the agistment she'd organised out at Samford. The torment of another long day stretched ahead.

She checked her reflection in the visor mirror and ran her hands through her hair, detangling the worst of the knots in her eastern spinebill locks, Olga's words momentarily warming her. Olga may have been onto something. Her hair certainly looked like a bird's nest right now.

She licked her fingertip and attempted to smooth her wayward eyebrows, then twisted her hair back up into a bun at her crown. Her lips were dry but there was no balm in sight. It was the best she could do. They passed the turn-off to their house and she tried to ignore the ache for a shower and a change of clothes.

'Come on, come on,' she urged the traffic.

'Have you planned what you want to say?' Zack asked. She nearly laughed. It was way too late to be wondering that.

'A bit, but it's tricky without knowing what they're going to throw at me. I'll try to stick to my main points.'

'I'll come with you,' he said.

She shook her head, sadly. 'You can't. You'll need to stay with this lot.' She tipped her head in the direction of their menagerie. 'They'll get too hot in the van. They'll need the engine running with the aircon on.'

'Damn,' Zack said, frowning. 'I want to be there. You shouldn't have to go alone.'

'True,' she agreed. 'But here we are.'

And there they were, pulling up outside the imposing set of multistorey red-brick buildings that lined the manicured lawns at the college's entrance. Three gardeners in high-vis shirts tilled, pruned and mulched the red-flowering bushes in preparation for the beginning of next term. Phoenix was glad, at least, that no students were there to see her in this state of disrepair, especially after that video.

The thought of it circulating among the students and their families made her so swiftly, acutely sick that bile actually shot to her throat. She closed her eyes, remembering to do a calming exercise, feeling herself only in this van in this moment. This van,

Zack and the animals inside it were her whole world right now. She took a deep breath as he parked in an empty spot.

Five things she could see. The dried purple lavender flowers in tiny white bags. The shining lights of the sunflower string. The small stone chip in the windscreen. The alien image of Ambassador Kosh on the front of Zack's faded *Babylon 5* tee. Her bitten and torn fingernails.

Four things she could feel. Her toes wiggling inside her scuffed boots, the seat at her back, her chest rising as she took another breath, her jeans stretched across her kneecaps and – she reached out and took Zack's hand – warm fingers threaded through hers.

Three things she could hear. The ducks shuffling in their crate, one of the kittens meowing, Humphrey panting.

Two things she could smell. The scent of the lavender and her stained shirt, unfortunately.

One thing she could taste. She leant over to kiss Zack. He tasted of minty chewing gum.

'You're going to do great,' he said, pressing his forehead to hers for a moment.

'Thanks.'

'But let me help you find a different shirt first. I promise it will be worth it to be a couple of minutes late.'

She snorted. 'Fair enough.'

33

In her not clean but not-too-smelly, not-too-stained green long-line tee, Phoenix marched up the concrete footpath to the administration building and pushed open the heavy glass door with a soft *whoosh*. It was quiet inside, save for the clacking of a keyboard as an office assistant typed. Phoenix was about to say good morning to her when Evelyn's assistant Linda popped out of Evelyn's office. She was wearing a white skirt suit, even though there were no students present. Phoenix had to hand it to anyone who could pull off wearing a white suit to work. She'd have slopped her coffee on it before even leaving the house.

'Hi, Linda.'

Linda returned the greeting with the smallest of nods. 'They're waiting for you in the boardroom.'

Phoenix put one foot in front of the other, down the hallway, past the executive offices, past the toilets where she'd locked herself on the day of her shutdown, through the staffroom, empty now, the only sounds the hum and shudder of the fridges and the thermostat tick of the wall-mounted hot-water dispenser. The boardroom lay beyond a heavy mahogany door. She paused at the golden name plate – *The Ferdinand McAlister Board Room* – and wondered again who Ferdinand McAlister had been and what he'd done to deserve this room being named after him. Maybe he'd done nothing at all other than pay for the addition of this wing to the building. She could hear muffled voices on the other side and resisted the urge to turn and run, forcing herself to knock twice instead.

'Come,' instructed Evelyn's penetrating voice.

The heavy door opened with an expensive-sounding *pft* of air. Linda's heels clacked behind her and Phoenix almost jumped out of the way to allow her to bustle through and take her place at the other end of the rectangular table, the first seat around the corner from where Evelyn sat like a grumpy crow in black at the head. Phoenix swept her gaze around those already gathered. Next to Linda on the long side sat a parent board member. Phoenix knew his face – she never forgot a face, no matter how many years had passed – but couldn't remember his name, because names were as easy to lose as her car keys, wallet and mobile phone. Here one moment, gone the next. He smiled at her though, and his eyes were kind – the same greyish blue as the suit he was wearing. She returned his smile, grateful.

Next to him, though, was Anthea, an arm's length from where Phoenix was required to sit. A wave of some sort of disagreeable perfume hit her. It smelled like a synthetic version of honeydew melon and it hurt her brain. She met Anthea's gaze briefly and Anthea wrinkle-twitched her nose, like a rabbit, a gesture Phoenix knew to be one of great discomfort. That knowledge did little, though, to ameliorate the sight of the person she had thought was her friend arrayed here with the attackers. It made her heart lurch so painfully she had to cough in order to breathe again.

Phoenix took her seat on the short side of the table, opposite Evelyn, finishing her visual trip around the table as she did so. To her immediate left was a second parent board member, also a man, also in a suit. She neither recognised him nor knew his name. His dark goatee made her skin crawl.

Last to finish that line was Robert Kendall, president of the P&C – the man who'd publicly called her intellectually impaired. She flared her nostrils at him. 'What are you doing here?' she asked. 'I thought the P&C was a separate entity from the board.'

Robert's chin jutted backwards, offended, but Evelyn spoke for him. 'Robert is not here in his capacity as P&C president but as a parent of students at this school.' Phoenix could barely contain an eye roll. It made no difference what they called him, his agenda was the same.

'Right, now that you're here,' Evelyn said, pausing a moment to make a show of taking in Phoenix's appearance, a matter Phoenix felt compelled to address.

'I would have liked to have had the opportunity to get suited up like the rest of you,' she said, gesturing around the table, 'but given I was in Dubbo when I received your summons for this meeting, I have barely made it back to Brisbane in a state of consciousness, let alone washed and dressed appropriately.' She turned to face Linda, taking the minutes on her laptop. 'Please ensure the record reflects that I am at a disadvantage in this matter, completely unable to present my best self, through no fault of my own.' She paused. Her poker face was most definitely not in place. The mask was down and she had little control over it at this moment. She didn't have enough capacity to play the game on their terms. Still, she attempted to find a part of herself that was at least a little less combative.

She cleared her throat and looked down at the tabletop, waiting.

'Phoenix,' Evelyn said, adopting an artificially gentle tone. 'The board has *concerns*,' she said, placing due weight and respect on the last word. 'My goodness, a lot has happened recently, hasn't it?' She offered a small, hollow chuckle, as if cajoling a toddler into considering her actions. 'Some choices have been made that, in hindsight, might not have been the wisest. Wouldn't you agree?'

Phoenix blinked, conscious of all eyes staring at her, and wondered which part of this she was supposed to agree with. A lot had happened, yes; with that, she absolutely agreed. She remained silent.

'There was—' here Evelyn paused, tipping her glasses down her nose a fraction so she could stare at Phoenix over them '—the incident in the classroom.'

Out of the corner of her eye, she could see Anthea offer a sympathetic look. No, not sympathetic – regretful.

'Then there was the extended sick leave, followed by some indecision about whether or not you were ready to return, then your abrupt decision to return, followed almost immediately by the disappointing footage of one of our teachers, bound by lifestyle expectations, kissing a young woman.'

'How many times do I have to say this?' Phoenix said, emphasising each word. 'Lily was my travelling companion, nothing more.' She paused. That wasn't actually true. Lily was a lot more than that. She was her very dear friend, a friend Phoenix was worried about and missing terribly. 'It was the angle of the camera, that was all.'

'Impressions have been made, though,' Robert Kendall interjected, crossing his arms at his chest. 'You can't deny that.'

'Oh, is that what we do now? We go along with what something *looks* like rather than what's true? To be truly in line with the *values* we are supposed to be living, wouldn't it be more appropriate to defend a person falsely accused? To protect and uplift a devoted member of your community?'

Robert Kendall raised his bushy brows and glanced at Evelyn, whose fingers were pressed to her forehead. Phoenix had never seen the principal look flustered before. It was intriguing.

'You have to understand the position the school is in,' Evelyn said. 'We've had'—here she cleared her throat—'two families pull their children from this school in the past two days citing the fact that they don't trust the integrity of St Clementine's any more.'

'Again,' Phoenix said, 'this has nothing to do with me. I would wager they've had longstanding issues and are seizing the moment now, using this as an excuse. You can't pin the school's bad reputation on me – a reputation that was started by Levi earlier in the year.'

'What about the footage from class?'

The question was asked in a small voice and Phoenix gasped, whipping her head round to stare Anthea in the face. 'Yes, what about that?' she challenged. She turned to look each of them in the eye, one by one. 'This school has had footage removed from social media platforms before. Indeed, all schools can and do so as the need arises. Yet the footage of me in extreme distress, doctored with beer steins, no less, has been out there for two days now, garnering thousands of views and shares, not to mention defamatory comments, and no one has done anything about it. I can only assume you have made the conscious choice to leave it there to embarrass me into resigning.'

'Now, listen here—' Robert began.

'No!' Phoenix said, pointing at him. 'You listen to me. You called me intellectually impaired on the public record. That is utterly false. My intellect is perfectly intact. I can, and well might, sue you for defamation.'

'How dare you—'

'Phoenix, there's no need to—'

'Let's be reasonable—'

'Everybody calm down.' Evelyn looked around as if searching for a gavel.

'Let's stop tiptoeing around what your real problem is,' Phoenix said. 'You have a problem with a senior teacher being autistic.'

There was a prolonged silence, in which Phoenix waited, eyeing them off. Robert's face bloomed purple. Anthea sucked on her top lip and stared at Evelyn, waiting for the woman to respond. Linda sat motionless, her fingers poised above the keyboard. Phoenix knew they were stuck. They had a problem but they weren't allowed to say it out loud and certainly not in a board meeting where minutes were being taken.

At last, Evelyn said, 'That's not true,' then cast a steely glare towards Robert to shut him up.

The parent with the kind eyes cleared his throat. 'Phoenix, would you like to tell us about autism and how the school can help you?' he said.

Phoenix gave him a grateful smile, while also noting the twitching jaw muscles of Evelyn and Robert.

'Wait,' Evelyn interjected. 'I'd like to make it clear that I pride myself on making sure that everyone gets treated equally in this school. Everyone gets the same treatment and level of scrutiny. Everyone is required to uphold the school's standards.' She pulled the bottom of her jacket with a sharp, shiny sound, to signal the end of her point.

'It's interesting you say that,' Phoenix said. 'Treating everyone the same is the *idea* of equality and yet it isn't fair, because not everyone is bringing the same resources to the table. Giving everyone what they *need* in life to have the same opportunities is fair. That's called *equity.*' Phoenix could see Linda frowning as she attempted to type this into the minutes.

'Speak English,' Robert snarled.

With supreme control, Phoenix smothered her rising impatience. 'Say you have three people standing at a fence, trying to watch a soccer match on the other side. One person is six foot tall and can see easily. One is ten years old, and can only just see over the fence if they jump up and down the whole time. The other is a toddler, who can't see anything. If you gave everyone a step to

297

stand on, they still wouldn't be equal. Now the tall person can see even better, the ten-year-old can just see, but the toddler still can't see anything.

'And then, what if there was a fourth person in a wheelchair? Would the step help them? No. To provide true equity, everyone gets what everyone needs. The six-foot-tall person gets nothing, because they don't need it; they could see perfectly well to begin with. The ten-year-old gets a large wooden box to stand on and now can see comfortably. The toddler gets a ladder to climb to a viewing platform. And the person in the wheelchair gets a ramp to the viewing platform.'

The man with the kind eyes smiled and nodded enthusiastically, his eyes shining. 'So, Phoenix, here is your chance. Tell us, what do you need us to do for you to be able to do your job?'

Phoenix blinked back tears as she tipped her head towards him in thanks. He got it. He really got it. But her chest was so full of emotion right now, and she was so sleep deprived, and she needed a shower so desperately, that her words dried up.

They were all staring at her, waiting, and the more they stared the more the glass wall came down. She could see them all, hear them breathing, shuffling papers, clicking pens, crossing and uncrossing legs and feet but her words had disappeared, and the more she tried to drag them back, the more they ran in the other direction.

'Would you like some water?' Anthea said, and despite all the things she'd done, Phoenix felt true warmth for her then. There she was – the person who'd been her friend, once. She'd been devastated when Anthea had withdrawn her support, aligning herself with those who had the most power, but she was thankful to have it here now.

She nodded at her and Anthea pushed her chair back to head to the staffroom kitchen.

'You know,' the kind man started, addressing everyone, 'maybe it would be easier for Phoenix to write down what she needs. She could type it up for us. I'm not sure any of us would be at our best after travelling the distances she has.'

Evelyn closed her eyes and took in a measured breath, noticeably suppressing her frustration at the suggestion of delaying this further.

Phoenix wasn't surprised in the slightest. What on earth had she expected from the woman who barely tolerated bereavement and maternity leave, two things considered utterly standard? There wasn't a version of reality in which Evelyn Godfrey was going to accept a disabled teacher in her ranks. Conversation continued around the table as they argued with themselves about the best way to handle this situation (Linda's typing noticeably stalled while she waited for the 'offline' discussion to end) and Phoenix retreated further into herself.

At last, she managed to hold up her pointer finger in a recognisable *just give me a minute* gesture and pushed her chair back to leave the room. She hurried past Anthea, now returning with the glass of water, and headed to the toilets, closing the cubicle door behind her.

So there she was again, stuck in the toilets, unable to put voice to her thoughts.

Fabulous, Phoenix. Way to go.

She sat on the toilet with her arms wrapped around her waist, rocking back and forth to calm herself, then pulled her phone from her pocket and called Zack.

'Hey, how's it going? Is it over? Where are you?' he asked.

'In the toilets.'

He paused. 'Do you need some help? Should I come get you, like last time?'

She very much wanted to say yes. She wanted him to come and get her and together they would drive away with their new animal family and put all this behind them and start again somewhere, anywhere in Australia where Zack could find another job doing what he loved, while she figured out what the hell to do next.

'Maybe. I don't know. What are you doing right now? Talk to me for a bit. Distract me.'

'Okay. Right now, I have the kittens out of their crate,' he said, a smile lifting his voice.

His words surprised her and had the immediate effect of halting her downward spiral. 'Jane as well? She's not really supposed to be very active yet.'

'I know. I remember. Milo is climbing all over the van. He's trying to play with the ducks and chickens through the bars and he's wrestling Humphrey's tail. Humphrey is really patient with him.'

'Oh, that's so sweet,' she said, calming further at the thought of their animals' happiness.

'Every now and then, Milo grabs hold of Humphrey's back leg with his front paws, lays his ears flat, screws up his eyes, sinks his teeth in and kicks. All Humphrey does is gaze at him like an adoring big brother and nose him out the way if it's a bit much.'

Phoenix smiled, listening to Humphrey's rhythmic panting. 'But what about Jane?'

'I'm holding her. I let her take a few steps across the seat, then I pick her up again and bring her back. It's some gentle physio for her.'

After another minute of listening to Zack's stories, Phoenix felt recharged. 'I better get back in there. It's the home straight.'

'You can do it – and whatever happens we'll be here waiting for you. Love you.'

'Love you too.'

She pocketed her phone, let herself out of the cubicle, and strode back to the boardroom.

34

Phoenix stepped through the boardroom door. Everyone stopped bickering and shifted their weight back from the table, where they'd been leaning towards each other, each trying to make their point.

'You're back,' Evelyn said, a statement, nothing more.

'Yes.' Phoenix hovered.

'Take a seat and let's get this sorted,' the new principal said, her patience decisively gone.

'No, thank you. I need to stand.'

Evelyn's face pinched then hardened, affronted.

'I'll try to keep this brief,' Phoenix assured her.

After a moment, Evelyn waved her hand. 'Say your piece, then.'

'Okay,' Phoenix said, then took in a long breath. She turned to the kind man for reassurance and he gave it with a small smile and an encouraging nod. It was enough. 'I would firstly like to say that I'm sorry.' She felt the weight of all eyes on her. For now, she directed her gaze to about a foot above Evelyn's head.

'It wasn't my fault that I had a shutdown in class. I'm not proud of it. I'm not happy it happened. But I do know it wasn't my fault.' She paused, allowing the feeling of self-forgiveness to sink into her bones. 'I am human, and all humans will break under the right circumstances.' The room was silent. 'I am a good teacher with a long history that proves that, and I pride myself on being there for my students. It may not be my fault,' she repeated, 'though I am still sorry it happened. Any day that I'm not totally present for my students is a day I'd like to do better.'

Phoenix felt, rather than saw, Evelyn's demeanour quaver. She went on.

'I am also sorry that I broke protocol in speaking to the media without permission. While I do not necessarily agree that teachers should be kept silent, as a careful follower of rules it took a great deal of pressure on me before I felt I needed to break one.' Here she saw the kind parent stare meaningfully at Evelyn, who had the surprising good grace to look sheepish.

She chewed her lip for a moment, thinking. There was so much she wanted to say but there was no way she could get through it all, and there was no way that Linda, typing speedily and glaring at the screen, could possibly keep up with the minutes as it was. She was swallowed briefly by doubt, but willed herself to go on.

'You've asked me what I need to continue. My identification is so recent, and my response to it is in its infancy. What I need in a month or a year might be different from what I've already learnt. But I love teaching. I love making a difference in kids' lives. I love acquiring knowledge and learning with my students, and learning from them. I love the days when I see those light bulbs go off in a student's head.' She smiled. 'Equally, I love being able to notice that a student is not doing well. I can invite them to put their head down on the desk and rest, to gather their strength for the next class, or a long ride home on the bus, or whatever it is they're going to find at home. I'm grateful if I can make a student's day better.'

She gazed around, taking in the faces of the board members. All eyes were on her and she welcomed them. 'I do need support.' She nodded, pointing to herself. 'Absolutely. And I'm not the only one. Right now, you're looking at me and thinking it's too hard to make changes for me – for one person – to accommodate my needs as something extra or special or as yet one more thing you don't want to have to do.

'But the things that will help me will help everyone. Our school has kids who go home to violence, to endless arguments, and students who are forced to play the role of parent for younger kids. Our students have experienced sexual violence, self-harm, bullying, eating disorders. We have kids with as-yet-unspecified conditions who have no idea why they struggle, why they're in trouble, and why they can't get help. Where other teachers see a student as lazy, I see anxiety so debilitating that the student can't even start the first sentence of an essay for the crippling fear of getting it wrong. I see kids with depression so deep they can't see a future, even just as far as making it to the next morning.'

She gestured above her head to the ceiling. 'We're working in buildings that are nearly a hundred years old and our classrooms still look like black-and-white photos from the fifties. Board at the front of the room. A teacher facing the students. Rows of identical desks and chairs where they have to sit still. Surely we can make some small changes that help to calm everyone's nervous systems, students and teachers alike?'

Anthea gazed up at her, taking in her words, nodding.

'Do we really need to have a screeching bell eight times a day? No one else in the world runs their life by bells.' She paused. 'Except maybe prisons.' That got her a couple of chuckles. 'The students start to pack themselves up ten minutes before the end of a lesson anyway because they are watching the clock the whole time. No one is going to forget to end a lesson.' She laughed, lightly. 'Though if both the teacher and the students were so deeply engaged with what they were doing and forgot to end the lesson, that would be marvellous.' Both the kind man and Anthea smiled at this, giving her courage to continue.

'Do we need bright fluorescent lights that flicker and hum? Can we not turn the air conditioning on in really hot rooms in summer? No one is happy when they're hot, sweaty and prickly. Can we not have a choice of seating in rooms, with wobbly chairs and beanbags and standing desks for those who need to shuffle around, or who have back pain, or are exhausted from working two after-school jobs, playing sport, taking care of younger siblings, managing their home life and studying as well? Can we not make more designated quiet spaces aside from the library, for students who need peace and those who are afraid to be out alone at lunchtime? Would it be so hard for every room to have a box of fidgets for students – any student – to use whenever they needed? Can every student, not just the autistic ones, have an *I need a break* card to hand to their teacher if they are overwhelmed and need to step outside for a bit? These are all human needs, not special needs. Everyone reaches their limit at some point and every human being has different abilities on different days.'

She looked straight at Evelyn. 'Surely caring for each other should be our number one "lifestyle" value.' She paused here, holding the principal's gaze, knowing her feelings had started to run away with her. She reminded herself to breathe. This might be the last time she got to say the words she needed to say.

She wasn't under any illusion she was about to change the school, let alone the world. But sometimes, the purpose of speaking up was simply about being part of something bigger, doing your own little bit to make the next step forwards a little easier for the person following.

'People like me are not the exception; we are simply the obvious. Once upon a time, I wasn't obvious. I've only become obvious due to stressors that have built up to unmanageable levels. Every student in our classroom could be the next obvious one in need of help, the next one like me. I would like to see us create change for them now, before they reach burnout.

'We need to make adjustments to support neurodivergent learners, absolutely. But we can do that in a way that is inclusive, rather than exclusive, that is welcoming, rather than stigmatising. If we help our neurodivergent students, we'll inclusively help everyone.'

The kind man began to clap, nodded at her and smiled. She returned his smile, grateful for his support. But no one else spoke.

Eventually, Evelyn asked, 'Is that all?'

Phoenix swallowed with some difficulty, suddenly aware her mouth was bone dry. 'Yes,' she said softly. She gestured over her shoulder. 'I'm going to go now. Thank you for listening.'

She turned and left the room, strode through the staffroom, past Evelyn's and Linda's offices, the clacking keyboards and the whirring printer, and into the sunlight. Zack was waiting for her on the footpath, pacing beside the van. He hurried to meet her.

'Are you okay? What happened?' He wrapped her in his arms and she leant into him, nodding into his shoulder.

'Let's go. We've got animals to take care of.'

35

Downunder Auties

PhoenixRising: Hi everyone! I made it back to Brisbane. I have so much to share with you all but I first needed to pop in to say a huge thank you to you all for keeping me going and getting me through this trip. All of Olga's animals, minus two chickens (rest their feathery souls), made it back to Brisbane, as well as the two kittens (Jane, who is doing much better and will be climbing the blinds any day now, and Milo, who is a gigantic ball of fluff and loves to chase Zack's shoelaces), as well as Linus the alpaca (sporting a bad eighties curly perm that falls over his eyes) and Lucky the piglet (who is hiding with us in our rental for a little longer yet until he's weaned and we can find somewhere for him to live).

Thank you, Bruno, for lending us your van – which I'm sure will never be the same again – and for coming to my rescue in Echuca, staying the night and teaching me to hitch and pull a horse float. (There's a sentence I never thought I'd say.) You truly were a lifesaver.

The Wonderful Thing about Phoenix Rose

Thank you, Shane, for your stellar accounting advice, Carla for finding me Lily (without her I'm sure I would never have made it through the trip at all), and Therese for midnight counselling and being my desk jockey, which meant I got to meet Mel, Jess, Kitty and your families along the way. Most importantly, Therese, you were right to call Zack and tell him about my ambitious all-night drive. Thank you ☺ Trust me when I say that all of you, not to mention the cakes and coffee you brought me (!), were invaluable in getting me to the finish line. I seem to be getting my kitchen mojo back and I see a lot of baking in my near future to return the favours.

I made it back to school in the nick of time to say my piece and now I'm waiting to hear from them. I'll let you know, of course. Here are some more photos from the last legs of the journey (as well as Lucky the piglet, who I'm sure you'll agree is criminally cute with his little milk beard), as well as a selfie of me and Zack at dawn this morning in Ipswich. That moment already feels like a lifetime ago. (Oh, and I asked him to marry me and he said yes! We're officially engaged, a thought that makes me feel less terrified this time and more . . . fluffy . . . and yellow.)

I also wanted to let you know that someone from the university replied to my email to let me know they have made progress on ensuring Olga's research work could be saved, which is such a relief.

Most importantly, though, I'm so grateful to every one of you for helping me help Olga rest in peace. I think our collective efforts have done her proud. x

36

Audrey's heavy weight landed on Phoenix's ribs early the next morning. The cat scooted on across the bed, with Marilyn in hot pursuit. When Phoenix groaned in protest, both cats jumped nimbly back up onto the mattress, Marilyn purring loudly and headbutting Phoenix in the eye.

'I'm guessing you want breakfast?' she said, rubbing the little cat's head.

'Sorry,' Zack said, coming to the door, wearing underpants and a faded T-shirt and one sock. His hair stuck up like he'd had his finger in a power socket. 'Lucky was banging on his crate door so I got up to make him a bottle and woke everyone up.'

The sight of him made her smile. 'Rough night?'

'Lucky's hard work,' he admitted, scrubbing the heel of his hand into one eye. 'It's a good thing he's cute.' The pink piglet skipped past the doorway on tiptoes, his trotters clicking on the floorboards and his tail wagging in post-breakfast glee.

'Is he trying to play with the cats?'

'Yep. I don't think it's going to end well,' Zack said, just as Milo skittered past, sliding across the floor, coming to a halt on his back paws, face-to-face with the piglet. The kitten fluffed to three times his size and hissed.

'What happened to your other sock?' she said, a smile in her voice.

'Milo stole it. Pulled it right off and dragged it away like lions do on nature documentaries when they've killed an impala or something.'

Marilyn headbutted Phoenix once more. 'All right, I'm coming,' she said, flinging back the covers. Outside in the yard the chickens were murmuring and the ducks quacking. It sounded like one was already in the paddling pool. 'What time is it?'

'Six o'clock.'

'No rest for the wicked, then,' she said, trying to rise. Zack got to her before she could swing her legs over, leaning down and kissing her, gently pushing her back against the pillow.

'Just a few more minutes,' he said, climbing in beside her. 'I've already called in sick today because I need to kiss my wife properly and for a long time.'

'We're not married yet,' she said, running her hand up under his shirt, her body humming as his skin met hers.

'Let's fix that as soon as possible,' he whispered.

They took their time to get ready and out the door and it was late morning when they made it back to the agistment paddock to check in on Rita and Linus. Both the pony and the alpaca had calmed since yesterday when they had practically bolted out of the float, snorting and careering around their new home, throwing high kicks that would put cancan dancers to shame. This morning, though, they were peaceful, lifting their heads from the grass as Phoenix and Zack approached, each carrying a bag of treats. They both came trotting to the fence to greet them.

'Here you go, babies,' Phoenix soothed, offering cut-up apple and carrot and soft bread as apologies for all they'd been through. She showed Zack how to offer treats to Rita with a flat hand, pushing up gently towards her mouth as she reached for the apple, so as not to get his fingers bitten by accident.

On the other side of their paddock's wooden fence, three sun-drenched women sat on a rug on the grass, wearing jodhpurs and glossy riding boots. Their horses were tall, sleek, muscly and sweaty, their saddles resting on the fence. Their thick manes were shiny – unlike hers, she thought, running a hand through her still-wet hair. At least she smelt like soap now. The women turned around to take in the sight of Phoenix and Zack, dressed in baggy pants and sneakers, feeding their dishevelled, hairy pony and skinny alpaca.

Phoenix raised a hand in greeting, smiling weakly, feeling like the girl at school who didn't fit in. But the three women smiled and waved back and raised their . . . beers? Phoenix squinted. Yes, they were drinking beers at eleven o'clock in the morning, possibly after having been horseriding. Huh. She gave them a hearty thumbs up because she had no idea how to respond to that. Zack gave her a puzzled look. She raised her shoulders and let them fall.

When Rita and Linus had finished their treats, Phoenix and Zack wandered around their allotted yard, shovelling manure into a pile and filling the water trough. A few moments later, one of the women in the next paddock squealed and there was a burst of laughter. Phoenix looked up to see that Rita had sneaked up behind them and stolen a beer bottle, tipping it onto the ground and lapping at it eagerly.

'Sorry!' she called, racing over there. 'She drinks coffee, but I had no idea she'd drink beer too.'

The women fell about laughing.

'It's fine,' the red-headed rider said, picking up the bottle. 'Harry over there loves beer,' she said, indicating her horse, who was rolling in the grass with a relieved grunt and groan. 'Happens all the time.'

'Really?'

'Lots of horses love beer,' said another woman with defined shoulder muscles and a sleeve of tattoos down her right arm. 'Especially Shitlands.'

'Oh, are you from New Zealand?' Phoenix asked, reminding herself not to copy the accent.

This caused all three of the women to guffaw, in on a joke Phoenix wasn't part of. She shifted uncomfortably from one foot to another, waiting for them to stop.

The tattooed woman took a breath. 'Don't mind us. We're celebrating Jilly's divorce with horseriding and beers.'

'Oh.' Phoenix didn't know what to say, and she had no idea which of them was Jilly.

The tattooed woman went on. 'Shetland ponies are often referred to as "Shitlands" because they're such little shits.' They all laughed again and Phoenix smiled to be polite, though in truth she wasn't amused. She quite loved Rita and thought she was marvellous.

'Are you new to horses?' the redhead asked, taking a steadying breath.

'Is it that obvious?' Phoenix said.

The redhead snorted, gazing at Linus, a bemused smile on her lips. 'A bit. I'm Jilly. Let us know if you need any help, okay?'

'Thanks, I will,' Phoenix said, waved goodbye and led the Shetland back towards Zack.

Although she wasn't entirely at ease with the three riders in the nearby paddock, she had to admit that the hour she and Zack had spent at the paddock, working up a sweat in the sunshine, had been otherwise enjoyable. As they left the property, she realised she hadn't once thought about school, Evelyn, the awful news-paper article, Anthea, the horrible P&C president or even whether she still had a job. She'd been there in the paddock, under a blue sky, in the moment, shovelling poo and brushing Rita – her very first pony – and it had all been rather unexpectedly enjoyable. She left with an easy sense of calm in her chest.

Back at the house, though, as the day ground on, there were reminders everywhere of Phoenix's career. Piles of notebooks and textbooks sat around on benches, her work clothes hung in the wardrobe, her yard duty hat hung on the hook by the door and tubs of resources from years gone by were stacked in the wardrobe. She even found a sports whistle in the bottom of an overflowing kitchen drawer. Each was a reminder of her valued identity as a teacher. As the minutes ticked by, her nerves grew sharp.

'I'm going clean out the van,' she announced to Zack, who was sitting on the floor of the loungeroom with Humphrey, carefully brushing the dog's coat. Humphrey sat still, occasionally nosing Zack on the cheek with great affection. There was no doubt about it, that dog was absolutely smitten with Zack. She cast her eyes to the heavens a moment and mouthed *thank you* to Olga.

Outside, she swung open the van's doors and peered down the runway of the space inside. The crates and cages had all been removed and were stacked in the yard, now empty. The sleeping bags were still there, and a random assortment of plastic bags, rubbish and tools. She pulled the shovel from the van, noting it would be of most use now in her horse paddock, then did the same with the broom, which reminded her she still needed to clean out the float and take it to the rental drop-off location. There was also the foam box with *Camping* written on the side. Phoenix remem-bered Lily putting that in the van before they left, thinking the tarps and ropes might come in handy. She stopped still now, staring at the box. Without warning, her eyes filled with tears.

She missed Lily so much.

She put herself to work bagging up rubbish and filling the wheelie bin to bursting. She longed to have Lily here too with her charismatic way of speaking, her willingness to sing to Phoenix to lift her spirits, her passion for bats, the ease with which they could talk for an hour or sit in comfortable silence together, her artistic flair and the generosity that would lead her to drop everything to save a kitten stuck in a tree. But the loss was more than simply Lily's presence at her side. It was the grief of yet another lost friendship that had flared and burnt brightly before abruptly extinguishing. At the very least, she wished Lily would simply return one of her text messages, simply to let her know she was okay, if nothing else.

As always, Phoenix had let herself fall hard and fast for her new friend. When she gave her heart to someone (people *or* animals, apparently) she gave it all, every last bit of it. Despite repeated evidence to the contrary, she assumed that others did the same. But they didn't. She was different. She'd thought Lily had been like her. And that hurt too. She'd thought she'd found someone equally willing to offer their loyalty.

Was this the way she would go through life? Forever wanting a friend who enjoyed her company as much as she enjoyed theirs? Forever looking for the same trust that Phoenix so willingly offered?

She let the lid fall on the wheelie bin and returned to the van. There was just the foam box of camping supplies left. She tugged at it, grunting with effort. It was heavier than she'd anticipated. She shook her head, bemused. Lily had hefted this box into the van easily. Phoenix put one foot up on the back of the vehicle to brace herself and tugged again, but the foam was slippery under her fingers.

Somewhere behind the horse float she heard a car pull up, its engine idling gently. Great, now she'd have an onlooker or two wondering why there was a zebra van and horse float parked in a suburban street of Brisbane. She heard the car door close and the vehicle drive away. *Keep walking,* she urged whoever it was that had stepped out. Climbing inside the van, she positioned herself behind the box, attempting to shove it towards the open doors. She could feel her face reddening with effort.

'May I be of assistance?'

Phoenix kept her eyes downcast. 'No, thank you, I'm okay,' she said, not able to make eye contact, not wanting to engage. But the woman didn't move. Phoenix had to stop and look up, puffing with exertion.

She was there.

37

'Lily?' Phoenix said, momentarily wondering if she'd passed out somewhere on the road between Dubbo and Tamworth and imagined she'd made it all the way home. The sleep deprivation in the past few weeks had been extreme.

'Hello,' Lily said. She was wearing a cream short-sleeved dress, a high-low hem revealing her pale, thin legs and more thigh than Phoenix had seen so far. A leather corset cinched her waist, her hands were gloved in lace, and a hat with driving goggles completed the ensemble.

'You look fierce,' Phoenix said, smiling shyly at her. 'What are you doing here?'

Lily dropped her chin and ran her fingers behind her ear, smoothing wayward curls out of the way. 'I wanted to surprise you.'

'You've definitely done that,' Phoenix admitted, moving to the edge of the van and hopping down to the ground to greet her. 'I've missed you.'

Lily's pale cheeks flushed and she gazed up to the sky. 'I have missed you too.'

Phoenix wanted so much to reach out and hug her. 'How did you get here? How did you know where I live? Why are you here? Not that I'm not happy to see you, 'cause I truly am, but what's going on?'

Lily dropped her gaze to the ground and ran her boot toe over a tuft of uneven grass. 'I arrived by aeroplane. Within moments of taking my leave with my mama in Dubbo, I was certain I had made a terrible error of judgement. Alas, I could not bring myself to say the words out loud to ask her to return me to your hospitality. So I continued, silently, the entire way back home.'

'Oh, Lily.'

'The moment we had completed our travels to Launceston, I began planning my return.'

'How did you leave things with your mother?'

Lily paused a moment, thinking. 'I do believe her tears of professed loss were, at least in part, genuine.'

'And your father?'

Lily shrugged, searching for words. 'Perhaps in time we shall come to some mutual understanding.'

'I hope so,' Phoenix said. 'And I'm really glad you're here now.'

'I contacted Carla, who contacted Therese, who informed me where you live,' Lily said, meeting Phoenix's eye now, a cheeky smile emerging.

'Of course she did,' Phoenix said, and laughed. 'Wait, does Zack know you're here?'

'I do not believe so.' Her face fell. 'Do you think it will be a complication?'

'No! Absolutely not,' Phoenix said, placing her hand on Lily's wrist in reassurance, before quickly pulling it away again. 'He'll be so happy to meet you. You will stay here with us, right?'

'Only if it is no inconvenience. I recall you said that you and your Zack would be working away from home and needed help with the animals.'

'Oh.' Phoenix grimaced.

'Has something happened?' Lily asked, alarmed. 'I can leave if you have changed your mind or if—'

'It's not that,' Phoenix said. 'It's not you, it's most definitely us. Turns out, it looks like both Zack and I might be jobless.' She shrugged. 'I'm still waiting to find out.'

'I am so sorry to hear this,' Lily said, gazing at the house. At that moment, two Appleyards came flapping and quacking down the side of the building, chasing each other merrily in some sort of game. Lily's face split into a huge grin. 'Look at them! They are so happy. Oh, Phoenix, I am very sorry to have abandoned you. I cannot imagine how difficult it was for you to get home again. Therese told me Zack went to your aid. I am awfully glad, though I also feel completely wretched that I left you alone.'

'It's all okay,' Phoenix reassured her. 'Look, we all made it back in one piece. I've only got this last box to get out of the van and then I'll take you inside to meet Zack and you can see all the animals again. Lucky is looking much better. His face is healing nicely and he's playing with the cats.'

Lily covered her mouth in delight. 'I cannot wait to see him.'

'You are welcome to stay with us as long as you like,' Phoenix told her.

Then to her surprise, Lily opened her arms wide and drew Phoenix to her, hugging her firmly. 'You are the very best of friends,' she said. 'I am grateful to have you in my life.'

Phoenix held her tightly. 'Right back at you.'

They released each other and Lily turned to the box. 'Let us remove this box together.'

'I don't know how you lifted this by yourself,' Phoenix said, approaching one side of it. 'It's so heavy.'

Lily grabbed the other end of the box and together they dragged it towards the edge of the van.

But then something happened. The box gave a little jerk.

Phoenix thought it must have been from Lily's efforts, them pulling against each other somehow instead of in the same direction. But then it happened again. They released their grip.

The lid moved.

It lifted.

And a scaly nose appeared.

Phoenix screamed and jumped backwards. Lily took a surprised step back too, with a small gasp. Like a scene from an old colonial movie, the lid of the box lifted and a diamond-shaped head appeared, rising like a cobra from a pot, summoned by a snake charmer's flute. Except this wasn't a cobra, it was an unmistakably Australian python. It had to be Henry, having hitchhiked all the way from Olga's dark pottery shed to the warmth of Queensland.

Phoenix leapt out of his way, back over the gutter, across the footpath and into her yard, where she stopped a moment to watch Henry drop himself elegantly to the road and pause to look around. Lily calmly stepped out of his way and he made for a jacaranda tree on the neighbour's lawn, slithering through the carpet of fallen purple flowers then up the trunk to take in the sights of the suburbs and plan his next adventure.

In the late afternoon, Phoenix, Zack and Lily sat in the lounge-room, drinking tea and playing with or snuggling a rotation of cat, kitten, dog and piglet in their laps. When Phoenix's phone rang, she shot to her feet, her heart kicking into action. The number was unknown, though she'd been expecting Evelyn's call all day, so she answered it, making her way to her bedroom and flicking on her sunflower lights automatically as she sat down.

'Hello?'

'Is this Phoenix Rose?' a woman asked. It wasn't Evelyn or Linda, and Phoenix didn't recognise the voice.

'Yes?' she said, suspicion creeping in. The last thing she felt like doing right now was telling a telemarketer to go away.

'My name is Marissa Brightside.'

Phoenix had no idea who she was but the woman's surname was enough to intrigue her into continuing the conversation for now.

'I'm the principal of a small independent school in rural Victoria. We've been up and running for three years now and are looking to expand next year. I have a teaching position I think you might be interested in, and I'd like to encourage you to apply.'

Phoenix struggled for words. 'I'm sorry, I'm confused.' She truly was. She'd been expecting a call from Evelyn, not a complete stranger. 'Why have you called me?'

'I read about you in the newspaper, and I read the response from your school. I watched the video from that guy, what was his name? The Cat Man?'

'Cat Man Ken.'

'That's him,' she said, clicking her fingers. 'And I saw the footage online of you in the classroom.'

'I see.' But she didn't. She could have sworn the woman had asked her to apply for a job, but she'd also read about her autism and seen her in shutdown while on the job in the classroom. The tops of her ears burnt. 'I'm still confused.'

'Phoenix, I'm autistic too,' the principal said, and laughed. 'I run a school that is inclusive of all students. We have quite a few autistic students here and they do well. I'm happy to talk to you about your needs and how the school can best accommodate you but, as I said, I'm autistic too so I'd like to think I'm a little ahead of the game already.'

'But you don't know anything about me,' she said.

'That's what LinkedIn is for,' Marissa said. 'The teaching world is rather small. I already know Claudette in Echuca, who wrote the first local story on you – and yes, I read that too – so I called her for a character reference first. Then I played dot-to-dot to find other teachers in senior positions who would give you a reference, and trust me, I didn't have any trouble at all. I even got one from your old principal.'

'Levi Backhurst?'

'Yes, Levi. But as his character is a bit tarnished, I also spoke to the principal before him, the religious coordinator, heads of department. It really wasn't difficult at all.'

'I can't believe this. Why would you want me to apply when you've seen what happened in the classroom?'

'You've completed an enormous road trip, with all sorts of obstacles and challenges on the way, I gather. That's impressive.'

'But I had to rely on so many other people to help me through it.'

'What you have actually demonstrated there is the beauty and necessity of human collaboration. No one is truly independent. The idea of independence can be weaponised against disabled people to remove agency. In reality, we all rely on other people to survive – unless you are a true wild man or woman living on the land in isolation from anyone else. We all rely on others to grow our food, to make our clothes, to provide our electricity, to provide transportation and communications, to repair our roofs, cars, teeth and plumbing, and even our minds.' She chuckled at her own joke. 'You have demonstrated you are resourceful, a leader, a team player and someone who, despite great odds, is tremendously adaptable under pressure. You are exactly the sort of person who could benefit this school and our students.'

'I don't know what to say.'

'Don't say anything,' Marissa said, and Phoenix could imagine her holding up her hand in a stop gesture. 'I'm going to email you through information on our school and the position. We prioritise our teachers' health here, too, so if you're keen to look at a job-sharing position we can arrange that.'

Phoenix turned to smile and nod at Zack and Lily, who were watching her anxiously from the hall.

'There is the fact that we're in Victoria, though,' Marissa said, groaning a little. 'I know it's a long shot to ask you to relocate from Brisbane. I'm sure you have a whole life set up there and—'

'Not really,' Phoenix said. 'It could actually be good timing for both me and Zack.'

'Wonderful!' Marissa said, typing on a keyboard in the background. 'I'm sending you this information through LinkedIn right now. There, done.'

'Thank you. I'll read it straight away.'

'I've included my mobile number too. Call me if you have any questions or want to talk anything through.'

'I will,' Phoenix assured her. She thanked her again and ended the call.

'Who was that?' Zack asked, coming to her side.

Phoenix grinned. 'That was a job offer.'

'What?'

'Well, not exactly an offer. A request to apply so, you know, but it sounds positive, right?'

'Where?'

'Ah, yeah.' She pulled an uncertain face. 'It's in rural Victoria.'

Zack's eyes widened with surprise, taking that in.

'I know your family's all up here,' Phoenix rushed to acknowledge. 'We don't have to go anywhere. Even if Evelyn doesn't let me go back to Clemmy's next week, we'll work something out. But it feels good to be offered something by someone who knows I'm autistic and actually sees it as an asset.'

Zack hugged her. 'I think you should take it.'

'What?' she scoffed, incredulous. 'You don't know anything about it.'

'I didn't know anything about you when we met for the first time but I still knew you were the one for me.'

She held his hands. 'Do you really think I should do it? *We* should do it?'

'I do,' he said, and kissed her before she could say another word.

After a moment of kissing, she stepped back, holding him at arm's length. 'You realise we'll have to pack up all these animals again and take another road trip back to Victoria, right?'

'We'll do it together.'

Phoenix leant to the side to peer past Zack and find Lily's face. She was hovering, staring at the floor. Phoenix led Zack over to her. 'Hey, Lils.'

She lifted her gaze, biting her lower lip. She looked at Zack, then back at Phoenix, as though waiting for them to ask her to leave.

'Did you hear all that?' Phoenix asked.

Lily nodded.

'Wherever we go, you can come too, if you want to.'

Zack nodded enthusiastically and gave her a thumbs up.

'Are you certain?' she asked, her lip trembling slightly.

'Absolutely.'

Relief washed over her. 'Then I would like that, very much.'

And so when Evelyn eventually called to tell Phoenix that she could come back to work on Monday with a comprehensive supervised return-to-work plan, Phoenix accepted, knowing that the last term wouldn't be easy, but that she would most likely be accepting a new role for next year anyway, in a new town, in a new school.

Change was coming. In just three weeks, Phoenix's world had turned upside down. But fresh new life was here, running around this house, and Lily was part of their family now too. Zack would find a new position in Victoria, of that she had no doubt. Radiographers, like teachers, were in constant demand. Her entire life had changed because of one word. Now, she'd spend the rest of her life helping to change the lives of others like her, Zack and Lily. She had no idea where the road was going to take her but she did know she had the power of community, and if she had the support of these two by her side, she'd make it.

Epilogue

Six months later

The best man wore a white bandana around his neck, with a little yellow bow tie at his throat, and the words *best boy* embroidered in yellow onto the material. Humphrey looked serious but happy in this honoured role, his jaw frequently dropping open to reveal his pink tongue and wrinkles at the corner of his mouth. His black coat was glossy and shiny, now brushed every day by his favourite human. In return, Humphrey shadowed Zack at every turn. The groom wore a misty blue suit and a yellow bow tie, his hair pulled back into a neat bun at the nape of his neck. The smile on his face was as wide as the dog's and together they waited at the archway, a masterpiece of yellow chrysanthemums and eucalyptus leaves.

Phoenix watched them for a moment from the kitchen window in their little stone home on two acres on the outskirts of Mansfield, in the foothills of the Great Dividing Range, a mere six-minute drive to her new school. She was ready to go but wanted to take in the sight of her handsome husband, letting the image soak into her memories. Her flowers were heavy in her hands, full of golden wattle and yellow sunflowers, with a train of green and silvery grey eucalyptus leaves from trees on their property, which a local florist had been keen to harvest and weave into the bouquet.

Lily walked towards the archway where Zack waited, leading the pony on one side of her and the alpaca on the other. Rita wore a neck garland of flowers and leaves, similar to Phoenix's bouquet, and Linus wore a yellow bow tie to match Zack and Humphrey. Lily looked tall and strong and fabulous. She had made her dress from reclaimed lace and silk that she'd cobbled together in her unique style. She stood tall. Phoenix was certain Lily's straight back and lifted chin were now less because she was trying to hold herself in a collected Victorian manner, and more because of her flourishing online business, the strides she'd made into clothing design, and her new role as a teacher's aide in the same school as Phoenix.

The heritage stone cottage Phoenix and Zack had bought was a renovator's delight and had come with a gatekeeper's cottage, which Lily had enthusiastically accepted as her own space. She'd worked hard on it, stripping it back and revealing its beautiful dark wood bones and quirky stone patterns in return for free rent. She loved it down there, being near the animals she tended so diligently, and having her own space to herself for the first time. She was welcome to stay as long as she wanted, though Phoenix didn't imagine it would be forever. Lily's wings were stretching, growing stronger every day, and her recent reconnection with her sister, Leonie, offered hope for further support.

As Lily, Rita and Linus disappeared through the archway to meet the celebrant beyond, Phoenix's heart jumped, not with nerves but excitement. It was time to go.

She pulled her glorious pale yellow cashmere wrap around her shoulders to brace against the cold, a beautiful wedding gift from Zack's mother. The weather there was certainly colder than she'd been prepared for, or would have ever thought she'd embrace. Aside from missing Zack's family, it was the one aspect of the move she struggled with. She didn't miss St Clementine's. She didn't miss Brisbane. But she did miss an abundance of warm days. Her first few pays from her new school had meant she could invest in 'highland' clothing to keep herself warm. That had helped. And she had to admit that the cottage's crackling open fire was a welcome daily event that unfailingly cheered her mood. Still, her wedding attire – a soft yellow pantsuit, flared at the bottom, the top not too tight and not too loose – needed that extra warm wrap even in autumn.

She stepped through the doorway and onto the pebbled path. The moment Zack saw her, his hand rose to cover his mouth for a moment. Then he dropped it, bent to Humphrey's ear and whispered something, pointing in her direction. She could see their smiles from here.

It was so peaceful over there, one of the strongest selling points for this property. Other than the sound of her boots, now swishing gently through the grass, all she could hear was birdsong, the rustle of treetops in the breeze and Lucky's snorts of pleasure as he snuffled in his trough.

She met Zack at the arch, her cheeks now aching from grinning.

'You look incredible,' Zack said, his eyes bright.

'So do you.'

She bent to pat Humphrey, then reached for Zack's hand, shifting her bouquet to one side. 'Let's go.' Together, they walked hand-in-hand through the archway and towards the lemon tree.

That lemon tree – aged, gnarled and massive – had been her sign that this was the place for them. It was surrounded by an opening bordered with trees and the small creek beyond. Phoenix could imagine it had been the place for picnics and celebrations for many generations. Finally, she had her very own lemon tree. She'd be making lemon meringue pies for months to come.

They stopped in front of the tree, greeting the waiting celebrant, Lily, the pony and the alpaca. Phoenix's principal, Marissa, had quickly become a firm friend and Phoenix's neurokin. She was there today as a witness to the ceremony and also offered a warm and generous welcome to Country.

On a table nearby sat their two-tiered lemon curd wedding cake covered in white buttercream, adorned with whole lemons and trailing greenery on top, a dramatic fault line around the middle revealing slices of candied lemon pieces inside. It was perfect.

It was all perfect. This was exactly the wedding she wanted, one that was a joy to be part of, not a stress. In a week's time, they'd head up to Brisbane and share an extended family mumu with Zack's relatives. Phoenix's mother would come too, probably. It would be fun because there would be no pressure to perform, no special clothes or hair or make-up, no one watching her speak her precious words to the one she loved, no one asking them to pose and smile on cue for hours at a time. No loud music. No speeches where words might get tangled or lost. No fancy tableware that could be dropped or used incorrectly, no procedures that had to be followed the right way, no too-cold air conditioning or sterile surrounds. Instead, there would be mess and river rocks and babes in arms and an expansive sky above them. But for now they had this, and it was everything she'd hoped for. Phoenix's heart soared high like the rising bird of her name. She was reborn.

Acknowledgements

I would like to acknowledge and pay respects to the Gubbi Gubbi/ Kabi Kabi First Nations people, on whose land I live and work.

•

Thank you to my publisher, Ali Watts, for your consistent and ebullient enthusiasm for, and encouragement of, my stories. I love that you always truly *get* them. It gives me confidence to keep going. I am a lucky author to have you.

Thank you to all at Penguin Random House Australia for the work you do, seen and unseen, to get my book out into the world and into the hands of my readers. And an extra special thank you to Kathryn Knight. (You know why!)

There are many small towns in this story. I always aim to present towns as accurately as possible, while still maintaining literary licence to make stuff up as needed. Usually, I like to visit my locations in person but, as most of this book was written under pandemic conditions, this time around it wasn't possible. Some of the businesses listed in this book may have now closed. Thanks for lending me your spirits. If these businesses are still operating, I encourage travellers to go visit them, take them this book and show them their cameos on the page. More than ever, we need to be supporting small businesses.

Thank you to my agent, Alex Adsett, for being a level-headed voice of reason. This book is in the world in no small part because of your assistance.

Thank you to Rosemary Galowa Duwaba for a chat about Papua New Guinean food – your passion for mumus is infectious.

The inspiration for this book was my own late-in-life autistic identification and the enormous support, acceptance, education and encouragement (not to mention new friends) I found in the #ActuallyAutistic community, at a moment in autistic history where things are changing rapidly but still terribly slowly. We still live in the shadows of a traumatic past and a barrage of false information but with the brightest of lights starting to clear the way. Finding and connecting with my neurokin has been the greatest blessing and I wanted to write a whole book to celebrate exactly that.

The autistic community is vastly diverse. (If you've met one autistic person, you've met *one* autistic person.) The views and opinions expressed by the characters in this book may or may not reflect another autistic person's experience. That's okay; it's kind of the point. There's space for all our stories out there. Let's go find them.

Thank you to Kay Kerr for your thoughtful sensitivity read and excitement for this story, and to Chantell Marshall (@shylittlepixie) for your generous reader's feedback and love for Phoenix and Lily's road trip. You both gave me so much confidence to let this book fly out into the world. Thank you Sophie Honeybourne for your teacher's brainstorm; it was much appreciated. My huge thanks, as always, to my dear friend Kate Smibert for relentlessly cheering me on, reading drafts, offering solutions, sharing writing retreats with me and never losing faith.

My animals are my furry family and no day would be complete without their licks, headbutts, side cuddles, snorts, fluffs, hugs and scratches, not to mention their thievery, escapism, hole-digging, bed warming and creative distraction.

I would also like to mention that there are without a doubt some great animal rescue organisations in Tasmania. I have personally been to visit Big Ears Animal Sanctuary Inc. and interviewed its founders, Jacqui and Brett Steele, while I was writing my book *Horse Rescue: Inspiring stories of second-chance horses and the lives they changed* (published by Penguin Books Australia under my other author name, Joanne Schoenwald, which you can still find at online retailers and as an ebook). Jacqui, who passed away in early 2022, and Brett put their life's savings into creating this sanctuary and it does incredible work. Obviously, I couldn't have Phoenix send all of Olga's animals to Big Ears or she wouldn't have had a road trip story to share! But if you are looking to support an animal charity, I feel Big Ears is truly a great one to consider.

Lastly, thank you Flynn, for handing us the map, and Alwyn, for taking the road trip with me. We've covered a lot of territory in a short amount of time. Thank you both for being the greatest lights of my life.

Book club discussion notes

1. What did you think of Phoenix's decision to care for all of Olga's animals herself? Did she make the right choice?

2. Did you learn anything about autism or neurodiversity from the characters in the book? Was there anything that surprised or enlightened you?

3. The Downunder Auties group is an invaluable source of advice, assistance and friendship for Phoenix on her journey. Have you ever been a member of an online community that shared advice and support in this way? Did your involvement in the group bring any other unforeseen benefits?

4. Phoenix and Lily make brief stops in many rural and regional locations during their journey up the east coast of Australia. How did the nature of these country towns influence the story?

5. In what ways do you think Phoenix and Zack are a perfect match?

6. Animals play a huge part in this story and in the lives of many of the characters. What do you think makes the relationship

between humans and companion animals so special? Are there any issues of animal welfare that are particularly important to you?

7. Phoenix uses her Pinterest board as a tool to calm herself and create a sense of order. Do you have any unconventional mindfulness or relaxation methods?

8. Instead of choosing to support her teacher, Evelyn does everything in her power to push Phoenix out of her job at St Clementine's. What prejudices are on show in her treatment of Phoenix? What benefits could a teacher like Phoenix bring to a school community?

9. 'Sometimes, the purpose of speaking up was simply about being part of something bigger, doing your own little bit to make the next step forwards a little easier for the person following.' Discuss.

10. Consider the role that trust plays in the novel, and why it is so crucial in the friendship between Phoenix and Lily.

11. Josephine Moon's novels are known for including a delectable variety of foods. In what ways do we see food being celebrated in this book and in other novels by Josephine Moon?

12. What do you know about the #ActuallyAutistic and #OwnVoices hashtags? What are the advantages of reading books by authors with firsthand knowledge of the experiences they're writing about?

These strawberry lemonade cakes taste like sunshine and holidays

(Gluten-free option)

I'm not even going to try and pretend I'm not crazy in love with these cupcakes! These are the cupcakes that Mel gives to Phoenix when they meet up in Coonabarabran. I had the character Olivia Kent bake them in my novel *The Cake Maker's Wish* but I knew they'd be perfect for Phoenix's love of all things lemon.

Years ago I found recipes online for these and thought they would be amazing. But when I went to make them, I found them seriously lacking in flavour. It was so disappointing. I love the intensity of lemon meringue pie and lemon curd so I wasn't going to accept that. I changed the recipe to boost the flavours, big time. Now they burst with lemon and the seductive aroma and flavour of strawberries. Every mouthful inspires hope and happiness, perfect as a winter warmer to chase away the blues. I'm not going to lie, though – these are not quick to make. But, oh, they are worth it, especially for a special occasion.

Ingredients

Cake part 1
125 g butter, room temperature
zest of three lemons
1 cup castor sugar
3 egg whites
1½ tsp vanilla extract

Cake part 2
1¼ cup all-purpose/plain flour (or gluten-free plain flour)
3 tbsp arrowroot or cornflour (check it's gluten-free cornflour if
    you want them GF)
2 tsp baking powder (check specs for GF)
pinch salt
½ cup sour cream
½ cup lemon juice

Strawberry buttercream
1½ cups frozen or fresh strawberries (hulled)
500 g pure icing sugar (check specs for GF)
250 g butter
¼ tsp vanilla

(Note: These quantities will make more than enough buttercream
for your cupcakes. You can reduce these quantities if you wish,
keeping the ratio of 2:1 for icing sugar to butter, or freeze the excess
and use later for biscuits or a loaf cake of some sort. I always figure
that if I'm making something I might as well make a lot of it to
freeze some for later.)

Method

Cake preparation

1. Preheat your oven to 180°C (160°C fan forced) and line your cupcake trays with paper. (This batch will make approximately 16 cupcakes.)

2. In a mixing bowl, beat your butter and lemon zest, then add in the sugar and beat again until well mixed and fluffy. Add the egg whites and vanilla and beat to combine.

3. In another bowl, mix the dry ingredients of 'Cake Part 2' together, then add half of it to the butter mixture, mix to combine, then add half the sour cream, mix to combine, then repeat with the remaining dry ingredients and sour cream. Finally, add the lemon juice and beat again to form a batter.

4. Fill your cupcake papers to two-thirds full and put them into the oven. The cakes will take 20–25 minutes, give or take. (I have a slow oven and mine took 30 minutes.)

Strawberry preparation

1. Place your strawberries into a blender and blitz until they reach a smooth consistency.

2. Transfer the strawberries into a small pot and heat on the stove until they are gently boiling, stirring often. Continue to cook them until they have reduced to approximate the colour and consistency of tomato sauce.

3. Cool the sauce before adding it to the buttercream, otherwise it will melt the butter. (Putting it in the fridge is helpful.)

Buttercream preparation

1. Make sure your icing sugar is as free of lumps as possible. You may need to dry beat it first. (Bashing the packet on the kitchen bench also helps.)

2. Beat your icing sugar, butter and vanilla until smooth and creamy. Add approximately three tablespoons of the strawberry sauce and beat until combined.

3. You may like to use a piping bag to pipe the cream or simply spoon it on. If you wish, you might like to decorate your cupcakes with extra strawberries or edible flowers for an added touch of beauty.

Enjoy! These really are divine.

Jo x

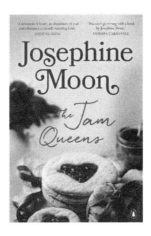

A sweet and soulful story about women being there for each other through life's stickiest situations.

Award-winning jam maker Aggie is determined to take her Barossa Valley cafe to new heights. She has put the pain of unsuccessful IVF treatments and a broken relationship behind her, and is focused on the many wonderful possibilities life still holds in store.

When an invitation to travel across Australia on the Ghan for her mother's seventieth birthday comes her way, she is at first apprehensive. But the trip offers a precious opportunity to spend some quality time with the other women in her family – all four generations of them.

As the iconic train chugs its way beneath majestic desert skies, she becomes distracted by the attentions of a handsome younger man on his own search for meaning. When long-held family rifts reignite, Aggie must learn the true meaning of love, and about sticking together even through life's trickiest situations.

'*The Jam Queens* celebrates the joys and sorrows of life, and reveals the essential ingredients of the true recipe for happiness.'
Better Reading

'A mountain of heart, an abundance of soul and a banquet of mouth-watering food.'
Good Reading

'Equally heartwarming and heartbreaking, *The Jam Queens* tells of a woman coming to terms with the joys and sorrows of life under the azure skies of central Australia.'
Stellar magazine

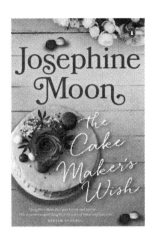

An uplifting and heartwarming story about the moments that change your life forever, human kindness and being true to yourself.

When single mum Olivia uproots her young son Darcy from their life in Tasmania for a new start in the English Cotswolds, she isn't exactly expecting a bed of roses – but nor is she prepared for the challenges that life in the picturesque village throws her way.

The Renaissance Project hopes to bring the dwindling community back to life – to welcome migrants from around the world and boost the economy – but not everyone is pleased about the initiative.

For cake maker Olivia, it's a chance for Darcy to finally meet his Norwegian father, and for her to trace the last blurry lines of her family tree. It's also an opportunity to move on from the traumatic event that tore her loved ones apart.

After seven years on her own, she has all but given up on romance, until life dishes up some delicious new options she didn't know she was craving.

'Josephine Moon just gets better and better . . . This is pure escapist delight, with a lot of heart and humour.'
Better Reading

'Utterly charming, sweet, engaging and carefully crafted . . .
This is the perfect single-sitting read for a lazy Sunday,
best accompanied by tea and a piece of cake.'
Apple Books

You've been given the gift of life, now go live it.

Gabby McPhee is the owner of The Tin Man, a chic new cafe and coffee roasting house in Melbourne. The struggles of her recent heart transplant are behind her and life is looking up – until a mysterious customer appears in the cafe, convinced that Gabby has her deceased husband's heart beating inside her chest.

Krystal Arthur is a bereaved widow, struggling to hold herself and her two young boys together since Evan's death, and plagued by unanswered questions. Why was her husband far from home in another city the night he died? And why won't his spirit rest?

Krystal is convinced that Gabby holds the clues she needs to move towards a brighter future. Gabby needs Krystal to help her let go of her troubled past. The two women must come together to try to unlock the secrets in Evan's heart in order to set free their own.

By the internationally bestselling author of _The Tea Chest_, this is a profound and moving novel about the deeper mysteries of love and loss – and the priceless gift of life.

'This story is a gift in itself.'
Herald Sun

'Reading a Josephine Moon novel is always a delicious treat.'
Goodreads

'Part mystery, part romance and all heart, Moon has crafted a great novel about the power of friendship, love and second chances.'
QWeekend

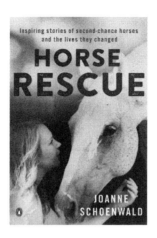

Inspiring stories of second-chance horses
and the lives they changed

HORSE RESCUE

JOANNE
SCHOENWALD

*'I really believe he knew I was there to help and make his
life better. It was my main goal that he would never
see a day of fear again in his whole life.'*
Eleisha, with her horse Phantom

The moment Joanne Schoenwald calmed her frail, dogger-bound accidental horse, he rested his forehead over her chest, directly over her heart. It was one of the most powerful moments of her life – and she would never be the same again.

This spurred a transformative journey of exhilarating triumph, inspiring connections, powerful self-healing and quiet meditative wisdom as Joanne launched a quest to change the lives of horses, one rescue at a time. The biggest miracle of this journey was learning the simple truth that – time after time – a person may set out to rescue a horse, yet a horse returns the rescue a hundred times over.

Written by the bestselling novelist also known as Josephine Moon, *Horse Rescue* is a beautiful and moving collection of true stories. Be inspired by rescue horses and their people, who shine in adversity, rise through the challenges of cancer, defeat all odds to go to the Olympics, and find light and hope after prison. Celebrate the incredible bond between humans and their rescue horses, proving that love, kindness and rescuing those in need are never an accident, but a life-changing gift.

Discover a
new favourite

Visit **penguin.com.au/readmore**